W9-BRD-210

A NOTE ON THE TYPE

Set in Linotype Sabon, designed by Jan Tschichold in 1964–6 on the model of Garamond types. First used in 1966, Sabon was available in identical form for both mechanical hot-metal composition by Monotype or Linotype, or for hand composition using foundry type, and has proved an enduring modern classic in revivals for film and digital setting.

My Heart Belongs in Castle Gate, Utah

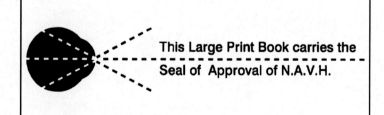

This Large Print Book carries the
Seal of Approval of N.A.V.H.

MY HEART BELONGS IN CASTLE GATE, UTAH

LEANNA'S CHOICE

ANGIE DICKEN

THORNDIKE PRESS
A part of Gale, a Cengage Company

Farmington Hills, Mich • San Francisco • New York • Waterville, Maine
Meriden, Conn • Mason, Ohio • Chicago

A Cengage Company

Copyright © 2017 by Angie Dicken.
All scripture quotations are taken from the King James Version of the Bible.
Thorndike Press, a part of Gale, a Cengage Company.

Thorndike Press® Large Print Christian Romance.
The text of this Large Print edition is unabridged.
Other aspects of the book may vary from the original edition.
Set in 16 pt. Plantin.

LIBRARY OF CONGRESS CIP DATA ON FILE.
CATALOGUING IN PUBLICATION FOR THIS BOOK
IS AVAILABLE FROM THE LIBRARY OF CONGRESS

ISBN-13: 978-1-4328-4546-9 (hardcover)
ISBN-10: 1-4328-4546-2 (hardcover)

Published in 2017 by arrangement with Barbour Publishing, Inc.

Printed in the United States of America
1 2 3 4 5 6 7 21 20 19 18 17

In loving memory of my grandparents. I'll never forget Yiayia Tom's village recipes, Papou Tom's Andes mints, Yiayia John's penmanship, or Papou John's stories — from the Utah mountains to WWII tours. I'm thankful for their rich Greek American heritage, and I'm proud to call it my own. I love you all and miss you every day.

ACKNOWLEDGMENTS

I want to thank my husband, Cody, for encouraging me to connect with other writers seven years ago. Wow. How much I had to learn and how daunting it would have been without your constant support. Thanks, Codeman. Yes, I really do love you.

My writing partner, Ashley Clark, thank you for believing in me, for speaking truth in love when I fall for lies (in writing and in life), and for sharing your beautiful stories with me. They will bless so many people! Pepper Basham, my lovely, talented friend. You've ministered to me so much through this writing journey, but more importantly, through my own personal trials. You've blessed me big, and I am forever grateful for you.

A huge thanks to the rest of my Alley Cats who make this journey such a joy! Thank you to ACFW for providing a stellar writing community. And thanks to the Barbour

7

publishing team, and my amazing agent, Tamela Hancock Murray, for making my dream come true!

Many thanks to my loyal bestie, Cami. You are truly my sister. To my four children — you all are my heart, and I am thankful every day for the chance to watch you grow toward bright futures. Mom, Dad, Chrissy, and Kate, thank you for your constant love and support. And to the rest of my family and friends, you don't know how much I appreciate your excitement for my debut year as an author. Everything I do is because I've been found by Christ. Thank you, Lord. Your inspiration and faithfulness have met me in every word. It is only because of You that I have any stories to tell.

CHAPTER ONE

Castle Gate, Utah, 1910

Leanna McKee pushed her hat by its brim, hiding her face as best she could. She would not let him see her. His large clumsy shadow had warned her as she approached the corner of the coffeehouse porch. She rushed to the other side of the road, so far over that her skirt skimmed the weeds. His gargling laugh tempted her to slip into the brush and weave through the scrubby trees, avoiding that Greek crook altogether.

"Pretty lady?" His thick accent tumbled across the afternoon air, and his shadow inched closer as she passed by. "I wonder where Meester McKee is, pretty lady?"

Leanna quickened her pace. No, she would not give this man any satisfaction in answering his question. If he had cared at all, he would have known what happened to Jack. The Greek man, with his slippery speech and beady eyes, could follow her home and beat down her door. She'd still not share one word.

"Excuse me, Meesus McKee . . ." He called from behind her now.

Maybe he would follow her home.

Her stomach soured at the thought, even amid the delicious waft of savory smoke pouring from the nearby restaurant's outdoor oven. As she turned up the path to her neighborhood, she stole a glance over her shoulder.

Good. The sloppy man had returned to the porch, scratching his balding head and staring at his pocket watch.

Leanna was certain what must be done now.

It was her only choice, no matter the consequences that might arise. After all, she had not chosen any of this. Besides the greedy Greek man harassing her on the streets of Castle Gate, she was surrounded by the filth of coal dust and grumbling, uncivilized miners. Unfortunately, though, her husband had become one of them.

But he was gone now.

She hurried into her home and hung up her hat and coat. Jack's empty chair snagged her attention, taunting her as she pulled out parchment and ink. She would not grow angry again. Her temper had brought nothing but regret.

The pen drank up the ink and her hand shook as the nib hovered over the paper. Were her parents truly the only way to a future without hunger and want? Would they ever take back the debutante who'd thrown away all her inheritance for the love of a common workingman?

Perhaps they would. Under certain conditions. There was a time when she'd have considered her parents' stifling expectations even worse than her lowly teaching position or the mining company's grocery store with inflated prices and limited supplies.

Yet she did not belong here. The belly of Carbon County, Utah, was the very last place she'd wanted to live.

"Must I return to Boston, though?" she spoke aloud, resting the pen on the ink bottle's edge. The desperate question was answered by a forceful knock at the door. Leanna's heart plummeted to her stomach, her arm hair stood against her cotton sleeves. Dusk's dimming light bled through the threadbare curtains. Who was there at this hour? Had the nosy man truly followed her? He had appeared to be harmless, aggravating beyond words, but harmless just the same. She'd welcome him over the dreaded visitors that intruded her imagination during these lonely days.

Her nerves frenzied, just as they had each time she'd caught a gawking miner staring in her direction. Would they dare prey on a new widow? She was concerned most by immigrant miners whose wives were left behind in their homeland, thousands of miles away.

Another, less forceful, knock startled her to her feet. A small whimper slipped from her lips. "Lord, protect me." She snatched the iron poker beside her coal stove and crept across the kitchen.

This was exactly why she needed to leave this place. There was nothing left for her. Just trouble.

"Who is it?" She threw her demand toward the bolted door.

"It's Alex Pappas." The deep cordial voice rumbled like the sound of breaking rain on a thirsty garden. Relief washed over her tense muscles. Alex was the one man who'd tried to save her husband in the mine accident.

He was not a threat, as far as she could tell. He was Jack's friend.

Leanna leaned the fire poker against the wall, straightened her woolen skirt, then slid the bolt and opened the door.

Alex's chocolate eyes brightened with his

kind smile, even in the dull afternoon. Before her gaze lingered too long, she noticed his nephew and niece, Teddy and Maria, waiting at the edge of the path.

"Good evening, Mrs. McKee," Alex said in perfect English. He pulled his hat off, releasing thick ebony curls across his brow. "I am sorry to bother you so late."

She straightened her spine trying to appear unaffected, even if she welcomed the friendly company. Perhaps loneliness had crippled her good sense. Jack's absence this past month was more detrimental than she'd thought. Before Castle Gate, she would have been lost without him. But now? After all she'd found out?

Leanna cleared her throat. "What can I do for you?"

"A favor, if you please." He gave a nervous chuckle then glanced at the children.

"Favor?" Leanna half whispered. Her eyes searched the neighbor's near-identical house to hers. What would anyone think of this Greek man asking an American woman for a favor? "Mr. Pappas, I don't know what you mean."

"Well, it is more of a business proposition than favor," he said, shifting his weight. "You see, my sister-in-law is expecting and she has taken a turn for the worse. Now,

13

she is restricted from walking. My brother and I have to work early in the mines," his voice lowered while he fiddled with his hat. "Perhaps, we can leave the children in your care before school begins?"

A protest formed on the tip of her tongue, but she only stared at him with wide eyes.

He licked his lips and began to explain further. "My parents must tend to the restaurant, and the children's mother, Penelope, does not trust the children to walk themselves to school. She fears gypsies might steal them."

"Gypsies?" She'd never heard of such a thing.

"Ena, dio, tria . . ." Maria and Teddy held hands and hopped across the path. The dark-haired boy fell to his knees and whimpered. His sister helped him up.

They were sweet children — for Greeks anyway. Of all her students, the Pappas children were at least the most tolerable, even if they forgot to use their English at times. They had women, the only two Greek women in their town, tending to them each day. Both children were always scrubbed free of lice and smelled of freshly washed clothes. The young boys who came over with their uncles and fathers were quite different. If they didn't take positions as water

14

boys at the mine, they tumbled into school in a thick layer of filth.

"Mrs. McKee, we will pay you." Alex wrung his hat in his hands. Coal dust blackened the bed of his fingernails, just as it had Jack's. How often had she complained to her husband to scrub his nails better? He never ignored her, but it became a useless task. She scrunched her nose as the usual shame spread through her gut. Perhaps, she wasn't so different from her parents. Civility was ingrained in her breeding to a fault — an added bitterness those last days of marriage.

What kind of person would she become if she returned to life under her mother's scrutiny?

"Your offer is interesting to me." Leanna clasped her hands and brought them up to her chin. "How long will you need me?"

"Until Penelope has the baby. A few months, maybe?" Alex shrugged his shoulders. "Here. This is how much we'd like to offer you." He pulled out a piece of paper.

The number was fair enough. Actually, plenty to cover her train ticket and meals. But she'd hardly eat if her final destination was Boston.

Her thoughts swirled in a brew. "There's little for me in this coal town."

"I understand." Alex nodded, a crease between his eyebrows marked him with compassion. She nearly smiled in gratitude for his kindness. "Will you go to San Francisco? Jack said you were hoping to be there by summer."

"Jack told you that?" She bit her bottom lip. Her eyes ached with the effort to dam her emotion. "That has been my dream all along, before . . ." *Jack gambled it away.* But she wouldn't share that with Alex. Her bitterness toward Jack while he was alive haunted her with remorse. She couldn't speak ill of him now in his death. Even if it were true that his vices had slashed her dream — and her heart.

Alex brought up a plan that had been smothered by her misery. But now? A grin appeared against her will.

"San Francisco is a fine idea," she said. Just speaking the name of the city out loud seemed to brighten the dreary valley all around her. Her heart quickened. Just a few weeks of helping the Pappas family and she might save enough to make the trip. All on her own. She'd owe nothing to her parents, and she could still teach — in a finer school than Castle Gate could provide — under her cousin in California.

Alex narrowed his eyes and hooked his

16

thumb on his suspender. "I am glad to spark your memory," he said. "And that smile." He offered a dazzling smile of his own. A rush of heat met Leanna's cheeks. She was trapped by his gaze, gold flecks dancing in his umber eyes. Only a high-pitched squeal from the children released his hold. The six-year-old, Teddy, sprinted to a cluster of trees.

Alex took long strides down the knoll. "What did you find?" Leanna followed, careful to stay a decent distance from the Greek man. Once again, she looked around for any onlookers.

"Ghata!" Teddy scrambled into the shrubs then stood up cradling the Coffey's tabby cat.

"Say *cat,* Teddy," she said, trying to make the visit more about teaching than the moment that had just passed between her and Alex.

Teddy copied her English, and Alex tousled his hair.

"We must return home before dark," Alex said. "Will you accept my offer?"

"I will, Mr. Pappas." She held out her hand, and they shook. Leanna prayed that the butterflies in her stomach had everything to do with San Francisco and nothing to do with his firm embrace of her fingers. "I will meet you at the corner by your parents' restaurant in the morning." Leanna silently scolded her girlish reactions to Mr. Pappas. He was Greek, after all.

"Good evening, Mrs. McKee," her neighbor, Mr. Coffey, called out from his porch. "What's he doing here?" His sharp stare pointed at Alex.

"Ah, Mr. Coffey. He is the uncle of two of my students." She cut through the sparse grass. "I believe Teddy has found your cat." She reached out to the boy and gently pushed him toward Mr. Coffey. He was reluctant to hand the cat over, but her neighbor plucked the cat from his arms by the scruff of its neck.

"Is that what brings them to these parts?" He referred to them as if they were already gone, not standing a few feet away. She bristled. He was rude and arrogant, no matter if it was an acceptable attitude around here. "My cat doesn't go as far as Greek Town." He glared at Alex.

Alex's face was cold as stone, and he barely moved his lips as he spoke. "We were not here for your cat —"

"They were here because I am their teacher." Leanna wanted to end this ridiculous interrogation. "I have arranged to care for the children before and after school."

She held her head high, then turned to Alex. He confirmed what she'd said with a nod.

Mr. Coffey grunted and flung the cat onto his front porch. The cat screeched, landing on its feet and arching its back.

"Ghata!" Teddy cried out. Leanna grabbed him before he ran out of reach.

"*Cat,* Teddy," she snapped then spun on her heel still holding on to him. "Be sure you two are ready by eight o'clock tomorrow." She reached her hand out to Maria, and the ten-year-old girl took it.

The scowling man retreated to his door.

"Good night, Mr. Coffey," Leanna called out as she walked away with a child on each side of her.

Alex's darkly dressed eyes glinted with admiration. Her overactive cheeks began to heat again. She begged them to remain a cool shade of ivory. No man should have such an effect on her. Especially a Greek man who treaded dangerously close to hostile territory by her neighbor's obvious calculations.

Alex ran a hand through his black curls then put his hat on. He spoke Greek softly to the children. With a tip of his hat in her direction, he led the children toward town. "Thank you, Mrs. McKee."

Leanna rushed inside, eager to discard the

19

letter to her parents and revive an old dream — teaching in San Francisco. Who would have thought such a chance would appear when life was at its lowest?

Gratitude filled her heart. She peeked out her window just as the tall, handsome Greek disappeared down her walk. One day soon she'd leave, never to return. Thanks to Alex Pappas, she'd finally found a way out of Castle Gate after all.

Alex arrived at the mine the next morning, trailing behind Leanna's neighbor. Besides the sour memory of Turks threatening life in his homeland eight years ago, Mr. Coffey was a pesky weed in his family's effort to grow American roots.

Yanni rushed toward Alex with their helmets tucked beneath his arms. "I see I am too late to help with the children."

"Yes, Brother. Don't worry," Alex said. "How is Penelope?"

"She's the same, resting with her feet up. Did Mrs. McKee arrive this morning?"

"Yes, the children are on their way to school now," Alex said quietly, even though they spoke Greek. Mr. Coffey had looked their way more than once since Yanni arrived. "That Coffey was not happy to see me in his neighborhood."

"He had a whole team of men hollering the other day." His brother shook his head. "Don't understand their words."

"Perhaps you should learn English alongside your children, Brother?" Alex had harassed him about this since he joined him in America. The Pappas family was here to stay, unlike the many Greeks who leeched off the land of opportunity. "Now that I understand their language, men like Coffey are more careful around me, even if they still hate us."

"Perhaps." Yanni rolled his deep brown eyes then handed Alex a helmet. "But we have to deal with Anthis now." He nodded toward the Greek labor agent who was gabbing at the water station with a new arrival. He patted his pocket then the man's shoulder.

"Quick, let's get to work before he sees us," Alex whispered, but the large man was already plodding toward them.

"Ah, just who I was looking for, the Pappas brothers." With arms wide, Anthis met up with them.

Alex shoved past the labor agent. "We can't talk now, Anthis. It's time to work."

"It's a funny thing, that." Anthis wiped his forehead with a handkerchief. "On one hand, you mustn't neglect the mine, but on the other, you won't have a mine to work if your fees are tardy." He rubbed his thick fingers together.

"Now?" Alex gritted his teeth. He had been wrong about Coffey and the Turks being his only nuisances. This man was just as much of a weed, and a stubborn one at that. "You come for fees now?"

"You should thank me. I save you a trip to Salt Lake City, eh?" Anthis said.

Alex motioned to Yanni to continue gathering their equipment. He then faced the agent, nose nearly touching nose, only to get a whiff of soured feta on his breath.

"I don't carry my wages in my pocket like a fool," Alex sneered. He was a fool, though. He'd listened to Anthis eight years ago and left his wife in Greece. All for fortune.

"Perhaps you know where that Scotsman is off to?" Anthis picked his tooth with his pinky nail. "He owes me a wager. If he pays up, perhaps it will give you some time." He chuckled, surveying the area. "Where is he? His wife is a mute, it seems."

"Mrs. McKee?" Alex blurted. Had Anthis pressured her to pay up for Jack?

"*Neh,* neh." He nodded then snorted. "She is not a happy woman."

"Jack McKee is dead, Anthis."

"Oh, really?" He scratched his jaw. "Well,

22

no wonder she wouldn't speak." He burst with a roaring chuckle. Wiping his eyes, he said from the corner of his mouth, "End of the month, Alex, no later."

Of course. Had he once skipped payment to this man? Many meals he skipped before Momma and Papa had come over and set up the restaurant. But, no, he had never denied Anthis the ridiculous amount of money that he demanded for Greeks to keep their jobs.

Anthis was almost as much to blame for Helena as —

Alex glared at the colorless sky above then sighed and ran to catch up to his brother.

"Jack was a good man." Yanni shook his head. "It's a shame that Anthis had suckered him into his money-making schemes."

Not only had the fat slime taken money from his own people all these years, but now it seemed he was finding ways to cripple Jack's widow, also. What did Mrs. McKee think of his people with a man like Anthis trying to settle her dead husband's gambling debt?

Alex shouldn't care what she thought — although she was mysterious to him. He'd seen pain and hope and kindness dance across her face yesterday. They shared more in common than this mountainous town. If

23

only Mrs. McKee knew that he had walked the same valley of loss that she was walking now.

Alex was glad that he'd helped her find some hope. He knew how important that was at such a time. Second best to having a comforter and a friend. But Alex Pappas could not be anything of the sort to Leanna McKee. What a dangerous notion that would prove to be.

After they replaced their fisherman caps for helmets and gathered their tools and carbides, Bill Coffey cut them off at the mine's entrance, his long spindly legs and wiry neck stretched up like a gangly rooster protecting the henhouse.

"That Mrs. McKee's a pretty gal, don't you think?" Coffey seethed.

Alex took in a deep breath. "Out of my way, Coffey."

"You've found quite legitimate reasons to weasel your way up our hill," he snorted. "Enough. You hear me?"

"Your imagination is carried away." Alex spoke quietly but with clarity. "Mrs. McKee's husband was a friend, and my niece and nephew are her students. I visited her for these reasons only." He pushed past the man and followed the glow of his lamp into the earth.

His reasons were innocent, and he had dismissed the idea of becoming anything more than an acquaintance to her. But he couldn't disagree that the fair-haired schoolteacher was pretty — beautiful, to be more precise. He'd tried to divert his attention from her loose golden curls and sparkling blue eyes, but he was as mesmerized as if he had discovered a diamond beneath all the coal. No doubt she was as strong as a diamond — in her decency to ignore Coffey and in her firm kindness with the children.

If he was not devoted completely to his family's success, he'd consider the tempting distraction of befriending Mrs. McKee, despite Mr. Coffey's warning.

A second chance to care for a woman — could he risk it?

He sucked in an aggressive breath through his teeth, the stagnant cavern air giving little relief to a sudden bitter taste on his tongue.

Risk it? This new life was full of enough perils. He didn't need one more.

Yanni laid a firm hand on his shoulder. "Coffey is worse than a Turk, and I don't even know what he said. But just the look of him makes me want to —" He took his fist and squeezed it in the dim light, twisting it like he was breaking a chicken's neck. "You are lucky he can't understand Greek.

25

I wouldn't be surprised if he's nearby."

"And you want me to learn English?" Yanni prodded his eyebrows up. "See how our secret language gives us a chance to spite our enemies?"

Alex chuckled and pushed his brother playfully.

Enemies. They left their country, the Turks, the poverty, and hardships, only to come to this land and make more enemies along the way. Alex mustn't let the beauty of a woman weaken him. He'd already found shame in such weakness and had proved to everyone that his heart was not to be trusted.

CHAPTER TWO

24 October 1910

My Dearest Anne,
I write this letter with dire news, even more than when I forfeited my position at your school to come to Utah. My husband has passed away suddenly, and I am left desolate in this godforsaken place. Fortunately, I have retained my position as teacher at the small coal-town school, and I have acquired a small job that will provide me with the funds needed to make the journey to San Francisco.

Do you still have a position available for me? I am sure, as headmistress, you hardly have time to worry about your desperate cousin, but I am just that, desperate to leave this place, to start anew in your well-reputed school.

As we have corresponded before,

Mother and Father have not revoked their disownment, and I am forever thankful that you are sympathetic to my circumstances.

You are a dear friend, and I look forward to your reply.

Your loving cousin,
Leanna

She placed her fountain pen next to the ink bottle and waved her letter to help it dry. Confidence coursed through her shoulders, and a smile nearly sprouted on her lips.

Thank You, Lord, for this new plan.

Maria and Teddy waited by the door of the classroom, their large brown eyes staring in question.

"Just a moment, children." She popped up from her seat. With a quick tap of her finger she made sure the ink was dry before folding the letter. It would be mailed first thing in the morning.

"Come now." She shooed the children through the door and sailed down the stairs, lighter than before. She would leave all this behind, forget about this miserable chapter in her life, and continue on to a dream that she'd once cast off because of Jack's foolishness.

Leanna shook her head and shoveled in

air. No, she would not allow bitterness to ruin this moment of clarity.

"Meesus McKee?" Maria came up beside her as they left the school building.

"Yes, Maria?"

"You dance in America?"

Leanna raised a brow in her direction.

With all the English words she didn't know, Maria knew *dance.* Of course, after seeing her dance in a most Greek way with her mother on their walks home from school, Leanna understood how this might be of particular importance to the little girl.

"We do dance. Not like you, though." She recalled her last ball as a debutante. It was a Lawrence ball, and her dance card dangled from her wrist while she chatted with her dear friend. Mary had just completed her first year at Simmons College. Leanna's dress was an appropriate green silk to match the envy that filled her torso as Mary gabbed about the lectures she attended and the courses she would take to complete her degree in domestic science.

Well, who needs a degree to be a house-wife? A comforting retort for her jealous heart.

She had yet to fall in love with Jack, then. Perhaps she'd chosen the wrong rebellious path. Fighting her family's tradition of

29

pomp for a college education might have put her in better circumstances than as the widow of a gambling man.

She swallowed away the ache in her throat. Regret was not beneficial, but it certainly was persistent.

Maria slipped her hand into Leanna's, pleading with large chestnut eyes. "How?"

Leanna sighed. "What is it you would like to know, Maria?"

"To know?" She crinkled her brow and twirled a curl with her finger.

Teddy's small feet carried him in a silent tune. "How you do?" He waved a hand to his feet then wiped his dark brown hair out of his eyes, giving a sideways grin.

Her heart melted. She couldn't help but laugh.

"I cannot show you how to dance here in the middle of the road." By the confused looks on their faces, they didn't understand. "I am a teacher of words, not of fancy footwork —"

A freckled child ran past her from behind, stopping and peering at Teddy with widened eyes. "Is that a jumping-bean Greek?" He poked Teddy with a scrawny finger. "Jump Greek, jump!"

Distant laughter carried down the road from some children looking on in the

30

schoolyard behind them. Leanna glared at the gaggle, but it didn't stop their teasing. One little boy called out, "Don't touch him, Billy! Your mother will scrub you for a week!"

Billy sniffed his fingers and scrunched up his face. "Eew, greasy Greek, you stink."

"That is quite enough, child," Leanna erupted and nearly boxed his ears right there. "Who are your parents?" She grabbed his arm. Billy bit his lip. "Well, who?"

"Mrs. McKee." The headmistress's high shrill pierced her ears. Mrs. Rudolf stood with the rest of the children. "That is my student. If you would kindly leave him be." Her thin spectacles slipped down her long nose, and her gaze bore through Leanna as if *she* were the naughty child.

Leanna released her grasp of Billy but cautioned him with an icy glare. He ran up to his friends. Leanna trailed behind him and said, "Mrs. Rudolph, I must tell you, their manners were quite unbecoming —"

"Thank you, Mrs. McKee. I trust you to provide for your own students as I provide for mine." She curled her lip as her gaze bounced from Maria to Teddy then to Maria again. She swiveled on her heel and disappeared into the school.

Leanna steamed with anger. How dare she

31

excuse such behavior? And reprimand her in front of the students? Gathering the children's hands again, they nearly ran down the hill.

"Meesus McKee?" Teddy whined.

"What is it, child?"

"That boy, want friend?"

Her anger fizzled, and she slowed her pace. Maria didn't look up, but Teddy waited with round eyes glistening up at her.

"He is no friend," she mumbled. Her throat knotted. These children would always fight such torment against their kind. Perhaps they would return to Greece with their family, as so many other Greeks did. The thought settled her nerves. The Pappas children deserved better than Castle Gate could offer.

They walked the rest of the way to the restaurant in silence.

When they arrived, Maria hopped onto the front step and her brother followed.

"You teach us American dance." Teddy's wide smile flashed in the afternoon sunlight.

"Will you?" Maria jumped up and down, her round face tilted upward.

"You'd be better off learning English. Dancing is not useful."

"It make you happy, though." Maria sighed, smiling like a lovesick woman. "It

32

make everyone happy."

"Good-bye, children." She waited until they disappeared inside their grandparents' restaurant, then continued home.

Happy. What a thought. These children had just faced the unhappy truth in that bully. The boy reminded her of the snobby schoolboys at home, the same children who received nothing but accolades for their schoolwork and a blind eye for their ill behavior.

Her parents had been just like Mrs. Rudolf — but with a wealth of investments behind their attitude. There'd been a time when casting off that kind of snobbery and elitism had made Leanna happy. But now? She could hardly consider herself happy regardless of where she resided. Perhaps if she hadn't been deceived by Jack, if he had proved his remorse by working their way out of this place, maybe then she could have been happy again.

Would she ever look back on her marriage with the joy she'd once felt in Jack's arms? He'd encouraged her long ago, sparking her desire to make a difference in the lives of children. But she didn't know his secret vice then.

Leanna was certain. Happiness was nowhere to be found in Castle Gate.

■ ■ ■ ■

Alex spied his nephew on the porch of the restaurant as he returned from work. "Hello, Teddy."

"Where's Papa?" Teddy ran up, his nose pink with the evening chill.

"He's at home with your mother. We'll take dinner to them later." He hooked his finger beneath the boy's chin. "Did you learn good English today?"

"I learned *dance.*" He thrust his arms to either side of him and began the traditional wedding-dance footsteps.

Alex chuckled. "That is an interesting topic for an English lesson."

"And he learned *jump.*" Maria leaned up on the porch's post, her arms crossed and her nose scrunched up.

"Really?" Alex tilted his head. He was familiar with that look. One of contempt mixed with a challenge. Every Greek woman had mastered it, and it seemed Maria learned quickly at ten years of age. "What is the matter, *kookla?*"

She stepped down into the road. "The other children tease us."

"What have I told you?" Alex crouched down and patted her nose. "We are as

American as they are. I've worked hard for you to have a home, and a restaurant, and —"

"A good teacher," Maria said. Her face relaxed, and she patted his shoulder. "Mrs. McKee was kind, at least."

"Yes, it is kind that she walks you," Alex said, surprised by the leap in his chest at the mention of the schoolteacher.

"No, she reprimanded the boy who made fun of Teddy, on our walk home." Maria offered her hand, and Teddy took it. "I just wish the boys would listen to her. And that Mrs. Rudolph." They began to walk back to the restaurant. "Mrs. McKee is our only friend."

Alex stood up, rubbing his stubbled jaw. "I don't doubt that. Jack was just as kind to me."

A long whistle pierced the air, and the rumble of a train shook the ground. As it grew louder, the children covered their ears and ran inside the restaurant.

"You've got to get used to that, children," Alex bellowed in the chaotic noise as the train approached from Price Canyon and the rest of the world. The engine's steam rose and clouded Alex's view of the two spires of rock that gave their town its name.

He continued through the restaurant's

door and a waft of Momma's cooking filled his nostrils. His stomach's grumble matched that of the loud train passing through the coal town.

The dining room was already filled with crowded tables of hungry miners. Momma bustled out of the kitchen, her graying ebony hair swept up in a bun, and all four feet ten of her slumped with the weight of the filled tray in her arms. She worked her way to the front, setting down bowls for Greek miners with black fingernails and dust-covered faces.

"Alex, where have you been? Your *avgolemono* is cold." She nodded toward the back where the children were sitting.

He wormed his way through the men, anxious for the frothy lemon soup to coat his dusty throat and empty stomach.

As he scraped the last of the rice and meat from the bottom of his bowl, Momma returned with a tray full of empty dishes. "The children tell me that teacher is kind to them. I have some chicken for you to take to her." She nodded her chin toward the kitchen, gesturing for him to follow her.

He set his bowl on the tray. "Now?"

"Of course." Momma threw up one hand as she balanced the tray on her shoulder. "Before dark, Alex. Go."

"I cannot go now, Momma. It's not right for me to be in that part of town at this hour," he said. The thought of Coffey soured his contented belly.

Her brown eyes narrowed with concern. "You've been here for many years, and still you're not welcome?"

"*Thios* Alex, you just told me that we're as American as those people." Maria's reminder encouraged Momma's eyebrows to a high arch.

"You are right." He pointed a finger at his niece, forcing himself to grin. He couldn't allow them to see weakness. He was the one person who'd given them this fresh start, this chance to prosper. He was their rock, and he could not allow anything to shake him. Not again.

How weak to abide by the lines drawn by men like Coffey. Alex was an upstanding man whose sweat and toil not only brought his family to this place but also contributed to the prosperity of the coal company.

"Okay, Momma. Make me a plate," Alex said, glancing out the window to note dusk falling at a rapid pace on Castle Gate. "It is best if I get there before dark."

The blaze filled the coal stove as Leanna stretched out her hands for warmth. She spied the unmade bed, the tangle of sheets from restless nights. Not much longer now and she'd be off to the rest of her life. Her heart fluttered with excitement — only for a moment. The shadows of regret began to crawl from every corner of her two-room shanty. How many times had she prayed forgiveness since Jack's death? Yet how many times had she thought ill of the man since he'd been laid to rest?

The single noise in her home erupted from her empty belly. "Hunger is not discriminatory," she mumbled, cradling a warm bowl of bland stew in her lap.

One bite, then two, and that was enough. Eating alone was more dreadful than she could imagine. Even ill-mannered Jack offered some sort of company.

"This is a good meal, Leanna." Jack would say, his lips smeared with coal slime. He'd then thud his fist on the plain wooden table as he coughed on his stew. Once his fit subsided, he'd continue to shovel in his supper.

When he was done, he would toss his spoon beside his bowl, evoking a cringe from Leanna, and then sit back in his chair with a smack of his lips.

"Thank you, lass." His pale blue eyes would shine through the layer of filth. "How was your day?"

She'd complain about the filthy Greek boys, and the tricky language they'd speak, talking about her without her understanding, she suspected.

"Aye, but their fathers and uncles are hard workers," he'd say, splaying his hands across his taut shirt, rubbing his belly. Leanna had doubted he was full, but he always seemed satisfied. "They are good men, those Greeks."

What did they think of Jack, she wondered? The ugly labor agent, trying to collect money from her came to mind. He probably thought Jack a fool, losing a bet on miner's wages.

But then there was Alex. He was Jack's friend. She saw him at his funeral — on the other side of the fence, but he had been there, nonetheless. Alex Pappas seemed to be a good man.

Jack was a good man, too, when she'd first met him.

A question nagged her heart with a searing burn like the fiery coals. If she had known the end was near, would she have made Jack's last days so miserable? If he had known, would he have tried harder to get them out of here?

Leanna grimaced, her throat so tight that

she couldn't manage one more spoonful. Frustration crept into every bone of her frame. She needed to leave this room where so many fights and disappointments clung to the walls. She burst through the door onto the porch, her lungs parched for a fresh breath of God's creation. Leanna longed for lush lawns and planted flower beds. Her view of a stark mountain range was less satisfying. There was no lawn for her simple house, only a rudimentary dirt path leading to scrubby trees lining the bald, rocky slope at her property's edge.

The sun had tucked itself behind the range, and dusk promised that nightfall was fast approaching. Her shawl did nothing to ward off the cooling temperature. As she turned to warm herself by her stove again, a nearing figure caught her eye.

Alex Pappas approached from the path to town. He jaunted toward her with an eager wave then turned up her path. "Good evening, Mrs. McKee." His dark eyes slid toward Coffey's unlit windows.

"Good evening," she said. "Is anything wrong, Mr. Pappas?"

He shook his head. "Nothing at all." He gave a reassuring smile, warming her from the inside out. She was content enough to stay outside a moment longer. "Momma insisted I bring you some chicken and potatoes. A recipe from our village in Greece." He handed her a warm pot. She lifted the lid and inhaled the same savory smell that met her each time she'd passed their restaurant. Butter and oregano and comfort.

"This is kind of your mother." A low growl erupted in her torso and her mouth watered. It smelled better than her unfinished stew.

"Think of it as a thank-you for your kindness to the children." He pulled his hat off and held it at his chest. "They told us about the teasing today."

So Maria did understand that Billy was mocking them.

"It was the civilized thing to do." She cleared her throat. "This is a miserable place to find civility, though." In her opinion, this canyon bred nothing of the sort. "When do they return to Greece?"

"Greece?" He pressed his shoulders back with confidence. "We are Americans now, Mrs. McKee."

"I just assumed." She furrowed her brow and cradled the warm pot against her waist. "Many of the children leave once their uncles have filled pockets." *Is it possible I'm envious of those lice-infested boys?* That bitter weed began to reach upward and wrap

41

around her throat. "How often I'd wished Jack's pockets didn't have so many holes so we could do the same," she muttered.

"Those Greek men who leave have sisters with dowries, or families who need them. They shouldn't take advantage like that, but they are desperate for work. Unfortunately, the same man who entices them here is the man who stole from Jack."

"Stole?" Her voice heightened.

"Yes, the labor agent took Jack's money, I am afraid. Not a good example of my people."

She'd avoided that man. He was persistent and obnoxious. But Jack had left her here linked to that rotten man, hadn't he? Leanna pursed her lips. "Mr. Pappas, Jack gave our money away. He gambled every last penny in Boston, and every earned one here." She bristled at this conversation.

"I understand your frustration. But Jack was a good man," Alex said in a hushed voice.

She gaped at him. The old anger was fresher than the air she breathed, and she could not talk herself out of it. Alex Pappas had overstayed his welcome.

"I must go inside now. Thank your mother, please." She turned a shoulder to leave.

Alex's lips parted as if to speak, but then he pressed them together in a consolatory smile. "I will tell her. Thank you again, Mrs. McKee."

Alex stepped into the shadow of the restaurant's back porch as Coffey and his friends turned up the path to their houses — the same path Alex had just taken from Mrs. McKee's. A close call. Thankfully, Alex had refrained from offering to dine with her. What assumptions would Coffey have made then? But Alex knew the loneliness of her circumstance and how a friend could soothe such pain. Where would he be now if Will Jacob hadn't been his friend those first weeks of his loss? His foreman taught him English and kept him sane when silence promised to strangle him.

Now he stood against the wall. The jagged brick snagged at his coat, but not nearly as gripping as the shame that ground against his conscience like sandpaper. This was a ridiculous posture for a man like Alex. To hide from those weasels? Eight years of working in the mines of Carbon County and those fools treated him as if he'd only just arrived off the boat. He was giving into their ignorance by hiding like a child.

It was better than confrontation, though.

That would only break his vow to remain indifferent to any jesting that would come his way.

After they were out of sight, he ran along the side of the restaurant, releasing his held breath. It formed a misty cloud in the cool night as he made his way to the coffeehouse.

He entered a room filled with his countrymen. Their chatter clashed with a wild pluck of a guitar and boisterous singing. Tonight was the first wrestling match against the boastful Japanese wrestler. The miners from the Far East talked up their fighting abilities, and no Greek would allow such bragging to go unmatched. The prize-winning fighter, Nick Lampropolous, was surrounded by his cousins in the far corner. With winners like Nick, Greek pride pulsed amid the tables of the crowded establishment.

Alex joined his brother at a square table by the bar. "Nick will be sorely missed when he returns to Greece," Alex said.

"Ah. Yes. But he promises to send over his nephew." Yanni tapped his foot to the music. "And he is twice his size."

"Perhaps his nephew will stay for good."

"We are lucky, you and I." His brother leaned back in his chair. "Momma's restaurant is prosperous, and we have nothing but time to gain our successes."

"And with time, comes wisdom." Alex winked, trying to convince himself that he had been wise more than foolish as he had cowered in the shadows.

"And maybe a life free from Anthis and those American bigots?" Yanni slung back a drink of ouzo. "I only envy Nick because he'll wipe his hands clean of those men."

"Men like Nick do not help our attempt to become respected by the American miners." Alex ran his finger around the rim of his glass. "He comes, makes money, and returns."

"Can you blame him, though? He has family back in Greece. You know what that is like, Brother. Helena needed the money you were going to send —"

Alex tossed a heated glare at his brother. Why did he bring that up?

Yanni lifted his hands up in surrender. "I am sorry, Alex. May her memory be eternal." He bobbed his head and lowered his eyes, clasping his hands together. After a moment, he leaned over the table and in a hushed voice said, "You can't point fingers at men like Nick and blame them for the ignorant Americans. Everyone is free to choose what's best for their lives, don't you agree?"

He spoke truth. But the mention of Helena only reminded Alex of a choice that he'd made — one that would haunt him forever. He dragged his fingers through his curls and sipped his drink.

Yanni shifted around the table, slid in another chair, and slapped Alex's back. "Brother, you seem too serious for such a night." He shook his finger. "Cheer up, or I'll offer you up to the Japanese fighter." He then rose to his feet and joined arms with another Greek. They began to sing their nation's anthem, as was custom before a fight. A bustle of Japanese miners entered the place along with a sprinkling of fat snowflakes.

Alex had little interest in any of it. Winter was upon them, and if there was one thing time did not bring, it was healing. This season only taunted him. Years ago, he had sworn his first winter in America would be his last. He'd worked hard for his wages, with every intention of returning to Greece. But it was all in vain, the lot of it. No help from God, no use to send back money. Helena died, and he was alone in a foreign land without reason at all. Just like Mrs. McKee, he had been abandoned because of money. Had Jack crippled his wife's wallet? This was difficult for Alex to imagine. His friend was a good man.

And his wife had been good to his family. Hurt flushed her face tonight. Her blue eyes were ready to burst with grief — and perhaps anger? He'd felt the same way when Helena had died before his chance to help her. But while it seemed Mrs. McKee's anger was at Jack, Alex was only angry with himself. For believing in answered prayer and foolish providence.

All these years, one thing remained the same — it was up to him alone to stay the course. Everything depended on Alex Pappas — his family, their success, and most of all, their happiness.

CHAPTER THREE

"Watch your step." Leanna tightened her grip on Teddy's small gloved hand. Patches of ice offered dangerous stepping-stones up the slope to the schoolhouse.

"We know. We have snow in Kalavryta." Maria walked ahead with her arms out like a circus performer on a tight rope.

"Be careful, Maria," Leanna called out.

The girl shook her head, spun on her toe, and tilted her nose to the sky. "See, I am not afraid."

Leanna clicked her tongue in disapproval then pulled Teddy closer to her side just before he stepped onto a shiny layer of ice.

"Thank you, Meesus McKee." He shivered as he spoke. She nearly picked him up. The urge to protect him surprised her. How could she grow attached to these children in such a short time?

"Thios Alex make snowshoes. We are ready for winter." Maria wobbled, caught herself, and giggled. Leanna winced.

Thios Alex.

It had been two weeks since Alex had brought her dinner. Beyond his dazzling smile and unexpected gift, he praised Jack, unleashing her bitterness into that cool night air. Why had she allowed her anger to admit Jack's shortcomings? Hadn't she spited him enough in his living? She was wretched with guilt as she ate dinner that night. The delicious food was wasted on her sour attitude.

Teddy's teeth chattered, and Leanna wrapped her arm around his shoulders. "We're almost there, Teddy. You need a thicker coat."

Maria squealed as her foot slipped and she began to fall back. With a quick jerk, Leanna let go of Teddy and caught his sister under the arms. "Thank you, Meesus Mc-Kee." Maria looked up with an apologetic look.

"I told you to be careful, Miss Pappas." She stood her up and crouched down to Maria's eye level. "You will walk beside us, now. No more silliness on the ice."

Maria nodded. Teddy clutched at Leanna's skirt. She reached for his hand, but with the next step his arms flew up and he fell back on his side.

49

His wail pierced the air, and he began to scream in Greek.

Leanna froze with panic. "What is it? Where are you hurt?" She tried to pull him up to standing, but he screamed louder.

"Quick, Maria, go get your grandfather," Leanna said.

Maria gave her a blank stare as the color drained from her face. She shook her head and lifted her shoulders. She didn't understand. Leanna took in a deep breath. She had heard them reference their grandfather when she dropped them off at the restaurant.

"Pa-pou," Leanna over-pronounced the name she'd heard them speak a handful of times. Maria's eyes lit up and she treaded carefully down the hill again.

"Shh, shh." Leanna adjusted Teddy's hat to keep the cold away, and brushed his forehead with her own gloved hand. The little boy whimpered and shivered.

Lord, protect him.

A sudden shriek of pain escaped his purple lips, and he began to sob. Leanna forced back her own tears. She unbuttoned her coat and took it off, placing it over Teddy like a blanket. Teddy's mouth began to tremble uncontrollably, and his face

50

paled to an off shade of his olive complexion.

"There, there." She wiped a tear from his cheek.

If she could talk to him in his language, she'd provide some sort of comfort. Even though she'd been surrounded by Greeks for nearly a year, she had done nothing to understand them. Jack had always revered the Greek men as strong workers, but Leanna couldn't see past his betrayal to care much for her students.

In this moment with Teddy, an old passion stirred inside her. He was in her care, and just as scared and in need as the American children who'd inspired her back home. Why had she let herself believe that teaching immigrant children was any less noble than educating the children of the Boston slums? This was the work she'd wanted to do when her sewing circle first spoke of education for all.

The frigid air bit through her thin cotton sleeves, and her lips quivered in the cold. Her teeth began to chatter just as she spotted Maria and her grandfather trekking toward them. "Papou is here," she said, stroking Teddy's hair.

Mr. Pappas ran up to them, mumbling in Greek. He was a distinguished man, with graying sideburns and a salt-and-pepper mustache. Concern puckered his brow, shadowing his pale blue eyes. "*Ella,* ella," he said in a hushed tone. The man carefully handed Leanna her coat and then scooped Teddy into his arms.

The boy screamed and grabbed at his left arm, which dangled loosely to the ground. Mr. Pappas sucked air in his teeth, grimacing in a regretful way. He gingerly helped Teddy rest his arm on his belly, then cradled the boy close to his body. Teddy snuggled against his broad chest, and Mr. Pappas kissed his forehead.

"Thank you to send Maria." His words rolled with an accent, but they were comprehensible.

"Of course." Leanna brushed her hand along Teddy's back, fighting the urge to kiss him also. She quickly stepped away.

Mr. Pappas, Teddy, and Maria made their way carefully down the hill while Leanna continued on to school. The school bell rang as she opened the gate, and the children ran to line up.

Perhaps she would learn some Greek from her students today. The Americans and Greeks stayed to themselves, yet the relentless jeering from Mrs. Rudolf's students filled the entire school yard. She shook her head. What good would learning Greek do? Unless the American children were taught differently, the dividing line would remain as deep as the mountain ore. And if their upbringing was anything like hers had been, they had been bred to know that lines were never to be crossed. Propriety was strong and powerful, just like prejudice. And the consequences could be dangerous. Teddy and Maria had more to worry about than broken limbs.

Why had the Pappas family chosen to live in such a stifling place as this?

Morning light shone before her, a stark contrast to the Greek priest hurrying along the road ahead. He wore a tall black hat, long dark beard, and a black robe as he turned toward Greek Town. A foreboding shadow cast across Leanna's spirit. The last time she'd seen a priest in Castle Gate, he'd stood solemn like a charcoal statue, waving incense over one of the coffins near Jack's gravesite.

She quickened her pace to the front porch of the Pappas restaurant, anxious to check on Teddy. Savory smells of roasted meat, garlic, and butter filled her nostrils.

"Good morning, Mrs. McKee." Alex stepped out from under the canopy of the porch. His olive skin was clean of coal, and his white button-up shirt was crisp and gleaming. "Maria will be out shortly."

"How is Teddy?" She adjusted her out-of-season hat — much too small of a brim to be fashionable now, but perfectly suitable for the widow of a common man.

"He has a broken arm, but more than that, a poor attitude." He smirked.

"I cannot imagine that. He seems like such a joy," she said, distracted by her thoughts. "Mr. Pappas, do you think his attitude is just about the arm? I fear that the children at school are unrelenting."

Alex searched her with a steady gaze. Not just her eyes, but her hair, her cheeks, and her mouth. She tried not to melt. Finally, she turned her attention down the main street lined with wagons.

"I would like to thank you." Alex cleared his throat. "*We* would like to thank you. You were a great comforter to Teddy, just as you helped ease the children's growing pains the other day."

Growing pains? A weight pressed against her heart, the same disappointment when Mrs. Rudolf affirmed the rude behavior of her students. "I fear the jesting is more than growing pains. Will the children ever feel welcome here, Mr. Pappas?" she asked.

"You have made them welcome, Mrs. Mc-Kee." His eyes sparkled beneath his fisherman's cap, and again she was forced to look away. There was so much life behind those eyes. So much curiosity and hope.

"I am one woman who is being paid to care for them," Leanna said. The burden of caring beyond that suffocated her. She could not grow attached. "What about every obstacle they'll meet along the way?"

His eyes narrowed. "What do you mean, Mrs. McKee? Do you expect us to give up on our chosen life because of ignorance?" He huffed. " 'There is no darkness but ignorance.' "

She widened her eyes and he did the same, but his was in challenge. "Is that Shakespeare?" she asked.

"Even Greeks know wisdom, Mrs. Mc-Kee."

She resisted the temptation to gape at him. Perhaps she was no better than Mrs. Rudolf and other Castle Gate residents — Alex Pappas was an educated man, and she shouldn't be so surprised. "Shakespeare was a wise soul," Leanna whispered. "If only others around here heeded his words. I fear the darkness is widespread." She'd fought it in Boston in a different way. Her parents refused to see the truth of her cause.

"And kind schoolteachers like you are a light to our children." He beamed, and she squirmed. Leanna McKee — a light? If he only knew her within the walls of her home with a disappointing husband bringing out her worst.

"I am but one woman, Mr. Pappas." She sighed. "Just the other day there was an anti-Greek riot in Omaha featured in the newspaper. The same sentiment of Castle Gate's foolish schoolboys is rampant across the country."

Alex snatched a coat from the hook by the restaurant door. "There may be miserable men who will get in my way" — he grabbed a sturdy walking stick — "but just like you choose to do what's right for my kinsmen, I, too, shall persevere." With each word, his height seemed to grow. Leanna caught her mouth from dropping at this strong, eloquent man. "Mrs. McKee, I daresay, you of all people should understand the need to persevere in this unforgiving land." Silence fell sharply between them. The roar of a train disrupted the quiet as it approached the nearby depot.

"I only persevere to find my way out," she said. "There is no hope here."

"Everyone I love is here in Castle Gate. They are my hope."

56

The restaurant door swung open, and Maria stepped onto the porch. "Kaliméra — ah, good morning, Meesus McKee."

"I apologize for offending you," Leanna said to Alex through a forced smile. He turned toward her, blocking Maria from view.

"This land of opportunity has its thorns." He lifted his hat, running his hand through his curls. "We can either let them bind us to a meager existence" — his brow softened, and he spoke through gritted teeth — "or trample them to reach a greater potential."

His wisdom was familiar, akin to Jack's advice when she chose education over a haughty inheritance. Leanna understood his optimism. It had once been her own.

"No matter what the rest of the country says, Mr. Pappas . . ." Her throat tightened. "We aren't so different." Discarding a life among wealth and snobbery was nothing she'd regretted, but it had brought her to a new briar patch to overcome.

"You are a kind, compassionate woman." His gaze trapped her once again. She couldn't look away because he'd filled up every bit of her world at this moment. "I am glad the children have you."

"Don't try to flatter me, Mr. Pappas." She swallowed hard, a stubborn sting of tears threatening her eyes. "I don't deserve it."

"Deserve it? You cannot deny who you are, Mrs. McKee." He stepped back and Maria appeared beneath his elbow. Alex muttered Greek from the corner of his mouth.

"Neh, neh!" Maria squealed and ran up to her with arms open for an embrace, but when she caught Leanna's glare she reached for her hand instead, giving it a shake. A warmth spread across Leanna's chest, and she couldn't help but chuckle.

Alex winked at his niece. "I am off for a hike before the graveyard shift. Good day." He tipped his hat then began up Main Street. His coat hung over his shoulder with one hand, and his hiking stick stabbed the ground with each stride.

"What did he say to you, Maria?" Leanna asked as they started up the hill to school.

"That you are our first American friend."

Leanna was tossed in a storm of thanksgiving and stubborn propriety. She was only the child's teacher, but Alex's opinion overwhelmed her.

The same Greek priest from earlier passed them on their way to school. He patted Maria's head, and she kissed his hand. Leanna was close enough to see the man's face. There was no sadness in his eyes or frown upon his bearded lips. He grinned, his pale blue eyes brightened beneath a scruffy mess of dark eyebrows. Her impression shifted from a dark mystery to that of a kind grandfather, like Maria's papou.

Shakespeare *had* said it best: "There is no darkness but ignorance."

From the corner of her eye, she saw the American boys mocking the priest and chucking rocks in their direction. Ignorance was rampant in Castle Gate. Even Leanna had contributed to the darkness at some time or other in her subtle prejudice against these people. Alex was either brave or foolish to hope for change around here.

CHAPTER FOUR

Clanking pots and a constant murmur of conversation flowed from the kitchen. Alex tossed his coat over the counter in the back of the restaurant.

His hike was useless today. Usually, it cleared his mind and gave him the same peace he'd found from the liturgy back in Greece. But the only peace he found today was in convincing the young American widow that his family was strong enough to prosper even here, in this place. And unlike the resistance he found among many of the miners, both Greek and American, Mrs. McKee had willingly considered all he said.

He shouldn't have complimented her like he did, and he shouldn't have encouraged Maria, either. But somehow, a friendship with Mrs. McKee gave him a strange hope. In what, he wasn't sure. And dwelling on all of this had disrupted his usual harmonious trek.

From now on when he worked late, he would stay in Greek Town. Leanna McKee had overstayed her welcome in his thoughts today, and no matter how many thorns he was willing to overcome, a friendship with an American woman would bring nothing but trouble to the Pappas family.

His father carried a bucket and mop through the kitchen door. "If we were back in Greece, all I'd do is sit outside and smoke with my friends. Now your momma puts me to work."

"Am I not understanding your Greek, or is your memory failing?" Alex walked around the counter and patted his father's shoulder. "I recall you mopping there, too."

Papa grunted. "How is Teddy?"

"I wasn't home."

"That Mrs. McKee is a kind woman. I can see it in her eyes. You did good hiring her."

Alex's heart leaped. Papa was slim with his compliments. Some days, Alex wondered if the only reason he came to America was to wait for this whole new life to fail and blame it on his oldest son. If he knew Leanna's concern for the children's well-being here, they'd be fine friends. At least the schoolteacher was willing to consider Alex's position. Stergios Pappas was as stubborn as any Greek patriarch.

Alex gathered up his coat again. "I am going home to sleep before my shift."

His father hesitated with the mop, narrowing his eyes at Alex. He gave a curt nod and continued to his chore. Alex released a long sigh as he made his way to the door. The slosh of the water and the slap of the mop on the floor echoed off the walls.

"When will you work enough to avoid such a shift?" Papa called out just as he reached for the doorknob. "I don't see why you are still shoved around by that coal company."

Alex winced. The same conversation as always. He turned but kept his eyes on the icon of the *Theotokos.* "You and Momma keep up the effort here at the restaurant, and I'll keep up the work in the mines."

"Your momma worries about you. She thinks you care only about work. What about a life, Alex? Maybe you should go back to Greece this summer. Find a bride and start a family."

"I tried that once. It did not go so well." The Virgin Mary stared at him from the painting. How often did he pray for Helena in those days? Nobody answered his prayer.

"Helena was sickly from the beginning," Papa said. "I don't blame you for leaving."

Anger infused his frustration. His father's

words chipped at the dormant guilt for his shortcomings — and his greed. "I left for her, to make money for her care," he said out loud to re-convince himself. "How many times do we have to go over this, Papa?"

"I am just saying, you cannot give up on a life because of a sad incident like Helena's."

"Give up?" Steam rose from his pit. He glared at his father. "Look at this!" His arms flung out to his side and waved at every established corner of the room. "Do you know how successful we are, Papa?"

"Do not talk to me that way," his father snapped. He lowered his eyes to his ever-moving mop. Defeat settled on Alex's weary shoulders. He had crossed a line — again. But having this conversation over and over was exhausting.

Maria tumbled through the doors. "*Yas-sas*, Thios Alex. Papou."

"How was your day?" Alex asked. As the door closed behind her, the petite blond schoolteacher hurried past toward the rest of town.

Leanna had recognized his quote — the wisdom he had learned from an old Shake-speare volume those days in the boarding-house where he practiced his English. *"There is no darkness but ignorance."* A bold declaration that shaped his resilience to men like Coffey. Dare he say this to his family, as well? They did not understand him fully at times like these.

"Mrs. McKee said she would teach me to dance if I learned my words by Christmas." Maria twirled on her foot, grabbing Alex's hand to steady herself.

"Oh, that is nice." Papa's voice grew higher and lighter — he was a good papou. "She is a kind lady, isn't she?"

"Who?" his mother entered from the kitchen.

"Mrs. McKee," Maria called out.

"She is. We should invite her to your name-day celebration, Stergios. I am making the *glyká* now."

"Imagine that. A schoolteacher among a roomful of Greek miners." Papa chuckled.

"No, leave her be. She does not belong here." Alex gently removed his hand from Maria's.

"We are American, too, are we not?" His father's sarcasm was thick. Alex left the restaurant without another word.

Cold air stung his face as he stepped outside again. His father had a point, and to admit that frustrated Alex even more. If they were Americans, then why did they have to worry about affiliating with one?

64

Momma and Penelope craved friendship, like all good Greek women did. What would it look like for an American to become friends with a Greek?

The street was busy, women strolling side by side and men in wagons or tending to horses. Perhaps Momma had a point, too.

Why not invite a family friend to a celebration?

He shook his head and crammed his hands in his pockets. Maybe one day, but not now, not with — Leanna? From the corner of his eye, he saw her beneath the post office sign on the other side of the coffeehouse.

She had her back to him, her blond hair in a bundle at her neck. She spun around on her heel, holding a piece of paper in her hand, with her hand over her mouth. She barreled toward him, but her gaze was lowered to her feet.

"Whoa." He held up his hands as she nearly ran into him.

"Forgive me, Mr. Pappas," she spoke hoarsely and stepped around him, continuing toward her neighborhood. When he caught a glimpse of her face, her cheeks glistened with tears. *Continue to Greek Town, Alex.*

There was no use befriending this woman.

65

This was not the time to blur those social boundaries. But how could he ignore her hurt?

"Mrs. McKee," he called out, jogging up beside her. "What is it?"

He pushed aside the vulnerable nag to look about them. This was his land as much as anyone's, right? Leanna continued with brisk strides alongside the restaurant then pressed her back on the wall, folding her arms across her chest. A small whimper escaped her lips.

"My plans to leave have changed," she muttered. "My cousin has no position for me in San Francisco."

"Oh, I see." He searched his pockets and found a handkerchief, offering it to her as she folded up the letter and placed it in her pocket.

She dabbed her eyes and her cheeks. "Blasted, Jack! He has cursed my life forever." She covered her face with trembling hands. Her sobs grated on Alex's heart like a pickax on stubborn ground. He pulled her by the elbow, finally looking about himself, and took her to the yard behind the restaurant, wrapping his arms around her shaking shoulders. She had nobody here. The mine had stolen Jack, and her family was far away.

A sorely familiar predicament for Alex.

"Leanna." He winced. Using her first name seemed inappropriate. But formalities were useless when tears were involved. "Please, stop crying."

"You do not understand." She pulled away. "You are happy here. I am not." She sniffled and returned his handkerchief.

He'd gained something other than happiness here. The mines had offered Alex a place to redeem himself. That was what made his choice to follow Anthis worth it in the end. Success against all odds. Even after his worst failure.

"You may not realize it, but I do understand." Alex curled his lips and looked away. What was he doing? He did not need to open that chapter again. But Leanna stood before him without hope, just as he had once stood on this mountain, holding a letter from his momma that declared the end of everything — for him.

"I have nobody, Alex," she sniffled. His stomach leaped at his name on her lips. "You have family here."

"That was not always true. I've felt just as alone as you have, Leanna," he admitted. "I am here for you, just as I was for Jack. He was a good friend to me."

Her glassy eyes searched his, and she frowned. "If that were the case, I do wonder what he said about me. Did he tell you the truth about me?"

"The truth?"

"That I was bitter. And hard. That no matter how much he regretted his mistakes, I suffocated him in shame." Leanna gasped on a sob. "I deserve to be alone. And I do not deserve your kindness, Alex." She turned to leave, but he clutched her arm.

"We are more alike than you think," he whispered at her ear. "Regret weighs us down like a heavy boulder."

She shook his hand away and tucked wisps of golden hair beneath her hat. "I have said too much."

He smoothed her last stray curl behind her ear. His pulse sped as his fingers skimmed her soft ivory skin.

Leanna's eyes closed then fluttered open. The topaz blues swam with tears and awe. Alex could not pull his gaze from hers.

"What regrets do you have?" she asked. "You are kind and courageous in this dark place."

He opened his mouth to speak, but he couldn't form the words. What was he doing? There was no reason to live his past all over again. No, he could not share with her the one thing that broke him in two. He walked away from everything that day long ago, when the heavens stole from him just as greedily as Anthis.

"Forgive me, I must leave. My shift will begin soon —" He tipped his hat and left the woman with a look of wonder.

What was he thinking? He had just discouraged his parents from letting this woman into their lives more than they should. His road to prosperity would not be distracted by such temptation. He had been distracted before and paid the price. And now, Leanna McKee had stolen his senses.

Leanna shivered on her way to pick up Maria. Winter was harsh this year. If only she could afford warmer attire. Alex's embrace on Friday crawled into her mind and its warmth filled her again. He was strong yet gentle, proud yet humble. Everything he would need to live by his philosophy of perseverance.

But what regret did he have?

He crept into her thoughts and prayers all weekend. Was it a coincidence that this man seemed to show up and offer her hope every time she found herself at her worst?

Leanna cringed. Regardless of Alex's optimism, she could not depend on him in a place like this. Perhaps loneliness grew her need for others, when her passion had always been to help those in need.

The Pappas family had clogged the leak of her own prejudice, hadn't they? The children, Alex, and even his father, who had displayed such affection to Teddy — a love deserved just like any other child in Castle Gate, in Boston, in this country.

Alex and the Pappas family had become endearing.

Leanna stepped onto the porch of the restaurant and peered in the window. It was mostly dark inside. Only a small light glowed in the back. The door swung open and Maria appeared, stopping it from closing with her foot.

"Good morning, Meesus McKee," Maria said, wiping her mouth with a gloved hand.

"Is Teddy coming —" Leanna bit her lip when Alex, instead of Teddy, filled the doorway.

"No," Alex replied, scooting Maria through. "He is better, but not ready to return to school." Yanni joined them, closing the door with a quiet click.

"I see." Leanna reached for Maria's hand. "We'll be on our way, then."

Yanni spoke to Alex in Greek, and Alex shook his head fervently. How irritating that they spoke so openly in a language she couldn't understand.

70

She winced at her attitude, which matched that of most Americans around — including her arrogant neighbors. Alex spoke her language perfectly, didn't he?

"Come, Maria." She started up the road toward the school while Maria lagged behind shouting her good-byes.

A loud commotion of Greek started behind them. The brothers' tiny mother was rambling away. She then gave Alex's arm a firm smack. He rubbed it and said something inaudible from where Leanna stood.

"Wait!" he bellowed, still staring at his mother. "Mrs. McKee, wait." He bulldozed toward her, setting off a rush of blood to her face.

"Is something wrong, Mr. Pappas?" Her eyelashes fluttered just like her stomach.

Alex stopped at a proper distance to converse, his hands clenched by his sides. "Mrs. McKee, my mother insists that I extend you an invitation to my father's name-day celebration," he said softly, but his brow was tight with frustration. "Please, don't feel obligated; it might be strange since she will be the only other woman."

Words lodged in her throat. Her sensibility agreed that it would be strange. Especially if she was the only American, too. Mrs. Pappas cast an eager glance her way,

the woman wringing her apron and nod-
ding enthusiastically.

Alex did not appear so eager.

"She is persistent, isn't she?" Leanna
whispered. "I do not want to cause your
family any trouble. And I am sure it
would. . . ." She glanced up the hill where a
group of miners trekked toward the mines.

"That is what I try to tell her, but then
again —" Alex stepped closer. His lips
curled inward as his exasperated expression
turned to one of thoughtfulness. "It is your
choice, Mrs. McKee. Perhaps changed
opinions start with you? The schoolteacher
who not only teaches Greeks but befriends
them?" He shrugged his shoulders then
sighed. "At least, that is a fleeting thought
of mine while Momma is unbearable." He
gave a lopsided grin, tipped his hat, then
signaled to Yanni who rushed up to them.
He kissed Maria on the forehead, smiled
kindly at Leanna, then walked alongside
Alex. "It is tonight, Mrs. McKee." Alex
waved to his mother. She gave a satisfied
smile then hurried back inside the restaurant.

"My papou like you. He say you love
Teddy like a momma." Maria giggled. "He
want you at his party."

"I see. What is your grandfather's name?"

If they were celebrating it, she should know what it was.

"Stergios."

"And you celebrate this?"

"All names have special day." Her English was improving nicely. If only Leanna could talk to her about what was truly in her heart. First, should she accept the invitation? And second, did Alex want her there?

She was distracted by the invitation all day. A month ago, there would have been no hesitation in responding with a polite no. But she was a prisoner to her cold, dank home with the puny coal stove providing the only warmth.

Alex had made it seem that she could make a difference around here. What if she could? What if this was the very reason she was still in Castle Gate? To scatter the darkness brought in by ignorant miners?

Leanna decided to accept the invitation. She and the other progressives in Boston had rebelled against the class who firmly pushed immigrants and laborers to a level beneath them. She would not allow old expectations to hinder her from spending an evening in their company instead of being alone and miserable.

CHAPTER FIVE

Darkened skies brought the dusty coal miners from the heart of the mountain. With the babble of Greek, Leanna shrank into the shadows of the restaurant, her ears pumping with nerves. She tucked her loose hair back into her bun. Her golden locks alone surely screamed that she was a stranger.

At least the past few hours after school had been quiet and pleasant. Alex's parents had made sure she was comfortable, while Maria taught her how to play jackstones. Leanna enjoyed the lull of small talk, even if she couldn't understand everything, and the warmth of family, even if they weren't hers.

"Meesus McKee, you like Yiayia's *patatas?*" Maria scooted closer.

"The potatoes are delicious. Thank your grandmother for me," Leanna whispered to the girl, who then sprinted toward the kitchen. Maria had sat beside her during the early supper, trying to translate her grandmother's chatter while the woman piled their table with food.

"Good appetite," Mrs. Pappas gleamed, proud of her food, or perhaps her English. Leanna wasn't sure. But they were her only two English words, it seemed. Every other communication was in smiles and hushed Greek to Maria.

Now Leanna kept an eye on the men filling the tables.

Only one or two miners glanced in Leanna's direction at first, but soon a dozen pairs of eyes gawked at her.

She turned to Maria and said, "I must go," and then pushed her chair back and stood up. Mrs. Pappas rushed over, speaking rapidly as she threw her hands about.

"You stay, Meesus McKee," Maria translated. "Papou play music, and we eat fruit."

"Thank your grandparents, Maria." Leanna spoke close to her ear, keeping her eye on the growing audience of men. "But I must —"

"You decided to come." Alex approached, his eyes shining brightly from beneath a layer of coal dust. He sidestepped between two tables and bent down to kiss his mother's cheek.

"I have been here for quite a while." Leanna smoothed her skirt and straightened the cuffs of her sleeves. "I think it is time for me to leave."

"Why? And miss my father's bouzouki playing and Momma's glyká?" He gave a bright smile and winked at Maria.

"Eh?" Mrs. Pappas stared up at her son, and he responded in Greek.

She shook her head fervently. "*Ohi!* Helena's glyká." Her dazzling chocolate eyes brimmed with tears, and she patted Alex's cheek. His jaw flinched.

"*Thia* Helena?" Maria grabbed her grandmother's hand. The woman nodded, drew the child close, and crossed herself in a variation of the manner Leanna had seen Catholics use.

Alex turned away from his mother in her apparent agony and said, "Mrs. McKee, it would devastate my mother if you leave before the celebration has begun."

The woman had been so kind, and it seemed that somehow Leanna was adding to an unknown misery. She pressed her lips together and slid back into her seat. This was a mistake. She was sure of it.

Maria sat next to her again. "I glad you stay." She slipped her hand into Leanna's. A smile crept across the girl's round face.

"Maria, who is Helena?" Leanna asked while Alex walked across the room and shook his father's hand.

"Thia Helena?" The girl's mouth dipped into a frown. "Thios Alex's wife." She fiddled with a spoon lying across an empty bowl. "She die after I was born."

"Oh." Alex was a widower? A chill spread across her arms as she recalled his compassion when she received her cousin's letter. The man understood her more than she could imagine.

As they ate again, Leanna was aware of where he was at each moment that evening. A growing wonder colored her impression of him. In their few interactions, he had appeared to be as steady as the Castle Gate rock spires, which announced the entrance to Price Canyon. His pursuit and his character were unmatched by any person she knew, yet he'd traveled the same tragic path she now wandered over.

Alex weaved in and out of the rows of tables, laughing with friends. Amid the houseful of Greeks filling their bellies, Leanna was not uncomfortable or impatient to leave anymore. This Alex Pappas had her attention like she was a debutante again, waiting for a signature on her dance card.

Stergios took up a seat with a strangely

shaped guitar. As he played, claps and shouts bounced off the walls. The miners began to push back tables, creating an open space in the center of the room. Men locked arms and spun around. Their serpentine line bounced and swayed, creeping closer to her corner of the restaurant.

Maria tugged at her hand. "Come, Meesus McKee, I show you my dance."

Leanna's stomach fell to her feet. "Absolutely not," she commanded, gripping her seat. Heat flushed her cheeks. What would happen if word got out that she was caught dancing among these men? Maria's shoulders dropped, but instead of persisting, she scurried across the room and knelt beside her grandfather, patting the beat on the floor.

Leanna wiped her brow with the back of her hand, anxiety creeping to every corner of her frame. She scoured the room for the nearest exit.

Alex drew near, blocking any view. "You look distraught," he said.

"Just a bit out of sorts. Your niece is unaware of my position here." She forced a smile, even though her stomach remained unsettled.

"I do not blame you," he said. "You are the talk of the miners."

Leanna's mouth dropped.

"Don't worry," Alex quickly continued. "I have told them that we are conspiring, you and me." He winked.

Leanna swallowed hard. "Your words are not comforting in the least. What do you mean?"

"I mean, that you and I are proving that Greeks and Americans can be on harmonious terms. Your presence is a good sign of that."

Besides his eloquence once again sparking awe, she wrestled with embarrassment. "This is all too forced." An ache crept around her heart seeing that she was just one person, and there was a whole town of miners who'd avoid this place at all costs. "I enjoy being a guest, not an experiment."

"Aw, you are a guest," he said. "Forgive me. My family thinks nothing more about you than a treasured guest who helped our children."

"And you?" Leanna's heart leaped to her throat.

His debonair smile fell. "I am grateful to you. I've told you before." Alex's clean-shaven jawline twitched, and his lips pressed together in a thin line. "But I admit that I was hesitant to invite you."

"And I was also hesitant to accept the

79

invitation," she agreed meekly. "You and I are alike in many ways."

The music swelled while his umber eyes steadied on her. Flecks of gold and brown glinted in the lamplight from above. He sighed then straddled a chair with the back pushed against his chest.

"Would you like a candied fruit, Mrs. Mc-Kee?" He slid a tray from the other side of the table.

"Thank you." She picked one and bit into the sticky fruit. A chewy cherry exploded sweetness in her mouth. "It's delicious."

"Momma certainly makes the best." He offered her a cloth napkin. "I joke and tell her she should open a candy store, too. If she wanted to, she would, she says. I believe her."

"I can see that. Your mother is a very persistent woman."

"She is that." They both chuckled. The men behind them began to sing in Greek while Mrs. Pappas carried a pitcher to each table, filling glasses.

"How long have you been in Utah, Alex?"

"Eight years." His forearm muscles flexed as he tightened his grip on the chair.

"My goodness, I was in a completely different world eight years ago. French tablecloths and fine silver — and parents who

80

were persistent in keeping strangers away. Unlike your mother who insisted I come inside." She gave a wry smile.

"It doesn't sound like we are alike as much as you think." His brow wagged playfully.

Leanna lowered her gaze, tracing the table's grain with her nail. "You have felt the same loss as me, Alex." Her pulse quickened.

"You know about Helena?"

"Maria told me."

"It was a long time ago." He looked away. "She was a very ill woman."

"I am sure you were a good husband to her."

His nostrils flared. "What would have you think that?"

"You are kind to me, a practical stranger."

Alex's brow furrowed. "You are right. We are strangers. You do not know me." Turmoil washed his eyes. He glanced around the busy room. Men were now singing with Stergios while Mrs. Pappas disappeared to the kitchen. "There's something about the call of this land. It's intoxicating. I am sure Jack felt the same way when he learned the work he could do and the money he could earn."

Leanna's mouth went dry at the mention

of her husband — and the decision that broke their marriage almost two years ago. "Did Helena come willingly to Castle Gate?" Did she want to know the answer?

He examined her face. The stark contrast between Alex's wife and bitter Leanna was probably blinding — more than her northern blond hair among the Mediterranean ebony locks. "She did not come with me. I left her in Greece. My plan was to return to her, but just like Jack, I was struck by fool's gold."

She stiffened in her chair. "Jack? You are nothing like him."

"You don't give your husband credit for who he was. He was a good man. A saint compared to some," he mumbled with seemingly much effort.

"Why do you tell me this?" Stubborn tears pressed against her eyes. Jack had good intentions — the very reason why she fell in love with him. Yet he left her with a heap of unmet expectations. "I apologize for bringing up your past. It seems you are using mine to hurt me." She pushed her chair back. Her heart banged against her chest as forcefully as the room pulsed with music and stomping feet.

"I do not mean to hurt you, just prove the truth. I am more like Jack than you think.

In the worst way." Alex's jaw flinched. "Because of my foolish gamble, I lost everything."

Leanna's mouth fell open. "You —"

"Thios Alex," Maria whined, tugging at his sleeve. She rubbed one eye and spoke Greek. Alex stood up. He stroked his niece's curls.

"I will take Maria home now. Yanni left a little while ago to check on Penelope and Teddy. Thank you for coming."

"You can't leave now." She shot up from her chair. How could he end this on such an uneasy note?

Regardless of her demand, he turned his back, starting toward the door. "Good-bye, Leanna." His words were swallowed by the noisy celebration.

Blood pumped thick in her ears. She felt as foolish as she had that day she'd discovered Jack's last exchange for their hard-earned wages, the very same day Jack died in the mines. And, the same day that Alex became a hero without victory — failing to rescue her husband. Leanna had trusted Alex enough to accept an offer to care for his family. She'd found relief from this dark chapter in her life, and she thanked God for the means to possibly escape this place.

But why would God use a man with the

same vice as Jack's?

Leanna crept out of the dining room while the rest of the crowd was focused on Stergios. In the kitchen, Mrs. Pappas stoked the coals in the iron stove.

"Thank you, Mrs. Pappas," Leanna said, buttoning her coat and continuing toward the back door.

"Ah!" Mrs. Pappas set down her iron poker and wiped her hands on her apron. *"Efcharistó."* She rushed over and grabbed Leanna's hands. Wrinkles fanned from her chestnut eyes and her genuine smile warmed Leanna for a moment.

The woman kissed her cheek, causing Leanna to squirm at such familial affection. She hurried out the back door, stepping away from a regretful evening. Or at least, a remorseful end to one.

Fat flakes plopped on the ground, leading the way to her cold, empty home. The thin blanket of snow shone bright from the moon, giving ample guidance in the late night hour. She glanced behind her before turning down the path. Far ahead, Alex disappeared along the hill's crest. His tall, broad figure was in silhouette holding hands with little Maria.

Of course he and Jack were friends. No doubt they plotted ways to throw away their

84

money together. Anger whipped through Leanna, enticing her to wave a fiery fist up to Jack in the heavens. Her constant prayer of forgiveness was just as useless as Jack's empty promises.

She clenched her gloved fists and swiveled on her heel. The ground was slicker than she thought, though. A squeal escaped her before landing on her backside.

"Mrs. McKee? Is that you?" Mr. Coffey appeared at the edge of the tree line. He rushed up to her.

"If you could please help me up?"

"Of course, ma'am." He offered his hand and she found her feet again. She dusted off the back of her dress and straightened her hat.

"I must ask, Mrs. McKee, why you're out and about at this hour of night?" The brim of Coffey's hat shadowed his pointy face.

"Well, sir, why are you out?" She pulled her shoulders straight, standing inches taller than him.

"I was looking for my cat." He let out a gurgling laugh. "You ain't got a cat, Mrs. McKee. What's your excuse?"

She offered a pretentious smile. "If you must know, I was invited to a party by Mrs. Pappas." But her grin relaxed, and she was genuinely happy to have played the part of the progressive she'd hoped to be — even if it was just for one evening.

He shook his head. When he pulled off his hat, the moonlight shone pale gray on his protruding forehead. "I know you are newer to these parts than most. Wet behind the ears on what's proper around here. But don't you think them Greeks aren't the best people to make company with? I mean, not for a fair American woman as yourself?" He wore a wide grin on his face, but Leanna swore his eyes flashed contemptuously.

"I do not intend to jeopardize my reputation or theirs, Mr. Coffey," she scoffed. If he only knew all the propriety she'd escaped. "The children are my students, and their grandmother is an exceptional hostess. Now, if you please, I would like to go home." She leaned forward in challenge, forcing Mr. Coffey to move aside so she could pass by.

"Them Pappas men don't seem to understand their station in America," Coffey spoke to the back of her head. "Just because they open up a restaurant, don't give them the right to skip ahead of their rightful place here."

She spun around, uncomfortably close to the man. "I understand, Mr. Coffey," she snapped. "More than you know. But they have more sense of hospitality to a widow than any American, I have found. Good night." She resisted sprinting the rest of her way home and carried herself tall and proud. Every ounce of her wanted to cower as she imagined the busybody's retaliation.

Leanna stormed into her small kitchen, discarding her coat and removing her hat. The chilled air shocked her to the bone. She forgot about Coffey in her urgency to light the stove.

She spied the empty hook next to her coat. Jack's coat rarely hung there those last days. He was usually drenched by the time he returned from work. Leanna insisted he leave it out on the line. As her gaze wandered around the lonely room, she remembered their last night together.

"I best get out of these trousers, then," Jack's Scottish lilt was more obvious when he was tired. *"The water was like ice in that mine. Came right up to the knee."* He staggered across the room and caught himself with a firm hand on the wall.

Compassion overwhelmed her, and she'd rushed to his side. "You are exhausted," she said. Jack leaned into her while she wrapped her arm around his waist and helped him to the bed. *"And dripping wet."* She knelt down and began to unlace his boots while he leaned

87

his elbows on his knees and hung his head above hers. "No use in catching your death of cold."

"Perhaps it would be an answered prayer, that?" Jack mumbled.

Leanna stiffened. Her hand froze just above the last hole to pull the lace through. Surely Jack spoke of their most recent argument. She had implied her hope in his demise, hadn't she?

Father, forgive me.

"Hardly." Leanna dropped her shoulders, tugging the lace through the hole. "You are all I have." Her quiet words hung on the air like the scent of the mildew that clung to her husband's muddied clothes.

Jack's rough hand caressed her chin and pushed her face upward. His eyes shown with intensity, his brow creased upward with a mixture of desperation and hope. "Lass, you warm my heart."

"Do I?" No matter how much her own heart iced at the discovery of Jack's secret vice months ago, it now flooded with a warm gush, no doubt rivaling Jack's.

He brushed his fingers against her neck and twirled the loose hair that fell from her bun. "Leanna, I miss you." Their foreheads touched. "When I am digging all day for that Mormon's fortune, all I can think about is my *broken promise." His lips brushed her fore-head. Leanna swallowed hard, begging the tears to evaporate. Why was he telling her this? She should tell him to be quiet, to let this moment remain tender and untainted. Did he not realize how easily his words could summon her bitterness again?*

His blue eyes faded, and all she saw was the red-hot coals of her stove finally providing the warmth from her encounter with the evening snow — and the chilled conversations with Coffey.

Leanna stomped her foot.

After that night of Jack's tender words, the next morning proved him to be a liar when she'd caught him with another lost wager.

Leanna bristled at her attempt to lash out, trapped by the memory. All her hatred bore as much sin as Jack's lies. Had she not learned anything from her constant prayer for forgiveness? And from God's obvious mercy in providing for her all this time?

She was at a crossroads of how to react to Alex. With Jack, she had rushed down the road of a hardened heart and withdrawn herself from their marriage. But Alex was not her husband. He was hardly her friend. And he had given her a place to fall when her hope was lost, twice. Even if he stood in

Jack's shoes, he was the one person who had shown her kindness.

Could Alex be her chance to prove that she could offer grace, even if she'd failed so many times before?

CHAPTER SIX

Yanni leaned over his steaming cup of Greek coffee, contorting his face as he spoke the English words, "How are you this morning?"

Alex stifled a laugh. At least his little brother was trying. He was the mule of the family, stubborn in all matters. To break him down enough to attempt to learn English was quite a feat.

"Bravo, Yanni."

Yanni blew out a long breath of air then continued in Greek. "These are not the words that will give me advantage over my enemy."

"You must be a civilized person, Yanni. It is the only way to win hearts." Alex had tried his best to work hard and show respect for his foremen. It gained him wage increases to at least compensate for the monthly charge Anthis demanded.

After Helena passed, Alex threw off the

idea of returning to Greece — a place of poverty and memories — when he was given the opportunity to leave the D&RG and work in the Bingham copper mine for a daily ten-cent raise. The dank work of mining gave him a purpose. He'd chosen to cooperate with the American foremen and the Greek labor agents. It was the best way to keep a job. Even when union talk arose among his fellow Greeks, he kept his mouth shut and refused to be part of the ruckus. He was for himself then, and he was for his family now.

"To hurl insults at our enemies will not get us anywhere," Alex advised. "Your English is only advantageous if you choose wise words."

"I see that your civilized way has gotten you much respect." Yanni raised a skeptical eyebrow.

"It has given me wages enough to give you a roof over your head."

"Yes, and I thank you for that, big brother." He sighed. "In this harsh winter, I am grateful we have a place for Penelope to rest." Yanni may be difficult to sway, but he was a weakling when it came to his woman.

"You are a good husband." Alex drank the last of his lukewarm coffee. "And a good father."

"All of a sudden, compliments?" Yanni smirked. "You are good to care for Maria and Teddy. If Mrs. McKee hadn't agreed to our arrangement, they would be helpless in this foreign place." Yanni examined him. What was brewing behind those eyes? He squinted and leaned forward. "That Mrs. McKee is quite a beauty, no? You had a hard time working Papa's celebration that night." He winked.

Heat filled his face. "You know nothing, little brother."

"What? Every time I looked for you, your attention was in her little corner. She is quite different than a Greek. Papa would be devastated."

Alex tossed his hat on the table. "Shut up. Look at you conjuring up fantasy like a gossiping *yiayia*. Mrs. McKee and I are nothing alike — you are right. She is nothing to me but the children's teacher." Even the words fell to the floor like hollow beads, shattering into slivers of lies.

Alex could not keep his eyes off Leanna the night of the party, that was true. Her beauty glowed as bright as her flaxen hair in the dark restaurant. She entertained Maria and delighted his mother. Quite a different woman than the one who cursed Jack and

93

worried about the children's future in this place.

A sudden sprout of affection for the schoolteacher had frightened him more than an unsteady mine shaft. So when she had grown curious about him, Alex found the chance to cut off her interest. He had implied that he had gambled. And in a way, he had. Even if the money was for his wife, his risk to earn more had led to disaster. Alex had fallen for Anthis's empty promises once, just the same as Jack had.

With the schoolteacher invited to his world, and the way his heart reacted, he realized that this next risk was too high. He couldn't allow an American woman to bring on weakness. Nothing good could come of a Greek man involved with an American woman. Jeopardize all his hard work and the fortune of his family? All would be lost.

Yanni waved a hand in front of Alex's face, pulling him away from his thoughts. "I am not the only one conjuring up fantasy, Brother." He burst into laughter and took a final swallow of his coffee.

Alex rolled his eyes then stood up. Of all things, he should not entertain any romantic notion. He must guard himself against the golden-haired schoolteacher. She was nothing but helpful to the family.

After cleaning up and wiping down the table, they parted ways at the restaurant porch. Yanni joined the rest of the Pappas family at the Greek Orthodox service, and Alex turned down the slush-covered Main Street. Sundays were the most difficult with his family around. They did not understand his choice to hike instead of kneel beneath clouds of incense in reverence to Christ.

God and Alex weren't on speaking terms as far as he was concerned.

Main Street was busy with horse-drawn carts, and men and women traveling to church services. He plowed through the soggy ground, glad that he would enjoy his Sunday hike with bare boots instead of his snowshoes. The sunshine dimmed when a golden mess of hair beneath a black brim caught his eye. A cart flung up the melting snow from the road, chasing Leanna to the door of the saloon just ahead of him. Alex slowly released his breath as he considered crossing the street to avoid her altogether.

She saw him, though, while she attempted to wipe off her dress. "Hello, Mr. Pappas." Faint music spilled from the saloon door where she leaned on the doorjamb.

"Quite an establishment to spend your Sabbath." He couldn't help but smile.

"Very amusing, Mr. Pappas." She continued to shake the tips of her slush-covered boots. "This is worse than snow."

"It makes for an easier hike," he said, tapping his hiking stick on the wooden walk.

"A hike? I saw your priests arrive at the depot. Are you not off to church?" She shook off her muff. "Is that what your people call it?"

"Church? Yes, that's the word in English. My people believe in the same God as you, Leanna, if that is what you wonder," he snickered.

"I assumed so, seeing the large cross around the priest's neck," she said. "Why aren't you going today?"

He used his hiking stick to push along some more slush from the walk. "Church is not for me." It hadn't been for nearly a decade. "I choose a Sabbath hike instead."

Leanna narrowed her eyes, examining him as if she thought he were bluffing. Or perhaps, remembering the kind of man he had painted himself to be at the restaurant. A gambling man who skipped church.

She could think what she wanted. After Yanni noticed the attention he had given the pretty schoolteacher, this was all probably for the best.

"I look forward to church. It gives me hope." She nibbled on her lip then said,

"Where do you go on your hike?"

"Ah, it's quite a view. You would be amazed at the beauty." A wagon rattled behind him, and he stumbled closer. His shadow slinked across her ivory skin. "Today is a perfect day to go."

Uncertainty flickered in her pale blue eyes. "Oh, I don't know if I could go today." She looked down at her attire. "Thank you, though."

"Oh, did you think I meant for you to —" His heart pounded erratically. Had she thought he'd asked her? "Would you go with me? I mean, you'd consider it?"

She gasped and then shook her head. "Oh, I misunderstood." Her cheeks reddened, and she cupped her hand over her mouth. "You were not asking me to go?"

He couldn't stand the embarrassment that flooded her face. "You, you are welcome to join me anytime." He was losing control of his good sense. "Yes, I did say today was a perfect day."

"Forgive me, Mr. Pappas," she said, not looking directly at him. She swiveled on her heel and started off down the street again.

"Maybe another time?" he called out then stepped into the shadows, suddenly aware of the attention he had drawn to himself.

She spun back around and seemed at a

loss for words.

"Hello, Mrs. McKee." The banker, Mr. Tilton, peered down from his approaching wagon, jerking the reins of a gray mare who snorted and danced about. "Ah, hello, Mr. Pappas." He tipped his hat, while his wife kept her attention straight ahead.

"Good day, Mr. Pappas," Leanna gave a cordial smile. "I shall meet Maria and Teddy tomorrow as usual." She stepped over to the wagon and greeted the banker's wife.

Alex tipped his own hat to Mr. Tilton then continued to the Castle Gate formation.

Frustration gripped him at every turn on his usual trek through town. Hadn't he just prided himself in being wise over these years with foremen and labor agents? How could he be so reckless now?

But his heart swelled as he replayed their conversation. What had he said to suggest that he'd invited her this morning?

And even more curious, had Leanna McKee really considered joining him on his solitary hike for all of Castle Gate to see?

Mrs. Tilton's big hat adorned with feathers cast a shadow upon Leanna as she stood between the wooden walkway and their wagon. "How are you, dear?" The woman patted her forehead with a white handkerchief just a shade off from her aging hair. "Was that man bothering you?"

"Of course not," Leanna snapped too quickly. "Forgive me. I just assumed you knew that he was my employer in a way. I care for his niece and nephew."

Mrs. Tilton lifted a brow. "Ah, Mrs. Rudolf has shared that you've grown affectionate for two of your students. A dangerous alliance to make, if you ask me."

"Dangerous?" What would she have thought if Leanna had not only presumed that Alex invited her this morning but had also decided to hike with him? Her pulse frenzied with the lingering embarrassment — and perhaps with anger from Mrs. Tilton's implications. "I have been employed to escort the children to their family's restaurant. How is that dangerous, Mrs. Tilton?"

"Do not be naive, Mrs. McKee. Have you not heard of the lynchings or the riots?" She nudged her husband and pointed a gloved finger ahead. "Whites do not need to mingle with such leeches."

"Some Greeks may leech off the land, but not all —" Leanna repeated Alex's words. She savored the grace in that. And the change in her own heart. The children were sweet and loving. And Alex was kind and —

99

Trapped by the same vice as Jack. He'd mentioned it clear as the icicles that hung from the roofs. Then why did she want to go with Alex this morning? Why did his dark eyes and dazzling smile trip her heart nearly every time he paid her attention?

Mr. Tilton gathered the reins tighter around his hand. "We always seem to pass each other to our places of worship, don't we, Mrs. McKee?" He changed the topic. She was grateful for that. The Mormon meetinghouse was just across the street from her own church. She'd avoided the splash from the Tiltons' wagon many times. Of course, they stopped today, with Alex there.

Mr. Tilton continued, "I do hope that you received our package the other day."

Leanna forced her lips to perk into a smile and said, "I did. Thank you very much." At first, she was shocked to find the package from the banker and his wife. After all, Mr. Tilton was the one person in town who was aware of the debt payments she had wired for Jack. The package was lovely, she must admit. It held a box of tea bags, a loaf of freshly baked bread, and an assortment of cheeses. Actually, it had given her supper for almost a week.

However, they'd hardly spoken two words

to her until now. She was certain it was due to her class, and perhaps their differences in religion. While many Mormon women seemed quite humble, Mrs. Tilton managed to put on airs as high as the Rockefellers. Leanna had never been snubbed before — it had been her own practice, one that she'd mastered in Boston. But Mrs. Tilton's sharp eyes and pursed lips undoubtedly affirmed Leanna's reasons for leaving the class of her upbringing.

"You must come have some tea before it is all gone, Mrs. Tilton." She flashed a wide smile.

"Ah," Mrs. Tilton shifted in her seat. "That would be" — she cleared her throat — "lovely, my dear."

To travel to that side of town? Of course not.

"Well, I do believe I will be late to church if I don't hurry," Leanna said, stifling a giggle.

"Let us give you a ride, Mrs. McKee," Mr. Tilton offered. "Hilary, scoot over."

His wife's face fell at his suggestion, but with a visible poke from his elbow, she slid herself toward him, gathering her skirt in her gloved hand.

"Well, that is nice of you." Filling her lungs with crisp air, Leanna heaved herself onto the bench seat of the wagon. This was an invitation she was certain of, and one she could accept. Leanna rolled her eyes discreetly. The effect Alex Pappas had on her emotions both frightened her and filled her with an overwhelming desire to understand him. The grace she'd hoped to bestow on him was easily found today, wasn't it?

"We usually take our covered carriage during the winter," Mrs. Tilton said with her chin high. "But it's such a sunny day, isn't it?"

"Yes, it's lovely. Except for the slush." She glanced at her soiled skirt and slid her hand along it.

Mrs. Tilton leaned in while her husband called the horse to go forward. "Mr. Tilton has it in his head that we will own an automobile in the near future. A cousin in Enterprise saw one this past summer. Ranted and raved about it. I doubt its dependability, though."

"In my head?" Mr. Tilton exclaimed. "I've already narrowed down the make, Mrs. Tilton." He chuckled deeply. "Perhaps Mrs. McKee here is more progressive than you, dear?" He craned his neck and gave Leanna a wink.

"Progressive?" Leanna laughed. "Well, I hope I am that. At least with education."

Mrs. Tilton joined in with a tumbling warble. "Teaching the Greeks has surely put a brake on your progress, hasn't it, Mrs. McKee?" The woman sounded like her mother.

"If a child is willing to be taught, that is as much progress as one needs in my profession." She stared ahead at the bouncing mane of the horse.

"Ah, that's the attitude we need." Mr. Tilton punctuated the air with his words. "Mrs. McKee, do you intend to remain in Castle Gate now that you have no ties to the mining company?"

She grimaced at his forward inquiry. "I hoped to find employment at a well-respected school in San Francisco." Speaking this half-truth aloud turned her stomach. She'd have to wait now, according to her cousin's letter.

"Perhaps you could lift yourself from the position with such" — he let out a forced cough — "with such undesirables and become a private tutor. In Salt Lake City, for instance?"

Mrs. Tilton gasped and slapped her husband's arm.

"What, Hilary? Bethany needs assistance with Tommy."

Leanna's eyes grew wide, her heart beating wildly.

The wide brim of Mrs. Tilton's hat nearly swiped Leanna's nose as the woman jerked back against the seat and nearly pouted.

"Our daughter is seeking a tutor for her son. Mrs. Rudolf speaks highly of your ability," he said, despite his wife's tight grasp on his arm.

"That is hard for me to believe, Mr. Tilton," Leanna said, remembering how the headmistress had not spoken one kind word to her in all her months at the school.

"Let me remind you, Mr. Tilton, of the one complaint we've heard over and over from Mrs. Rudolf." Mrs. Tilton lifted her hand to her mouth so Leanna could not see, but she could hear the whisper: "She's attached to those Greeks."

Mr. Tilton bounced the reins and cleared his throat. "We must offer her an interview with Bethany. Provide an escape from her current commitment." He called, "Whoa," to the horse as they stopped near the entrance of the church.

His wife huffed, her arms planted firmly across her waist.

"What do you say, Mrs. McKee?" Mr. Tilton hopped down from his seat. "Shall I take the liberty of arranging an interview with my daughter?"

A position? In the city? *Lord, is this my way out?*

If it was, then why did she hesitate? Just like she mistook Alex's mention of a hike as an invitation. Both wavering moments had something to do with her heart. She may as well have stumbled down a tricky cliff than climbed out of the Tilton's wagon.

"The heart is deceitful above all things . . . : who can know it?"

She did know it. Months were spent arguing with Jack, shaming him for the consequences that had led to his death. And now, her very wish to leave this place could come true, and she might let her heart ruin even that.

Her recent days here had reminded her of the one thing she'd still clung to — her hope in education. And she had the Pappas family to thank for that. It was the children's love for life, Alex's kindness, and the whole family's hospitality to a widow that had removed the mud from her eyes. Now, it was time to move on.

"Well, Mrs. McKee?" Mr. Tilton stepped around the horse, helped her down, and returned to his seat.

"Of course. I would appreciate an interview with your daughter very much."

She looked past the houses across the

street and stared at the spires of Castle Gate. They probably loomed over Alex this very instant. If she had joined him on the hike, the opportunity to leave this place would have been lost.

But if she had gone on the hike, would she have considered leaving, after all?

Her cheeks flushed.

Lord, I must leave now. To stay would be as dangerous as Mrs. Tilton implied.

CHAPTER SEVEN

Alex turned toward the towering rock, the slush splashing up at each stride.

"Alex!" Constantine ran across the street from the boardinghouse. "Where are you off to?"

"Going up to the rocks today. Are you going to church?"

"Yes. My sister's betrothed is the priest's cousin. How can I not?" He grinned and shrugged his shoulders.

"Ah, I see." Alex had little desire to converse. Not with the confused battle between his heart and his mind. "Have a good morning, Constantine."

"Wait, I would like to speak with you." He put his arm around Alex and offered him a seat on a nearby bench. "I have wanted to talk to you for quite some time."

"What is it? We will both get a late start to our day off if we sit here and gab."

"I know, I know." The young man took a

seat. He blew on his bare hands.

Alex sighed, trying to tamper his agitation.

"My parents struggle in Greece. They write often and beg for me to return with a dowry for my sister, Kristina. At least she could marry off and have some future." He was hardly twenty, but his worry appeared like that of an old man.

"I know times are hard over there, which helped convince my own family to start new in America."

"I try to convince my parents of the same thing." Constantine's face lit up with expectancy. "That is why I ask you. How do I do that?"

"Each situation is different. My parents desired to open a restaurant, and with this place growing like weeds, I convinced them."

"But what of you marrying a Greek woman? There are none here. Do you plan to go back?" The young man crossed his arms, waiting for an answer. Alex understood his concern. There was hardly a day that went by without Papa offering to send him to Greece to find a bride.

"Is that what is stopping your family? A bride for you?"

Constantine shook his head and sighed.

"Can I trust you, Alex?"

Alex grimaced. What was this young man going to ask? Alex was not concerned for someone else's family dilemmas.

"I am in love — with an American," Constantine whispered. "And she loves me back."

Alex pushed his back into the bench. "I see."

"How can I tell my family to come here and not worry about a bride for me? What if they bring one to me? If I could just get them here without worrying about a Greek woman, then I could convince them of my own match." He spoke the last words with much animation, as if he'd rehearsed that line to perfection.

"What country are you from, man? And what family? You cannot take the Greek way out of your parents just by moving them across the ocean. Besides, there are plenty of Americans who would give you trouble for tempting one of their own."

Constantine looked deflated. He leaned forward, his elbows on his knees. "Susanna and I have already received the blessing of her parents, which helps with naysayers. I know it will be hard at first, but we are going to make it work. I just can't find a way to convince my parents to move here."

"Is it worth it?" Alex asked himself as much as Constantine. "I mean, is a woman worth risking your family's happiness and American hostilities?"

Constantine swiped his hat off his head and twisted it. He looked over at Alex with bright hazel eyes. "Yes, Alex. It is worth it. I will work for my sister's dowry a little longer. And then after that? Susanna and I are supposed to be together. I know it. I can't risk leaving her out of my future."

The young man reminded Alex of himself when he had first decided to come to America. Such determination for a better life. All for love.

Alex thought love was lost when Helena died. But now his heart was waking up. He and Constantine had more in common than he thought.

The young man stood up and crammed his hat on his head. "One more question, and then I must go to church."

"What?" His mouth was dry, the word slurred as if he spoke from a deep sleep.

"Would you give up everything for a woman?"

Alex rose and tapped his hiking stick on the ground as hard as he grit his teeth. "No. Constantine. I would not." He promised himself no distractions long ago. That was what made his choice to follow Anthis worth it. Success against all odds. Even if he'd started out failing the one person who'd counted on his success — Helena.

Constantine's hopeful expression melted as quickly as a falling icicle landing on a burning bed of coal. He shook his head then started toward Main Street.

Suddenly a rock, heavier than those along his hike, settled in Alex's stomach. "I am sorry, Constantine," he called out. "But we have duties to our families."

Constantine turned back, narrowing his eyes at Alex. "Yes, but we are men. Our choice in whom we love should be our own." He spun around and sulked off to church.

Could Alex be that brave? Turn his back on his promise to himself and love another — an American at that? What would it cost him? His family?

They would only accept a Greek woman. His father had made that perfectly clear.

Alex shuddered.

The greatest question would be if an American woman would consider him at all. He fluttered his eyes upward and scowled. If God weren't so far away, Alex would beg him for an answer.

He ground his stick in the earth ahead

and pushed forward in the bright winter morning. He tried to form words of an old tune that he often mumbled to empty his thoughts. But he couldn't. Only one word came easily to him that morning.

Leanna.

The next week, snow appeared again, covering the weeds along the road. Leanna was careful to avoid any ice as she turned toward the restaurant. When would she let Alex know of her plan to interview in Salt Lake City? She felt an urgency to tell him, especially since he'd made it clear how much his family depended on her.

Yesterday, Mrs. Tilton had reluctantly stood in the doorway of the classroom with her daughter's address scribbled on a piece of paper with a date and time. She barely spoke to her and sniffled as she bustled away. Leanna would certainly put her best effort into impressing her daughter. It would make the pompous woman squirm.

Maria rushed out of the restaurant door with a smile pushing up her rosy cheeks. "Teddy is coming today!"

Leanna returned her smile with a broad grin. "Wonderful. Where is he?"

The door to the restaurant barely closed before it swung open again and Teddy tumbled out. "Look, Meesus McKee." He held up his arm and wiggled his fingers from a cast.

"It is good to see you, Teddy. We should —"

"Ella," Alex's deep voice called from inside the restaurant, and soon he appeared at the door. He switched to English and said, "I will take you, Teddy." He reached his arms to his nephew.

"Mr. Pappas, I am capable of taking the children," Leanna insisted.

"Yes, you are," Alex said with a gentle voice. "But there are slick spots and I am free this morning. Yanni and I work the graveyard shift this week." He bent down and lifted Teddy up. The boy hitched his scrawny legs over his uncle's shoulders.

"Very well." Her words were stuck in her throat. Why did her insides tumble so?

She reached for Maria's hand and took long strides toward the road. She must focus on Salt Lake City now. Surely this tutor position was God's provision to leave this dark place behind. But what perplexed her was that she didn't notice the dark near as much. The sun shone bright, the joy of children surrounded her, and Alex stirred a reminiscent longing that she felt as a debutante long ago.

113

"How is the children's mother?" she asked, walking beside him.

"Penelope is okay. Momma thinks she might walk around soon enough," Alex said.

They wouldn't need her anymore. "The winter break is coming. Perhaps my duty to you is coming to an end." A gloom covered her heart and she remembered the darkness of this place after all.

"Perhaps."

She looked up at him. His jaw was tight, twitching beneath a slight stubble.

Maria broke the silence. "Meesus McKee, I like you to walk me to school." She tugged at Leanna's arm.

"You are a sweet child, Maria." She stroked her curls. "I will leave here very soon, though." From the corner of her eye she noticed Alex's head turn in her direction. "I have an interview in Salt Lake City this Saturday." An icy patch glistened to their left. She pulled Maria closer to avoid it.

"I suppose a hike is out of the question." His voice seeped with a challenge.

Her lips parted, and she stared at him. He stopped walking and she did the same.

"I apologize for my assumption the other day," she mumbled. Humiliation coursed through her veins.

114

"I wish I'd thought of it first." His smile did not brighten his face like it normally did. His eyes were soft and eager. "But now you might leave. You must see the Castle Gate spires close up, not from the window of a train." Alex breathed in deep. "There are few things in this world as beautiful as the carved mountains, and to have you there would be the perfect —"

"Thios Alex," Teddy whined from over his shoulders then spoke in Greek. Alex nodded and shifted the little boy up, tightening his arms around his nephew's legs.

Alex's words hung between them, aggravating and exciting her all at once. She shouldn't think on them one moment longer, but her skin tingled at all he implied — that she might be beautiful to him.

They continued ahead while Alex conversed with Teddy. When they reached the school gate, he helped the boy down then kissed Maria on the head.

He turned to Leanna. "Good day, Mrs. McKee." He sighed then headed back down the hill.

The school day could not have started on a more frustrating note. Her time here was coming to a close, and she must do everything in her power to make that happen. If she stayed in Castle Gate any longer, she might regret more than her life as a bitter wife — following that man into the wilderness was becoming a tempting notion — and her heart was wild in anticipation of his every word.

Thankfully, the week continued on as quiet as usual, and she had plenty of time to prepare herself for the interview. The children met her in the morning with no sign of their uncle, and they ran into the restaurant at the end of each school day without a greeting from any Pappas member.

She was relieved that Alex was nowhere to be found. This was her chance to step away from all the memories and prove that she could follow her dream to the full. Her thoughts must remain only on the gratitude she felt for Alex — that he revived her love for progress without prejudice. If she lost sight of that, she worried that she might discover more than her overactive debutante heart — but an adoration worthy of Mrs. Tilton's warning.

Saturday arrived, and she hurried down her path to catch the train to Salt Lake City. As she neared Main Street, familiar laughter soured her excitement. The Greek labor agent stood at the corner by the Pappas restaurant. He rubbed his hands together,

116

his chin tucked deep in the fur collar of his enormous overcoat.

Unfortunately, her hat could not hide her face today. Leanna assumed her proudest position, tilting her nose to the sky and keeping her eye on the road ahead. She tried to calm the furious shudder inside. The last time she'd actually spoken to the avaricious man was the day of Jack's death in the mine.

"Ah, pretty lady!"

She pressed her lips together and ignored him as best she could.

"Meesus McKee, is that it?"

"Leave her be, Anthis," Alex growled. She stopped and saw him on the porch behind Anthis. He stood with his hands on his hips as if guarding his family's restaurant.

"What, Alex?" Anthis raised his eyebrows and pushed his chin farther into his fur collar. "I want to give my condolences." The man laid a heavy hand on Alex's shoulder and said, "Okay?" He spurted a gurgling chuckle then turned to Leanna.

"Jack was a good man, Meesus McKee." He held his hands out as if he expected her to embrace him.

She shot a look at Alex. His gaze was so intent on her, dancing with a glimmer of affection, her proud defense nearly slipped away. Was she imagining his attention? She swallowed hard, looking away.

"Meesus McKee? Has the cat got your tongue?" Anthis whispered then erupted in laughter.

A wall crumbled down inside her, unleashing a fiery flood. She could not avoid him any longer. "Do not tell me that Jack was a good man, sir." Narrowing her eyes, she stepped closer. "You had little conscience when stealing whatever good remained in my husband." If she wasn't a lady she would spit on his shoe. His astonished look gave her only small satisfaction, and she breathed deep, ready to retort to his next dismissive comment. But Mrs. Pappas's voice distracted their heated exchange. She called for Alex from inside the restaurant.

"Excuse me," Alex said before slipping inside. She imagined he was breathing a sigh of relief at that moment, and she wished she could also be excused from this icy atmosphere.

Anthis began to wring his gloved hands. "Look, I am sorry for taking Jack's money. It was a friendly wager. I tell Alex all the time, I am not always here for business." He shrugged his shoulders.

"Business?" She scoffed. Jack had told her about the scoundrel's fees for his own countrymen. All the more reason she was furious when she caught Jack feeding the beast with his minuscule wages. "If I recall, your fellow Greek men disagree with your ways."

"Who? Alex?" Anthis waved a hand as if swatting a fly. "He's been bitter since his wife died before he could send her money for medicine. I tell him it's not my problem. All labor agents collect money to live. How else do we eat?"

"He gambled her money away?" Her throat tightened.

"Alex? Gamble?" Anthis's whole body shook with his obnoxious outburst. "That man takes life too seriously for that! When I met him in Greece, he practically begged for me to bring him to America to make a fortune and save his wife." He shook his head and sucked air through his teeth. "Even if he had made enough for her treatment, how could he expect to get the money to her in time?"

Leanna squeezed her hands inside her muff and resumed her glare, even though her ears rang with the news.

"He came here to make money for her?" She nearly whispered, "Not himself?"

"Neh, neh." Anthis nodded. "He's like your husband in a way, eh?" He pointed a finger to the sky. "Jack mentioned making

119

some money to get you out of here. These men doing what they can for their women, when in the end, life is full of disappointment." He shook his head. "Good day, Meesus McKee. It was a" — he cleared his throat — "pleasure." He tipped his hat and crossed over toward the coffeehouse.

Alex poked his head out from the door. "Are you okay?"

She just stared at him. His love for money did not lead him to America. His love for his wife did. The chivalrous immigrant crossed the ocean and foreign land to save his wife's life.

"I am fine." Her voice rasped. Shame flooded her. "I must go."

As she hurried down the street, Leanna wiped hot tears from her face. Thank heavens the journey to Salt Lake City would take hours or she'd run the risk of showing up to her interview flustered.

That labor agent brought her a different type of turmoil than usual. Jack's last bet had stirred up a mighty fight between them, hadn't it? She shuttered her eyes, her guilt only sharpened at remembering her angry words. Would she have lashed out so, if she had known he was trying to please her — even if it was in a pitiful gamble?

She continued toward the depot, confused

as to why Alex would compare his deed to Jack's. A gamble was a gamble, but Alex's venture was nothing of the sort.

The man went to the ends of the earth to help his dying wife. Not difficult to believe from a man whose loyalty to his family and kindness to her was a shining light in this dark coal town. His attempt to save his wife was a great feat, even if it failed.

Perhaps Leanna did not need to leave Castle Gate for her own future, but for the protection of those who deserved to prosper most — the Pappas family and especially the hardworking, compassionate Alex Pappas, who seemed too enamored with someone as broken as Leanna McKee.

Alex skirted around his mother at the heavy wooden kitchen table. The little woman rolled out a thin sheet of dough, using her whole body to create the paper-thin pieces of phyllo. She stretched her arms across with one movement then pulled the pin back just before her torso dragged against her creation. What effort it took, but how delicious the outcome. Alex's mouth watered imagining the sweet baklava filled with honey and nuts between crispy phyllo layers.

"Who did you talk to out there?" Momma

didn't look up, keeping her attention on the job at hand.

He rocked back and forth on his heels. "It was Anthis." Momma rolled her eyes and muttered under her breath. He added, "And Leanna — Mrs. McKee."

"Ah, I wish she would stop in every once in a while. She needs some fat on her bones."

"Why? So then you can whisper to Penelope about how much weight she's put on?" He laughed at the double-sided standard of every Greek woman — to offer food abundantly, but criticize privately when the effects become visible on the partaker's womanly figure.

"Well, she is beautiful, and a little food would only give her more of a healthy glow. That's all." She shrugged her shoulders before rolling the pin again.

If she knew all the animosity of Coffey and his friends or the incidents around the country involving Greeks, would she be so persistent about feeding an American woman? He couldn't tell her the truth — it would only cheapen the roots they were growing here. After all the convincing he did to bring them here, how could he admit they weren't welcome by many?

"You like her? No?" she asked. He caught

Momma's smirk before it faded with her continued baking efforts.

He studied her, sure that her question was a trap. But what if it wasn't? Could a blessing from his family be enough to follow his heart regardless of the others' expectations?

"She's not Greek," he said. He would not dare share more than that — yet. If his mother's inquiry was a snare, she'd enjoy nothing more than throwing a fit of disappointment about what kind of Greek he'd become. Just like when he stopped going to church after Helena passed away.

"Ah, but she is a beauty and a kind soul." Momma continued to work on her baklava. He narrowed his eyes, but his pulse raced with anticipation. "She must find a good American man to get her away from all these miners," she continued. Alex's stomach dropped.

She set aside her rolling pin. Pushing her silver-dusted hair from her forehead with the back of her wrist, she added, "Stergios adores Mrs. McKee," with a nod toward the back window. Papa was stoking the fire in the outdoor oven. A thin stream of smoke from his pipe joined the oven's cloud. "He trusts her with his grandchildren." She curled her lips. "But he's not keen on seeing you gawking over her like you did at his name-day celebration."

Did everyone notice? Heat crawled up his neck as he recalled Yanni's jest at the coffeehouse.

Yes, he was smart to not agree with such accurate descriptions of the schoolteacher.

His mother was testing him.

"We were talking about my dead wife that night, Momma," he spat out sharply.

Momma sucked in air between her teeth with a glare then crossed herself three times. "May her memory be eternal." She pointed her rolling pin at him. "Whatever you talked about, you must stop entertaining public conversations with the woman. Papa gets nervous that she will distract you."

"Then stop inviting her in," he mumbled.

"He'll find you a good Greek girl, either in Salt Lake or back in Greece —"

"I am not going to Greece, Momma," he said. "I don't need his help. I am nearing thirty years old. What man asks his papa for an arrangement at such an age?"

Stergios swung the door open, ushering a blast of cold air into the warm kitchen. Momma raised her brow and set her mouth into a thin straight line. He'd seen that look before. The one she'd given him many times when the priests would visit and he'd have to bite his skeptical tongue. The one look that screamed, *Don't you dare think about it.*

"Alex, you should get to bed," Papa said. "You'll be exhausted for your shift tonight." He tossed his gloves on the counter and blew on his hands.

"I don't like you going into the mines so late. I have no sleep on these nights." Momma shook her head and furrowed her brow with worry. "All I do is pray. You should, too, Alex."

She never did miss the opportunity to remind him of the lack of prayer in his life.

Alex gave a curt nod, giving her neither hope nor disappointment. "See you tomorrow."

He grabbed his coat and left the kitchen, his mouth watering as he caught a waft of the chicken roasting in the outdoor oven.

At least life had not ended when he broke free of the church that seemed to bind most Greeks together in this land. He was still accepted — even if Momma tried to guilt him into forgoing his hikes. He was not shunned.

A group of miners trudged down the hill from the mine, most waving at him. He had made some friends — Americans, Polish, even some Japanese. Coffey and a few of his friends trailed behind the group. They didn't even look at him.

125

How could Constantine be brave enough? He had her parents on his side. And they weren't planning on staying here. There was a whole slew of men against Alex in Castle Gate. If Alex showed any interest in the schoolteacher, the men who already hated him would no doubt cost him his job.

He ran his fingers in his curls beneath his fisherman's cap then turned toward Greek Town. As much as he did not want to admit it, he must take his mother's advice and stop listening to his heart. Besides, Leanna McKee would have nothing to do with him, would she? He was a miner in Castle Gate, Utah. A place she'd soon leave behind.

CHAPTER EIGHT

By the time Leanna arrived in Salt Lake City, the town was fully awake, clattering with familiar city sounds. She boarded a trolley at the train station and found a seat near a window. The trolley was alive with conversation — some in foreign languages and some American men talking about Admiral Murdock and British relations.

"The Brits declare us to be an important part of the English-speaking family," one man said loudly. He then chuckled. "If only they knew the jibber jabber we contend with day in and day out." He flicked his head to the back of the trolley where a huddle of immigrants were carrying on.

Leanna sighed, the tug of her heart and reason were forever at odds. She prayed the rest of the way, begging for her prejudice to never surface again. These loud opinions grated on her, and she wondered if her place was to shed light, or allow the darkness to continue?

When the trolley stopped at the corner of South Temple and O Streets, she hurried down the steps, assuring herself that staying silent was the wise thing to do.

The street was lined with newly built four-square homes. Inviting porches were flanked with bay windows, some framing cozy parlors lit by roaring fires. The idyllic neighborhood was nothing like the poorly built one of the mining company. Her excitement grew with each step, and gratitude filled her at this opportunity.

She could never get past all the shame that filled her in Castle Gate, especially with men like Anthis triggering her old bitterness. And then there was Alex — but all he brought about for her were new, bright memories, and the promise for more on the horizon.

No, this was where she belonged. Leanna straightened her hat and turned up the Scotts' walkway. She climbed the brick steps and knocked, fiddling with her overcoat and gloves.

Soft footsteps drew closer on the other side of the door. A freckled boy answered, half-hiding behind the cracked door.

"Hello?" he said.

"Good afternoon." He was about the same

age and height as Maria, but not nearly as animated. "Is your mother in?"

"Are you Mrs. McKee?"

"I am. And you are?"

"I am Tommy. I am to show you to the parlor." He pushed the door open and leaned his back against it. "Come in."

"Thank you." She stepped inside and waited for Tommy to show her to the parlor. He took her to a square room with a settee and two high-back chairs.

"I'll get my mother." He ran off and clambered up the stairs in the foyer.

A fire licked the fireplace, filling the room with the warm smell of cedar. The mantel boasted watercolors displayed on miniature easels. In the center was a photograph set in a silver frame. A small boy, most likely Tommy, and a man and a woman, most likely his parents, stood at the gate at Temple Square. Leanna had seen the magnificent architecture when she'd first arrived in Salt Lake.

"Good morning, Mrs. McKee."

Leanna spun away from the artwork. A short woman with a pile of blond curls pinned to her head sailed into the room. She carried a tray of china that she placed on the coffee table. Her round face was aglow with rosy cheeks, and her sparkling green eyes offered kindness. "I am Bethany Scott," she said, extending her hand.

"I am Leanna McKee. Thank you so much for meeting with me." They shook hands.

"Do you like watercolors?" Mrs. Scott asked while turning her attention to the tea service.

"I do. These are wonderful."

"Thank you. It is a hobby." She began to pour a cup of tea. "Please make yourself comfortable. Would you like some?"

"That would be nice." Leanna sat on the settee across from Mrs. Scott. Could she remember exactly how to carry herself in such a pretty setting as this parlor? How long had it been since she was surrounded by such civility? Three years, maybe four?

Mrs. Scott handed her a teacup and saucer then served herself. "I must say, it shocked me when Mother told me she was sending you for the interview." She raised an eyebrow.

Leanna shifted in her seat. "To be honest, your father seemed more enthusiastic than she did." She sipped her tea, praying that a woman like Mrs. Tilton wouldn't ruin her chances.

"Ah, that makes sense. Mother would never jeopardize her reputation with her gaggle. You see, we haven't been on the best terms with my parents." She sighed. "They do not understand my leaving the Church of Latter Day Saints."

"Oh, I wasn't aware." Leanna's nerves settled a bit.

"It is quite an embarrassment for them. They are resistant to change and we are very open with our Protestant belief. So to have them recommend someone like you, who attends Castle Gate's Methodist church, was a shock to say the least."

"You don't know how much I understand the predicament." She had not expected the conversation to take this path; however, there was an easiness about Mrs. Scott. "I chose a different lifestyle than my own upbringing. My parents have hardly spoken a word to me since."

Mrs. Scott placed her teacup on its saucer and set it on the table. With genuine interest, she leaned in and clasped her hands in her lap. "Where are you from, Mrs. Mc-Kee?"

"I am from Boston. I married a Scottish worker from my father's factory." Leanna also set her tea down. "It dashed all my parents' hopes of my remaining in high society with a rich husband and a social calendar."

131

"Ah, marriage is at the crux of it, isn't it?" In one dramatic motion, Mrs. Scott collapsed into the back of her chair, a disapproving posture for any socialite. "My husband is to blame for my conversion, in their opinion." She studied Leanna with smiling eyes. "We are similar in a way, aren't we?"

"We are." Had she found a kindred spirit in Mrs. Scott?

Mrs. Scott began to ramble on about her own history — how she met her husband at a social with a mutual friend, and when her parents chose to bank in Castle Gate, she got married and made a home in the city. The woman was animated in her storytelling, and Leanna's cheeks hurt from smiling at the tale.

How strange to feel such a wave of familiarity toward a person she hardly knew. Their conversation was reminiscent of her talks with her sewing circle in Boston. She'd forgotten the need for a friend in all of her recent hardship. Sitting in the sunlit parlor refreshed her spirit. Would their meeting linger into the late afternoon hours? She hoped so.

"My parents tell me you teach English to the Greeks. My son has trouble with reading and mathematics. We're considering hiring a full-time tutor instead of enrolling him in the local school." She topped off each of their cups. "Are you inclined to modern education, Mrs. McKee?"

Her spirit leaped at the question about one of her greatest passions. "Absolutely. It is my mission to teach children, especially those in greater need than others," Leanna said. "The two Pappas children I care for have shown such potential in the short time I've spent with them. I am confident that Tommy could excel with individualized attention —" Her throat tightened at the comparison. The Scott's child might excel, but would he capture her heart like Maria and Teddy?

Mrs. Scott continued on about the many activities they were involved in, and how her husband, Dr. Scott, was often busy with hospital affairs. She patted Leanna's knee. "I certainly wouldn't mind having a friend around here also. I think we could be good friends, Mrs. McKee." She beamed, her eyes flashing adoringly.

Leanna's bittersweet thoughts melted away and she smiled once again. "I agree."

"I must first speak with my husband about your credentials, but I am certain we can work something out. Would starting at the end of January give you enough time to tie up loose ends in Castle Gate?"

January was only a month away, and she had to give Alex time to find help. Her stomach turned. Why did she feel allegiance to him? She cleared her throat. "It should be enough time. I would need to find room and board in Salt Lake, too."

"Oh, do not worry about that, dear." Mrs. Scott bit into a piece of shortbread. She wiped the corners of her mouth and continued, "We have a spare room. Stay with us until you are settled, and then you can look come spring."

A house servant interrupted their conversation, and Mrs. Scott excused herself to assist in the kitchen. Leanna finished up her tea and cookie alone, admiring the window scene. A red-breasted robin flew into the yard outside then two more joined him. Life seemed more abundant in a few hours here than in her entire first year in Castle Gate.

But what of this second winter? This one amid the Pappas family? This one with a strong Greek man's arms holding her when times were difficult?

Bethany Scott offered her a tempting alternative, one that would secure her a steady position and a much more suitable lifestyle. The Lord had plucked her from her misery and given her this amazing gift.

Perhaps she could just stay here this evening, in Salt Lake, and become better acquainted with the town. Sort out her thoughts and spend time away from Castle Gate for a while. A few weeks ago she'd have longed to do so. But even if she tried to talk herself out of it, she urgently desired to return.

As much as she resisted admitting it, Alex Pappas was a loose end mentioned by Mrs. Scott. He had become a part of Leanna's life as an employer. But he had also become a friend — first to her late husband and recently to her, as well. Why did he try to keep her in the dark about his intentions during his first days in America?

Mrs. Scott returned to her seat and offered Leanna a truffle. "The cook enjoys making candies. Not so good for my figure, but such a treat." She grinned.

The chocolate was filled with cherry, reminding Leanna of Mrs. Pappas's glyká. Even after she swallowed, a lump sat in her throat.

Leanna began to put on her gloves. "I look forward to hearing from you, Mrs. Scott. It was a pleasure meeting with you today."

Yes, speak eagerly and willing. Mostly for her own heart to hear such wise affirmation.

Mrs. Scott clapped her hands saying, "Of course," then sprung up from her seat, holding her hand out. "You are such a delight, Mrs. McKee. We'll soon have you away from the grim Castle Gate and in a proper home where you obviously belong." She chuckled as they shook hands.

Leanna stepped into the orange glow of late afternoon. Mrs. Scott's assumption of her current home being a less-than-proper one crossed her mind. She was certain Mrs. Tilton had painted that picture. But Leanna could not muster up any sense of embarrassment or pride — her mind was too distracted by an attractive Greek man who'd made the chance to leave Castle Gate a more difficult decision than it should be.

Alex spied her from his trek down the hill before she saw him. She stood with her arms crossed over her long overcoat, her ivory skin aglow beneath the shade of the porch roof. Even her reflection in the window glass beside her was nearly as intriguing as her actual figure.

Resisting his heart was becoming more difficult. The brave woman who had put even Anthis into his place, also seemed vulnerable — cheated from love and security — two treasures that the Pappas family held most dear. Alex Pappas could offer the first, but security was the one thing that might fail, for them both.

He must remain strong, perhaps even encourage Leanna to leave once and for all. Who could he find for the children, though? And could he imagine life in Castle Gate without Leanna McKee brightening up the town?

Mrs. Coffey stopped to converse with Leanna when Alex was halfway down the road. He ground his teeth and slowed his pace. How could such a tiny woman block his view?

Wasn't it perfectly ironic, though? The counterpart of the one man who hated him most would steal away his sight of the one who'd given him hope in —

He muttered, "You are a fool." In several ways. First, he was irritated by such a wiry lady, and second, he was playing with a lit match, a flame that could surely burn him and the golden-haired schoolteacher if they weren't careful.

In eight years, Alex had never felt so drawn to a person. His mind had been on one goal only: to better the life of his family. But just as his parents had nagged him to live life beyond work, his heart began to long for such a chance at living. Not in the way his parents hoped for, however. Could Leanna give him that? He didn't know how yet, but even if he wanted to find out, he must resist.

He stalled until Mrs. Coffey continued on her way down Main. Leanna's shoulders sagged with a sigh, and she blew a stray curl from her face. When she caught Alex's gaze, she waved halfheartedly.

He jaunted across Main Street. "Good morning, Leanna." He tipped his hat.

She adjusted her coat, lowering her eyes behind long lashes. "Hello, Alex."

He diverted his attention, glimpsing Mrs. Coffey disappearing into the bank with a quick look over her shoulder. He must covet that as a warning. For his family, for his heart.

"Where are the children?" Leanna asked

"Their mother is not feeling well today. They begged to stay close by, and well" — Alex smirked — "their papa gives in too easily."

Leanna faintly smiled. "I see."

A silence fell between them. He should ask about Salt Lake City and her interview. But did he really want to know?

The patter of horses dragging wheels along the dirt road and the chatter of men and women preparing for the day faded away. He held Leanna's sparkling blue eyes in an entranced lock.

What was she thinking?

Her lips pursed. "Why did you lie to me?" She cocked her head to one side and put her hand on her hip.

"Lie?"

"Yes. You told me you were a gambler like Jack. Do you *want* me to detest you?"

"I did no such thing. But I am not much different than him. I left Greece for money — a foolish endeavor."

"You left for your ill wife, though. The money was for her, wasn't it?" Her words heightened with emotion, as if all her faith depended on the truth in her assumption.

"How do you know this?" he grumbled.

"That labor agent told me," she said. "But why would you compare yourself to Jack?" Her voice was softer, fragile in a way. It seemed weighted with hurt.

He'd failed one woman, he couldn't fail Leanna, too. He was good at the success, the work, the providing — but matters of the heart? Not so much. He was misled by love and faith once before. The best way to avoid such pain was to end this now.

"Did your interview go well?" he blurted.

"Alex, are you listening to me?" She held her arms across her torso, and her glare turned to ice. "Why are you changing the subject?"

"Because it is good for you to leave this place. My history should not concern you." Alex stepped closer. "Leanna, you deserve better than anything Castle Gate can offer you."

Her eyes became large topaz gems. A small crinkle appeared between her eyebrows, and her lip trembled. "You know nothing of what I deserve. It is by God's grace that I breathe another day and that I have found a second chance in Salt Lake."

"God's grace?" He scoffed. "What of God? You are a strong woman, Leanna. Your unbelievable strength is what has gotten you this far."

Her mouth fell open. "What of God?" she shook her head. "Are you trying to cast a lie about yourself again? Everything you do and most everything you say have been blessings to me, Alex. I see His hand in my life more and more because of you."

"I think you see what you want to see," he said, but his chest constricted with the temptation to wonder at her words.

"Alex, you are wrong in that," Leanna snapped. "You are less like Jack than you think. He was at least a man of faith."

Now she stung a place in his heart that he

offer warmth and love, or one that could burn whatever heart he had left.

Leanna took long, determined strides toward the school — not because she might be late, but because she suspected she was being watched as she ascended the hill. Most likely, that busybody Mrs. Coffey was making sure everyone was getting where they needed to be. By the time Leanna reached the school gate, her jaw ached from gritting her teeth. She dared not look back. Mrs. Coffey's interruption was rude and uncalled for — but Leanna could not expect anything less from the woman, could she?

Earlier, while she waited for the children, Mrs. Coffey had stopped on her way to town, carrying on about the Greeks who'd supposedly disrupted her quiet evening with their obnoxious music and drunken hollers the other night.

"I believe it was the same night you ate there." Mrs. Coffey had shot a hot glare at the restaurant door, her lip pulled up in a sneer. "My husband told me he ran into you that night."

"Yes, I was invited by Mrs. Pappas to a fine celebration," Leanna had said, determined to snuff out any lies this woman was trying to conjure up. "There was not one

143

drunken holler or any loud music that I recall, Mrs. Coffey."

The woman narrowed her eyes and said, "Seems we have different opinions on many things, Mrs. McKee. Good day."

Why had the good Lord given her a spy as a neighbor, instead of a friend?

She opened the gate to the school, glad that winter break would arrive soon. Icicles encapsulated the fingers of the lone tree in the schoolyard, as cold and rigid as the headmistress of the school.

If there was one thing Leanna missed about Boston, it was friendship. When she first arrived at Castle Gate, she hadn't expected to live here indefinitely, so she did not attempt to grow any roots in the way of friendship.

But now? Without a husband to at least fill the void of silence at night, she craved conversation. Salt Lake City offered that. The Tiltons' daughter was more than a potential employer, but a pleasant woman who seemed to anticipate their future friendship with great joy. The letter to her parents became ashes that very night she had returned from Salt Lake City. Her hope was vibrant at the thought of working for such a woman.

Even Alex seemed to think that Salt Lake

was best for her. Hadn't he said that she deserved better than Castle Gate had to offer her?

What did he know of what she deserved, though? By God's grace alone she could hardly believe that, but the man seemed to know her better than she knew herself at times. They were alike in many ways, yet he complimented her at her worst and offered her hope in something she shouldn't even consider.

She breathed in deep, the smell of winter carrying on the icy air. It was a smoky and ironically warm smell, no match to the warmth she felt now, thinking about Alex.

"Lord help me." She wagged her head as she headed across the yard.

He was curious, for sure. One moment, he seemed to try to aggravate her with sharp remarks, hidden truths. And then other times, he drew her in with his unwavering attention, affirming words — holding an impression of her that was much too lofty. What strength had she truly shown him, and what lie did he believe that she managed anything on her own?

It was only by God's hand. Nothing came to her by her own effort, no matter how she'd tried to be that guiding hand during her marriage. A terrible way to be, and now she suffered the shame of it.

She pulled the door to the school. It was heavy, needing a quick jerk to release it from its stationary position. When she stepped into the hall, it creaked shut and then rested against the jamb with a thud. As she hurried up the stairs to her classroom, the gaggle of Greeks scurried down the hall ahead. A smile crept across her face.

Before she'd roll her eyes and curse Jack for their predicament. How quickly her heart changed, though. The Pappas family had much to do with it. Alex's kindness had much to do with it.

When she reached the classroom, the boys were clambering into their desks. She hesitated and examined each of them. Something was different.

Their clothes were bright and clean.

"What happened to your clothes?" she asked an older boy, Petros.

"Mrs. Pappas clean them. She scrub us, too." He frowned, pressing down his somewhat groomed hair.

"Did she?" Leanna grinned.

"She say we are no good dirty," he said.

"She mean," a younger boy said. "She like my yiayia." He crossed his arms over his chest and pouted.

Leanna laughed out loud, and all the boys

widened their dark eyes and stared.

That woman had brightened life nearly as much as her eldest son had. She was a kindhearted soul. Life in Castle Gate was better because of the hospitality of such a person as Mrs. Pappas. If she stayed, what else could she expect here?

A life of frustration, for sure. If these once-filthy boys became as endearing to her as the Pappas children, and if the owners of the town's Greek restaurant became her adopted family, she'd grow weary in hiding a forbidden friendship with Alex. Friendship would only last so long, before she'd hope for more. Or perhaps, there was something more already.

CHAPTER NINE

"Ghata, ghata." Teddy's call carried down the path from Leanna's house. When she approached the knoll, the little boy came into view, sitting on her front step. He wrestled with the Coffeys' cat, trying to pin him on his lap.

"Teddy, what are you doing here?" She strode across the yard to the porch.

"The ghata ran away." Teddy nodded at her neighbor's house then shrugged his shoulders. "I come give it back, but he gone. I wait." He gave a crooked smile, his light brown eyes flashing with amusement.

She pulled him up by his good arm. The cat struggled and meowed while Teddy held it tight. "Does your mother know you are here?"

The little boy peered up with apologetic eyes and shook his head.

"We had better get you back. Leave the cat be, Teddy. He'll be fine."

"No!" He put the cat to his shoulder, holding his arm over it.

Leanna sighed. She pulled him by the arm and walked over to the Coffeys' house. Surely they wouldn't have a window open in the winter. Should she try to open one herself?

Before she could muster up courage to investigate her options, a familiar clearing throat startled her.

She spun around with a firm grip still on Teddy. Mr. Coffey stood before them, dusted with coal, shadowed with suspicion. His chin prodded forward and he grimaced. "What you doin' round here, Mrs. McKee? You look mighty interested in that window." He set cold eyes on Teddy. "You trying to steal somethin' and got caught, little boy? I'm thinkin' it may be my cat." He reached over and snatched the cat from his arms. The cat screeched then settled against Coffey's chest.

Teddy whimpered.

"Mr. Coffey, the boy was returning your cat. There's no reason to assume anything. We were trying to find a way to keep it safe and sound."

"Don't be too trusting, Mrs. McKee. D'you hear 'bout them Greeks carrying their weapons and shooting them off the train cars? They think they're goin' to make waves like Butch Cassidy did at the old coal company office." He scowled at the little boy.

"I daresay, the Greeks that I know care nothing for the outlaw's notorious history with Castle Gate." She rolled her eyes. "There is plenty of crime by American folk these days also, Mr. Coffey. Let's not take our social qualms out on a child. He was returning your cat, that is all. Come Teddy." She pushed him forward and followed him down the knoll.

"He mean," Teddy mumbled after they passed through the scrubby tree line.

Leanna didn't speak. She tried to tame the anger stirred by her neighbors twice today.

When she and Teddy neared the restaurant, Leanna suggested, "Let's go through the back." No use feeding the Coffeys' gossip by entering the restaurant from Main.

Smoke rose from the outdoor oven. Her stomach grumbled at the smell of baked bread. Teddy opened the door and ran inside, leaving her at the doorway. She peered into the dim room.

Mrs. Pappas spoke loud and frantic, shaking her hand at Teddy. The little boy carried on in Greek and pointed at Leanna.

Mrs. Pappas went from a scowl as she'd reprimanded Teddy, to a look of surprise. "Meesus McKee! Come, come!"

"I just wanted to be sure he is okay." She smiled, trying to back away.

"No, no. You come eat." Mrs. Pappas grabbed her by the hands and smiled wide. "You save Teddy twice. You come."

"Save? I didn't —" But before she could insist, she was dragged across the small kitchen and through the door to the dining area. Maria sat at the table in the corner, playing cards with her grandfather. The restaurant was empty. It was not near suppertime.

"Meesus McKee." Maria ran over, holding her hand of cards against her chest. "Why you here?"

The ever-persistent Mrs. Pappas gently pushed Leanna toward a seat. "Your grandmother is determined to feed me." She giggled at the woman. Maria slipped her hand in Leanna's and they sat at the table together.

"How is your mother?" Leanna tried to retrieve her hand. There was no use getting attached. But Maria squealed as if it were a game and relentlessly grabbed at her hand again.

"She okay. Just tired. We miss school to be

151

with her."

Her grandfather left the table, tipping his cap to Leanna before going into the kitchen. "Papou thinks you pretty." Maria giggled into her cards.

Leanna couldn't refrain a smile. "Oh?"

"And Thios Alex." The girl now had her whole face leaning into the flayed cards, chuckling loudly.

Leanna's smile disappeared and her stomach jumped. "Did Alex say that?" She suddenly felt like a schoolgirl herself.

Maria's big brown eyes peered over the cards. She nodded. "Don't tell him I said so, but Papa teases him about you."

The strum of the Greek instrument floated around them. She looked over at Mr. Pappas who played in the corner. He gave another nod.

"Meesus McKee, will you dance now? Look, no one is watching." Maria pointed at the empty room with her cards then set them on the table.

The little girl took her hands and pulled her from the table. "Come, I show you first."

She found a clear area. Teddy sat on a tabletop, leaning his chin on his fist. His sister positioned herself beside Leanna, gripping her hand.

"Watch, and you step with me."

With each movement of her feet, Maria's curls bounced. Leanna pulled her skirt just at the ankle and tried to keep up. As the music sped up, they moved around the space faster. It wasn't complicated, but she stumbled a few times. She laughed out loud at herself each time. By the end of the song, she was out of breath just as if she had waltzed the night away at a ball.

"Bravo!" The children clapped.

"Who is the teacher now?" Alex asked from behind them. Leanna spun around. His broad shoulders nearly filled the kitchen doorway. Mr. Pappas set down his instrument, patted Alex's arm, and said something in Greek. It was more serious than a greeting. Alex's jaw flinched, and he gave a quick nod. "Good afternoon, Mrs. McKee."

"Maria is as persistent as her grandmother," Leanna said, adjusting her bun. She wondered if everything was okay with his father.

"You are a good dancer." Alex smiled, seemingly unaffected by Stergios now. The children ran up to him.

"I taught her, Thios." Maria clung to his hand now, swinging his arm back and forth. All the while, Alex's attention remained on Leanna.

"You are a good teacher, Maria." It was

153

more comfortable to look at Maria than Alex. Leanna's heartbeat at least slowed this way. When they had last spoken, Alex had been cut off by Mrs. Coffey, and Leanna had said they'd finish the discussion later. She was afraid of what he might say. Afraid and curious and expectant for the words to be what she assumed. Thank goodness Maria was here. Leanna was not ready to fortify her heart today. She was enjoying herself way too much.

"Will you teach me your kind of dance, Meesus McKee?" Maria called out.

"Perhaps," she said.

Mrs. Pappas pushed Alex out of the way, carrying a platter of food from the kitchen. She rushed everyone to sit and eat.

Once again, the tiny woman served a delicious plate, better than any that Leanna could make for her table of one. And sharing a meal with Alex and the children only made her eat slower, procrastinating her lonely walk to her dreary house.

Another reason to look forward to Salt Lake City. She would have a family under the same roof. Although, she'd yet to make a first impression of Dr. Scott.

The thought of Salt Lake City was brief in the warm atmosphere of the Pappas family.

Alex guided the conversation, and it was a gentle one, unlike their several heated conversations before. He spoke of Greece and the land they owned.

"Thousands of sheep grazed in our pastures, and our crops produced large yields. We were in need of nothing." That was before the drought, he said. He even mentioned his wife, Helena, and her sickness consuming her just as the drought heightened. "A bad omen, Momma would say. She still curses the sun for stealing the rain *and* Helena's health." Alex rolled his eyes then continued on with talk about his journey to Athens.

His descriptions of the classical architecture that Leanna had studied in school were interrupted by Maria asking about American dances. Pictures of the Parthenon and memories of debutante balls spun in Leanna's mind.

"More?" Mrs. Pappas scooted the platter of chicken and potatoes next to her.

"No, thank you. It was wonderful." She shook her head with a wide grin, wondering if Mrs. Pappas understood. The woman shrugged her shoulders and walked away, mumbling in Greek.

Alex chuckled. "It's okay. No Greek woman likes her food to be turned down,

155

even if you've eaten all night." He leaned back in his chair and patted his belly. "Momma!" When he got her attention, he winked and spoke in Greek with enthusiasm.

"*Efcharistó,* Alex!" The lady blew her son a kiss and continued preparing the tables for supper. The miners would be there any minute.

"I really must go." Leanna cringed at the truth in the words, torn between enjoying the company and being caught in a roomful of gawking miners once again.

As she scooted her chair back reluctantly, Alex leaned forward on the table and cocked a smile to one side. "Perhaps we can show Maria how to dance before you go?"

Her heart skittered beneath her blouse. "Do you even know how?"

He sat up straight. "Do I? You think your dance is so much more difficult than the Greek way? It is nothing."

He poked his finger at Maria's arm, keeping his bright eyes on Leanna. "Shall we take this to the kitchen, Maria?"

His niece clapped her hands together, jumping up and down. "Yes, yes! Let's!"

He held out his hand to Leanna.

She should not let this go one minute further, yet Alex's warm gaze, kind smile, and eager brow were difficult to resist. She may never take that hike to Castle Gate's namesake, but she could show his niece how to dance. Dancing was another piece of her past that she missed.

"This, this isn't proper . . . is it?" she muttered.

Alex raised his shoulders with a nonchalant shrug even though a slight grimace shadowed his face. He quickly looked back at his father. The man was sitting in the corner, cleaning his instrument and glaring at Alex.

"Perhaps your father doesn't think so," Leanna whispered, but Alex just grabbed her hand, and Maria pulled them along.

She followed closely behind him, wondering what her neighbors would think. She clung to his hand even more assuredly. Alex Pappas was no less than any of them. If anything, he was more — more passionate, determined, and kind than any person she'd ever met.

The kitchen was empty. He turned around and slid his hand to the small of her back. Staring down at her, his curls fell across his forehead. Their eyes danced together before any footwork began.

Was she the one person he mentioned this morning — who he'd found to care for in addition to his family? Could she allow herself to be lost in this moment, with the memories of her misery with Jack so close to sabotaging this feeling?

Who was it that Alex stared at? A schoolteacher or a lonely widow in need of a friend? Was there a chance she meant even more to him than that? Because right now, Leanna wanted to be nowhere else but in the arms of this strong, handsome man. His shirt smelled fresh with soap, and his peppermint breath tickled her forehead. She inhaled deeply, trying to contain the conflicting emotions inside her.

An inch closer and she'd sink into his chest. Her conscience screamed, *Leave.* She was in danger of turning her back on the chance to be free of her old self and start new in Salt Lake City.

But Alex stroked her cheek, and she couldn't imagine wanting to be anywhere else but Castle Gate.

"Thios Alex," Maria whined. They immediately stepped back, dropping each other's hands, giving full attention to the little girl. She blushed and bit her lip. "Will you dance now?"

"Maria!" Mrs. Pappas called from the dining room.

She let out a big sigh and stomped her

foot. "Don't leave, Meesus McKee," she pleaded.

"We will have to demonstrate another time," Leanna said. Yes, that was the best thing to do.

"No!" Maria looked back and forth between them. Alex placed a hand on the girl's shoulder.

"Maria, I promise. We will show you how to dance soon enough." He kissed her forehead. She slumped her shoulders on her way out.

"You promise?" Leanna placed her hand on her hip.

"Sure," he said. "You said we would demonstrate later."

"But I may not even be here —"

The light in his eyes dimmed, and the corners of his mouth turned down. "I see."

"My interview in Salt Lake City went well."

His disappointed look made her throat ache. "That is good. For you." He shoved his hands in his pockets then kicked his boot on the floor like a schoolboy. "For me?" Alex walked across the room and pulled his coat of the hook. "It is a burden." With an aggressive tug, he opened the door and left.

Leanna froze for a moment, the air pouring in from outside just as cold as Alex's abrupt absence. She hurried and gathered her coat and hat from the hooks on the wall.

Dusk was almost consumed by the night sky. When she approached the road to look for Alex, he was gone.

If he felt like Leanna had in his arms, then she understood his anger. She was angry, too.

All her plans to leave waned in comparison to the security Alex offered her in a dance. Was Alex burdened for the same reasons as Leanna?

She should not stay in Castle Gate long enough to find out.

She could not.

Alex hammered the nail through the wood crate, securing the western wall of their makeshift home. Several crates had come loose in the last snowstorm. While his hands worked, his mind was somewhere else entirely.

How could he let Leanna go? After eight long years, he'd finally found that life was worth living more than to make a penny or keep this house secure for winter.

Life was not all work; it was love, too. And as much as he resisted admitting it, his emotions could not be tamped down much longer. Love was boundless. Hadn't Shake-

speare alluded to something like that? His days of reading the poet were during his early English-speaking moments. But one thing was for sure, his heart awakened on the wrong side of the boundaries set in place. And no matter how much he tried, he could not find peace in the lines drawn by men. Not when Leanna stood so close to the edge. With the golden-haired schoolteacher about, Alex could not soothe his heart back to sleep.

"It is early to bang on the wall, Alex," his father said, fixing his suspenders and yawning.

"Sorry, Papa. I needed to get it done before work today." He looked up at the gray sky. "It looks like we might get snow again."

"The spring cannot come fast enough." Stergios sat on a discarded mine crate and pulled out his knife and carving wood. "You remember Georgios from Kalavryta?"

Alex continued, "I do. He was on his way to Athens when I left, eh?"

"Neh. His daughter is only a few years younger than you. You may have gone to school together, I don't know." He shrugged his shoulders and whittled away, but Alex could only stare at him.

"Papa, where is this going?"

161

"He has a dowry, Alex. And you need a bride."

Alex tossed the hammer to a patch of dead grass. "I need nothing but some peace and quiet."

"Well, you will get none of that if you keep entertaining that Mrs. McKee."

"You are right. There are too many eyes about. But do you understand my predicament?" Alex wanted to continue at this even pace of conversation. Too often their emotions got the best of them when they discussed his father's expectations for him.

Papa nodded, continuing his whittling. "I understand that she is a beautiful woman, and you have been single for too long. America has its lure. And even Georgios's daughter is willing to come this way —"

"You've spoken with Georgios?" Alex's voice hitched. "When?"

"We write letters. He shared the amount of his dowry with me in the last letter. It's not bad," he lifted his shoulders. "But I don't care so much about that." He stood up and placed a hand on Alex's shoulder. "You are a good son, and you deserve a good Greek family."

"Deserve?" Frustration filled his chest. "Why do you push and push when I've done enough? I brought you out of poverty and into a prosperous life. If I deserve anything, it is to make my own decisions. Why should I worry about a dowry or a Greek woman I know nothing about?"

Papa's mustache twitched at one corner. He dropped his hand. "This is the way it is done."

"What about love, Papa? The way it is done isn't always the only way."

"Love? Do you love the American woman?" Papa gaped.

"I — I . . ." He clenched his teeth. No, he couldn't say it. Even if his heart nearly burst at the thought, there was a dangerous power in words right now. And he knew that whatever he said would be used against him more than bring him the peace he longed for.

"Alex, enough." His father lifted his hand in finality. "There are few things that have better options than tradition. This is tradition. You are Greek, and you deserve a good Greek bride."

"We are American, too," Alex muttered without looking at him.

Papa sucked air through his teeth and glared. "Your blood is Greek. Do not cast off your obligations for an American woman. They are a different breed, nothing like a Greek woman who will care for you

163

and feed you and pray for you."

"You are no better than the Americans who sneer at us," Alex seethed without guarding his tongue. His father's eyes flickered with hurt. He curled his lip and stepped back. "Papa, I didn't mean to —"

"You are a disappointment, Alex." His bottom lip trembled. "You turn your back on heritage as if everything you've done with your own hands is most important." He turned away. "If you forget that American teacher, then I will no longer speak of a match." His slouched figure disappeared around the corner of the house.

With great force, Alex kicked the mining crate and it split with a crack. He had done so much with his own hands. Everything up to this point had depended on it. Life was what he made it. If he hadn't worked so hard, where would they be?

They would be Greek and poor and no doubt starving.

His heritage was one thing, but he had survived and brought them along with him.

Wasn't that enough for his father? He had been strong and determined and had accomplished much on his own.

But it wasn't enough, and it didn't hold as much weight as he thought it should. Even Leanna couldn't admit her strength

was her own — she cast it off on God.

If there was a God willing to help him, then wouldn't He have done so long before now?

Alex picked up the hammer and began to work. It was what he did best, but he wasn't at his best now.

He wasn't so sure he'd ever measure up to his father's expectations. Just like God hadn't measured up to his.

CHAPTER TEN

Jack haunted her thoughts all night long. The blasted stove-door hinge broke again, reminding her of another fight she'd had with her husband.

Guilt crept around her heart, and she prayed forgiveness in and out of sleep. Her head began to ache at the midnight hour.

She was beginning to forget his mannerisms. Her heart grew anxious. Why had her guilt not left her? What would it take to forgive herself for the wife that she had been to him?

When light finally spilled about the edge of her curtains, she got up and dressed.

There was one vow she must make to herself now.

"Stay away from Alex," she mumbled. How could she be trusted by another man? She'd proven her heart was nimble in its pursuit of forgiveness. Stubborn and tough. Alex Pappas and his family did not need

anyone like her about. It would only be a matter of time before he would see her true self and the ugly mess of her unforgiving heart.

Leanna began to boil water for tea. While she ate a meager breakfast of oatmeal and dried fruit, a tap at the door startled her.

"Who is it?" she called as she gathered her dishes and placed them in her wash bin.

"It's Bethany Scott."

Her heart leaped. Perfect timing for her most recent vow. Leanna opened the door to find Mrs. Scott beaming with a pink nose and a delighted smile. "Good morning, Mrs. McKee."

"Good morning," she greeted. "Please, come in out of the cold."

Bethany bustled past her, and Leanna closed the door against a harsh winter breeze.

"What brings you to Castle Gate?" Leanna bit the inside of her cheek. Perhaps she knew the answer?

Bethany fiddled with her gloves. "My husband has offered to help the town doctor this week due to the influenza outbreak, so we have stayed with my parents for a few days." Her brow became worrisome beneath her wide hat. "My mother has done well not to argue with me in front of Tommy.

167

The very reason that I keep him close by at all times."

Leanna gave her most apologetic look and offered her a seat at the table.

Bethany sank into the chair with a resolute smile. "Tommy went back to the city with his father, and I will be on a train this morning." The kettle began to whistle and Leanna quickly removed it from the heat. "I had to pay a visit to my newest friend before I left." Her face brightened once again, and Leanna smiled also.

"Well, you arrived just in time for some tea."

"How perfect," Bethany said, unbuttoning her coat. Leanna hung it up on a hook. The soft fur was fine, a reminder of the luxury she'd once taken for granted.

"Ever since your interview, I cannot help but think of you alone here, in this place." Bethany examined the small room.

Humility snagged on a pesky remnant of Leanna's pride. She plopped one of the last tea bags from the Tiltons' gift basket into a cup.

"The remainder of interviews were a mere formality," Bethany continued, her eyes flashing as she sat across from her. "My husband agrees that you are the best fit for the position." She pulled in a breath and seemingly held it, raising her eyebrows in excitement.

"I am?" Leanna held her breath also. The timing of this escape was too good to be true.

"Yes!" Bethany clapped her hands together. "Nobody has the same qualifications as you do. We hope for you to move your belongings to our spare room and begin lessons next month."

"Thank you, Mrs. Scott," Leanna exclaimed, Bethany's excitement a sure contagion. "Of course I'll accept."

"Oh, good!" She patted the table. "It will be nice to have another female around the house. Men can be so boring at times." She chuckled. "And please, call me Bethany."

Leanna nodded. *Thank You, Lord, for this providence.* She released a sigh, indulging in the relief of finally leaving all this behind.

Unwelcome in this moment, Alex barreled to mind. A stab sliced through her heart. He'd said her leaving was a burden. And for that, she could not fully rejoice. He was a good man, and his family had been good to her. But her feelings for him were becoming dangerously inappropriate.

She must tell him right away that she was leaving Castle Gate. Give him a chance to find her replacement and end whatever that

169

dance had stirred in each of their hearts.

December offered clear skies for his Sunday hikes. Alex passed the boardinghouse on his way to the Castle Gate formation. Several swarthy Greeks sat on the porch, smoking and jabbering.

"Shouldn't you be at church?" he called out to his friend Nick, who rattled off a similar interrogation in jest.

"Alex, you've been here long enough," another friend called out. "It's about time you go back to Greece and find yourself a bride. We have plenty of sisters to choose from!"

"Perhaps your sisters should come to America." Alex chuckled. The Pappas women were weary of limited gossip sessions between just the two of them.

The sun shone bright, but the air was still bitingly cold. There was enough hardship to focus on the elements and ignore the war raging in his thoughts — between everyone else's expectations and the selfish desire to follow his heart. Over and over, he recalled the afternoon in the kitchen — Leanna's tight grip on his hand, the floral scent of her hair, and the threads of gold in her sapphire eyes.

Even though he hated to hear it, it was

good that she'd mentioned Salt Lake. Her chance to leave was probably the best way to end this torment.

How could he expect her to stay in this town filled with men?

He stomped harder as he trekked toward the looming rocks.

Why did he allow his heart to depend on a woman again? After eight years of persevering, why did he invite weakness in so quickly? Perhaps he wasn't as strong alone as he hoped to be.

Hollering grew loud behind him. He peered over his shoulder. Leanna stormed toward him, taking wide strides along the dirt road while the men at the boarding-house teased in Greek.

When she approached him, she pulled her hand from her muff and dug it into her side. "My, this is quite a climb," she spoke breathlessly, adjusting the high collar around her throat.

"We are not beyond the town yet," Alex challenged with a wag of his eyebrow. They should not go any farther — especially with everyone below still in an uproar of laughter and gossip. His father's opinion came to mind. "Leanna, is there something —"

"I'd prefer not to stand here with ill-mannered men gawking at me from behind." She gestured to the path. "Shall we hike?"

The sparkle in her blue eyes sent a current through him, enticing him to take the risk. He'd deal with his father later.

The sparse ground cover crunched beneath his boots, and Leanna followed him. When they reached the snow-covered path that wrapped around the base of the rigid cliff, he paused.

"My, I've never been this close," Leanna whispered.

The rocks loomed ahead like a sandstone castle.

"I only have one pair of snowshoes. May I help you put them on?" he asked.

She hesitated then lifted her dress just enough to stick out her boot. Alex knelt down and placed her foot on the snowshoe, adjusting it until it was snug. He did the same for her other foot then stood up.

"Thank you." She tried to walk. "This is awkward."

"You'll get used to it. Here, let me help." He hooked arms with her and they walked along the fresh snow.

"It is so quiet here," she marveled. " 'Our peace shall stand as firm as rocky mountains.' "

"Shakespeare?" His heart leaped. "This

172

hike is my sure peace every week." Until this woman took hold of his thoughts.

"It's nice to get away from the busy miners, and the busybodies for that matter," she grumbled.

They continued on in silence. Occasionally, she would lose her balance and hold on to him. Each time, he hoped she would keep hold of him. An urge to help her grew stronger with each step.

When they turned the corner, the rocks towered on each side, a grand entrance to the whole of Price Canyon. Mountains stood as far as they could see.

Leanna gasped. "It's beautiful, Alex."

He swallowed hard, trying to take in the beauty that captured her, not the beauty that she was. "You are the first person to join me at my personal sanctuary." He took in a jagged breath.

A gray storm flooded her eyes. "I see why you come so often." She pulled off her hat and laid it on a boulder. She tilted her face to the sunshine, with eyes closed. "This is so peaceful." Her hair was gathered back in a loose bun. Strands of hair framed her face, tempting Alex to brush them away.

"I tried to catch you before you left today," she said, opening her eyes and staring into the expanse of rock. "I have accepted the position in Salt Lake City."

His stomach twisted. Disappointment flooded him, just like when the next foreman position was given to someone less qualified.

But Leanna's opportunity was for the best. Everyone would be happy.

"That is very good for you. I am sure you will find the city a much better fit." He forced a smile. He must remain strong, unaffected, and ready to continue life as he had planned.

Leanna's eyes only darkened and her lip trembled. A deep crevice carved between her eyebrows. "You said that my leaving Castle Gate was a burden to you." She plucked at the fur of her muff. "Why?"

"That doesn't matter," he said. "I was foolish. How could I fill my promise to dance with you if you leave?" He winked and laughed. But she remained unmoved. Could she tell that he was bluffing? That no matter how much he talked himself into keeping a distance, he found himself increasingly drawn to her? But he could not tell her anything now. His weakness was growing, and everything he thought valuable was falling away, leaving a void that he thought had been filled up with his effort all these years.

Her cheeks grew red, and she raised an eyebrow. "Alex, I must know."

Through gritted teeth, he muttered a benign reason, "You are Maria's and Teddy's teacher, are you not?"

Her mouth parted and she placed a hand on her cheek. Her gaze scattered about and fell on her cast-off hat. She snatched it up. "Yes, of course." He'd seen her embarrassment before, when she'd first assumed he had invited her here. "I shall inquire about my replacement. Thank you, Alex." She tried her best to turn down the path with the snowshoes still strapped on her feet, but she stumbled.

"Wait." He grabbed her arm.

She shook his hand off. "I — I should not have come out here. This was foolish. I don't know why I was so anxious to tell you —"

"You are kind to let me know." He wanted to assure her, to release her from the humiliation. "Please, you deserve this new position. It's a better place for you, no?"

"Deserve?" Her eyes glistened, and she spun away. "You think awfully highly of me." The woman had been through enough with the loss of her husband and the pesky neighbors casting judgments on her.

"Don't cry, Leanna."

"I rarely do," she blurted through her tears. "Cry, you know? Although, you've caught me before." Wiping her face with a handkerchief, she continued: "I wish I agreed with you. That I deserve this and can move on. I thought that I would be lighter, more free now. But I am burdened by so much regret."

With a gentle hand, he swept away the strands of hair by her face. "Forgive me for my words."

She sniffled then sat on the boulder. "It's not you, Alex. I pray and pray, and I'm never released of this burden."

His jaw tensed, and he understood the frustration. There was a time when he prayed and prayed and nothing but guilt came from it.

"You are hard on yourself." He crouched beside the boulder. "We should just sit. Enjoy the beauty."

"Yes, no more talking," she whispered.

The distant rush of a train rumbled below; then all was silent. He focused on the slopes ahead, trying to spy any wildlife like he usually did on his hikes. One day last spring, he had spotted a magnificent elk, and since then he had hoped to see it again. Leanna's profile was more interesting now. He couldn't keep his eyes off the woman who seemed perfectly content in their quiet solitude. She'd almost left, but now, she was choosing to stay.

The moment was just as fragile as finding the elk. The slightest movement and Alex feared she would disappear.

"Look, a fox," Leanna whispered, pointing down the slope. The animal slipped in and out of the dormant bushes, disappearing into its hole. "Beautiful." Her face lit with excitement. He imagined he wore the same expression when he caught sight of wildlife for the first time.

"You are beautiful, Leanna," his words slipped out, and he wished he'd spoke Greek instead.

Her ice-blue gaze settled upon him. The corners of her lips twitched. "Is that what you tried to tell me on our walk to school?" She gave a genuine smile. "You don't realize how much a woman wants to be told such things."

He swallowed hard. "I've wrestled with all I want to say, and all that I should say." His father's bargain irritated him now — leave her alone and he would forget the match. Yet how could he abandon his heart right now?

Her loose bun grazed the back of her neck, begging to tumble out and show its length. Light from the open view of the mountain range reflected on her ivory skin, and she fluttered her eyes to a close.

Everything fell away. The world was this woman and his beating heart.

He lifted his hand to her cheek. She didn't flinch, just gently pushed into his palm. With trembling fingers, he brushed down her neck and wrapped his hand around her gathered hair. With little effort, he released the knot. Golden hair fell down her back in one glorious wave.

"Beautiful," he whispered. He cupped his hand beneath her chin. The pale blue shimmer of her eyes awakened. "Leanna, your leaving is not Maria or Teddy's burden. It is my own."

"Is it?" Her voice was small.

"My father is right about one thing, I need to live more. Working in the dark mines is not much of an existence." He chuckled at his own blindness all these years. "But there was a time when I needed to bury myself in the effort." The loud piercing whistle of the train below interrupted his confession, awakening his good sense. He should not speak further.

"To forget?" Leanna questioned. "You loved her very much." She gave a sad smile. "I can tell."

"I did. And I thought that I followed a good plan. Yet all the effort was in vain. Helena died. A foolish mistake on my part. One that I shall never make again."

"You couldn't have known. What could you have done?"

"Depended on reason instead of an empty prayer," he grumbled.

She tilted her head and frowned. "I wish I leaned more into prayer during my marriage and less on my own reason." Her teeth rested on her lip as she appeared lost in thought. "Perhaps then I wouldn't have been such a bitter wife to Jack. And maybe I could have understood him better. Anthis said Jack was trying to work our way out of this place — for me."

"Like I said before, you are too hard on yourself."

"And you aren't too hard on yourself?" She narrowed her eyes. Perhaps he had been. Could he have known how long he had to save Helena? Nobody knew. "Look at all that you've accomplished, because of following your heart — or a prayer?" She raised an eyebrow.

His first step in America was because of his heart, wasn't it? "We are both difficult people, aren't we?" They laughed together and in the midst of it, they twined their fingers.

Leanna laid her head on his shoulder. "You are a good man, Alex."

Anxiety mixed with joy frenzied in his veins. How natural this seemed. They may be from lands thousands of miles apart, but they were together now, and all the darkness of his past faded away. "I have not been honest with you, Leanna." He leaned his cheek into her soft hair. "I am finding an even greater burden to bear — I've never wanted to be out of the dark mines and in the sunshine more than when I know I might see you. And now you are leaving."

She squeezed his hand. "You have brought more light to my time in Castle Gate than I'd ever imagined could be so."

"Then why don't you stay?" He lifted his head.

She slipped her fingers from his, taking all the warmth that made him bold. A sad smile crossed her face. "I've only brought you scrutiny from the Coffeys and trouble with your father. I saw how he looked at us that last time I was in the restaurant." Leanna sighed. "And the good Lord knows that I will never find forgiveness amid all the bitter memories."

"Forgiveness?"

"I haven't forgiven Jack, not really." Leanna searched his eyes. "God's hand has been in all of this. I am inclined to think that leaving Salt Lake City is my greatest hope to move on."

Alex looked away. She sounded like he did when he left for America. "You see, God and I don't align much," he frowned. "I don't think He deserves such credit."

"It is okay to be angry. He can handle it." Leanna slipped her hands in his again.

"I am not angry." Alex stood up, her hands falling away.

"Oh?" She stood, too, compassion filling her eyes.

He diverted his gaze and looked around for his hiking stick, without really seeing. "Come, we must go before all the Americans fill the streets after church," he said, finally noticing the stick at his feet.

"See, it's best that I go." She knotted her hair and put her hat on. "Neither of us can live life in hiding."

She was right. As they trekked back down toward town, the usual torment of his thoughts were just as apparent with Leanna by his side as they were when he was alone.

Had he been living life in hiding from more than just his foes, but from God as well?

In his mind, He had been his greatest foe all along.

CHAPTER ELEVEN

"Meesus McKee, you promised to show me how to dance." Maria begged as they walked down the hill on the day before winter break — Leanna's last day to walk with the children. Teddy skipped ahead.

"I will not show you here, in the middle of the road, Maria." She tried to maintain a firm tone.

"Thios Alex would love to dance with you. Come to our house." She began to walk toward the path to the Greek neighborhood.

"Maria. We will not go to your house," she snapped. "Come here this instant."

How could the mention of Alex bring such a fluster of emotion? Their hike was not the finality she had hoped for. She should have left much earlier than she did. Why did she prod into his heart so much? Only a few more weeks and she would leave Castle Gate, never to return. If she thought too much about Alex, her own heart might lead her in the wrong direction.

"This way, Miss Pappas." She steered Maria away from the path, to the street toward the restaurant.

"Hmph." Maria crossed her arms on her chest.

Teddy tugged on Leanna's coat sleeve. "She likes you good." He smiled.

"She likes me very much?" She corrected with a raised brow. Teddy nodded.

And to think, just months ago, she cursed her pitiful position to teach English to little Greeks. How easy it was to trick a heart into misery.

When they reached the restaurant, Maria yanked the door, but it was locked.

"How strange." Leanna peered into the window, but darkness revealed nothing.

Teddy began to cry. "Where are they, Meesus McKee?"

"Let's go around to the back door. Perhaps they are outside?" She ushered the children around the corner of the building, but the yard was empty. The outdoor oven, unlit.

"Walk us home, Meesus McKee." Maria snuggled up next to her as if more than just the winter air had gone cold.

"I can walk you to the path, then you can find your way from there, right?"

"No!" Teddy wrapped his arms around her skirt.

"Do not be ridiculous." She peeled him off and placed her hands on her hips.

"We cannot walk alone." Maria's eyes were round like chestnuts. "Please, the gypsies will take us."

"There are no gypsies —" Before Leanna could convince them, they both began to sob.

"Please, no go alone." Teddy grabbed her hand and held it to his cheek.

"Please, Meesus McKee." Maria sniffled.

Leanna glanced at the tree line that led to her house. What eyes were watching her?

Nobody was about. She walked to Main Street and saw no one of concern. She had sat in the restaurant twice now, and both times were of little consequence except the harmless judgments by the Coffeys.

"Come on, children." She took each child by the hand and walked to Greek Town.

Only a handful of houses lay nestled in the neighborhood. A couple were simply old railroad cars serving as shelter. After her hike with Alex, she was certain that most of the Greeks chose the boardinghouse.

Leanna rushed the children along, thankful for the biting chill keeping everyone inside.

"This is our house." Maria ran up to the door and her brother ran around the back. "Yiayia! Momma!" The house seemed well built. Better than Leanna's. She noticed a wall of mine crates making up part of the house, extending it far wider than Leanna's little home.

Mrs. Pappas appeared in the doorway. "*Tiepethis*, Maria?" When she saw Leanna she gasped and looked about.

"The restaurant was closed." Leanna pointed back toward town.

Maria interpreted and Mrs. Pappas's eyes popped as she pursed her lips.

"Stergios!" She yelled louder than a train engine as she walked in the middle of the path. "Stergios!"

The door of the house across the way flung open and Stergios stumbled out, yelling in Greek.

When Mrs. Pappas retorted, he grew pale and clutched Maria to his frame, mumbling words and stroking her hair.

Mrs. Pappas returned to their door. Her face was pinched in anger, but in a weary voice she said, "He forget," then paused a moment and stared at Leanna from toe to head. "Come. You help."

"What?"

"Penelope." She darted a glance at Maria

then flicked her head to the door. "Come."

The forcefulness in her voice and the seriousness of her look gave Leanna little choice but to obey.

She entered the home. It was warm with a blazing oven in one corner, and the sweet, spicy smell of cinnamon. Delicious, just like the scents of the restaurant. A long table with a bench on either side and chairs at each end lined the wall opposite a kitchen boasting a sink and a wall of cabinetry. A bed in the corner was made up as a settee, a small table was decked with a Grecian statue, and a wall was laden with a wooden crucifix and icons with grave expressions.

She followed Mrs. Pappas to a bedroom. The children's mother, a petite lady with wavy hair, who'd walked with the children this fall, knelt on the floor, her arms and head resting on a bed. Her body lurched forward, and a long moan escaped her while she gripped the bedsheets with white knuckles.

Mrs. Pappas whispered continuously as Penelope groaned, wiping the hair from her neck.

How could Leanna help? What would she do?

"Yiayia?" Maria cheeped at the door. Leanna turned and ushered her out.

"Come, Maria. Your mother is having the baby today."

Maria shook her head, her face filled with panic. "No! It's not time."

"When is she due?"

"January, Meesus McKee. It too early." She began to cry.

"Come, Maria. There is only one thing to do now." She led the little girl to the long table. They sat together, and Leanna bowed her head. "Heavenly Father, You are the God who sees. Watch over Penelope, and give her strength. Bless the baby, and protect its tiny body. Give Maria, and all the family, a peace that surpasses all understanding. I pray this in Your name. Amen." She looked up to see Maria still reverent. The child crossed herself like she'd seen Greeks do before then lifted her head.

"God will protect her, sweet Maria." She brushed a stray curl from Maria's forehead. The girl wiped her eyes and gave her a hug. How she would miss this girl. Leanna gently pulled away, begging her own eyes to stay dry.

The door burst open with a whipping blast of freezing air. Yanni and Alex stepped into the room. Both men gaped at her. They were tall Greek statues dusted in black.

"Papa!" Maria ran into her father's arms.

"Don't worry, we pray for Momma," she then continued in Greek.

Yanni put her down and hurried into the back bedroom.

"What are you doing here?" Alex tossed his gloves onto a counter then took off his hat.

"The restaurant was closed, and the children were afraid to walk home alone."

"I see." His voice was cool, harsher than the wind. "Thank you, Mrs. McKee."

She narrowed her eyes his way, but he cast his attention on Maria. Leanna swallowed a lump in her throat. They'd grown close in that hour on the hike, but they'd left with more heartache than before. Would he be cold to her the rest of her time in Castle Gate?

"Oh!" Maria clapped her hands together. "You dance now?"

"Your mother is having the baby. Go to your room, Maria," Alex snapped.

The little girl sulked out of the room.

"I should go, too. It seems your mother thought I could help. I don't even know what to do."

"She will tell you in time. Or at least, I will translate for her." He stood with his fists by his side.

"It is getting late, I should go home."

189

"Please. There are no other women to help. You are the only one." He softened his tone, but his expression remained grim, like the faces on the icons.

She pulled the chair out once more and sat down. The longer she stayed in this house, with the handsome man tripping her heart, the longer her walk home would be, and the longer it would take for Salt Lake City to become her home.

Mrs. Pappas called for boiled rags and Leanna helped Alex, trying to ignore the ache that spread across her chest. Alex nudged her to take them in the room. She hesitated, but he placed his hand on the small of her back and said, "You are stronger than you know, Leanna." She stepped into the room.

"Here you go." She set a bucket next to Mrs. Pappas who sat at the end of the bed, quietly instructing Penelope.

Leanna leaned on the wall, nerves tumbling and thoughts racing as Penelope began to push. Her mother-in-law prepared for the entrance of their newest family member with rolled-up sleeves and a fresh towel slung across her chest.

Leanna gasped at the sight of a head, a small head covered in dark hair. The excitement electrified Mrs. Pappas's squeal and her rambling words. One more push and a baby boy, no longer than Leanna's forearm, screamed into the stark black coal town.

His mother wept with joy and his yiayia laughed. Leanna stepped over and helped clean the baby with a warm washcloth.

"Efcharistó, Meesus McKee." Penelope's cheek rested against the fuzzy head of her baby. "Tell Yanni, please."

Leanna opened the door and faced three anxious men. Alex, Yanni, and Stergios sat frozen around the table, cards in their hands.

"You have a fine baby boy." She laughed as she spoke, elated at the privilege to invite Yanni in to meet his new son.

Cheers bellowed in the house. Yanni slipped past her. Stergios shouted in Greek as he entered another room. Soon, Maria and Teddy's voices bubbled with excitement.

Alex stood up, his curls unruly and his eyes bright with joy.

"I have never . . ." Seen anything so beautiful, so perfect. A deep breath rattled her body.

"Thank you for staying." He gripped the back of a chair and rocked forward. "It is good for Momma and Penelope to have a friend."

Friend? They could barely speak to her!

"Friend?" Mrs. Pappas stood at the door. "Who? Meesus McKee?" She took Leanna's face and pulled it down to her level. "You family now!"

She kissed both of Leanna's cheeks then turned and spoke to Alex. A cloud shadowed his expression, but when he shook his head no, Momma slapped his arm. "She insists that I walk you home."

"That won't be necessary," Leanna said, although she hoped he would oblige. Her heart was full. She feared that a quick return to her lonely home would deplete every ounce of joy by the midnight hour.

"It is necessary with Momma." He grabbed his coat. "I will walk you to the road at least."

"Very well." She pressed her lips tight, suppressing a grin.

Dusk fell fast on the makeshift neighborhood, as did the temperature. They walked in silence for long, treacherous minutes.

"I am in awe of your sister-in-law and your mother. What a family you have, Alex." She had nothing of the sort. "Your family is blessed."

"Ah, remember the words of my mother. It is your family, too." Alex chuckled. Leanna dipped her chin into her coat and swallowed away a sprout of pity, knowing that words meant less than actions. Soon, she'd be on her way to a new family.

Alex continued, "Momma and Penelope enjoy being with other women. Even in childbirth." He laughed again, this time, she joined him. "When will you leave?" His question tumbled out like an avalanche crashing into her joy.

"After Christmas," she said. "The Scotts invited me to stay with them until I am settled."

"What will all the Greek children do? They must learn good English." He stopped walking, shoving his hands in his pockets.

"Mrs. Rudolf is looking for my replacement."

"A replacement? For you?" He searched her face, his eyes warm with affection.

"Alex —" She placed her hand on his arm. "We've gone over my leaving — it's best for both of us, remember?"

"God's plan," he half-laughed. "I just wonder, is it His plan to have such division among us?" Alex mumbled.

"You've thought about our conversation, I see."

"We could create good memories, together, Leanna," he challenged. "And now, my momma will be on our side. She adores you."

"But we have a whole country against a match like ours." She bit her lip at the mention of a match and all that it implied. Alex loomed over her, his broad shoulders and dazzling smile tempting her to linger on the idea.

"We are strong, you and I. Have we both not proven that?"

"Our memories trap us, Alex. We are difficult people according to you," she jested.

"Perhaps all the good memories could outweigh the bad?"

"I wish that would be so." Everything triggered her memory — the smell of coal dust, the ragged miners returning from the shaft, that greasy labor agent filling up the porch of the coffeehouse. She trembled as a breeze sliced through her coat.

Although, this afternoon was an amazing one indeed.

"You are shivering." Alex drew near.

"See. This place is not kind to me." She rolled her eyes at her poor joke.

"Leanna —" He moved closer still, his strong hands resting on her arms. "Jack would have wanted you to be happy. I know it."

The mention of her husband welled up

bitter tears behind her eyes. "Why? When all I did was make him miserable."

"Because, he cared for you. He wanted to provide for you."

Anthis's words came to mind. "I do not deserve happiness, and I cannot bear to find it here. It isn't fair."

"To whom?" He tightened his grip. "To Jack?"

"Yes, to Jack. I still hate him for what he did to me. Bringing me here because of a gamble back in Boston. But I am no better. I gave him no grace, no kindness when he was alive."

He pulled her close, and she didn't resist. She buried her face in his wool coat, warmed by the scent of firewood trapped in the fibers.

"I will spend the rest of my life replacing those memories if you stay." He caressed her cheek with his finger then lifted her chin. Nothing but determination outlined his set jaw. Nothing but desire shone in his vibrant eyes.

Could he be right? If a Greek family could enjoy God's blessings in Castle Gate, Utah, then why couldn't Leanna start anew, on the arm of a capable, adoring man?

"Alex —" Before she could speak any further, he pressed his lips against hers. His gentle mouth caressed her own with such tenderness — an unimaginable contrast to his strong, chiseled figure. Her stomach leaped as she savored the softness in his movement. She gripped his arms. Firm muscles flexed beneath her fingers, sending her pulse into a frenzy. She melted against his chest. The kiss grew so impassioned that Leanna pulled away with surprise. She stepped back.

Her old roots of propriety surged with doubt. It had been difficult to leave her class behind with ill-mannered Jack. What troubles would she face crossing a different boundary, one that Mr. Coffey had warned about?

"I am sorry, Alex. This is not our time. The only thing that feels right about this is based on my heart — not my reason." She could not look at him. "You even said there was no wisdom in that."

"But, Leanna —" He tried to take her arm, but she twisted away.

"Good night, Alex."

The black cloak of night fell on the path ahead, and she walked away from the warmth he offered. When she came to the road, she sighed. Alex would make life worth living in any place — she was sure of it. Her heart was heavier than it had ever been in this town.

A group of men approached from the direction of the depot. Their low conversation urged Leanna to hurry down the road.

Their voices grew closer and she walked faster. She did not want to encounter any boisterous miners or troublemaking vagabonds.

"Mrs. McKee?"

Leanna groaned and dropped her shoulders in defeat. It was Coffey. At least she was not in danger. She stopped and waited.

Five men stood in front of her, with Mr. Coffey in the middle. Their breath puffed in the cold air like the smoke of a mining blast. Most of their faces were black with soot. Jack's usual appearance came to mind. *How can I forget?* Nausea threatened Leanna to swoon.

Not here. Not with them.

"It's a cold night to be out and about, Mrs. McKee." Coffey looked around at his friends. "This is a brave woman, boys. She is often caught tiptoeing around at night." A chorus of chuckles shattered like fallen icicles. A rush of humiliation met her cheeks. Did he know what he implied?

"And the one who catches me? What is your excuse, Mr. Coffey?" But she knew his excuse by the soot-covered clothes. She cringed at her poor retaliation.

"It looked like she came from them Greek parts to me," spouted a younger man with a tall brow beneath his cap.

Coffey glared at her, his beady eyes filled with hindsight.

"This was my last day to take the children." Her spirit fell as she realized that she failed to say good-bye. "The family was tending to a serious matter." No need to tell these men the details. "And I escorted them home, if you must know." The dense stares of the miners grew her courage. "Last I knew, you have absolutely no authority over my whereabouts, Mr. Coffey. If you please, I will continue on home." She swiveled on her heel, only to be caught in midspin by Coffey's quick hand.

"Ain't none of my business what you do, Mrs. McKee. But when you get muddled with them scum up yonder, it becomes every hardworking American's business." His sour breath offended Leanna, and she leaned her body back.

"What have you against them? What have they ever done to you?" She understood social prejudices, but this man's persistence was more than a snub of ignorance.

"Don't be a fool, Mrs. McKee. A white woman don't need to mingle with a Greek.

It ain't proper."

"Especially if that Greek tries to move up where he ain't supposed to be," the younger man blurted.

"Hush, Jed," Coffey spat out.

Yet Jed continued, "Them boys told me that those Pappas think they're better than everyone else. Opening a restaurant on Main and all. None of them 'cept the kids and Alex will even learn English. Ain't American."

"No, it ain't." Coffey steadied his glare at her.

She refused to release her own stare. "Jealousy is a dangerous thing, Mr. Coffey. It makes perfectly decent human beings appear rather unbecoming." Her heart thumped at her bold statement. What would he say next? Or do?

His nostrils flared, and his lips curled inward. If she wasn't a woman, she would probably prepare herself for a good fist to the jaw.

"Now," her voice trembled, as did her hands, "I must go home. The temperature drops by the second." And not just from the icy winter.

She turned to leave, and this time, she was not stopped.

Her nerves only relaxed once she came to

the corner of the restaurant. A wave of comfort overwhelmed her. She'd treasured the few moments about this place, feeling like she was part of this family in a way.

Salt Lake City would also provide belonging — eventually. Sweet Bethany was sure to make her feel comfortable in no time.

But for now, as she turned away from the empty building and toward the old path to her current residence, Leanna felt like a child without a home.

CHAPTER TWELVE

"Alex Pappas, good to see you." A familiar man appeared before Alex as if he'd walked along the track right out of the days from his time on the D&RG railroad.

"Will Jacob?" Alex shook his hand fervently. He was glad for this reunion — it lightened his dull mood from a sleepless night of newborn cries and his tortured heart. Leanna's life was over in a mining town like Castle Gate. And his, well, his life was tied to a family with deep Greek roots and expectations. The circumstance had only one logical conclusion.

Let her leave.

Then why couldn't he talk himself out of praying?

All night he prayed to Someone he'd never wanted to speak to again.

Even in his work, he couldn't wrestle away his distress.

Now, with Will standing here, the man

who'd helped him with English using an old copy of Shakespeare's *Greatest Works,* Alex shoveled air into his exhausted frame and shook hands with him. "My friend, it is good to see you. What brings you to these parts?"

"I just came on with Utah Fuel. Overseeing operations in Price Canyon." Will's shoulders pulled back a little, his pride shining under his fur-lined frontiersmen cap with long flaps covering his ears.

"You're moving up in the world." Alex laid a strong hand on his shoulder and gave his friend his proudest smile. "And you even have a fancy hat." He tugged at an ear flap and burst with laughter.

Will chuckled. "You are doing well also, my friend. I am here to offer you the foreman position over the a.m. shift." His eyes twinkled at his news.

Alex's heart leaped. "What?" He couldn't contain a grin. After years of working hard — filling carts with maximum coal for weighing, standing in freezing water below the black earth — he had gained enough notice to move into a higher position.

"I take that as a yes?" Will cocked his head and raised an eyebrow.

"I — I am so grateful." He thrust his hand out and shook Will's with enthusiasm once restaurant once more? Please, Meesus Mc-Kee?"

"We'll see." She was distracted by Mr. Pappas's urgency to leave after insisting he come instead of Alex. The man was protecting his son — from her. And the rest of Castle Gate. She understood because she'd also walked away from Alex to protect him.

Maria returned to her grandfather and gave a sad wave. The two continued down the path to town, passing the grimly dressed Mrs. Coffey. She stepped around Maria, her boots sinking into the new layer of snow.

"Good afternoon, Mrs. McKee." She approached Leanna's door wearing a summer straw hat held in place by a knit scarf tied beneath her chin. She looked quite ridiculous, but it was the best the woman could do on a miner's wages. "May I come in?"

"Of course." She widened the door, shivering at the icy bite of the elements. Mrs. Coffey breezed past, taking her perch by the warm stove and untying her makeshift winter hat.

"Would you care for some tea?"

The woman didn't answer and hung up her hat and scarf. "I never saw such a personal relationship between a teacher and her student's family."

Leanna chose to ignore her and prepared

more. "Thanks, boss."

"Don't thank me. You've worked hard. You deserve it." He patted Alex's arm then continued toward the small fire in the center of huddled miners.

What would his father say? He would finally understand that his work paid off and maybe stop pestering him so much. His thoughts turned to Leanna, and a sudden burst of hope filled him to the brim. This promotion was a rolled-away stone from the dark hole of ignorance in this place. He could almost see the light shining brighter not just for him but for all his countrymen, for his family, for the chance to love whom he chose to love.

Love?

He shook his head and let out a laugh of surrender beneath his breath. It was true. Alex Pappas was falling in love with the American schoolteacher.

The chance at convincing his father and other miners that the American schoolteacher was Alex's perfect match was all the more probable. Could he convince Leanna, though, that she might just belong in Castle Gate, after all?

"You look more delighted than I do, and I am the proud papa," Yanni declared, walking up with an armful of broken carbide lamps.

"Delighted?" Alex crammed his helmet on his curls. "I am very happy. I am the new foreman of the morning shift." Again, his smile grew large without his permission.

"Congratulations," his brother bellowed in Greek. "I am happy for you, my brother. Now we work on that blond beauty becoming a Pappas." Yanni wagged his eyebrows.

The hair stood up on Alex's neck. He looked around. "Hush, we should not tease about that." Alex shifted his weight and leaned closer to his brother. "Do you think Papa would relent?"

Yanni's happy expression faded into a thoughtful one. "He may find Leanna to be a friend to our family, but he is Greek. I'm afraid even if you owned all of Price Canyon you would still have to fight for his blessing."

"Even if Momma helps me?" He sounded desperate and young.

"Momma?" Yanni shrugged his shoulders. "I think she expects Leanna to be more of a daughter than a daughter-in-law."

Alex's stomach grew heavy. This was true. He knew it, deep down. How much further could he push his parents? The arguing about leaving the church had subsided, but forgetting a Greek bride for their eldest son? Greek parents were more stubborn than any American's bias. Tradition was steadfast even if the country soil changed. And a Greek wife was a long-standing tradition indeed.

"Yiayia and Momma ask me bring you *koulalakia.*" Maria stood shivering at Leanna's door. Stergios waited at the end of her path, with a cigar hanging from his lips. He lifted a hand in greeting. Maria pushed the tin into Leanna's hands. "They are Greek cookies."

"Thank you, Maria," Leanna said. "I was afraid I wouldn't have a chance to say good-bye." She crouched down and brought herself level with the bright brown eyes watering in the cold. "I am going to miss you." She wrapped her arms around the girl, who immediately squeezed back.

"I hoped Thios Alex and you would dance," she whined. "I begged him to come with me."

"You did?" Leanna swallowed hard. "It's probably for the best —"

"Maria!" Stergios called out and waved for her to come.

"Papou wanted to come instead." Maria took a couple steps away. "You come to the

204
205

another kettle of water. She'd taken the busybody's unsheathing of winter clothes as a sure sign that she would stay awhile.

"Is it not yet winter break, Mrs. McKee?" She traced her finger along the square edge of the windowsill.

"It is." She clenched her teeth. "I assume you are curious as to why the Greeks would dare visit me in broad daylight?"

Mrs. Coffey laughed a thin, tin chuckle. "I suppose if you're goin' to volunteer the information, it'd ease mine and Mr. Coffey's minds about why them folk are 'round these parts."

Leanna bristled, reluctantly placing two teacups on the table. She hoped Mrs. Coffey would decline the tea, gather up her things, and leave. But the woman sat in the chair, waiting for an answer.

"It was my honor to assist in the birth of Penelope Pappas's newborn son. It was a matter of providence that I happened to walk the children at the same time an extra pair of hands were needed to bring the child safely into the world." With each word, she marveled as Mrs. Coffey's stony facade crumbled into one of mortified shock. "They repaid me with some delicious cookies, which they brought today." She reached for the tin on the counter and placed them on the table with a loud thud. Mrs. Coffey jumped. "Would you like to try one?"

"Um, no." Mrs. Coffey stared at the tin. "Truly? You assisted in a birth, Mrs. McKee?" Her face was suddenly vulnerable, childlike in a way.

"I did."

"All these years I wanted a babe," Mrs. Coffey spoke low, her attention still on the tin. "Ain't ever worked for us. Course the only childbearing Greek in town gets three of 'em. Why doesn't that surprise me?" A sour frown appeared on her face. When she looked up, she shook it away and glued the pieces of her usual facade into perfect stone.

"They are mightily blessed." Family and love. Prosperity really had little to do with it.

If only I had known that with Jack. . . .

Would her bitterness have sprouted at his first mistake? Would she have pushed him to work so much, increasing the risk of accidents all the more?

"Enough about them," Mrs. Coffey blurted. "They are a thorn in the side of any American trying to make a decent living. Them strikebreakers are stealing our jobs. You ain't goin' to get me to agree otherwise." She gripped her empty teacup and tapped a quick finger on the rim.

208

"What is the purpose of your visit, Mrs. Coffey? To criticize my student's family?" She was losing her patience. Just as she had done with Jack. Her anger was forming sharp words on the tip of her tongue. These walls had heard it all before. They knew her to be a haughty woman with an uncontrollable tongue.

Guilt began to awaken once more, and she feared it would not stop its nagging anytime soon.

"I assume you are going to the mining company's winter dance next week?" Mrs. Coffey folded her hands on the table.

"No, I am not." She never went to any functions sponsored by the mining company. "I am planning on leaving —"

"Mr. Coffey asked me to invite you to come along with us." The woman shifted in her seat, refusing to look at her. "He's got someone he'd like you to meet."

Her mouth dropped at the forwardness of her neighbors.

"It ain't that bad, Mrs. McKee." Mrs. Coffey swatted her hand in the air. "You can't live here alone forever. Ain't you scared some dirty fob might take advantage, knowing that you have no male protection?"

With your husband's intrusive eyes, do I really have anything to worry about?

209

Leanna stood up. "I am leaving after Christmas, if you must know. I have accepted a position in Salt Lake City."

The woman chewed on her lip. "Well, that's interesting news." She stood up and planted her hands on the table and leaned in. "But you should still go to the dance. There's talk goin' around 'bout you and that Mr. Pappas. People seen you walkin' about town with him. It ain't right." She walked around the table and stopped beside her, stretching her neck to peer out the window. "My husband came home drunk as a skunk from the saloon the other night, cursin' you and your Greek friends." Her face turned from a gossiping old crone to a concerned citizen. "I fear he might find trouble with the law, things he was sayin'. Talkin' about lynching and the sort."

Leanna's mouth went dry. Would Mr. Coffey become a monster just because of prejudice and a little jealousy? Although she had read the papers and knew that men would take it into their own hands if American women were involved with Greek men.

But not here. Not in Utah.

"What good would it do," Leanna nearly whispered, "if I go to a silly old dance?"

"You'd clear the gossip for one thing. Just because you'll leave doesn't mean trouble's

210

over for the Pappas family. But dance with some American miners, prove you're just a schoolteacher with a weak heart for immigrant children."

Weak? Leanna's heart was stronger than ever. And it beat fiercely for the Pappas family, for Alex. With each encounter, her heart grew stronger. Even enough to consider staying.

What was it about Castle Gate? She had ruined Jack's life here, and now she might even destroy Alex's life, too. And worse yet, risk hurting his family.

It wasn't Castle Gate.

It was her.

"I will go to the dance if that would lessen the presumptions." She began to gather Mrs. Coffey's items and handed them to her, one by one. "If you please, I would like to rest now. My stomach ails me."

"Mr. Coffey and I will escort you to the dance." After buttoning her coat she barely looked at Leanna as she hurried out the door.

There was one person she worried about in all of this — Alex. If he saw her at the dance, what would he think?

She had been so close to giving in to his plan to stay and find a second chance at love in Castle Gate.

But these walls —

She didn't deserve a second chance. Not when her failure at the first chance soiled her heart like coal dust on a miner's hands.

The chill lost its bite on the night of the company dance. Why had she agreed to this arrangement? When she had a husband, she didn't go to such social things. What was the point now — mingling with miners and their families — when she would leave and never look back?

More than that, though, she wondered if she would see Alex. They had not spoken since the night of the baby's birth. What would he think of her attending a dance after refusing to stay for him? And even if he was there, she could not talk with him, knowing that there was a very real danger.

Mr. and Mrs. Coffey waited at the end of her path. Their dark garb blended in with the dim evening, only their pale faces shone bright in the moonlight.

"Good evening, Mrs. McKee," Mr. Coffey said. He was more chipper than usual.

For the briefest moment, her old bitterness for Jack transferred toward her neighbor, and she near-stomped down the walk, tempted to snap, "Let's get this over with."

Instead, she said a prayer, managed a

smile, and waited for them to lead the way.

When they arrived at the dance hall, a small band played a lively tune, and several couples were on the dance floor. A reminiscent wave lapped along Leanna's memory and she nearly checked her wrist for a dangling dance card.

"There are the fellas." Mr. Coffey gestured to a group of men. "Mrs. McKee, I'd like you to meet someone." Her stomach twisted as Mr. Coffey grabbed at a scrawny fellow by the arm and marched him toward her.

"Howdy. I am Mike Griffin." The young man tipped his hat and flashed yellow teeth. Mr. and Mrs. Coffey headed to the dance floor.

She plastered a smile. Perhaps she could find a nearby exit and slip out while they danced. As she scoured the place, a group of men in the back corner caught her eye — a handful of Greeks from the restaurant. She scanned their profiles for one tall, handsome, curl-topped man. The man she would have to say good-bye to sooner than later.

Lord, give me strength.

"Leanna? What do you say?" Mike came into focus again, his eyebrows eager and his mouth open like a dunce.

"What?"

"Can I have this dance?" He spoke with

certain hesitation, as he should. He was no match for her. And he knew it. She deserved someone —

You don't deserve anything. Remember Jack?

Alex had almost made her believe otherwise. Almost had her believing that she was worth loving. But the cold truth was that she had fumbled miserably in her first chance to love, and now the risk was too great to consider anything Alex had to offer.

A figure moved toward them, from the direction of the gaggle of Greeks. She squinted. Was it Alex? The dimness of the room did not serve her well, until the man was nearly upon them.

Familiar broad shoulders, the confident jaunt, the perfect hair, it was —

"James?" Leanna stumbled backward.

It couldn't be.

But James Winston Alcott of Boston, Massachusetts, shuffled around the puny miner and stood before her like some spectacular hero. Mike faded away. "What on earth are you doing here?"

"My fairest Leanna Willingham — ahem, McKee." James wore a cheeky smirk, bowing slightly. His emerald eyes sparked off a familiar tumble in her torso. "I have searched far and wide for you, my long-lost friend." He straightened, clutching the edges of his pressed jacket just along the curvature of his puffed-out chest.

"James Alcott. You did not answer my question." Her nose found its rightful position, in a slight tilt to the rafters, and she carried herself as if she wore the latest fashion instead of her simple wool dress. "What are you doing here?"

"Why, looking for you, of course." He found her hand and held it to his chest. "You owe me a dance, remember?"

"I —" That was so long ago. It seemed like a different life altogether. Well, it was in a way. Her first party of the season and she'd promised the last dance to James Alcott, the only man who had the appearance and personality to make her ridiculous debut worth pursuing. They never did reach the last dance, as James's father suffered a stroke, right there in the parlor of the Preston mansion. And the next week Leanna met Jack and gave her heart away.

"How is your father, James? I know it has been a few years." She furrowed her brow in concern.

James's jaw twitched. "He is —" His gaze left hers and fell to his feet. "He is no longer with us."

"I am sorry." She squeezed his hand.

The band changed tunes, and couples began to flood the dance floor. His audible breath released the sore subject into the past.

He gave a wry smile. "You, my darling, are stalling." He held up her hand as if they were dancing side by side. "May I have the dance you never gave me?"

"If you promise to explain your sudden appearance immediately after," she said just as he playfully swung her away from himself and teasingly bowed, with her hand still cradled in his own.

"Of course." James laughed, and the handsome man captivated her just as he once had years before.

Alex's stomach was one large knot as he headed toward the dance hall. When he passed the turn to her house, he had to force his boots to head down Main instead. He had not seen Leanna in quite a while, and the way she'd left things, Alex wondered if he would ever see her again.

This first day as foreman of the crew kept his mind busy — work had always been a welcome distraction. But the pushback from disgruntled miners having to take orders from a Greek only justified the reason Leanna refused to stay. Alex feared he could not work his way out of this. He could not think his way out, either — the only hope was prayer.

He blinked several times and stared up at the cloudy sky that was as hazy as his willpower in all of this. He should just return home and spend the evening with Yanni and his family. But some of his friends urged him to come to the dance and celebrate his success. Since the only Greek women in town were home taking care of his new nephew, and American women would dance with their own men, the dance was nothing more than a change of scenery from the coffeehouse.

This would be good medicine. He'd spend time with his friends and away from his thoughts. If his people could do anything better than most, it was celebrate.

"Alex Pappas! You came," Nick declared as he approached their corner in the loud dance hall.

"Of course he did." Another friend came up and patted him on the back. "He must show that he cares as our newest foreman." He winked. A ripple of laughter went through the rest of them.

"Or he came to watch that pretty bird who joins us at the restaurant from time to time." An older gentleman nodded toward the dance floor.

Leanna?

He swiveled on his heel. The knot in his stomach tightened, threatening to fray at its strength. Leanna danced around the hall on the arm of a tall stranger. She was beaming and laughing, her attention only on her dance partner.

And he was certainly not a miner.

As the music swelled, she threw back her head and let out a tinkle of giggles that burned his ears. Who was this man? Why did Leanna look so comfortable in his arms? And why had Alex fought so hard to have her stay, if her attentions would flitter to another so soon?

Her fit of laughter ended and she faced the man who held his hand at her waist. As if Alex's hard stare had a magnetic pull, her eyes found his and all joy blanched from her face. How awful it was to be the one person to erase the light from such a face as Leanna McKee's.

His willpower was no longer a concern. He took heavy strides toward her.

"I am surprised to see you here, Leanna," he seethed, fully aware of her dance partner's glare at his left.

Leanna looked about like a frightened deer. "Please, Alex, do not do this here. You

don't realize the trouble it might bring —"
She looked over her shoulder at the Coffeys
who were still dancing.

"Oh, believe me, I understand your concern about trouble. You've perfected such
an excuse."

Her blue eyes pleaded with him.

"Leanna, can I help?" Her dance partner
placed his hand on her arm, sending a mad
frenzy of anger through Alex's chest. The
manicured gentleman set a cool, reprimanding gaze in his direction.

"Do not worry. I will leave you to finish
your dance," he said, now catching the eyes
of those around them — including the
gawking Coffeys.

Fine. He'd give in to their scrutiny and
leave.

He stormed across the hall and out into
the crisp night air. His heart was laden like
a frail limb piled high with snow.

A desperate prayer tumbled from his lips,
one that had been ingrained in his heart
since he was a child sitting beside his papa
at church — the only prayer his family
spoke aloud together.

Thy will be done.

All these years, Alex had found his own
will to be sufficient in his pursuit. After all,
the last time he'd prayed for God's will, it

led him to leave Helena to die alone.

But perhaps that wasn't all God then. Perhaps Alex depended too much on the counsel of men and less on the stirring of his heart.

Faith was what gave Leanna the strength to continue on — and right now, Alex felt nothing but weakness. Every fiber in his being split with the truth that Leanna would never be his. The only way he could survive such knowledge was casting the effort away from himself. He needed someone to take this from him.

Thy will be done.

At this moment, giving up his burden to the God he'd forsaken was his only choice. Would He accept such a prayer from Alex?

Alex assumed He had, because somehow he continued to step away from the woman he loved — by no strength of his own.

CHAPTER THIRTEEN

Leanna nearly ripped herself from James's arms, but the Coffeys danced into view and she thought better of it.

"You have quite a different class of friends here, it seems," James said, staring down his nose at the group of men that Alex had left in the corner.

"Class is nothing compared to the heart," she mumbled.

"You sound like a progressive." James laughed.

"You know that I am. Why else did I leave my parents?" She continued to watch the door Alex had gone through, while James sighed at her ear.

What did Alex think?

She knew what he thought. If he had known that James was an old friend, one she had not seen in a very long time, perhaps his envy would have faded. His hurt was so bright, it scorched her conscience.

The music ended and everyone clapped.

"Now it is my turn to hold up our bargain, is it not?" James placed her arm atop the crook of his and grasped her hand.

"Of course." She pushed away the urge to chase after Alex.

James led her to a table, and she sat in the chair he offered. During her debut, she never sat so casually. It was difficult in the stiff dresses and tight corsets. Now she felt small next to the tall gentleman. There was no dress filling up the space.

"Why are you here, James? We are quite an odd pair now, don't you think?" She swatted at her wool skirt then tugged gently at the cuff of his jacket.

"I still see the beautiful girl beyond that poor imitation of a dress." He chuckled. "And, your family will be jealous that I have been first to lay his eyes on her, as well," he marveled, studying her lips.

"My family?" Her hand clamped on her chair as if the world would soon spin out of control. "Do my parents forgive me for leaving?"

"Of course. They are worried for you. Your cousin from San Francisco wrote a letter of some urgency to your mother. Seems that she was concerned about you and your desperate situation." He peeled away the layers of her heart, leaving her sitting there, vulnerable and embarrassed.

"My desperate situation?" She mustered the courage to be offended.

"You said it yourself," he spoke softly. "I was there when they read the letter from your cousin. She quoted your very words."

She had said that to her cousin in confidence — or so she thought.

"That does not matter, though." He gathered her hands in his and leaned forward. "I was devastated at your elopement. And now, it seems, your God is one of second chances."

The words stabbed at her heart. "My God?"

"Darling, you act as if I know nothing. Your heated arguments with your family did not go unnoticed. Especially since Paul is my best friend." Her brother's classmate sat before her and unveiled yet more of her past as if it were a gnarled tree growing at a rapid pace. She had defended her faith to her family. Her call to teach the underprivileged was one from God — she was sure of it. Jack assured her of that.

James continued, "Don't you see? My being here brings us so close once more. I would have won you over if you had not given in so quickly to Jack. This is our second chance."

"A second chance for what?" she muttered.

"Do not be silly, Miss Willingham." He tucked his manicured finger beneath her chin, tilting it up. "A second chance to win your heart." His eyes flamed with determination. "Come home to Boston, Leanna. Let us try to start anew."

"I — I can't." Her pulse thudded in her ears. "I have accepted a position as tutor for a family in Salt Lake City." Bethany had offered her a second chance, and she'd taken it. Alex offered her a second chance at love — but she was not brave enough to accept.

"Come now, Leanna." He spoke like her father. "Will you work all your life and be a spinster, when I can offer you all the happiness in the world?"

She swallowed hard. "What do you know of my happiness, James? The life my parents expected, to marry and sit like a china doll in the parlor of my rich husband? That is not happiness for me." But this life hadn't made her happy, either. She had lived among the people who struggled to survive. She had taught the children who deserved just as much education as the next child. Happiness was only found in one place during her whole stay at Castle Gate.

And it was with the man she was forbidden to see.

Alex gave her a ridiculous desire to stay in this unhappy place. He made her happy. She was falling in love with him. Yet he was a strong eagle, and she, a minnow. Castle Gate had no place for them to live.

All the more reason to leave quickly. But what should she choose? The arm of her old beau whisking her away to her hometown, or the lonely train ride to Salt Lake City?

After the dance, Leanna left James at the hotel lobby on Main. Hurrying along the sleepy street, she thanked God for the electric lamps providing light along the path. At least the coal town was progressive in this way. If she were to go back to Boston, what a wonder it would be after her long stay in the less-civilized West.

She wrapped her arms around her body, more for comfort than warmth. Tears threatened to blur her view as she tilted her head toward the sky — the clouds shifted, revealing a glitter of stars.

"What of your light?" Her question sliced the winter chill and echoed against the quiet buildings. " 'There is no darkness but ignorance.' " Shakespeare and Alex. She smiled sadly. Too much was known now, and everything here seemed driven by ignorance.

What about at home?

She would shine bright in Boston as a daughter redeemed to society again. Life would no longer be a struggle. All her bitterness toward Jack would fade along with the racing train tracks as she headed east.

Lord, can I be a better person in Boston?

Could she forgive herself for the mess she made of her first marriage once she embarked on the hope of a second? James was kind and attractive. He would treat her well and lavish her with anything she asked for. He was here for a few days and hoped that she'd join him on the long train ride home.

Yet the darkness was thick at home, too. The same ignorance toward the immigrants in Castle Gate would be praised among her parents' circle, and James's. Could she compromise her passion for progress and find light in finery and comfort instead?

Across the street, the restaurant's dark windows reflected her image as she passed under the streetlamp.

Alex knew her differently than the Willinghams and Alcotts. He understood her struggle as a guilt-ridden widow. They were more alike than most of Leanna's acquaintances. And Alex gave her worth in more than the things of the earth, but in the ways of her heart as well. She was not the same person her family had once known. The person Alex saw her to be was so much better than a stuffy debutante. Perhaps she might be worth his affection, just as he claimed?

If only the risk to love him wasn't so great a threat.

Her reflection crumbled when the door to the restaurant opened, nearly slamming against the window. Alex emerged from the darkness, his body quickly lit by the halo of a streetlamp.

"Good evening." She fought the urge to run across the street and embrace him. Instead, she toed the dirt, waiting for his response.

"Is it? A good evening?" His cynicism sobered her. She recalled his face when they spoke on the dance floor. She must explain herself to Alex.

With a quick glance up and down the street, she hurried across. "Please, can we go inside? I must speak with you." Her teeth began to chatter. His stormy eyes searched her for a moment, then he allowed her to pass through.

He hadn't waited for her, but he had hoped

to see her before the night was over. Le-anna's face shone with excitement, even with the dim cloak of light. His heart skipped, and a sudden numbing washed over him, making him forget why he was upset. That was until she ran to him and asked to speak with him. Her lip trembled beneath dread-filled eyes.

Was this God's answer to his prayer? His well-established cynicism pushed aside the thought. He shut the door behind them.

"The fire is dying now but gives heat nonetheless." He led the way to the kitchen, her soft steps distracting him as he tried to avoid knocking over the chairs on the tables.

He grabbed two stools from the wooden table and placed them in front of the small kitchen fireplace. Flickering embers promised little heat.

"It is so quiet here." She lowered to the seat. "I miss the Greek ramblings of your parents and Maria." A soft smile crept across her face.

"They are sound asleep, no doubt." He kept his eyes on the fire. No use tempting his heart to indulge in her beauty when she was so comfortable in the arms of another man.

"Tonight was quite a surprise for me," she said.

Alex scoffed. "For you? It was a surprise for more than you."

"Please, let me explain. That man is from Boston. He is a dear family friend from years ago." Her voice was barely audible above the sound of the crackling embers. Her brow crinkled in an upward plea, and her mouth wore an unsure smile. "You can only imagine my surprise to see him here, in Castle Gate."

"I see." Despite his sadness, he grinned. "It hurt a little when I saw you laughing with him." What was it with this woman that turned his thoughts into unguarded words?

She reached across and placed her hand on his. "Alex, I am sorry that I hurt you." A warm comfort radiated through him. He twisted his hand beneath hers, entwining their fingers together. She beamed with delight, just like she had on the dance floor. But as quick as the embers faded to gray, her face twisted with a sorrowful sob.

"Forgive me," she managed as she lowered her head. "I promised before, I rarely do cry."

He leaped from his stool and knelt in front of her, gathering her into his arms. This was the only place he wanted to be. Holding Leanna and offering relief. He surged with the fulfillment in being her strength right now. He'd felt the most alive when he was a strong refuge for the woman he loved. Many years had passed since he felt the same purpose as he did at this moment with Leanna. Hadn't he desired to be the same for Helena even if it ended up being a mistake?

All he wanted was to save her.

But perhaps that wasn't his purpose. Perhaps his purpose was simply to love her, and God had a greater plan, just like Leanna believed? Fear iced his spine as he considered the devastation if he were wrong. Even if it was true, could Alex trust that God would help him at all after all these years of silence? What destruction could happen now if he followed his heart, just as he had followed Anthis's lead eight years ago?

Leanna pulled away. Her blue pools sparkled, tears clinging to her lashes like tiny diamonds. She placed her hands on his cheek. A runaway tear slid down her ivory skin. "If I could choose, I'd choose you," she whispered.

His heart pounded in his chest, a flood pressed against his own eyes. This was his answer, wasn't it? Nothing felt so heaven-sent than loving Leanna McKee and being loved by her in return. Alex wanted nothing more than to believe that God was on his side in this moment. If ever there was a chance for a deal to be made, it would be a promise to cast off his anger forever if God weaved His plan for Leanna with Alex's own.

Before he could speak, she placed her finger on his mouth. "That was not proper of me. I couldn't help —"

He removed her finger. "Proper? Since when is love ever held in the bounds of propriety?" He grinned as big as his heart swelled within him. He heard her breath catch. She pulled him in with her vibrant, longing gaze. Her soft lips waited. Another kiss and she'd choose him. Surely she would? Why allow expectations to stop this — a pure second chance at love for each of them? They were a perfect match under something greater than his papa's thumb or the prejudice of a people. Perhaps under something he could not wrap his mind around yet. Their noses met first. The warmth of her breath on his lips sent shivers along his arms. He gathered her up, relishing her warmth.

"Alex, I cannot continue." She pushed away. "We cannot continue this." Her eyes diverted to the fireplace. She pressed her lips together as if trying to contain a new rush of tears. She seemed more shaken than ever before.

"What is this about, love?" He wanted to hold her again, to comfort her and love her with all the strength he'd borrowed from God earlier this evening.

She sniffled. "This is too dangerous now. No matter how much I love —" She stopped herself as if the very word was snagged by a hook. "No matter what I feel for you or you for me, there are people who will do you harm. And I fear for your family, as well. Prejudice is a very real evil in this town, Alex."

"Of course, I know this. But I will not allow fear to keep me from happiness." He smoothed the hair behind her ear.

Her eyes fluttered closed, and she grabbed his hand. "Can I truly bring you happiness? My flaws are many. Besides, there is so much at stake. You may not be afraid, but I am. I will not allow you or your family to suffer because of me." She stood abruptly, the stool knocking back to the floor. "I already made one man suffer for my willfulness. I will not ruin an entire family." And she turned around and ran to the back door.

Before he could speak, Leanna was gone.

Someone had scared her. The very thought of that kindled a roaring fury within him. He stood, his own stool teetering over. He

232

raced to the back door, threw it open, and tumbled into the icy night. As his mouth opened to call her name, he was startled back into the shadows of the building. Mr. Coffey and his wife were just up the way to their house.

If the threat was from Coffey, Alex was certain the man had many words and few intentions.

But how could he convince Leanna of that?

"Good morning." James hopped down the stairs of the hotel and met her in the fine parlor. Crimson velvet cushions dressed an elegant settee and winged armchairs, while a fire blazed beneath a polished mantel. But none of the furnishings were nearly as fine as this handsome man from her past.

Leanna's heart skipped. His tall, trim build held an air of royalty. Even the wisp of his gold hair stayed in perfect place across his strong forehead. He was groomed to near perfection.

"Are you sure you would like to go to church with me this morning? It is very plain compared to church in Boston." When was her last service sitting in the Willingham pew? Those days of tending meticulously to her beauty and opulent wardrobe were hazy now. Wouldn't James's pressed waistcoat and shined cuff links have been more interesting to her than the sermon from the pulpit? Now she absorbed every word from the minister's lips, praying that her heart might stay as soft as the moment Jack's faith became her own.

God bless Jack for peeling the mud from my eyes.

An ever-gracious wash of sadness crossed her heart, fading the tarnish of Jack's mistakes and polishing the truth of all the good in Jack McKee.

"Where is that pretty head of yours?" James waved his gloved hand in front of her face.

She breathed deeply and ignored his inquiry. "This is a lovely parlor, isn't it?"

"It is quaint," he offered, the word dripping in arrogance.

She smirked, less embarrassed by her fall from luxury and more secure in it by all she'd gained from slipping through society's talons. "If you mean, common, then I beg to differ. Our tastes have grown apart, I am sure."

"But I assure you, my heart is still near." He winked, charming her with his dazzling smile once more. Nerves tickled her stomach while she accepted his arm before entering the cold winter day.

There was little to hide on the arm of this man, unlike the fear that had her hover in the restaurant's shadow last night. The Coffeys were turning up her path as she rounded the corner of the restaurant, and Leanna wouldn't dare make her presence known. Not after all the strength it took to turn her back on Alex like she did. If only Bethany or James had arrived earlier — before Alex showed up on her doorstep, inviting her into his world — his heart. How could such a strong, determined man risk everything for her? But she'd given him the chance, hadn't she? She'd kissed him back, and spoken her feelings. Only the truth fell from her lips last night. And in her weakness, she was strong enough to step away.

She loved him and couldn't bear to bring trouble to one more man. Just like Jack had given Leanna the courage to find God, Alex gave her the strength to persevere in this place. But what had she given to either of those men? A bitter heart to one, and a scrutinizing neighbor for the other.

She squeezed James's arm closer to her, secure in the fact that at least a fresh start was on the horizon. Perhaps with James, or maybe in Salt Lake City. Either way, she would be more careful to tread gracefully, wherever she ended up.

"Leanna, did you hear what I said?" James stopped on the wooden walk. "You are in another place today. That is the second time I've failed to keep your attention." He pushed his bottom lip out in a playful pout.

"I am sorry. I have so much to consider." She fiddled with her lip, tasting dust on her glove.

"It seems to me you only have one choice." His mouth grew into a wide, confident grin.

A splash of water from a passing wagon elicited a gasp from her. "One? What is that?"

"To accept the fact that you are more suited for luxury, my pet." He whipped a handkerchief from inside his coat and assisted her in drying off the spots on her overcoat. She glared at his head, struggling to maintain a frown instead of the threatening smile. His suggestion was offensive but somehow intriguing.

What if Leanna McKee could reenter society with all she'd learned in Castle Gate? Could she be the one to bring ignorance to light? The thought of that formidable task exhausted her more than a climb to the Castle Gate rock formation.

James flashed a dashing smile in her direction as they carried on, and she was certain of one thing only — the attention of a pampering gentleman was more enticing than she wanted to admit.

From the corner of her eye, Leanna spied Alex, with his walking stick and his fisherman cap, heading their way from the restaurant.

"We are going to be late." With a quick jerk, she hurried James along. No, she couldn't face Alex, not on James's arm. Not with all the emotions flaring up inside her.

No matter how much she considered the crossroads set before her, she knew for sure that there was one token neither Bethany Scott nor James Alcott could offer Leanna — the piece of her heart stolen by Alex Pappas, a piece she'd given away, never to retrieve again.

Jealousy raged within him. He stormed down the street like a dog following its owner. What a pathetic man he had become, set off by the golden hair shining beneath her hat. A stark contrast to the dark overcoat of the man who clung closely to Leanna's side.

His fists squeezed the snowshoes that hung from his hands. He should continue walking out of town, but something inside of him, some forceful current of entitlement, kept him ducking into doorways and sliding between buildings whenever he supposed Leanna would turn her head.

When the couple slipped through the doors of the Protestant church, he halted. He was only acting upon the devastation of losing her.

"Hello, Mr. Pappas." Ten-year-old water boy Tommy Prior stood beside him. He was washed and shiny, unlike his usual muddied face and disheveled clothes from crawling into the mines to give water to the men.

"Uh, hello there." He lifted his fisherman's cap and ran his fingers through his hair. What was he doing in this part of town? He swallowed past a lump in his throat, glaring at the church door. The agony of Leanna's choice weakened any common sense, a sure sign that this was not worth the trouble.

"Would you help my grandmother?" Tommy asked. "She can't make the stairs into church, and my pa is sleeping for the graveyard shift."

A woman appeared from behind a cart. Her back was hunched as if she'd carried the weight of the mountain for much of her life. She leaned on her cane, catching her breath.

"Good morning. I'd sure love a hand. You

238

can share a pew with us." She smiled sweetly.

"Oh, I don't belong to this church —" He backed away. "I am Greek."

"Belong? You Greeks believe in Jesus, don't you?" She hobbled over to him. Alex nodded on behalf of Greeks like his momma. He wasn't sure what he believed anymore.

The woman's hat did not hide her bright countenance as she continued, " 'There is neither Jew nor Greek . . . : for ye are all one in Christ.' So the Good Book says."

"Does it say that?" His eyebrows perked up. He knew more Shakespeare than scripture. He was worn out wondering about God's plan. Everything seemed helpless now.

"I pray that one day we will all see one another for our hearts and not our origins." She shuffled across the path and forcefully placed her cane on the bottom step.

Alex glanced down the street, quieter and more settled as the town dissolved into their places of worship. Behind him, music began inside the building. He was indeed a stranger, no matter the optimism of this woman.

"It's what the Good Book says," she continued.

"What?" he asked.

"That we are one, not divided, you know?" Her glassy gray eyes settled on him, and Tommy tugged at Alex's coat, also looking up expectantly.

"I need to read that Good Book, I think," he muttered. "I once thought it could be so." He'd hoped that Leanna's presence at Papa's name-day celebration would be the start of erasing boundaries. Yet it didn't change the minds of the ignorant — it only created fear. What greater evil would be stirred if they chose to love each other? Was Leanna right?

"How can we change hearts, though?" The words tumbled from his mouth.

"That's an age-old question, isn't it?" The woman chuckled. "We do our best. And we love, I guess. There's no fear in love. Another nugget from —"

"The Good Book?" Alex half-smiled. The woman grinned wide, and he held out his arm, carefully guiding her up the steps.

We love?

Did she just say that? Coincidence? He wasn't so sure. He narrowed his eyes to the clear steel-gray sky. But he couldn't make his smile turn to his usual grimace at the heavens.

His stomach quivered, and he longed for

240

something — beyond Leanna, beyond this path to success — he could not be sure of what it was, but he had a hunch.

Singing poured from the doors of the church — similar to those songs sung by certain men as they worked the mines. Nothing like the liturgy of his people. But different didn't mean less.

The Greeks and Americans worshipped in different ways, but they worshipped Christ with all their hearts. At least his momma did, and Penelope, and . . . Leanna, it seemed.

All the anger inside him began to fizzle.

When they reached the porch of the church, Tommy ran to open the door.

"Thank you, sir." His grandmother patted Alex's arm. "Would you be my guest?"

A glimpse of golden hair in the back pew caught his eye while Tommy leaned against the door.

Leanna.

He followed the grandmother inside but stopped at a column.

"Mister Pappas," Tommy whispered and tugged at his coat. "Would you like to sit with us?"

"Oh, no. I can't stay. Just warming myself a bit," Alex said, but the warmth inside him had nothing to do with the building, and everything to do with the beauty he fixed his eyes upon.

There was no fear in love, according to the Good Book — or the old woman. Then why was Alex so afraid as he studied Leanna from a distance? Fear gripped him like it did when the mine caved in and Jack was stolen away.

Everything was changing inside him, and the ground he'd worked so hard to claim as his own was crumbling beneath him in the face of his desired, ridiculous future. A pipe dream, as they say.

Foolishness.

Leanna had spoken of prejudice being an evil in this town. And regardless of the old woman's optimism or the hope he'd found in Leanna, there might not be a place for such a love as theirs. For the sake of his family, he had spent eight years surviving the evil. It took every ounce of effort. There was no room for love.

He turned to leave at the same moment she turned her head. Their eyes met. He stood, frozen behind the column. Her brows knitted together. Alex clenched his teeth and stormed out of the church.

It was time he tried to forget. If only he had good practice at that. Eight years was hardly enough time to forget his late wife.

Wouldn't it be just as difficult with a woman such as Leanna McKee?

The crisp air was never so welcome upon his face as when he escaped the heat of Leanna's wonder. But before the door closed behind him, she slipped out to join him.

"Alex?" She touched his arm as he leaned against the rail of the steps.

"I apologize for the intrusion. I — I don't know what got into me."

"Did —" She dropped her hand and descended to his step. "Did you want to come to church?"

He glared at her. "I wanted to see you. But you seemed rather comfortable on the arm of your *friend,* so I don't know why I bothered." *Walk away, Alex. Begin to forget.*

Her eyes widened, a magnetic sapphire pull. "I am sorry. He really is an old friend, but —"

His heart plunged when she hesitated.

"But he offered to take me back to Boston." She stepped farther down the steps, wrapping her arms around her waist. A nipping breeze swirled past them. His reason wrestled with all temptation to gather her in an embrace. "My mind is made up that I will leave this place; I just have another option besides Salt Lake City. I will not lie to you — he hopes to marry me one day."

"Marry?" Misery melted his motivation to leave her be. "I thought you didn't want to return to Boston."

"I was certain of that — until James showed up. Don't you see, Alex? I do not belong here. Perhaps I was never meant to live this meager lifestyle. I may never have to worry about surviving again —" Her chest swelled and she let out a sigh. "And then there is Salt Lake City, where I can still teach. But I will be alone just the same. How long will it be until I am in need again?"

"You wouldn't have to be hungry or alone if you would stay here." His voice was low and scratchy. He trembled with a mixture of passion and fear. But he was not as afraid of being caught with Leanna as he was of never seeing her again.

"Mrs. McKee?" Mrs. Tilton crossed the street from the Mormon meetinghouse. She glowered at Alex, but spoke to Leanna. "Is this man bothering you? I can get my husband —"

"That will not be necessary, Mrs. Tilton." Leanna swiped her eyes with the back of her finger, bounced a quick look to Alex, then rushed up the steps. "I was just settling some loose ends with Mr. Pappas. You

244

know I taught his niece and nephew?"

"Very well. I was retrieving my reticule from our wagon and thought I'd offer some help."

"Good day, ladies." He tipped his hat and left them briskly. His heart still sat low in his chest, but a sudden wash of clarity splashed the air at Mrs. Tilton's interrogating stare.

He felt like a new strikebreaker, a Greek who recently arrived to work when others would not. They all started out lodged beneath the fat thumb of Anthis, constantly at his beck and call for more money and careful to tread only in the agent's favor.

Mrs. Tilton made him feel small. Just like he did his first days here.

How could Leanna live life here with him and not suffer from the criticism and judgment that shone so keenly in Mrs. Tilton's gaze? If Alex loved her at all, he would not allow her to go through that. Just like he would have never let Helena suffer disease if he'd had the choice.

He'd have to let Leanna go. It was the only way.

CHAPTER FOURTEEN

"At least allow me to join you on the train." James coddled her hands in his as they sat on the settee in front of the parlor's fire.

"I must do this alone." She was firm, as if he were a student begging for trouble. His vibrant green eyes tripped her heart with all their eagerness.

Leanna sighed. "Very well. Just the train ride." The more time she spent with him, the more she felt like a naive debutante — a feeling she used to abhor. But now she found comfort in the security of being cared for. Yet hadn't Alex also offered to care for her if she'd stayed?

What would that look like in a town like Castle Gate?

This strange predicament was exactly why she needed to visit Bethany today. They were fast friends, having met for breakfast at the Italian bakery before Bethany returned to Salt Lake during her last visit.

Bethany deserved to know that Leanna's commitment teetered, but more than that, Leanna hoped to seek advice from her only female friend.

James cupped her chin and hesitated just inches from her face. No. She should resist. Her decision had yet to be made and — "James Alcott," she said in weak reprimand.

"Let me buy you a hat," he murmured as if he spoke the language of a sweetheart.

"A hat?" She pulled away, straightening her shoulders.

"I can't bear to see you in such drab clothing, Leanna." He picked up his coat, which lay beside him, then stood up. "You are too beautiful to dress so, so . . ."

"Common?" She stood next to him, chiding herself for getting so caught up in his charms. Of course her old self would love for James Alcott to buy her a hat. But she remembered that she was no debutante. "Be careful, Mr. Alcott. You still have no answer from me. Do not spend your money so quickly." She tilted her nose up and breezed past him in good Willingham fashion.

The train ride was long. James caught her up on all the marriages that had taken place since she left. She really couldn't care less, and by the time they arrived in Salt Lake City, she wondered if she had any intention of going back to Boston at all. All the people James had spoken of wore the same puppet strings that she had bravely cut off when she married Jack. Did she really want to reattach herself so quickly?

They hurried to find a taxi since James had refused to take public transportation.

"Tell me more about my parents. Do they truly want me back?" Leanna asked as they pulled into the quiet neighborhood of four-square homes and shade trees.

"Of course they do. Your mother was sick for a month at the thought of you in the Wild West." He chuckled.

"Yes, but I hesitate to return if they will not accept me for who I am. Do you understand? I cannot be their puppet any longer."

He put his hands on her arms. "Darling, if you were to go back, you'd be with me. And I will lavish you with whatever you'd like. I adore you, Leanna." His passionate confession sent a warmth through her, a welcomed sensation on such a cold day. Entranced in his loving gaze, she could almost convince herself that God had sent James as her second chance for happiness. After all, he looked rather angelic — in a masculine, rich sort of way.

Before he parted to explore the city, James escorted her to Bethany's house but had the taxi idle as she walked up to the door.

The taxi waited until Bethany appeared, then slowly continued down the street. How strange it made Leanna feel to be pampered so.

"Leanna? I am so glad to see you," Bethany exclaimed with a gleeful expression. She ushered Leanna into the foyer, taking her coat and chattering away. "I hope I didn't miss a letter or a message that you were planning a trip."

"Oh, no. And I am sorry for the intrusion, Bethany. But I do have quite a dilemma."

Bethany put her arm around her shoulders and gushed, "Oh, dear. I do hope you are okay."

Leanna gave a weak smile, ever thankful for this kind woman. They sat together in the parlor. Bethany had an assortment of chocolates on the table, as if she knew a visitor was due. The room was still as warm and pretty as the first time Leanna had visited. Light sparkled through crystal beads of a lamp shade, casting a rainbow across her dark skirt. She smiled faintly.

"Every day at this hour, the sun is positioned just right to give us a light show," Bethany giggled. "Tommy tried to trace the rainbows on his slate, but that is easier said than done."

"You have live art in your parlor. How wonderful."

"It shall soon be yours, too." Bethany offered her a chocolate.

"Thank you," Leanna said, unable to look her in the eye. Instead, her mind's eye was trapped in a prism of sorts, admiring the glimmer of three colorful fractals. Which would she treasure as her own, and which would she turn away from forever?

"You are deep in thought, dear friend. What brings you here today?" Bethany asked.

Leanna shoveled in air, finding courage in her friend's kindness. "You see, since I accepted the position here, I am suddenly caught between my heart and my family."

Bethany set down her half-eaten chocolate and folded her hands.

"That is a difficult place to be." Her expression shadowed. "I am someone who knows that very well." She smiled tenderly.

"Yes, and that is why I feel I can confide in you, even though it might be difficult since you are my employer." She winced. Bethany nodded for her to go on. "These past months I have fallen in love with —" Mrs. Tilton's condemning face transposed on her daughter's and, even though it was her imagination, she didn't dare mention Alex.

She mustn't consider Alex. Not with Coffey's threat.

Her choice was between two bright fractals, not three.

"A particular man in Castle Gate. But the place bears so much regret, I can't possibly stay there. Now an old family friend, my brother's best friend actually, waltzed into town and is begging me to come back to Boston with him. Partly by my parents' request, but partly because we both had feelings for each other before I met Jack."

Bethany slouched and leaned back on the settee. "My, my." What did she truly think? Was Leanna out of place coming here?

"I am sorry," Leanna mumbled. Humiliation was becoming a regular visitor to her cheeks. She suddenly felt exposed, uncertain that this was the best way to vet her circumstances. "I would never have come to you, but you are my only friend, to be quite honest. And I know that you made the choice to leave your family's religion for love and conviction —"

"Oh, Leanna. I understand. Please, do not justify yourself. This is a matter of your happiness. I will not be so persuasive to guilt you into a position in my household." She

251

laughed as she said, "I am no queen."

Leanna sighed with relief.

Bethany's smile faded into a determined look. "I will confess something that I have not told a single soul." She looked around the room and then into the foyer and the rest of the house. "I followed my husband purely for love. To speak in truth, I was rather lukewarm about the whole religion thing. It was only after we married that I accepted this new religion as my own. But you have done quite the opposite of me. Your conviction about your beliefs as well as love had you cast off your family. You have a strong sense of self, Leanna. It would be a pity for you to follow only your heart, or just your head. You need to go where you are loved and appreciated for who you are."

"Those are very wise words, Bethany," Leanna said softly. All her insecurity fell away and she knew that at least Bethany affirmed what she had known to be true.

"Let me ask you this. What holds you back from each option?"

"In Boston, I will be comfortable and adored. Yet I am still leery that my parents will not accept me for who I am now." But as James's wife, did they have a say at all? She could find employment in Boston. Still teach children, join a humanitarian society, and find happiness as James's wife — eventually. She was attracted to him, but did she love him? "And then, here, I will have my mind to keep me busy, and while my heart will surely grow fond of your family, romance will be put on hold for a while."

"And Castle Gate?" Bethany lifted a brow. She had mentioned that, hadn't she?

"Well, that is hardly an option at all. It is Castle Gate. There are people that I love very much, and people who make life miserable there." Just like she had made life miserable for Jack, too.

What was it about that tumultuous piece of Price Canyon that could harbor such a cauldron of emotion?

"Well, those are strong points all around." Her eyes sparkled deviously. "But you know, there are quite a few single men here also." She shrugged her shoulders and winked. Leanna's stomach only soured, even if she appeared to jest. Her heart was sagging from all the pressure.

"Oh, look at you. You've gone green. I am teasing, Leanna. Like I said before, you must decide for your heart *and* your mind." Bethany swatted at her lap playfully. "In all seriousness, it sounds to me that you should go where you can be yourself. All of yourself. And while I might find disappointment in your decision, I will be happy for you regardless." She leaned in and hugged her.

"Thank you, Bethany. I will let you know very soon."

"Let us have some tea before you leave." She bustled down the hall, returning in no time with her tray.

During her visit, Leanna became more acquainted with Tommy. The truth was clear that she'd find employment here to be a pleasant opportunity — one with a loving family and a decent dwelling to live in. But she would feel like an outsider for the most part — an old spinster, even if she was twenty-two. Her loneliness might not be so abundant here, but it would be quite obvious in a different sort of way.

She hadn't felt that way with the Pappas family. The Greek family embraced her even if she was quite different. Loneliness was squelched there. No matter how she scraped her brain for a flaw at the thought of the Pappas family, she could only find one — the risk that would lurk about if she followed her heart to Alex's arms again.

If she was to follow her heart and her mind, without the threat of loneliness and worse, she knew of only one choice.

After saying her good-byes to Bethany and Tommy, she spied the carriage waiting for her just as James had said — at three o'clock on the dot. Every corner of her being thirsted for air and courage. She breathed deeply with each step, her pulse in a fury and her thoughts racing.

Her mind was made up, and her heart would be satisfied with the decision, too.

James hopped out of the carriage and held open the door. "Good afternoon." He seemed excited and bursting with news.

"What is it, James?" She gave a coy smile as he helped her into the carriage. He hurried around, whipped open the opposite door, and scooted close to her.

"Oh, Leanna, you will be beautiful." He reached down and produced a large round hatbox from the carriage floor. "I bought you a hat, and you will adore it!" He slipped off the lid and retrieved the most magnificent hat imaginable. A rich violet brim trimmed with a satin edge and topped with a gorgeous arrangement of silk flowers and wispy feathers.

"Oh, James. I told you not to —"

"Please, Leanna. You've weighed your choices long enough. Now accept the hat and come with me to Boston."

"That's quite an offer."

"Really. I am falling madly in love with you more and more each day." A strand of his perfect hair fell across his forehead, and his cheekbones were bright with color. She believed him. The man appeared to be a lovesick fool.

Leanna bit her lip then admired the hat once more, skimming her fingers over the delicate trimmings and gorgeous contour.

James placed the hat and the box tenderly on the floor of the carriage then pulled her hands to his chest. "I can give you whatever you'd like, Leanna," he whispered, brushing his lips along her forehead. "But you will make me a better man. Please, come back to Boston."

This was where she was meant to be. Her life detoured for a reason — she learned much about faith and life's hardships. But now, she could return and continue the good work near her home, with a man who loved her and would provide for her — and perhaps, join her in the progressive cause. How much they could do together. "Very well, James Alcott," she said, annoyed that her throat ached. "I'll come home with you." She laughed at his bobbling eyes searching hers in disbelief.

His brow lifted, and he laughed a hearty, triumphant laugh. "Wonderful!" He gathered her in his arms. "I am so happy. Your family will be ecstatic."

"I hope so." She also hoped to feel relief in this moment of finality, but she only felt a headache spreading behind her eyes.

The carriage moved forward and its rocking was nothing compared to the swaying of her emotions. She tried to push Alex out of her thoughts, but what small joy she felt with her decision was only trampled by her grief in leaving him behind.

James held her hand, squeezing it occasionally, and observing the city as they trotted along. "What will you do first when we arrive home? I am ready to give you everything you can imagine." He kissed her gloved knuckles.

"I suppose I will look for a position at a school. It would serve me best to get settled with the children as soon as the spring semester begins." She thought about January in Boston. It was even worse than Utah.

"Ah, yes, but if your father agrees, I hope to marry soon. No need to get too settled."

She squeezed the bridge of her nose, the ache was radiating. "Why not?"

"You will be a wife, of course. Mine, at that. There is no need for you to work."

"But I want to, James," she said quickly, ignoring the pain. Her choice to leave with him was of heart and mind, just like Bethany said. And education was closely knit to both. "Even if it's not needed."

He sneered. "Who does that? Really, Leanna, you have forgotten all that life in Boston holds. Perhaps you can join a league or something." The charm and handsome physique fell away. "Volunteer when you have the time." His grip on her hand was weak, his hand — limp. Leanna could hardly look at him. For the first time since Jack died, she felt an old longing for her husband — the man who at least encouraged her dreams.

"Well, then." She sniffled, and pulled her hand away with the excuse of finding her handkerchief. "You have made my choices very clear, James."

At least one of them.

CHAPTER FIFTEEN

Leanna threw back the covers and wrapped her blanket around her shoulders. She was quick to light a fire and avoid the streams of frigid air entering through the cracks around the door and windows. She poured water into the pot on her stove then slumped into her chair. The flames grew and flickered like the uneasiness in her stomach.

Lord, how could I be led astray so easily?

Why did she even consider returning to Boston? Of course she would be expected to conform once more. And deep down, she'd known that to be so. But the comfort, the luxury, the distance from Jack's final resting place had tempted her to compromise her character.

She may have failed Jack miserably as a wife, and he may have died believing he was a poor excuse for a husband, but she was still Leanna Willingham McKee, the progressive debutante who had walked away from arrogance on the arm of the man who inspired her.

A strange relief met her the moment she refused James once and for all. All heaviness left her in that carriage ride to the train station. A sudden revival of her self-worth had her sit tall on the silent train ride to Castle Gate.

Her small home seemed like a refuge from all that had occurred. As she sat in the shifting shadows of this early morning, she could credit her good decision to one man only. And in doing so, something greater was in store, she was sure of it.

Leanna forced herself to use cold water to wash. After a cup of tea and a small meal, she put on her overcoat, gloves, and hat, and abandoned a cooling stove.

Most of the snow from the last fall had melted away. Only patches of the white stuff splattered here and there. If she were a child, she would purposefully walk right through the middle of them, even though the path was perfectly clear.

A meowing came from the Coffeys' porch, and she thought of Teddy and his fascination with the silly old cat. How those children had brightened her life. James had been quite the distraction, but now, with only two weeks left in December, she longed for their sweet faces. Her heart leaped knowing that she would be choosing a life of purpose over one of luxury.

Her long walk to the cemetery numbed her toes and her fingertips. It was a mountain winter for sure. The last time she'd walked through the cemetery gate, she recalled noticing Alex paying his respect at quite a distance from the funeral. After all, he was the only miner to see Jack breathe his last breath before the rock tumbled down.

So much had happened since Jack's funeral.

Her breath caught as she considered that, for the most part, many good things had occurred. Mostly due to Alex and his family. She forced herself to calm her racing heart.

Soon she came upon the simple gravestone that read:

JOHN HAMISH MCKEE
1886–1910

Leanna was only a small part of that life of twenty-four years. She knelt down, the cold earth slicing through her skirt and stockings to her bare knees.

"Jack." Her voice was hoarse. Her warm

breath formed a cloud in the air. She closed her eyes for a moment, trying to remember Jack when she first loved him.

They had strolled through Boston Commons together, when she'd left James Alcott without a dance partner at the most anticipated ball of the season. Jack's inspiring words had kindled a fire in her spirit, and she dared to believe her worth was not in the wealth of her parents. He had quoted scripture and given her reason to listen in church for the first time in her privileged life.

They married and made a home in a part of town that her parents would never visit. She tried to embrace it, thankful for the chance to teach at a nearby orphanage. It was a step in her heart's direction. But when Jack confessed his addiction to gambling after the loss of their money saved for San Francisco, Leanna could not forgive him. For a very long time, she wondered if his noble talk was just a pretense to drag her into his pathetic world.

Now she knew better. Each moment she remembered was wrapped in both misery and love. The man struggled with his vice, but not once had he struggled in his love. She was the one who wrestled with a bitter weed. Her hurt was so tightly wound around her heart that she could hardly go a second without firing hateful words to her husband from the same mouth that begged God to help her. She was as much of a hypocrite as Jack.

The gravestone's chill pierced through her glove to her palm. "Forgive me, Jack. Wherever you are, forgive me. Yesterday, I took your advice, 'To thine own self be true.' " She smiled at the thought of Shakespeare popping up again. Jack had shared that line with her, and Alex had shared another.

If the old bard wrote her story, what would he write? A comedy or a tragedy? She hoped for a happy ending. Only God knew that.

After all that had been stripped away from her, the faith Jack had first awakened remained. "I will be forever grateful to you, dear Jack." She narrowed her eyes. "Even if you did light my anger on occasion." She wagged her head and laughed gently.

Leanna released her bitterness at last. With palms lifted toward the white canopy of clouds above, she spoke through a downpour of tears.

"I beg Your forgiveness, too. All these months, I've clung to my hate. But I know now that I am better because You placed him in my life. Please forgive me, Lord."

As she continued toward the gate, her path ahead was unclear, but she felt lighter than before. Freedom had found her this morning. Over these many months, her stubborn Willingham pride would not allow her heart to forgive the man who could be credited for giving her a heart in the first place.

"There is no darkness but ignorance." And today was a bright day.

Her heart lurched as she neared the path to the Greek neighborhood.

Maria's dark curls bounced into view. "Meesus McKee!" The little girl ran up to her, flinging her arms around her waist. "I have missed you."

"Why are you here alone, Maria? Surely your mother would not approve?" Leanna looked past her with a leap of expectation in her spirit.

"I am not alone. The others are coming to open the restaurant." Her big brown eyes filled with tears as she searched Leanna's face. "Please say you've changed your mind. You stay?"

She bit her lip. "I am afraid not." She would rather teach Maria than Bethany's son. Her heart and her mind begged her to reconsider. She'd tossed out Castle Gate in Bethany's parlor and then once again in that carriage with James.

Castle Gate was more of a battleground than fresh soil for a new start. In a way, Castle Gate held little more than Boston. "Perhaps I can visit." She tucked the girl's hair behind her ear, wiping a tear with her thumb.

Maria sulked. "I want you to be my thia."

"Thia?" The word was vaguely familiar.

"I want you to marry Alex," Maria blurted.

Heat scorched Leanna's frozen face. Thia Helena was Maria's aunt. "We mustn't say such things, dear —"

"Maria!" A rich bellow belted through the trees along the path.

Alex appeared. His clean-shaven face was bright beneath a dark cap. When their eyes met, he stole away his gaze and focused on his niece.

"You do not run ahead, Maria. Your mother will have your neck." He grabbed her arm and held her to his side, acknowledging Leanna with a quiet, "Good morning."

"Good morning." Last they spoke, she had tried to convince herself, more than him, that Boston may be her only choice. "I am not going to Boston, Alex."

"You aren't?" The tension in his face fell,

and he gave her an expectant look.

Leanna's heart pounded, tempted to put Castle Gate back in her future. She could give him her full heart now. Her guilt was finally laid to rest.

"Why are you staying?" he asked.

"I turned down James's proposal," she said. " 'There's no darkness but ignorance,' right?" She gave a lopsided smile. "Boston would only push me back."

His broad grin warmed every bit of her heart. "You are a strong woman, Leanna McKee."

Mr. and Mrs. Pappas joined them from Greek Town. Mrs. Pappas rushed up and kissed Leanna on both cheeks, but Mr. Pappas only nodded then gave his son a sharp look, speaking in Greek.

"We are in a hurry to open the restaurant," Alex seemingly translated.

"Is that all he said?" Leanna smirked, remaining playful and light, even though all her hope deflated with the reality of what was at stake — not only was the town against them, but Alex's own father was as well.

She'd lived a life of broken ties in her own family. How could she allow Alex to strain his? Not with this sweet family. They were here for her season of healing. And perhaps that was enough. "Go ahead, Alex. Don't upset your father by wasting time with me."

He narrowed his eyes and shook his head slowly. "Walk with us," he offered. "You were walking this way, weren't you?"

She nodded. Maria grabbed her hand then her yiayia's, and they began walking down the hill. Alex walked ahead with his father.

When they got to the porch, she continued toward the path to her house. "Good day," she spoke to Mrs. Pappas who took her hand, giving it a squeeze. "I'll be sure to stop by before I leave," Leanna said to Maria, aware of Alex's stare.

"So you are going to Salt Lake instead?" he asked.

Mr. Pappas spoke impassioned words to Mrs. Pappas, and they went inside.

"Come in, Meesus McKee." Maria ran and grabbed her hand. "Yiayia made cookies for Christmas. You try?"

"No, Maria. I don't think it would be wise."

The little girl sulked and disappeared through the door.

Alex fiddled with his cap in his hands. "So?"

"Alex, I think we know what's best, don't we?"

"I wish I didn't know, but I have to agree,

Salt Lake is best." His face grew dark. His agreement was agonizing.

"It is good that you understand." She tried to appear resolute, but all the heaviness that left her yesterday, now threatened to return.

"In the city, you'll have nobody to scrutinize you. Here, they will sneer at you just as they do me." He kicked at the dirt with his toe.

"I don't care what they think of me," she said. "But your father does not approve of us, and you are a good son —"

"Papa? He has no hold over me, Leanna. I want you to go for your own sake, not mine."

"For me?" If she could tell him she would stay if there was a guarantee he'd be safe, his family secure, she would. She wasn't leaving for herself. "I am leaving for you. Trouble will find you, and your family —"

"Yes, I know. I don't worry about trouble. But I don't want you to live a life condemned by every passerby." He swiped his hat from his head and twisted it in his hands. "I can't bear to think that my love would never be enough to bring you happiness."

Oh, but it would, it is enough. "There is no need to protect me, Alex —"

Maria ran outside again. "You come for

268

Christmas!" She whipped her attention to her uncle. "Thios Alex, Yiayia said so."

His mouth opened slightly.

"What did your grandfather say, Maria?" A lump formed in her throat. How could she come between a father and a son and find happiness?

Maria's brow furrowed. "Yiayia say not to ask him. Just you come."

"Why would she do such a thing?"

"Because you are family, remember?" Alex said, swiping a curl from her forehead. "They think you are going to Boston, anyway. I am sure Momma just wants to send you off well fed." He winked.

"Should I come?" Leanna's voice was meek.

"You know what I would want." Alex rocked on his heels. "Even if it is our last night together."

She wanted all that he did, even if it would fade away in dawn's light.

The expectations in Castle Gate weighed more than the tall rocky spires outside the town, and the chance to love each other seemed a greater indulgence than all the hats James Alcott could buy.

Momma bustled through the crowded tables as she always did. The smell of *zimaropita* and bowls of butter-milk tempted Alex to join his fellow miners for a hearty meal. But his stomach may as well have been piled with coal as deep as a cart from the mine. He anticipated sharing one last evening with the schoolteacher. How could he say good-bye?

"Petros Papamichael ordered a bride last week." Nick's mouthful of food did not stop him from talking. "He thinks he might be cursed from his dead momma. He is sick as a dog now. Laid up at the boardinghouse." The group around him began to laugh.

"Stupid superstitions," Alex said to himself as he helped clear a table. Everything was a blessing or curse according to these Greeks. And curses helped conjure a reason for most ill predicaments. Even Momma once declared Helena's illness a curse but did not have an answer for why she deserved it.

Alex was too practical to believe in curses. He had believed in a God who withdrew His hand and played tricks on His people. He cringed. Lately, he'd not just resorted to prayer, his heart longed for it. He needed the assurance of God's watch and hand.

Alex ground his teeth at the question lurking from his time at the base of the Castle Gate formation. In all his effort to work the mines, had he been hiding from God? Every day he worked hard, trying to make up for all he lost. But now that everything he wanted was out of his control again, he didn't want to hide. He wanted peace. And he only found it when he opened his heart in prayer.

Nick grabbed Alex's arm on his way to carry a dish bin to the kitchen. "Alex, tell this stupid-as-a-Turk that finding picture brides is not foolish."

"I have to agree with the Turk. If I need a wife, I'll find one the old-fashioned way."

"What Greek women will you two find, then?" Nick and his friends laughed as he put his napkin on his head like a veil.

"You stop that." Momma hit the back of Nick's head. "If your momma saw you —" She waved a threatening hand in the air and narrowed her eyes like a spying fox.

Alex slipped past his mother into the kitchen. He set the bin on the counter then escaped out back into the quiet of the yard. The oven smoked with the Christmas lamb, filling the evening air with scents of oregano and lemon. Heavy gray clouds snuffed out any sign of stars.

He blinked back tears. Fear swelled inside him. Everyone stepped toward a chance to love and flourish, even enough to order a bride and please their pure Greek lines. There was a reason for tradition — it gave sure guidelines to live life on purpose.

But what if his life's purpose was best lived with Leanna? Was she any different than a Greek bride? Her allegiance to his family was just the same as any Greek.

What had Tommy's grandmother said? That they were one according to the Good Book. Alex loved his people, and their origins, but his love for Leanna was beyond all that. He had never been so sure of a plan for his heart than he was right now.

Alex couldn't help but smile.

He'd have to get a copy of the Bible.

The restaurant was full of miners who were desperate enough to marry a stranger. But Alex did not need to resort to such things. No matter what Papa or the Coffeys said, his plan, maybe God's plan, was obvious.

He'd encountered more Americans who might help erase these steadfast boundaries, too. Will Jacob had promoted him, Leanna protected him and his family, and Tommy's grandmother had summed it all up as a greater belonging — to a people under God.

Could the death of prejudice start right where the old lady implied? With love?

"Lord, if You are listening, take away our

fear." He dropped to his knees, the hard, frozen earth doing little compared to the pangs of his emerging heart. "And Lord, take me back." Everything seemed connected in this moment. God and Leanna and the chance to peel away the darkness at last. At his next breath, the clouds dissipated and the bright light of a half-moon appeared. A breeze whipped through his hair, and sudden relief radiated through his chest. The urge to run up the dark path to Leanna's was hard to fight off, but he did so with all his strength.

Nobody would stop him from loving her. God may have used Leanna to awaken his faith again, but Alex was certain that she had more purpose in his life than that.

Leanna McKee was his future. And he would not let her leave Castle Gate without his promise to love her no matter what.

CHAPTER SIXTEEN

The familiar smell of cloves and cinnamon was not nearly as sweet as spying Leanna's hesitant entry from the shadowed dining-room threshold. She shut the back door behind her while noticing Momma at the fire. Her rosy lips grew into a genuine smile. She adored his family. A broody frustration unleashed inside him. The only thing stopping his father from embracing this near-perfect Pappas addition was his stubborn old pride.

But Alex had a plan tonight, in spite of tradition — and propriety.

"Meesus McKee. So glad you here." Momma's carefully crafted English did not damper her enthusiasm for their guest. Alex chuckled silently, unnoticed by either woman. Momma cried out, *"Kala Christuyenna!"* and grabbed Leanna by the shoulders, boldly kissing her on each cheek.

"Merry Christmas to you," Leanna

blurted behind a giggle. She still hadn't seen him, and he was fine with that. His new favorite pastime was admiring Leanna McKee from a distance. Her beauty, her confident cadence, and the flicker of abundant life in every expression. "Can I help?" Leanna motioned to the spoon, her brow filled with eagerness.

Momma nodded vigorously, handing her the spoon. She held up a finger signaling for Leanna to wait here then hurried past Alex, patting his chest as she went into the dining room. In a flurry of Greek she called out, "Hurry, Maria, finish setting the table. It's almost time."

Leanna's back was turned to him as she stirred the wassail. Every second slipped past like the steam leaving the pot. The fire beneath the pot was no different than the circumstances forcing her to leave.

But he was there to snuff out all their obstacles tonight.

"Merry Christmas," he near whispered, suddenly aware of this quiet moment alone. Her head lifted, and she turned, only slightly, finding him from the corner of her eye.

Her lips pressed together in a coy smile. "Merry Christmas, Alex." She rested the spoon on the edge of the pot and spun around. The dim kitchen did not hide her delicate features — high cheekbones prodded upward by her smile, her perfectly straight nose, and those eyes, blue topaz pools swimming with affection.

"I am glad you came, Leanna." He approached her and gathered up her hands. "This is my greatest gift."

She squeezed his palms, her eyelashes fluttering as she sighed. "I tried talking myself out of it, but I —"

"Shh," he hushed her with a finger to her lips. They were soft, her breath warming his skin. Her eyes brimmed with expectancy, and he brushed her bottom lip with the back of his finger now. A quiet hitch of her breath triggered his heart to a wild beat. He marveled at her once again. "I want to share with you —"

"Meesus McKee!" Teddy popped his head over the counter and waved a hand covered in powdered sugar. "Yiayia wants to cut the *Christopsomo!* Come!" He jumped up and down.

"Teddy, you are a little rascal." Alex sighed. "Momma will be in here next, hands flying." He glanced at her with a playful grin and gently tugged at her hand. "We better join them." She drew close to him as they shuffled out of the room, bolstering his assurance that she was worth fighting for.

The entire family sat around the large table at the back of the restaurant. Snow blew sideways beyond the glass window in front. Nothing cold met them in this room, though. Even Papa gave Leanna a cordial smile and tipped his fisherman's cap as Alex guided her toward her chair.

"Kala Christuyenna!" A chorus greeted.

"You are our guest of honor," Alex whispered in her ear while she sat.

"Me?" Leanna lowered to her seat.

"The children learn so much from you," he said. "And I shall never be the same, Mrs. McKee." She stared up at him, her knowing eyes seeming to dance with both sadness and love. If only he could speak with her now, but the Christopsomo would not wait for them. A delicious Greek tradition, indeed. He sat next to her.

"So tell me, Alex." Leanna leaned closer to the table. "What is this?" She pointed at the round bread with the star baked on top.

"Christopsomo — it is Christmas bread. Many Greeks make it this time of year." He winked at Maria, who'd grown more eager to listen to his English. "We decorate it for our family. Momma used to make a sheep out of the bread dough on top, but now she chooses the star of a persimmon fruit.

277

Persimmon is a symbol of prosperity."

"And fertility!" Yanni declared then roared with laughter as he stroked his baby son's black hair.

"I see your English is coming along nicely, Yanni." Alex chuckled with him. "Perhaps we should begin working on good manners?"

Yanni dropped his grin and tilted his head with a look of confusion.

Leanna giggled, and Alex just shook his head. Her laughter was a sound he hoped to hear for the rest of his life. It was authentic and melodious, just like her singing voice, which had carried to him in her church.

Momma lifted a knife to her masterpiece and Papa sucked air through his teeth. Each year, she took care to collect the finest ingredients, even sending Alex to Salt Lake City to hunt down anise seed. All Momma's effort would soon fill their bellies with the sweet, spiced bread fading into the memory of another Christmas on American soil.

When Alex was in the boardinghouse, the men would often reminisce about the Christmas bread, the cookies, and the syrupy baklava of their home country. A roomful of Greek miners sat with mouths watering while their only morsels were bland meat and bread from the American cook at the local saloon.

Now, he and Yanni were blessed more than any other miner in this town. His whole family sat here, including the only two Greek women in Castle Gate. His Christmas dinner would be nearly as satisfying as keeping Leanna close to his side.

He pushed out a staggered breath, probably mistaken by the others as one of regret when Momma pierced the bread. He must find a proper time to speak with Leanna before it was too late.

"Maria, pass out the bread, please." Momma placed generous pieces on plates and pushed them toward Maria who was careful to stand and take a plate to each person.

"Meesus McKee, you come back and visit at Easter. The *Tsureki* is just as delicious," Maria said.

Leanna's lips parted, and then she gave a resolute smile. "Perhaps," she said, glancing at Alex with an apologetic quirk of her eyebrow.

"Thios Alex, Salt Lake City is not so far?" Maria's earnest expression brought an ache in his heart. Leanna watched him, as if waiting for his answer, too.

279

"No, it is not so far," he said.

When they had all finished their first piece, Momma was eager to dish out seconds to anyone who was willing.

"No, thank you. Would you like me to bring in the tea?" Leanna asked.

Momma scrunched her nose in confusion. Alex translated.

"Oh, neh neh!" she agreed. Leanna excused herself and went to the kitchen.

He pushed his chair back, his heart thudding like a train barreling through the valley. This might be his chance —

"Alex. I have something for you," his father announced. He cleared his throat and rummaged in his pocket. "I received this from Athens a while ago." He handed him an envelope. The seal was broken.

"What is it, Papa?"

"You will see —" His voice caught when he diverted his attention over Alex's shoulder. Leanna sailed through with a kettle and mugs on a tray. "Perhaps, you should wait until this evening." He went to reach for the envelope, but Alex snatched it away.

"You gave it to me. Now you want it back?" A nervous pang scattered his anticipation to speak with Leanna. He pulled out a letter. Something fluttered to the ground. Maria hopped from her seat and picked up a photograph.

She stared hard at it then handed it to Alex. "Who is that, Thios Alex?"

The photograph was of a plain young woman. Alex gave his father a quizzical look, his spirit overcast by a foreboding shadow. Papa sat back in his chair and began to fiddle with his worry beads. Alex skimmed the letter while Leanna passed out mugs of steaming tea.

He did it. His father went ahead and followed through with his scheming, hadn't he?

If it wasn't Christmas, and if the woman who stole his heart was not standing so close by, Alex would slam a fist on the table. Instead, he crumpled the letter in his hand, shoved it in his pocket and tossed the picture on the tabletop. He dared not look at his father. He was afraid of the contempt that would surely shine from his eyes.

How could Papa suggest this, on such a day, with such company around?

But the letter made it perfectly clear that his father had gone back on his word and made arrangements for a Greek match anyway. The woman's voyage to America had been purchased and set for arrival in January.

■ ■ ■ ■

"You like babies." Penelope spoke English to Leanna, who cradled little George in her arms. Was it that obvious? The baby slept soundly until his lips grew into a smile then a sudden pout. He whimpered and with a contented sigh settled back into a peaceful sleep.

"He is so beautiful," Leanna whispered, consumed with all the life that pressed on her arms. Never before had she held a baby so small. He was perfect. His thick black hair, soft as velvet, had a natural part to one side.

When she was married to Jack, she had been so wrapped up in her departure from society and trying to adjust to living in a household without servants, she had never considered a family of her own. She was learning to be a wife, without a thought to motherhood. But deep down, she knew she wanted it. Now holding baby George in her arms stirred her soul deeply, mixing maternal instinct with a fear that she may never hold her own child. Like James had teased, she might just be a spinster for the rest of her childbearing years.

A ruckus of Greek chatter rose from the

men at the counter behind them. Penelope gave her a wary glance as they looked over their shoulders. Alex slammed his hand on the counter then stormed into the kitchen. Mrs. Pappas's high-pitched voice carried through the door.

"What is the matter?" Leanna whispered.

Penelope glanced down at Maria and spoke Greek in a hushed voice. Maria looked up at Leanna with much seriousness. "Papou found a wife for Alex."

The slight weight of the baby was featherlike compared to the rock in her stomach. Is that what the letter was about? She had wanted to ask about it, but it seemed that once Alex crumpled it in his hands, everyone moved on and finished their spiced tea. The picture appeared to be that of a woman, but she could not make out the details when he flung it across the table.

"Mama says Alex is very upset. He does not want a prearranged marriage. But the woman will be here in January." Maria petted her baby brother's hair.

"January?" Her mouth fell, and the heaviness inside pressed so much she could hardly swallow.

Was this a humorous turn of events on God's part? Scoot her out of the picture to make room for a proper Greek girl? She

283

looked back at Mr. Pappas. This man would make sure that the American did not enchant his son, wouldn't he? Perhaps he was more persistent in these finely drawn boundaries than even Mr. Coffey.

"Your papou must not like me at all." Leanna squeezed out the words beyond her tightening throat.

Maria looked sideways in her grandfather's direction. "He like you, Meesus McKee. He like Greek women better." She giggled. "I want you to be my thia, though." She shifted her chair close and slipped her hand in the crook of Leanna's elbow, just beneath the baby's head. Little George squirmed. His face grew red, and he began to wail. Leanna carefully handed him back to Penelope, who excused herself to feed the baby in the kitchen.

Leanna should leave. The warm evening that she'd hoped for was turning out to be a sign that every decision was for the best. This was exactly what she should've expected. The Pappas family would move forward just as she would when she boarded that northbound train.

But the piece of her heart stolen by Alex was larger than she thought. Perhaps she'd given too much away to a man who'd never be hers.

Alex sat beside her. "I am sorry for leaving you alone so long."

She couldn't look at him. He was so close, but come January he'd be a stranger again — another woman's hope and affection.

"You didn't leave me alone." She folded the small blanket left behind by George. "I was with Penelope." Maria grabbed her arm again. "And Maria." She forced a smile for the girl, but it was short lived as her mind spun out of control. She would love to be her thia, too. A grimace tugged at her lips. Foolishness was inevitable when she allowed her emotions to control her. She'd learned that with Jack. Expectations were fool's gold.

Alex leaned an elbow on the table and clutched the hair at his forehead. He sighed loudly and deeply.

"Are you all right, Alex?" She tried to keep her gaze set on anything benign, anything that would curb the battle inside her.

"I was, until —"

"I know." She couldn't bear to hear the truth again, especially from him. "I should leave." She pushed her chair back.

Alex dropped his hand and threw her a desperate stare. Through gritted teeth he said, "Maria, go help your yiayia." Maria began to protest, but he snapped, "Now."

She dashed across the room, and Yanni and Stergios followed her into the kitchen. Crying and voices were muffled on the other side of the wall. Leanna hung her head, trying to form the strength to leave. But nothing inside her wanted to go just yet. Once she left this place, she'd never return.

This was not how she'd hoped to end this season of love and second chances with Alex Pappas.

"Some Christmas." He shook his head then ran his fingers through his hair. "I apologize that you must witness a family dispute."

"I'm family, remember?" She gave a tender smile. "There's nothing to be embarrassed about. I am quite familiar with family disputes."

"I can't believe my father. If I were a boy, or a daughter, I would understand. But this? I am a grown man who has been married before."

"How long has the arrangement been in place?" Every fiber of her heart begged her to change the subject, to not wallow in the devastation of it. Yet she must know what she would leave behind. What life Alex might have after her.

"He had written his cousin in September.

Momma worries about me, especially on Sundays since I don't attend liturgy." He shook his head. "She hoped that a good Greek wife would change my heart for church. But when Papa overheard men talking about our hike —" He hesitated, his expression darkened. "They offered to pay the girl's way to expedite the plan."

A dagger twisted in her heart. Her insides quivered with shame for her desperate decision to forgo church and follow Alex on his hike. She'd provoked his parents to take such drastic measures.

Her eyes ached with a flood of tears. She could only whisper, "I didn't realize how they felt about me."

Alex tilted her chin up. A tear slid down her cheek. "This is not about you. They adore you. This is about me and their efforts to change my ways." He gathered up her hands in an impassioned grip. "But I have changed, Leanna. And you are the reason. I am a better man for it." He rested his teeth on his lip and searched her face with intense eyes. "I did not think I could love again after Helena. I blamed God for it, but it was my pride that hardened my heart. Then you came to me, with your tender spirit and your unwavering faith and —"

"Unwavering?" Leanna grimaced. "I did not have faith like I should have. Faith to forgive Jack and myself."

"You have faith in God's plan for you." He leaned forward. "And I assumed God had nothing for me. But then He gave me you and this uncertain dance of ours," he said, his lips forming a faint smile. "How could I be angry anymore when the only sane thing I could manage to do was pray?"

An overwhelming rush of love and awe forced her to laugh. She placed her hand on his cheek, thankful that they were alone in this moment.

Alex continued, "I will not marry that girl. There are plenty of men who want a wife. Her father may be upset, but I refuse to touch his dowry." He squeezed her hand, and his deep brown eyes lit with enthusiasm. "It is ironic that I've formed a plan for us just before Papa revealed his."

"A plan?" Her spirit leaped within her. "For us?" She braced herself. There was nothing they could do to continue this way. Even if she loved him, their time together was ending on this cold Christmas night.

"I am going to find work in Salt Lake City," he blurted.

Her heart skipped. "But your family. You've built all this —"

288

"They tell me to live more than work. Yanni says that I've done plenty." He held her hands tighter. "This is the life I want."

"Even in Salt Lake City, you are still Greek and I am American." Her eyes ached with frustration. She wanted to leap into his new plan, but her reason was strong and challenging every ounce of joy. "What is the difference in a lynching in Castle Gate or one in Salt Lake City?"

"Why must we worry about those around us?" He was unaffected, still glowing with excitement. "If we cower to such prejudices, we are no better. There is nothing to stop us but our own fear." His brow flinched with determination. " 'There is no fear in love.' "

Tears threatened as she drank in the scripture that had soothed her soul long ago, now being spoken by the only man who could make her heart whole. "I once said that to my parents and they scoffed."

"It's from the Good Book." He winked.

"You say it to me. And I want it to be true." She brushed her fingers against the curls at his forehead. This man had been a strong rock all these weeks. Someone who'd broken through her grief and given her a new glimpse at who she wanted to be.

Alex caught her hand. He took it and put

her palm up to his lips, gently brushing it with a kiss. "Marry me, Leanna. We'll prove that love is bigger."

Twining her fingers with his, she basked in the beauty of his words. Tears spilled, and her good reason was flooded by hope. Or perhaps this was good reason. Why cower in the face of hardship when she had something as grand as love on her side?

She mumbled, "There's no darkness but ignorance. And there's no fear in love." Nothing in the world seemed so wonderful — and so daring.

Her heart skittered beneath her blouse, and her cheeks rushed with warmth. Alex waited like a child longing for a Christmas present. His face was so pure in its willingness, so filled with love.

"But what if you find nothing in Salt Lake?" Her mind raced with the possibilities — both beautiful and tragic.

"Then we'll go to San Francisco. Or wherever God takes us. It might be difficult, but with love, there is always prosperity, right?" His face beamed.

"San Francisco? You'd go with me?"

He nodded and hooked her chin with his finger, pulling her close.

"What about your family? Your father will be devastated. I am afraid to hurt them,

Alex. They will be so hurt."

"Do not worry about them." He brushed his lips on her forehead. "Like I said, they love you, Leanna. They might be shocked at first, but with time, we will spend Christmas with them once again, you'll see."

"The last time I turned my back on love, look what happened." She sighed. "If we do this, we mustn't say a word while we're still in Castle Gate." She tried to sound firm, but he was kissing her cheek then her nose. His brow pressed against hers, and he drank her in with his gaze. "I don't want harm to come to you, and believe me, there are people who want to harm you."

He gave a sideways glance to the kitchen, and said, "Don't you worry," then pressed his soft lips to hers. He pulled away slowly, Leanna allowing herself to indulge in his tender way. She opened her eyes and he cupped her cheek. "We will leave quickly. Tomorrow if you'd like. We won't have time for danger."

CHAPTER SEVENTEEN

They joined the rest of the family in the kitchen and helped pack up the leftover food. Leanna's insides jumped about like the fiery flames beneath the mantel. She tried to douse them with the hope of this plan.

She would marry Mr. Alex Pappas, a man who cared not only for her heart, but for her dream to educate.

A niggling in her gut did not allow her to fully revel in that.

His dream was for his family, and she would steal him away.

"We leave Meesus McKee." Maria interrupted her thoughts.

Leanna knelt on the kitchen floor and embraced her. "Good-bye, sweet Maria." She heard the sniffles from the girl and stroked her soft curls. "Don't forget your English."

Yanni gently pulled his daughter from the

embrace and held her hand. "Come, we go home now." He smiled at Leanna and said, "Good-bye, Meesus McKee."

Teddy stole Maria's spot and wrapped his arms around her neck.

"You be a good boy, Teddy. No more chasing cats. Okay?" She tousled his hair and kissed his forehead.

"There cats in Salt Lake City?" he asked, his eyes wide with curiosity.

Leanna giggled. "Yes, there are."

After she said her good-byes to Penelope and baby George, the young family bundled up in their blankets, coats, and hats and headed home.

Mrs. Pappas offered her a tin of cookies, catching her own sniffles with a handkerchief at her nose.

"There is no use declining," Alex whispered close to her ear. His minty breath tickled her skin. He lingered longer than he should. She stepped away shifting her eyes to Alex and scolding him with a glare. But the playful wag of his eyebrow captured her in an affectionate current more powerful than the lighted Main Street.

"Meesus McKee?" Mrs. Pappas shoved the tin toward her and then gave Alex a serious look.

She'd noticed. Of course.

Leanna adjusted her hat then pulled her gloves from her pocket. She took the tin. "Eff-ah-di-sto, Mrs. Pappas." Did she say that right?

The woman's face brightened and she clicked her tongue. Wildly, she tossed her hands up and exclaimed, "Bravo! Bravo!" She pulled Leanna's face down and kissed her forehead then leveled her eyes with Leanna's and said, "You be careful."

"Yes, I will." She smiled brightly, but a deep uneasiness roused within her. Could she truly keep that word to Alex's mother?

A blast of cold bit through her layers when Alex opened the door. Momma squealed and moved closer to the fire. Leanna swept past him and stepped onto fresh snow. With a quiet click of the door, he followed her along the back of the restaurant.

She spun around, tilting her head back so she could peer up beneath the rim of her hat. "You are brave, Alex Pappas." She placed both hands on the center of his chest and fiddled with his coat button.

"And so are you. We are the perfect match." His grin hooked the corner of his mouth.

Her lips parted in awe. She then swallowed hard. "Is it foolish that we dream up such a plan?"

"Foolish? I was a fool before. But now I am finally wise again. My path is set straight, Leanna. There is a plan, I can feel it. And you are part of it. I am sure of that." He pulled her even closer still, until the only warmth in the whole of Castle Gate kindled between their pulsing hearts. With a slight tilt of his head, his lips hovered over hers.

"Alex —" Before she could finish, he kissed her. The warmth exploded, defying the cold around them. His firm lips explored her own, and he pressed harder. She gripped handfuls of his coat; his heartbeat pounded against her fists.

A sudden crack from behind startled her, and she ran to the far edge of the porch.

"Who's there?" she demanded into the darkness of the nearby path.

There was no answer but the rustle of dead leaves.

"It was an animal, Leanna." Alex walked up to her. "I am sure it was a raccoon. They are rampant here."

She stiffened, taking a step back. "What if it was Coffey?" Fear iced every vein. The warmth of his lips, a distant memory.

"Would he leave us in peace or come out and reprimand us?" Alex chuckled, calming her nerves.

She sighed. "True."

"I'll meet you next week, at the trolley stop near Temple Square." Their plan was set, but she wanted to speak of nothing right now. She only nodded and hurried toward the path to her home.

Was this the beginning of a second chance at love, or an inevitable disaster?

Leanna's eyes popped open as she lay on her mattress. Her mind raced with all that happened this Christmas night. The thrill of Alex's proposal sent chills down her arms, but her stomach swam with anxiety at what they were about to do. In just a couple of days, she'd arrive at Bethany's, only to decline her position — if everything worked out according to Alex. Were they fooling themselves? Dreaming up such an easy elopement seemed naive.

Gusts whistled under the door, piercing her nerves. She pulled her quilt to her chin. She had yet to find peace in living alone. And she wouldn't have to, would she?

Leanna groaned, trying to muster up the same excitement she had felt in Alex's arms.

If only she could have his faith in their future together. Faith and determination. Both of which she lacked right now. Her heart fluttered, and she sank farther into her mattress. Where could this dream come true?

San Francisco could be a possibility for her with Alex by her side — he even suggested it. Perhaps the coast was more progressive and more accepting? Her hope swelled to the far corners of the future. Yes, they could find a way. Life for them both was out there, somewhere.

She rolled over on her side, pulling her knees up and squeezing her eyes tight.

Lord, let it be so.

The high-pitched gusts turned into a distant growl. No, that was not the wind. Straining her ears, she could make out far-off shouting. She pressed her ear to the outside wall against Jack's side of the bed. The loud pulse of blood forced her to hold her breath. Yes, living alone was miserable. Was she imagining this? It was late and she was exhausted. Perhaps —

There. Another shout, barely audible.

Tiptoeing across her house, she made sure the door was locked properly. What drunkards were causing a ruckus at this time of night? Probably some young miners celebrating without any thought to sleeping families and rattled widows.

She turned the key once more for peace of mind and slipped it in her nightgown pocket. Her whole body froze at the sound of smothered voices. She ran to the window, pressing her ear against it. Mr. Coffey's low voice eclipsed his whining wife's words, and the distant shouts continued to erupt.

Why was anyone up at this hour, in this cold, unless something terrible had gone awry?

A sudden realization gripped her with dread. She had left Alex for fear of being watched in the back of the restaurant. Did this strange disturbance on Christmas night have anything to do with that? She thrust her bare feet into her boots and flung her coat around her shoulders. Her icy hands fumbled with the key as she unlocked her door.

The bite of winter did not stop her from rushing onto the path. The Coffeys stood on their porch arguing back and forth. They both stopped as she passed.

Mr. Coffey edged out from the porch, fully dressed. "Why, Mrs. McKee, you sure are up late this evening." He laughed nervously as he fiddled with his gloves.

"Mr. Coffey, I must say the same —" Leanna gasped. A funnel of smoke rose to the sky, just beyond the trees.

"Mrs. McKee, I trust you to be a smart woman and go back inside," he spoke with authority.

The restaurant.

Leanna ignored her prying neighbor and began to run. Yelling grew louder, and when she came to the end of the path, whipping flames lashed into view.

Several of his countrymen spilled out of the Greek coffeehouse across the street with pails of water and blankets.

"Quick! It is spreading fast." Alex held open the front door of the restaurant, broken glass crunching beneath his boots. The men shuffled inside. He took one of the pails and tossed it at the burning dining room. Anger coursed through him. He ground his teeth and blinked back tears induced by the smoke.

This was no accident. He was sure of it.

He had stayed in the kitchen after Leanna left, praying and considering his words with Papa about the arranged marriage. Once the embers in the kitchen fireplace died, Alex began to gather his things. It was late, and he was exhausted.

The shatter of glass had pierced the silence, and he ran into the dining room just in time to see a bolt of fire land on the front table. He was quick to fill up a pail to extinguish it. But by the time he'd returned, two more fiery bricks had been tossed inside, and the front half of the room was ablaze, smoke filling fast.

His shouts down Main Street were answered by his friends at the coffeehouse. The bachelor miners were no doubt wallowing in the misery of another Christmas without family.

Like ants upon a fallen crumb, his friends aided him immediately.

"The roof! It has reached the roof!" someone shouted, running across the street and tossing the water up as best as he could.

Alex ran to the back of the restaurant to fill up his bucket, panic swelling in his body. Leanna rushed toward him from her path.

"Oh, Alex, what happened —" she exclaimed, her face blanched and her eyes dark beneath her brow.

"Follow me. Help me get water." He jogged around to the back and went to the pump while Leanna retrieved another pail near the porch. He filled his, then Leanna began to fill hers. The water sloshed as they carried the pails along the side of the restaurant and through the dining-room door. She began to cough, and he fought the urge to aid her. She would leave if she needed to. He could not tend to her, no matter how much he wanted to do so.

The fire was somewhat contained to the front of the dining room. Most of the men were dealing with the fire on the front portion of the roof. They doused water on the last of the burning chairs. A billow of smoke swarmed them.

"Leave, Leanna." He coughed into his arm and followed her out and around to the back of the restaurant. She headed to the pump, but coughing racked her posture and she stumbled back.

Alex grabbed her by the elbow and led her to the kitchen. She collapsed on a stool. "Stay here. If the smoke reaches you, go outside."

He filled his bucket once more and sprinted around the building.

"We think it is out, Alex." Constantine bent over with his hands on his knees, catching his breath. "The roof is slightly damaged, but the fire is gone."

Alex tossed the water through the door for good measure then threw the bucket to the ground.

"What caused this, Alex?"

He shook his head. "I don't know. But it was malicious, I am sure of that."

"You have no enemies," Constantine assured him by words, yet his brow was cumbersome.

"What?" Alex sneered. "A Greek foreman over American men? No enemies?"

"But on Christmas? What could have sparked such an action?"

Alex ran his fingers through his hair, clutching at his curls tightly. That pain was nothing to what pinched him on the inside.

He knew what started this. The knowledge ripped through him, tearing apart his heart.

There was no animal in the woods that evening. At least, not the kind of animal he had assumed was out there.

"Thank you, friends." He inspected the damage once more. It would take time to fix, but it was not hopeless. "Go. We've had enough excitement this evening." He patted Constantine on the back and shook hands with the remaining men. They trickled across the street, their mumbling bumping against the thoughts in Alex's mind.

Only a few hours earlier and the result could have been disastrous. Hadn't he watched Teddy and Maria play hide-and-seek behind the tables at the front of the restaurant?

Their screams filled his imagination.

He slammed his hands on the wall, trembling at the possibilities. Darkness tormented him as he returned to the kitchen.

If only he would have listened to Leanna

from the very beginning, none of this would have happened.

Exhaustion crippled Leanna as she leaned against the brick wall of the kitchen. A seed of fear burrowed in her stomach. Perhaps the smoke had gotten to her head — the smoke from the fire that she had started. She suddenly became aware of a massive expanse that she'd stumbled into, a blindfold slipping from her face as she fell, fell, fell into the blackness of all that was the coal town — the very antithesis of God's plan for her.

Hot tears slid down her chilled face, and she dragged herself up from the stool, wiping them away with the cuff of her coat.

"Everything I feared has happened, all because of my wayward heart." She spoke into her hands, shaking her head with remorse.

"What do you say?" Alex entered through the kitchen door held ajar by a pile of loose bricks. Weariness cloaked his face, and the usual glint in his eyes was gone.

"The fire — is the damage terrible?"

"It is what it is." He lowered his eyes, pulling off his gloves.

"There is a reason for this, Alex. No matter how much I stand up and embrace your

303

family —" She folded her arms. "No matter how much I love you, we are not invincible to the ways of this place. This is exactly why I accepted the position in Salt Lake City."

He took wide strides and gripped the fireplace mantel with both hands, hanging his head below his shoulders. "Do you think it really could've been . . ." Torment seeped from his voice. "Could it really have been someone like Coffey who would do this?"

"I know it is." She wanted to wrap her arms around him and weep apologies into his familiar embrace. "He was arguing with his wife outside at this late hour. When I noticed the smoke, he did not act surprised at all."

A deep groan escaped from Alex, and he slammed his palms against the mantel. "How dare he? What if my family was inside? What if —" He kicked the iron grate at his feet, the clanging irritating the quiet.

Leanna's spine shuddered with the thought of Maria, Teddy, and baby George sitting in that dining room just hours before. "Your family, Alex, is more important than a hidden relationship."

"Or a discovered one."

"Yes." She swallowed a ball of emotion.

He kept his body turned away from her. "You were right. There is no place for us."

304

The words found their way around him and bit her ears with venom. She had tried to convince him, but he held on with all his heart. Even though her fear came true, Alex's surrender shattered every ounce of strength.

"It is best that I leave." Her voice cracked, and she covered her mouth to stifle a sob.

She longed to look in his eyes one more time. To warm her hands on his strong jaw and bid him farewell with one final kiss. But he was still as a statue, his broad back acting as a defense — against her. His posture was similar to the wall that she had built in her own heart when Jack was alive. Once again, she took part in destroying a relationship because of her lack of discipline. So impassible was this expanse between Alex and her. Such a firm declaration that she did not belong here. She was no longer welcome. There was no one begging her to stay. All the destruction she caused in this place was not laid to rest in the forgiveness of Jack, but now consumed a family she loved deeply.

As far as the owners of the Pappas restaurant were concerned, she may as well have lit the match.

CHAPTER EIGHTEEN

Spring 1911

The gravel crunched beneath their feet as they approached the small gate to their back garden. The mine crates had endured another Castle Gate winter with little repair, and now the bright spring sunshine bathed them. Building the house had been unforeseeable practice for Alex when he and many other miners reconstructed the restaurant after the fire. To have accomplished opening his parents' business in a matter of weeks was impressive and a start to laying to rest what was left undone.

Alex followed Yanni through the gate. "This spring promises much fruit. Momma and Papa have more business than ever," Alex said aloud. "Why are you so quiet, brother?"

Yanni stopped walking and spun around. "English is my enemy, now."

"What?" Alex scratched his head. "You

have learned so quickly. It is best to know —"

"Coffey admitted the fire to his friends," his brother seethed. "Today they joked about it, Alex."

Rage burrowed through him as he latched the gate behind him. It took every ounce of control to not yank the gate from its post. The case was never solved and was tossed out quickly by the authorities. Every Greek took it as an insult, and a notion that danger was at their backs.

His brother continued, "He said your ugly fiancée was a poor replacement for the English teacher, and bragged about how he ran her off before things got unruly around here."

A familiar fire ravaged Yanni's eyes. He was tormented by the injustice of it all — and the peril his family had barely missed. Some nights, Yanni would yell out in his sleep, shouting the names of his children, dreaming that Coffey's fire had consumed their little bodies.

Most days, Alex not only managed the crew but also had the task of keeping his brother away from Coffey and his gang for fear that his vengeful thirst might be quenched. He should have never told Yanni that he suspected that it had been Coffey.

307

But now? His brother had heard it for himself, from the very mouth of the arsonist. What could they do? He couldn't shake it out of Coffey in front of the authorities. He was certain if he laid a hand on the man, it would destroy all his hard work to become foreman. Years of breaking backs and breathing dust would be wasted.

Yanni cursed beneath his breath then disappeared inside.

Alex stormed across the yard, passed by the smoking oven, then kicked an old wash bin with his boot, sending it crashing into the wire fence. These were the moments when he spoke candidly with God. His first inclination was to raise a fist to the heavens, but how could he when the children were safe and business was booming? He could not blame God; he could only thank Him.

"Alex, you look as angry as a bull." His father carried a bucket and a shovel over to the garden in the back corner.

"Yanni overheard that Coffey admit to the fire."

"Does that surprise you?" The old man began to dig up the last of the leeks. "At least it's all past us now. Goes to show how much more important family is than a silly whim."

Alex clenched his fists, pushing away the

thoughts of the woman who his father implicated. Leanna was no whim, she had been his heart.

"Filling your obligation will prove you are committed to this family," Papa added.

"I work hard as foreman, Papa. And it's all for my kin. Marriage will prove nothing." Not a day went by without him trying to convince Alex to go against his vow to never marry, especially now that his supposed bride was living under their roof.

"Come now, Alex. You know what I mean. Kara is anxious to fulfill her own obligation to her father."

"What? To take his dowry?"

"To marry as she should." His bottom lip curled inward.

Alex considered offering to pay her way back. But he knew the ways of his fellow countrymen and the shame it would bring to the family and Kara. Nothing could be done except to marry her off. He had tried playing matchmaker around Castle Gate, but the prospects were fading fast. Unfortunately, the plain young woman did not attract even the most desperate of men. When Alex insisted that she had a good nature, all consideration left each man's eyes. There was no use. Kara would either remain a spinster in a foreign land, or Alex would have to give in to his duty and forgo his will.

"Every woman is blessed by marriage." His father pointed the hand shovel at Alex. "And every man."

"Enough." Alex's temper boiled. "I married once. That is enough."

"Enough? What children do you have to show for it?"

"Papa —" He seethed.

His father stood up and tossed his shovel to the ground. "Do not talk to me about love again, Alex. Your momma will die a sick woman knowing you refuse to make that poor Kara an honest woman!"

"Honest? She is your guest here, not mine."

"You choose hikes instead of church, and you fall for an American. How much can we take? Now I arrange a good match. This discussion is over." Papa threw his hands in the air and strode back into the house, leaving his leeks waiting in the bucket.

Alex sighed, resisting the urge to kick the bucket holding his father's vegetables. Papa said everything was in the past. Yet all was left undone. Especially one matter that was of no concern to his father — his broken heart. How could he talk his heart out of loving a woman he'd never see again?

He could not face Papa right now. He

310

headed back down to the restaurant to work on his walking stick.

The restaurant was quiet this afternoon. Sunshine poured through the pristine window he and Yanni had installed together.

"Watch the *zimaropita*, Alex. I have to get to the grocer's," Momma said as she headed to the door, wrapping a scarf around her head.

"Okay." He pulled a chair into the flood of light pouring in, finding joy in the warmth, forbidding any other thought to torment him right now.

Around three-thirty, Kara and the children appeared at the top of the hill beyond the coffeehouse. Alex tried to forget the woman who Kara replaced after school each day. Yet he could only imagine Leanna's beauty blossoming all the more on a spring day like this.

He abandoned the bright window and headed to the back table and sat with an unfinished hiking stick and his carving knife. The new bell on the door jingled as Maria and Teddy ran inside. Kara followed behind.

"Hello, Thios Alex!" Teddy raced around the chairs and tables and called out to Maria, "I am first!" He disappeared through the kitchen door to the backyard, no doubt.

311

"You are a weasel!" she called, not far behind him.

"Good afternoon." Kara smiled in her usual shy way, taking a seat across from him.

"Hello. The sunshine creates little monsters this time of year." He tossed his head toward the kitchen door then chuckled as he continued to carve.

"Yes. The streets are very noisy back in my village once school is out," Kara said, a wash of sorrow filling her face. She was plain, thin, and quiet. Poor Kara was as subtle as a mouse nibbling when it was time to eat, squeaking to be heard only when it was necessary. Mostly, she ducked in the shadows and seemed to spy everyone from a distance.

Guilt tore Alex's heart in two different directions. One was in his regret for allowing Leanna to leave without any information on how to reach her, and the other was his compassion for Kara. She'd traveled all this way, patiently waiting for his acceptance.

He continued to slice off more and more of the knobby stick.

"Are you making that for your Sunday walks?" she asked.

He nodded, not looking up. His hikes had become filled with prayer and reading a

312

Bible — or the Good Book as Tommy's grandmother had said.

Kara sat and watched as curled wood shavings hit the floor and the table. Alex grew agitated at the silence. He opened his mouth to speak, but the knife slipped and sliced his thumb.

"Oh, no!" Kara sprang up and ran to the kitchen. She hurried back with a wet cloth and helped Alex wrap it around his gushing finger.

"Thank you," he mumbled. The searing pain lessened with pressure.

"Are there any bandages?" Her eyes were big and round with concern.

"Do not worry, Kara. It is just a cut." He could not shake the tenderness in his voice.

Didn't she deserve to be cared for a little, though? In a way, he was the reason that she was one of three Greek women in this teeming town of bachelors. What would it hurt to show her some of the compassion that she was so ready to give him?

A thin layer of fog fell early on Sunday. Alex crossed the street cautiously, dashing past the rear wheels of a rattling wagon.

"Alex!"

He looked over his shoulder. Kara ran up with one hand clutching the corners of a black head covering beneath her chin, and his hiking stick in her other hand.

"You forgot this." She handed him the stick. "It would be a shame to not use it after spending so much time working on it."

"Who told you to bring it?" Was this Momma's scheme to get them together once again?

Her brows dipped with hurt. "I just thought you'd miss it for your hike."

He tapped the stick on the ground. "I am sorry."

"Do you mind if I join you?" She lowered her eyes. "I don't feel like sitting among all those men at church this morning."

He shrugged his shoulders then turned to hide a grimace. Only one person accompanied him on his hikes. First, she takes Leanna's place in caring for the children, and now she is here with him on Sunday. Life was spinning like a top, and he had lost control of where it would stop.

Perhaps this was the best thing, though. Replacing all those memories that tortured him day in and day out.

They walked for a long while without speaking. The fog lifted once they started on the rocky path to the formation. Indian paintbrush speckled the grassy patches on either side of them — colorful freckles that brightened the otherwise stark landscape.

As they trekked farther ahead, he barely looked at the place where he and Leanna had sat, and continued around the rock wall.

"This is nice." She wandered around the area, seeming to avoid crushing the pretty red wild flowers. "So different than the mountains back home, though."

"Yes. It feels like the desert here most summers."

"Why do you choose this place on Sundays, instead of church?"

Alex was taken back by her forwardness. It was so unlike her. "I find God is closer here than anywhere else."

Kara stared at her feet. "I see."

"Do you?"

"Not really." She looked up and laughed. Her face gleamed. "But I see you when you return on these days, and you have some peace that you didn't have before. So I guess, in a way, I see." Her smile was more comforting than it had ever been.

He grinned. "My peace doesn't last long with my mother nagging and my father meddling in my affairs."

Her expression faded to one of distress. "It is all my fault."

"No." Alex wished he could shovel it back in. "Don't say that." He enjoyed her smile much more than her frown. "They are like that always. Long before you arrived."

"I understand that," she said. "Each parent has their specific way to irritate us." She laughed again, and Alex couldn't help but chuckle, too. "My mother nagged me the entire way to the boatyard. I guess she had good reason. I promised to run away as soon as —" Her eyes wobbled with regret.

"Run away?" He raised his eyebrows in a teasing way. "So I am not the only one who did not agree to this arrangement wholeheartedly?"

Kara shook her head quickly. She slumped down on a boulder, removing her head covering and tying it around her wrist. "If we weren't struggling so much, I think my father would have allowed me to stay. But my dowry is not sufficient for the man who —" She bit her lip.

He knelt down beside her. "Did you have another proposal?"

"I am — was in love with another man," she whispered.

Alex smiled with a fresh wave of relief washing over him.

"We were in love with each other," Kara continued. "But his father expected a much larger dowry. There really was no hope for us —" She sniffled. "And then when your father began to correspond with us, Papa took it as a sign that there might be some future for me. America seems to promise such things to many people."

"Yes, I know America's lure." But how long ago that seemed now. Now that he had forgiven God and himself. "America has much."

"You fell in love with an American woman," she blurted simply. As a fact.

He nodded.

"Perhaps we are meant to be together, Alex." Her lip quivered. "Neither of us can promise our hearts to each other, but then again, we find ourselves here with much expectation from our families."

He grimaced. "To marry without love? Is that enough for you? I have married before. But you? Will you deny yourself love for the rest of your life?"

Her face fell.

Alex realized that he spoke a harsh admittance — that there was no chance at loving her. "I cannot promise love, Kara. I don't know how to forget yet. Maybe one day, but memories are everywhere in Castle Gate." He looked about the place, remembering how difficult it had been for Leanna to live here with memories of Jack. He understood her pain now. But his was worse, because

317

they were both living and breathing, even if they were worlds apart. He clenched his jaw then relaxed it enough to say, "A marriage between us will only work if you are sure that love is not expected."

Alex stood up and shaded his face from the sun. He searched himself once more and knew for certain.

He could marry again.

But to love? That was impossible.

CHAPTER NINETEEN

Salt Lake City

Leanna had bought a hat. A fine, simple hat — white as the temple in Salt Lake's center, and nothing that would suit a coal town. Salt Lake City promised to be a refuge from all that she left behind, at least for a season. Now, an opportunity rose to leave behind more than just her past, but her very present.

Leanna folded the letter, tossed it on her desk, then peeked down the hallway.

Bethany bustled about the foyer, primping the bouquet of flowers in the alcove and calling out her final directions to the cook before the guests arrived.

"Oh, hello, Leanna!" She waved a feather duster at her.

"I'll be out soon." She quickly ducked back into her room, biting back a frown. How could she consider a position in San Francisco, now? Her cousin's letter, offering her employment, had mentioned Leanna's "dire predicament among miners," triggering the very thing Leanna had promised not to think on during these weeks at the Scotts — her changed opinion of Castle Gate.

No matter the comfort of this tidy home, she lay her head on her pillow each night, wrestling with her longing to return to Castle Gate one last time. What would she do when she got there? Scold Mr. Coffey and beg Mr. Pappas to reconsider his own tradition? And then there was Alex — the greatest reason that she refused to think about Castle Gate. Alex's dismissal had been as clear as the mountain sky. They were over. She could not expect anything more.

Leanna sighed, pinning her loose locks beneath the wide-brimmed hat. An old dream might finally come true. She'd consider the offer from her cousin another day. Nothing could be said until Tommy moved to the next grade in school.

She would not run away just yet.

Bethany had become a dear friend, more than an employer. She even trusted her with all that happened in Castle Gate. And it seemed she valued Leanna's friendship just the same, especially being married to such a man as Dr. Scott. Leanna might be more useful as a friend than a tutor around here. Bethany needed encouragement often as her self-esteem was at Dr. Scott's mercy, just like their son's.

Tommy's slate sat atop her desk, a stark black-and-white example of life under this roof. She picked it up and shook her head sadly. His letters were absolutely perfect. Just as expected by Dr. Scott. The poor boy had rubbed his fingers raw fixing them upon his father's request.

"This will have to wait." She took the letter and tucked it in her drawer.

"They are here, Leanna." Bethany's voice warbled with excitement outside her bedroom door.

"I'll meet you outside," she said, pinching her cheeks and praying for peace — and patience.

The french doors were propped open at the end of the hall, the scent of blooms drawing her to the gathering. The bricked patio was dressed with colorful potted plants and ivory, wrought-iron furniture. Bethany and her visitors had already taken seats around the table, and she motioned for Leanna to do the same.

"Priscilla and Mildred," she said, "I would very much like to introduce you to my good friend and Tommy's tutor, Leanna McKee."

A tall, slender woman adorned with a tight graying bun reached out her hand for a shake. "Very pleased to meet you. I am Priscilla Edmond. This is my younger sister, Mildred."

A pretty young woman smiled brightly. "Very nice to meet you, Miss McKee." Two dimples graced her cheeks, and her blue eyes sparkled.

Bethany began to serve lemonade in fine glasses. "Tell me, Miss Edmond, have you enjoyed your tour with St. Mark's? I do hope that my husband treats the nursing students as kindly as he does the nurses, so I've been told."

"I am certain Mildred hasn't the time to converse with the doctors," Priscilla spoke for her sister. "She has already begun classes." She placed her glass on the table while her younger sister lowered her eyes, sipping her lemonade.

"As with all the physicians at St. Mark's, Dr. Scott has a wonderful reputation." Mildred stirred her lemonade with a spoon and glanced up with another smile. Her eyes danced as if they spoke of debuts and balls, not the nearby nursing program.

"Good afternoon, ladies." Dr. Scott appeared at the door, and every woman straightened in her seat. His fists rested on his chest as he clutched the lapels of his waistcoat.

"Dear! Are your ears itching? We were just talking about you." Bethany offered him a genuine smile.

"About me?" Dr. Scott returned a rare grin. "That must be quite a boring subject for such a pretty party as this."

"Absolutely not," the older sister said, much too seriously for such a conversation.

Mildred swatted at her hand, all the while keeping her eyes on the doctor. "Oh Sister, you must recognize when one speaks in jest. If you know Dr. Scott at all, you would realize he is quite the opposite of boring." She giggled then turned her attention to Bethany. "Your husband gives quite an interesting lecture for our nursing class. A perfect mixture of seriousness and entertainment."

"Entertainment?" The word slipped from Leanna's mouth. How unlike his philosophy for strict instruction of his son. She gave Dr. Scott a respectful nod. "My perceptions of nursing school are certainly misguided."

He clamped his lips above his smartly trimmed beard then puffed his chest a bit. "*Entertainment* might not be quite the right word, but it is a welcome challenge to teach beyond handwriting and simple arithmetic."

He cleared his throat. "I must tend to paperwork, ladies. Good day." He bowed his head, spun around, and was gone.

Heat crawled up Leanna's neck. Why had she spoken at all? It infuriated her that Tommy's father was quick to criticize him — and her, it seemed. Was her work not valued at all? She picked up her glass and gave a sideways glance to Bethany as she sipped. There was nothing on her face to reveal she'd been offended. But then again, Leanna was certain that the only thing on Bethany's mind was how to turn on her husband's charm so effortlessly when guests were not present.

"A kiss good-bye." Leanna muttered the subtitle of the newspaper article as she slowed her pace on the city sidewalk. More than a hundred young women were burned alive in a shirtwaist factory fire in New York City the day before, and the *Salt Lake Tribune* gave graphic detail to the horror of it all.

Women flung themselves to their deaths, chased by flames. The immigrant men, women, and children wept while waiting to discover if their loved ones had perished. The article sent daggers into Leanna's soul, and the wailing she once heard from a

Greek funeral in Castle Gate unleashed itself in her mind as she continued to read.

But her heart ceased to beat for a moment at the part of the article subtitled "A Kiss Good-bye." She scoured the sentences with burning eyes:

> They looked out of the window at the rapidly spreading flames and then the man enfolded the girl to his breast and pressed a kiss on her lips. She jumped to her death on the pavement below and he followed a moment later.

She looked up from the paper, regretful that she had continued reading. Crowds of people passed by in solemn quiet. Everyone knew what had occurred thousands of miles away.

If Leanna had returned to the East Coast, she was sure that she'd get caught up in the uproar this article would bring to her activist friends. No doubt they were planning now how to demand better working conditions in Boston. Her parents would have been appalled if she'd joined that effort — owning a large factory of their own.

Yet she'd rather stand here on this spring morning in the heart of Salt Lake City, thinking about the cruelty of her parents' creed. It was better than what her heart begged her to dwell on — the two lovers who perished together. The two who kissed their last amid the flame.

A wicked fire stole away her love just the same — but by God's grace, Alex lived. Even if they both left the fire unscathed, her heart was singed forever.

She hurried to church and settled in a pew. The incident was mentioned from the pulpit, and a prayer was spoken for the victims and their families. Leanna prayed for Castle Gate. Fresh gratitude spilled from her prayers as she thought about the time she spent in that town. Her heart softened there, and she'd learned much in the face of dangers similar to those faced by the New York victims — a mine was dangerous work, having stolen her husband, and the prejudice of certain men had proved nearly as dangerous.

Perhaps an article like this would stir their compassion, too?

She rolled her eyes for even considering that Mr. Coffey was capable of such a thing.

After the service, Sally Crawford came up beside her, wrapped her arm around her shoulders, and gave a squeeze. "Hello there, Leanna."

"Hello." She smiled at her friend. It was a

relief to smile. "How are your nursing studies going?"

"They are progressing along. I see your employer often." Sally searched Leanna's face with a determined look. "Do you want to take a stroll?"

Leanna narrowed her eyes, wondering why she'd asked. They often walked together to the trolley stop out of habit. Sally hooked arms with her, gave a quizzical look, then tugged her along. The noise heightened with each step as a couple automobiles buzzed past carriages and the churches emptied onto the walks.

Sally pressed close, speaking beneath their hat brims. "Dr. Scott's demeanor had me pay close attention to him these past weeks."

"I have learned he might be quite a different man when he's instructing you in nursing school," Leanna said. "If he's anything like he is at home, I wonder if you are crippled by his expectations." Not any different than her own father, really.

Sally's green eyes glistened in the bright spring sunshine. "At first, Dr. Scott's stoicism was obvious when he assisted in demonstrations, as well as in his lectures. Mrs. Scott is a saint, isn't she?"

"Bethany is a wonderful friend." Leanna sighed. "And receives similar attention, or lack thereof from the doctor."

"Lately though" — Sally flicked a glance at Leanna — "I've noticed that he is only a man of stone . . . to some."

"What do you —" Her stomach dropped, not because of Sally's words, but what she saw ahead: a familiar couple with a dark-haired woman by their side.

Penelope and Yanni.

"Sally, this must wait. I have someone to speak to. . . ." She rushed through the crowd, desperate to talk with them. If she couldn't return to Castle Gate, how wonderful to be able to speak with them right here in Salt Lake City. She had so many questions. Had they recovered from the fire? Was everything back to normal in Castle Gate? Were restaurant repairs under way? And —

Her mouth went dry. She slowed her pace.

What else would she discover? She shouldn't find out. Three months was hardly enough time to mend her broken heart. Witnessing such tension in her employer's marriage hadn't helped her heal quickly. It only tempted her to regret all the love she'd given up and the person who'd let her go.

She approached the awning of the dress shop where Penelope chattered in Greek to the other woman. Just ahead, Yanni admired a parked automobile along the curb.

"Penelope?" Leanna's voice cracked, and she cleared her throat.

"Meesus McKee?" Penelope's brown eyes widened, so similar to Maria's. She looked back at the woman next to her, and Leanna realized what they had been admiring in the window. The shop was closed, but its display was obvious.

A wedding dress.

Was this the woman sent from Greece to marry Alex?

Leanna stumbled back. Yes, the photograph. It was the same woman.

Life had rolled forward for everyone. Just as it should have. The woman meant for Alex had arrived, hooking arms with Penelope as if they were — sisters.

She was right. She did not need to find anything out.

"I must go." Leanna nodded quickly then spun on her heel.

Yanni's voice called out, "Meesus Mc-Kee?" but she didn't respond. How could she? It was much too obvious that she had intruded on a family outing.

And she was not a part of that family. Nor would she ever be.

Perhaps San Francisco was a wise place to go. At least she would have true family. Even if her cousin was closely knit to relaying

329

information to her parents, at least she would not have to borrow kin. She'd done so with the Scotts, and she'd considered it with the Pappas family. Perhaps it was time to move on for good.

Everyone else appeared to be doing so.

CHAPTER TWENTY

Alex jaunted across the street, taking determined strides back to Salt Lake's Greek neighborhood where he stayed with a friend. Tomorrow, he would ride the train back to Castle Gate. His heart was shadowed in defeat. He couldn't bring himself to continue on this ridiculous venture.

What was the point?

At first, he had convinced himself that a trip to Salt Lake City was necessary. After all, he needed to find a new waistcoat for the wedding and Momma needed ingredients for Easter. Yanni reluctantly gave him the name of the shop where they had seen Leanna last Sunday.

Yesterday, he forwent enjoying a beautiful Saturday and boarded a train instead, staying the night with an old friend from his days in the copper mines. This morning, he stood at the corner near the dress shop and a busy trolley stop, keeping watch for a blond beauty.

Last time they saw each other, he'd kept his back to her and demanded that she leave. Would she ever know how much he still loved her? He must tell her before he closed his heart forever in an arranged, loveless marriage.

He could never marry Leanna, but he could not live in regret like he had with Helena. She had begged him not to leave Greece, and so he left a note before boarding a boat to Athens. He hadn't known that he'd never see her again. He must share his heart with Leanna one last time and move forward with his life.

His pulse sped up when he saw her leaving the steps of a church, and she had no idea that he was there, watching. Leanna's smile glowed from beneath an elegant hat, and she hooked elbows with another woman.

He began to slice through the crowd toward her. As he did so, he caught heated looks from miffed gentlemen and their china-doll wives, and he received the same narrowed stares as he had from Coffey and his friends.

A Greek in Castle Gate was frowned on in Salt Lake City, just the same.

" 'There is no darkness but ignorance,' "

he muttered to himself. Then realization dawned on him like the bright light of the exit after rounding a curve in the dark mine.

He admitted the truth to himself. He partly hoped Leanna would convince him to forgo marrying Kara. To rekindle the plan to leave Castle Gate and prejudice behind and start life together — somewhere new.

But was there any such place? Salt Lake City was certainly not.

And besides, why would he expect Leanna, this beautiful woman who seemed happy and settled, to leave all this comfort for him? She'd done that once with Jack.

It seemed that both Leanna and he were given past mistakes to learn from and move forward. She had. Now he must.

Perhaps he was trapped by a different darkness — led down an ignorant path of his heart's whim.

No, he couldn't intrude once more on Leanna McKee.

"Alex Pappas?" The unwelcome voice of Anthis turned his head. He sat on a stoop with a newspaper spread out in front of him. "You come on a Sunday to pay me?"

"Pay you?" Alex sneered. "We are square, Anthis."

The labor agent shrugged. "Well, then, tell me, when is the wedding? I have yet to receive an invitation." He stood and folded the paper.

"It is next month," Alex said, gritting his teeth. He hesitated then continued reluctantly, "We will be sure to send one."

Anthis chuckled. "My, you don't seem like an eager groom at all." He let out a snort. "You are past due on one thing, and that is a family, Alex. One of your own, and in-laws. Perhaps, you will convince your bride's family to come over, too? There's no better place than America, is there, Alex?" He patted his shoulder.

And for once, Alex agreed with the man. Yes, America was his home and his family's home. But why did he feel like a stranger to so many of his adopted countrymen? He'd become an unwelcome guest. Especially when love led him astray.

"You are proving my life motto," Anthis continued. "Greeks are strong enough to carry on tradition no matter if it's in the Uinta Mountains here or the Pindus range at home. You are a good man to marry that woman. Now bring her family here." The agent rubbed his greedy fingers together. He no doubt counted his future profit right there on this Sabbath morning.

"One day, Anthis, you will go out of business," Alex said, holding in his anger.

334

"Greeks will come and find their own work and need nothing from you."

"Let's pray that day is far, far away."

Alex left him. His need to speak with God increased each day. He was David, surrounded by enemies, heartbroken by his own folly.

He tried to convince himself that even if he believed that a future ahead would be free of Greek labor agents, old traditions, and American prejudice, he could not break free just yet.

The next day, he returned to Castle Gate and headed straight to bed. Sleeping was his best escape lately, and filling in for the foreman on the graveyard shift was a good excuse. After eating baklava left over from Sunday lunch, he headed to the restaurant to find Yanni.

"Maria, what are you doing?" Alex stood at the door to the kitchen. His niece was dancing with no music, her hand held out as if holding the hand of an imaginary playmate.

"I am dancing, Thios Alex."

"I see that. But to what music?" He chuckled and leaned on the counter in front of him.

"The music in my head. I must practice for your wedding." She put her arm down and stopped her dance steps. She bit her lip and asked, "Would you teach me to dance American?"

"Maria." Alex swatted his hand, not only at her but at the memory stirred by her question. He swallowed hard, trying to dissolve the rush inside him.

"Perhaps if Meesus McKee comes to the wedding, she can teach me then." Maria clasped her hands together out of delight. "I miss her so."

"She is not coming," Alex said firmly.

"Who will not come to what?" Yanni and Papa came in from the kitchen.

Heat filled Alex's cheeks. "Come Yanni, we must go."

Yanni picked Maria up under the arms, kissed her forehead, then set her down again. With a playful grin, he asked again, "Who?"

"Meesus McKee, to Thios Alex's wedding."

Papa looked at Alex then at Yanni. "Why would she think such things?"

"Meesus McKee was a friend to the family, Papa," Yanni said quietly.

"Papou, she helped us. I love Meesus McKee." Maria wrapped her arms around her grandfather's waist. "She should come."

Papa set his eyes on Alex. He lowered his

brow and dipped his chin. "What do you say?"

"No. I cannot have her at the wedding." Alex spoke as if he were under water. His mouth ached and his throat seared as he held back the emotion. He was up against a wall, containing an inevitable avalanche.

"Of course not." Yanni patted his shoulder. "Maria, that would not be fair to Alex or Leanna."

"Fair?" Their father asked, not taking his eyes from Alex. "What do you mean?"

"Papa." Yanni bounced his hands as if trying to physically lower the tension. "How would you like to show up to Momma's wedding to another man?" He quirked his lip, as if he expected a laugh from his poor joke.

"Enough, Yanni. Let's go." Alex swiped his eyes, infuriated that he was being cast like one to be pitied.

"Love is learned," Papa said. "Look at Yanni. He adores Penelope."

"I loved her since I was five, Papa."

Their father swatted a hand then pursed his lips as he walked back around the counter.

Alex picked up his pail of food and headed to the door. "Hurry, Brother. We will be late to the mine."

Yanni said good-bye to Maria then followed him through the restaurant door.

"I am not sure if I should hit you or thank you," Alex seethed.

"What?" Yanni shrugged his shoulders. "I stuck up for you. You should hug me." He chuckled. They walked in silence across the street, past the coffeehouse entrance. "Did you not find her?" Yanni spoke on a long breath.

"Of course not. It is meant to be, this arrangement between Kara and me." Alex kicked a rock in the road that skipped alongside the wall they passed.

"Love is not always learned." Yanni groaned. "I am sorry, Alex. But perhaps you can get her address from the banker; he's her employer's father, no?"

"I saw her, Yanni."

"You did?" His brother stopped walking, his mouth hanging open. "Did you speak to her?"

"No, I did not. There is too much against us, isn't there? What good is it to send Momma to an early grave and stir up more anger toward our life here?"

"It is a shame." Yanni shook his head.

"It's okay. I have peace now." Or he was begging God to bring him peace. Surely it would come after the ceremony, when everything was done. "I am marrying Kara. That is a fact."

As they approached the crown of the hill, a group of miners appeared in front of them, nearing the mine.

"I feel sorry for you, Alex. Why can't a man follow his heart?" His brother ran his hand through his hair. "Perhaps I should have Maria talk to Papa — and Coffey?" He snickered but gave Alex a sympathetic look.

"I cannot be with Leanna, even if I tried. It was a foolish attempt to find her."

"If I can prove Coffey started the fire, maybe there would be a way?" Yanni hooked his finger on his chin. "I'm already working on Papa."

"The wedding is in a month. What would you have me do?" Steam rose in Alex, as powerful as an engine on the rails. "Where would we go?"

Yanni placed his hand on his shoulder. "You do not have to get married next month. It will not solve anything."

"That is where you are wrong." He exhaled, releasing the rest of his anger. "Kara deserves a marriage. She left love behind in Greece for me. I cannot keep her a spinster for my own lost love. I will not let it ruin her."

"Alex Pappas. Always a man to come to the need of a poor woman, even at the cost of himself." Yanni mocked on dangerous ground.

"Do not bring up Helena," he said in a threatening tone. "What's done is done." Yanni lurched forward to speak and Alex stopped him with a raised hand. "Enough, Brother. It is what it is. I will get married."

CHAPTER TWENTY-ONE

Tommy ran ahead, jingling coins in his fist. "Please, can we take the trolley?"

"Very well," Leanna said, hoping that the busyness of the city would distract her thoughts for a while. It was a fine day for an outing, the sunshine and fresh air were the perfect medicine to ground her to the present. After all, life back with the Pappas family was bitterly cold, at least the weather had been. She sighed. They walked through the neighborhood, and once they arrived at the corner, Tommy sprinted farther ahead.

"Slow down, Tommy. It is not proper to run ahead of a lady like that." She adjusted her hat and tucked her parasol under her arm. He ran back then walked beside her with exaggerated wide, slow strides. His blond hair shone white in the bright day. "Thank you, sir." She smiled. An outing was just what the child needed after working so hard on his assignments.

They arrived at the trolley stop just as one pulled up. Tommy scrambled up the steps first but turned around and held out his hand to help her up.

"Thank you, gentleman," she said, then followed him back to the seat of his choice. He offered her the window seat.

"I want to watch the driver," he said.

"Ah, I see." She slid into the seat.

Tommy would not sit yet. He reached into his pockets then pressed his hand to his freckled forehead. "Oh, no," he exclaimed. "I forgot."

"Forgot what?"

"To place a penny on the rail." He opened his hand and three shiny pennies gleamed. He crumpled into the seat.

Leanna refrained from chuckling. "I am sorry." She patted his knee and the trolley began to move. "I'll do my best to remind you next time."

They sat in silence, Tommy peering out into the aisle with his back nearly turned to her. She watched through the window, enjoying the breeze that poured through the open-air trolley. Buildings and trees passed by, and busy pedestrians streamed past carriages and an occasional automobile. She was certain that her father had an automobile by now. They seemed to be the most

342

prestigious thing among men these days.

At least, men like her father.

A familiar language snagged her attention to the back row of the trolley. Two Greek priests, with their tall round hats and bushy long beards, gabbed together. How had she not noticed them before?

Her throat tightened, and she turned her attention to Tommy's fingers tracing the coins in his palm. Tears sprung in her eyes. Even the sight of a strange priest not connected to Alex except by nationality caused her emotions to roll.

"Mrs. McKee, is that my father's hospital?" Tommy pointed to the window. A horse-drawn ambulance rushed down the drive to St. Mark's Hospital.

"It is." She swiped away the moisture, chiding herself as she returned her attention to the outside world. Three nurses bustled to the stopped ambulance, their hands clutching stark white aprons that crisscrossed in the back. Two of the nurses wrote in a small book, while the other nurse assisted a man being lowered onto a stretcher.

The trolley lulled at the hospital corner while several people shuffled on and off. Two young women hurried toward the nurses, spoke with them, then rushed inside as they took off their spring hats. No doubt exchanging their civilian attire for nursing frocks.

Leanna searched the crowd for her friend Sally. She spotted her in the scene while the trolley paused. Another familiar woman poised studiously, taking notes with her posture noticeably perfected. Leanna leaned closer — yes, she was sure of it. It was Mildred, the pleasant nursing student she'd met at Bethany's.

Even from a distance, she had a spirit of cheerfulness amid her somber surroundings. Perhaps she did deserve Dr. Scott's compliment, after all. She appeared eager and engaged.

"There's my father!" Tommy pointed again, his arm reaching across Leanna's shoulder. She narrowed her eyes to spot Dr. Scott. He stood at the door where the men carried the stretcher inside. Mildred was swarmed by the crowd of nurses and students and injured men. But while most disappeared into the building, Dr. Scott had grasped one of the nurses by the elbow, holding her back from everyone. The nurse stepped back outside along the brick wall, and Dr. Scott remained slightly pressed against her with one hand on her elbow and his other arm around her waist.

In a frantic motion, Leanna tossed her parasol to the floor and leaned forward, blocking the view from Tommy. "Give me my parasol, please." Her voice shook.

"But my father — should we go see him?" Tommy wiggled this way and that as he tried to get another look.

"No. He is working. We will see him at home."

The boy relented and reached down to gather up her parasol. The trolley jerked forward, and Leanna whispered a grateful prayer that Tommy had missed the intimate gesture. Then she begged that when she looked back she would discover she had imagined it all.

She whipped her head around to catch one last glimpse to be sure. Dr. Scott was twirling a curl that had been loosed from the bun beneath the nurse's cap.

Sally's forgotten words buzzed in Leanna's mind like angry bees. *"The man is hardly cold — to some."*

She could only see the back of his head, but the nurse was in plain view. The Scott's sweet guest, Mildred, turned her flushed faced up to Bethany's husband, beaming with rosy adoration.

Leanna flung her parasol to the cushions of

her bed.

For an hour she had tried to convince herself that she had misconstrued the circumstance. But it was too obvious. Mildred's improper affection had stirred up her memory of that cold December night when she found herself lost in the rich airs of James Alcott on the plain dance floor. No doubt Alex felt just as betrayed as he would have if he'd been her husband. They had both admitted their feelings for each other, yet how quickly she had considered another man when Alex was nothing but devoted.

Had she been so heartless as to put Alex through that torture? The Coffeys had frightened her, and she was scared to love Alex, or at least show it.

She had been a coward for good reason, though.

But now, she would have a choice to be brave. Should she keep Dr. Scott's secret or tell his wife and risk shattering the heart of her dear friend?

Bethany's call down the hallway pierced Leanna's thoughts. Could she pretend to think on anything besides Dr. Scott's horrific secret?

Her stomach soured.

How could that blasted Dr. Scott have

346

such a hidden way about him? He was not only a coldhearted fiend but a bigger cheat than that Greek labor agent. Hot tears seared her eyes as she remembered discovering Jack's wager. How betrayed she had felt. It took his death followed by life alone in a coal town to find forgiveness for her husband. Betrayal was a powerful destroyer. Leanna feared that a man like Dr. Scott would hardly care to mend the broken trust with his wife.

Bethany called once again.

"Coming!" Leanna's voice rang higher than usual. She hurried down the hall, hoping that a quick swipe at her eyes and a pinch of her cheeks would paint her healthy, not burdened.

A stout figure stood in the parlor offering her fashionable hat to Bethany. A groan threatened to escape her. Mrs. Tilton was here. Leanna hesitated before entering but decided she must at least make an appearance, especially if Bethany summoned her twice.

"Good afternoon, Mrs. Tilton." Leanna offered her brightest smile.

"Hello, Mrs. McKee." She smiled without looking away from Bethany then followed her into the parlor.

"Leanna, are you well? I rarely have to

call you more than once." Bethany gave a forceful laugh. She glanced at her mother from the corner of her eye. The tension was almost palpable between the mother and daughter. Leanna understood why Bethany might want an ally in the room.

But today? If she only knew.

She bit her lip. "I am well, Bethany," she fibbed.

Once they were all seated, Bethany began to pour tea without saying a word.

"I've often admired Grandmother Bartlett's tea service." Mrs. Tilton eyed the teapot as her daughter carefully set it on the tray. "How are Tommy's studies?"

"Leanna has worked wonders," Bethany was quick to say.

"Wonders?" Her mother snorted and reluctantly settled her gaze on Leanna. In a hushed voice she said, "Well, he's not a Greek, at least there's that." She raised her cup to her lips.

Bethany rolled her eyes with more good nature than Leanna would have ever mustered up in the face of her own parents. The woman had abundant patience for those in her life who deserved much less.

Mrs. Tilton lifted her eyebrows at Leanna as if she expected a response. "So, Mrs. Mc-Kee, do you have anything to say?"

348

Both women waited for an answer with eyes cast in her direction. If she must sit there and bear such a tactless woman as Mrs. Tilton, she may as well ask a question she had so often wondered about. "Whatever happened to that restaurant on Main? It was scorched to a crisp last I saw it." She took a sip of her tea. "At least it was Greek." Her emphasis on the last word was a sharp weapon, one she couldn't resist.

Could this woman, or any of the arrogant miners back in Castle Gate, realize the danger in their prejudice?

Mrs. Tilton paused before taking another sip. She then gulped, loudly. A sneer transformed her face, and she narrowed her eyes. "Funny you should mention that. It seems that you would know such things according to Mr. Pappas."

Her heart stopped. She nearly dropped her tea in her lap. What rumors had spread?

"Good heavens, Mother. What do you mean?" Bethany exclaimed, shooting a knowing look at Leanna.

"That Greek man visited Father the other day, insisting on obtaining your address." Mrs. Tilton shook her head. "Did he really think your father would hand out your address to any old immigrant?" She swallowed a sip of tea. "He claimed that our tutor here was a good acquaintance of his family's." Mrs. Tilton scoffed.

"I was a good friend. His niece and nephew were in my care just like Tommy is now —"

"I believe it was their father, not their uncle, who inquired." Mrs. Tilton fluttered her lashes and took another sip.

"Oh," Leanna murmured, flooding with embarrassment.

"It is a good thing that it was not the uncle, wasn't it, Mrs. McKee?" Mrs. Tilton glared at her. "Your interest in that man was quite known around town."

Leanna's nerves shook with anger and humiliation. "Mrs. Tilton, I was a good friend of the family. The children —"

"The children, the children. Yes. We know," she snapped. "It doesn't matter anyway. What's done is done."

Yet so much was left undone it seemed. Why would Yanni search for her? Perhaps San Francisco was a safer place to be? Salt Lake City was proving to be a poor bandage to her easily affected heart.

"Bothering a busy banker for an invitation to a wedding that you would have no time to attend. It just seems foolish for him to ignore —"

Leanna's cup tumbled from her fingers

350

and spilled tea down the front of her dress. She popped up and dabbed at it with a napkin, not sure if she was soaking up anything. Her vision was blurred with tears.

"Here, let me help you." Bethany stood, blocking Mrs. Tilton from further view of Leanna's face. "I will find out more. Go, now," she barely whispered.

Leanna rushed out of the room, down the hall, and threw herself on her bed.

The wedding was soon. Penelope and that woman were most likely shopping like all brides-to-be and their families. She grabbed a handkerchief and wiped her eyes then opened her desk drawer. San Francisco seemed her only option. Surely the western town was more progressive. At least she didn't know most anyone there — the bitter thread that attached her to women like Mrs. Tilton was much too easy to slice with her anger.

A wild storm set off at the woman's remarks about Greeks — it was nothing short of the ignorance of her parents or the many factory owners who took advantage of poor immigrants, driving them to work in hideous conditions, just like the papers reported.

She was one woman. Not a sewing circle with political connections to make a difference. What could she do? She wanted so badly to fight the injustice, to prove the value of women like Mrs. Pappas and Penelope, and men like Yanni, and of course, Alex.

"Darkness is but ignorance."

And the darkness snuffed her out. And she let it. Mrs. Tilton only reminded Leanna of her cowardice.

"May I come in?" Bethany peered into her room through the ajar door. She did not wait for an answer but sailed through the room and sat right next to her on the bed.

"I apologize if I've put you in a tight spot." Leanna sucked in a jagged breath.

"Don't worry about her." Bethany patted her knee.

"I thought I was at peace with it all. Perhaps, Castle Gate is not far enough —"

"If you love him as I love Dr. Scott, then you would give up everything for him no matter society's cost." Bethany's words were quiet but seeped in conviction. She had given up her own religion to follow Dr. Scott. If only to be deceived. An unbalanced price.

"Bethany —" Her throat twisted shut. How could she add to the sorrow of the day with such tragic news for her friend? She couldn't. It would be selfish to push aside her problem and present a massive one for

Bethany.

"Yes?"

"You are stronger than I am, to give up so much for love." Leanna sniffed. "Besides, nothing would change if I went back." Nothing, except finding out that Alex might be in love with his soon-to-be bride.

CHAPTER TWENTY-TWO

Bethany sat in her usual spot at the simply laid dining table wearing a gorgeous dress of royal blue silk. Her face was aglow. Had Dr. Scott's charming interlude on the back porch given his wife undue hope? Leanna ground her teeth, unable to eat her salad. The man gave more attention to his food than to his beautifully adorned wife.

"I am famished," he admitted as he tucked his napkin onto his lap and began to eat.

Hurt glanced Bethany's brow, and then she also ate, chattering between bites as always.

Leanna refrained from yanking the man's stiff collar to force him to pay attention. "Bethany, you look beautiful tonight," she declared during a moment of silence.

Bethany appeared startled by the compliment. She let out a giddy laugh. "Thank you, dear."

"Don't you think so, Dr. Scott?" Leanna

challenged.

His wife gave her a quizzical look but then looked at Dr. Scott with expectancy. He stared at her for a moment, his face without emotion. He nodded and said, "Lovely." When he looked down, his jaw flinched.

If it came with such ease for the guilty man to ignore his wife, Leanna doubted that he'd ever reveal his secret. There wasn't an ounce of confession in his cold spirit.

"The hospital is busier than usual," Dr. Scott continued. "A cartful of miners came in." He raised a fork to his mouth then stopped and shot Leanna a look. "Actually, they are from the mine at Castle Gate. Your neck of the woods."

Bethany slowed her utensils and gasped.

"Oh?" Leanna swallowed hard, resisting to appear too eager. "Any serious injuries?"

"A Greek has several broken bones, and the Japs have serious methane poisoning. Seems to be an all-out rescue mission down there. They say some of the miners are trapped. Don't know who is alive. Our beds are full now. If we have any more men brought in, we may have to set up tents outside like we did for typhoid a couple of years ago." Dr. Scott shook his head and continued eating. "What a mess."

She shot a panicked look at Bethany.

"Which Greek man?" Her voice was barely audible, her breath trapped beneath the lace trim at her diaphragm.

Dr. Scott was oblivious to her question as he began on his soup.

"What is the name of the Greek, darling?" Bethany arched her brows. "Perhaps Leanna knows him. She did teach the Greek children for several months."

Leanna mouthed "thank you" to her dear friend.

Dr. Scott shook his head. "I cannot recall." He snapped a bite from his fork then cocked his head. "Those Greeks have the most horrendous names. Nick Georgio-something? I cannot remember."

Was it the same Nick who was Alex's friend from the restaurant? He'd sat in front of the boardinghouse that day of their hike. A shudder went through her. The thought of that mine devouring more men frayed her nerves. Jack had been its last victim.

Fear strangled her heart. Who was trapped that might need saving now? She'd lived three months without answers to her questions about the Pappas restaurant and Alex's arranged betrothal. There was no doubt in her mind that she would never live fully without knowing if Alex was safe or —

There was only one way she could be sure.

She'd have to find out for herself. She barely touched her food. Bethany's continuous chatter was distant noise.

Leanna must visit the hospital tomorrow and find out whatever she could. She glanced over at Dr. Scott, consumed by his food.

Would she witness more of his charades, though? Perhaps her reason to visit would be twofold.

Dr. Scott stood at the end of the hospital corridor, standing over a silver tray and pulling on cotton gloves. All sorts of tools sparkled in the afternoon sunlight. Leanna prayed for courage as she continued toward him. Her pulse thumped in her ears. If this did not go well, she had only one choice ahead. San Francisco. Perhaps that was where she belonged all this time. But two people stopped her from making a final decision — Bethany, who'd soon need a friend more than ever, and Alex.

"Good afternoon, Mrs. McKee." Dr. Scott peered over his glasses.

"I hoped to visit the Greek miner brought in yesterday," Leanna said. Her mouth snapped shut. Could she be so bold? The doctor's manicured mustache twitched and he raised an eyebrow. "And there's —"

"Mother Tilton had mentioned your favor for the immigrants," The doctor interrupted her just as he did so often his own wife.

She narrowed her gaze. "*And* you have your favorites, too, don't you, Dr. Scott?" She instinctively placed her hands on her hips. Employer or not, he was scum. She glared at him.

He took a step back and straightened his coat. "Mrs. McKee, what is this about?"

"Ah, I cannot possibly know your secret, can I? How could a person such as myself, the mediocre tutor, know anything of the good doctor's affairs? And by affairs, I do mean one in particular." She lowered her voice and leaned forward. "How do you bear the weight of betraying the one woman who's remained loyal to you all these years? And with a woman whom she's so cordially invited into your home."

Dr. Scott's lip trembled, and he clutched the silver tray. The clatter echoed down the hall.

His reaction was satisfying. Leanna continued, "Yes, Dr. Scott. I know."

He fumbled for a handkerchief and wiped his brow. "This really is no concern of yours —"

"Your dear wife is my friend. It is my concern," she snapped. "Bethany adores you and will do anything for you. If there is any decent bone in your body, you would cut off Miss Mildred Edmond at once. If you do not tell Bethany about your folly, then as her friend and confidante, I must." Brushing past him, she recalled feeling this justified when she scolded Mr. Coffey for his jealous hatred.

What would it have felt like to have confronted him after the fire? She never approached him, didn't even see him after that night. She slipped out of Castle Gate without so much as a squeak of courage.

Leanna's mouth was dry like the cotton on the tray. She'd taken courage in fighting for her friend's heart.

But what of her own?

How did she walk away from Castle Gate, months ago, without so much as a complaint to the man who destroyed her second chance at love?

"Can I help you?" A nurse asked, stopping her at the double doors to the next wing.

"Yes, can you please take me to where the miners from Castle Gate are recovering?"

"Of course," she said and pushed through the doors, waiting for Leanna to pass through.

The nurse led her to a large room lined

with beds. She searched for a familiar face as she walked the aisle. The Japanese miners were sitting up, speaking among themselves. Their faces were covered with scrapes and bruises.

About halfway down the aisle, she saw Nick. Yes, he was the same man she'd first thought of when Dr. Scott mentioned him. His olive skin was a stark contrast to the white bandage on his forehead. His dark, unruly hair stuck up every which way, and his leg was suspended in a cast.

"Hello, Nick. Do you remember me?" She took timid steps toward him.

He stared at her with a look of confusion. She drew closer, unsure if he would know her at all. They never spoke. When she was in the restaurant, though, her blond hair was hard to miss. She stopped and leaned closer. "Do you remember me?"

"You the schoolteacher?" His accent was thick, triggering a spreading warmth in her heart. How she missed the Pappas family!

"Yes, I am Leanna," she said. "How are you feeling?"

Nick let out a raspy chuckle then winced. "Better than most." Darkness fell in his already black-as-coal eyes. He squeezed them shut and slowly moved his head from side to side. His hand, smudged with coal dust, gripped his mouth.

Leanna's spirit somersaulted and grief stabbed her without even knowing —

He slid his fingers down and gasped. His eyes popped open, and the whites glistened. "You wonder about Alex?"

She nodded slowly, taking a step back. Her spirit quivered. It might shatter into pieces at his next words.

His jaw twitched, and he pushed his head into the pillow. "I do not know. He was not in the count."

"The count? For what?"

"Those who survive."

Panic crept in from each side of her. The cold shiver of Jack's death reverberated from her memory. The morning he had died, she'd scoured the list of names provided by the coal company, but there was no Jack McKee. That was when Alex approached her, his coal-dusted cheeks streaked with tears.

"I tried, Mrs. McKee. I tried to save him —"

The darkness of not knowing where Alex was now depleted her sanity. She lurched toward Nick, gripping his blanket. Her throat burned with desperation. "Tell me, Nick," she rasped. "Is there a chance that he lives?"

His eyes grew wide again, and he scooted back. "They try to get them out. They find him." He looked away. "If he's alive."

That evening, Leanna prayed when she heard heightened voices behind the Scotts' bedroom door. Before she dressed in her nightclothes, Bethany came to her room and explained all that had occurred — that her husband had told her the horrid truth. And Leanna told her what had taken place just hours before.

"Should I have told you first?" Leanna's eyes filled with tears, mirroring those running down Bethany's cheeks.

"It wouldn't have mattered." She gathered Leanna's hands in hers, sucking back a sob. "I should have known."

"How could you have known?"

"Please, Leanna. Have you not noticed the man whom I live with day in and day out? He was not always this way. Once we settled in at church and began to mingle with his friends, it was as if a stony facade encased him." She widened her eyes, her brow furrowed with such sorrow. "He said it was me." She sat heavily on the bed and covered her face with her hands.

"No. It is not you, Bethany." Leanna wrapped an arm around her shoulders. "You have no control over his attitude or actions. Those are his choices alone."

"But he said it was the way that I am. The less eloquent, the least versed in the ways of the church and formalities. He said . . ." Her eyes bobbed with fresh emotion. "I am not good enough for him." She flung back on the bed, her head burrowed in the crook of her elbow.

"How dare he?" She bit her lip, fighting back an outburst of bitter words. She waited for Bethany to calm, stroking her disheveled hair. "Expectations are great destroyers of happiness — and love." In a quiet voice, much quieter than the fury within her, she said, "It was you who told me to follow my heart where I am most accepted for who I am. You helped me turn away Boston one last time. Bethany, no matter his criticism, you are who God made you. Do not doubt yourself."

"Thank you, Leanna. It will be difficult now — to not doubt. Especially having to spend so much time under my mother's roof."

"You are going to Castle Gate?" Leanna's stomach jilted.

"I must. He doesn't want me here —" Her lip quivered. "Tommy and I will leave tomorrow. You are welcome to come with us. There is room at my parents'. I will continue your pay as long as I have the means." She sighed then pulled herself up from the bed and turned to leave. With one last glance over her shoulder, she said, "Thank you for being here, Leanna. Funny how my one true friend was given to me by my parents." She let out a soft laugh. "Everyone has a purpose, I suppose. Even if they do wield the most impossible expectations." *Impossible* was a very fitting word. Impossibility and an expectant hope tugged within Leanna.

"I do hope you will consider returning to Castle Gate with me." Bethany stepped into the hall. The swift air from the closing door blew a strand of gold hair across Leanna's cheek.

Consider it?

She bit her lip and walked to the window to pull the shade down on a charcoal-gray dusk.

Consider returning to Castle Gate?

Leanna had already bought the ticket.

Chapter Twenty-Three

Castle Gate

The arid mountain range seemed to lean against the blue sky, threatening to pierce a giant hole against the canvas. How could such majesty wreak destruction at its foundation? A whip of panic licked through Leanna's core. She stepped off the train, clutching her one bag.

Main Street was busy with carts and horses and people. None of whom she recognized. Her eyes were hardly open during her early days in this town. And then, once she removed her pride, there was only one place where she cared to know the people here. She hurried along the street, the blazing sun promising a hot summer. Although she'd lived through a Utah summer with Jack, she could only think of the warm encounters with Alex during winter's chill.

The restaurant's newly constructed facade

appeared sturdier than before. Leanna marveled at the pristine window as she crossed the street. It was dark through the glass, yet she tugged at the door, and surprisingly, it opened.

Weaving through the empty tables, silence buzzed in her ears, and her heart was an erratic drum. Each empty chair whispered a horror into her imagination.

"No," she shouted out, gripping a chair and making her way back out the door. She must go to the mine.

"Signomi?" A sniffle in the darkness startled her.

As her eyes adjusted, a huddled figure took shape at the back of the restaurant. "Mrs. Pappas?"

Her back was hunched, and as Leanna approached, she could see shaky hands cradling a coffee cup. The woman stared at an icon on the wall.

"Meesus McKee." Without looking in Leanna's direction, she said, "I hope you come."

"You do?" She swallowed hard, forcing away memories of all that had gone awry and clinging to the hope that she was still welcome.

"Maria ask for you. She want you to pray for Alex, just like you pray when George born." Her reddened eyes searched Leanna's. "She feel God in your prayer."

"I have prayed ever since I heard, Mrs. Pappas." The whirl of emotion flooded her, and she dropped to her knees beside the woman. "Is Alex still missing?"

The woman nodded, bulging tears tumbling down her cheeks. "Yanni and Papa help."

Leanna wrapped her arms around her. Together they rocked back and forth, Mrs. Pappas wailing into her shoulder. In a desperate motion, she pushed away from Leanna.

"Go, Leanna. Go to the mine. Beg God to be with my son."

Leanna could not move fast enough. The weight of reality pressed down on her feet as she dragged them through the restaurant and up the hill to the mine.

Alex was still missing, and it had been over a day's time.

Please, Lord. Protect him. Give him strength.

She tried to focus only on the people dotted about the entrance of the mine and not the pile of empty coffins at the far side of the tracks. They waited hungrily, ready to be filled.

Yanni ran up to her with wild eyes. "Meesus McKee?"

367

"Any news?" she asked.

He shook his head, diverting his attention abruptly and taking a step back. She spun around. Mr. Pappas approached from the crest of the hill, his face unmoved as they locked eyes. A woman ran up beside him, the same woman from the front of the bridal shop. Leanna breathed in deeply, grounding her heels into the earth. From all the wavering in her past and all the silence in her heart, Mrs. Pappas's plea at least had assured her that God had her here for a reason.

"Thank you to come." Stergios tipped his fisherman's cap as if he were a stranger. His sad face was pale and tired.

"Of course, Mr. Pappas." She squeezed his hand.

The woman stepped forward and took Leanna's hands. "I am Kara." She smiled softly. "You, you are Leanna?"

She knew her name?

"Maria say you pray?" she said with a thick accent.

How had such a small prayer on that day of George's birth impacted sweet Maria? That day was filled to the brim of memories that threaded Leanna to this place.

"We pray now?" Kara motioned for the men to draw in close.

They all huddled together. The busy rescue operation continued behind them, but these men and this woman cast expectant looks at Leanna.

Faith like children — spurred from the testimony of a child. There was nowhere else Leanna should be right now — not Boston or Salt Lake City or San Francisco. All her plans faded in the light of Castle Gate.

Leanna breathed in a jagged breath. She turned to Yanni and said, "I don't speak Greek."

"Maria says you pray with power." Yanni crossed his arms on his chest. "We need that now. There's no time left."

Fear jolted through her spirit. She spied the black mouth of the cave over her shoulder.

A prayer with power.

"Heavenly Father, pour down Your power on Alex and the other men trapped —" Leanna's voice broke as Yanni muttered after her, translating her prayer for Kara and Stergios. She begged God silently to give her strength to speak as angst burst within her. "For You did not give us a spirit of fear, but of power, and love, and sound judgement." Love. Alex had more love waiting for him than most people. And Leanna's love, no matter how steadfast, was no match for the love of a father, of a brother, of a soon-to-be wife. She sighed and squeezed her eyes tighter. "Lord, protect Alex. Give him mighty strength to survive this —"

While Yanni continued muttering, Leanna opened her eyes. Kara stood across from her, her head bowed and her brow determined as she listened. This was Alex's betrothed. Leanna's own hands were in the tender grip of his rightful match.

Yanni cleared his throat. He caught her staring. She flushed and squeezed her eyes shut again. "Lord, give Alex direction now. We pray this in the name of Christ. Amen."

Kara's eyes sprung open when Yanni muttered, "Amen." She spoke in Greek to Yanni.

"You are kind to pray," Yanni said. "Kara says you pray like Alex." His jaw twitched after mentioning his brother's name. He sighed then strode over to the mining entrance. Stergios took Kara by the arm and followed his son.

Alex prayed with Kara? The man who'd cast off prayer because of his unanswered ones for his late wife? Had the same healing Leanna found in forgiving Jack, now moved Alex forward, too?

Perhaps, this was God's plan all along —

for the coal miner's widow and the Greek immigrant to break free from their past regret together. They'd conquered prejudice and expectation for a season and arrived at a place of healing.

There was enough peace in that to secure them for a lifetime apart.

Leanna tried to convince herself of that.

Darkness tricked Alex's mind. Was he awake? Asleep? Dead or alive? A deep breath filled his lungs with the familiar dust that coated him each day. He was pinned in a chamber of rock. His leg throbbed as he tried to shift his position. He was trapped beneath a fallen ceiling. If he reached his head up, he'd bang into rock, and if he tried to squirm forward, pain surged through his leg beneath a heavy weight. He was certainly the prey caught in the trap of a stony monster.

His fingers traced the low rocky ceiling until he fumbled on the mass above his leg. Could he move it? What destruction would that trigger? Perhaps it was safer to sit and wait to be rescued, something he had little faith in. He was in a small alcove of the mine. Coffey had called him there, saying that the reinforcement frame was splitting and he needed help.

371

Some help he needed.

"When you gettin' married?" Coffey had leaned up against the wall with his arms crossed while Alex did the work — alone.

"Hardly a matter to talk about down here, Coffey."

"Oh, right, boss." He saluted and chuckled. "Too bad that little kitten from your homeland didn't come here sooner. Save a lot of trouble for you and yours, huh?"

Alex stopped what he was doing and turned toward him. Was he confessing to the fire? "You are treading on dangerous ground, Coffey." Alex gritted his teeth.

"What, Mr. Foreman?" The man held up his hands with a challenging grin on his face. "Don't let me get you all in a tizzy." That was the last thing Alex remembered before the room came tumbling all around them.

His breath caught. Was Coffey nearby? He strained to listen for any breathing. All he heard was his own heartbeat pounding in his ears. He dragged his fingers along the rubble beside him and hit the base of the wood reinforcement frame as solid and upright as before the collapse.

How ironic that the very thing he had tried to repair, survived such a disaster. If it hadn't been destroyed by the fall of rock, then he knew where the entrance of the tunnel was according to the location of the post. He grabbed a fist-size piece of rubble at the left of his hip and placed it next to the post.

"Show me the way out," he muttered, squeezing his eyes closed then mumbling a prayer from his heart. "Lord have mercy," he said the supplication rising from his memory of liturgy. God was near. He could feel Him. The bright memory of Leanna beside him at the Castle Gate formation and the glow of her face as she sung in the pew overwhelmed him with strength. Such light, such beauty. He craved the light.

He must find his way out.

He continued moving rock, over and over. A small pinpoint of light suddenly pierced his eye. He worked faster. Gratefulness poured from his heart as the dot of dim light became penny-sized, then the size of his palm, then bigger and bigger. He could make out the rock around him, the ceiling above him. His throbbing leg was lodged between the ground and a flat sheath of rock. When he tried once more to wiggle it free, the pain pierced straight through his kneecap.

"Oh, dear God," he groaned, the pain producing sweat beads along his hairline.

Tears squeezed from his eyes and he rested until relief coursed through him.

"Alex?" Yanni's voice funneled through the small opening.

"Yanni, I am here!"

"We'll get you out, Brother." Footsteps padded away, and Yanni shouted for help in the distance.

Thank You, Lord.

Several minutes passed as he wrestled with the throbbing pain of his leg and the joy of the light growing wider and brighter. He relished the sound of his brother's voice among that of Greek and American miners together. Soon, Yanni's face shone down on him as if he were a looming giant.

Alex shielded his eyes with his arm and chuckled. "You are my angel, Brother."

"Say that to your bride. She refused to let us leave this morning. Said she prayed all day and all night and knew that God would protect you."

He praised God for answering that prayer, but when he closed his eyes, he could only envision Leanna.

Yanni shouted through the tunnel for a stretcher. "They'll be here soon. Is it your leg?" Now that the rock was moved, he saw the unnatural angle of his leg and winced.

"Who else was with you, Alex? Do you

374

remember? We are missing a handful more." Yanni was now crouched down, one arm leaning on the rock just above Alex's head.

"Coffey. He was with me," Alex said. If his mother were near, she'd blame the accident as a curse for the fire.

"He is missing still." Yanni did not look at him, just at the ground. As if his words declared some sort of challenge to fate, a deep moan came from his right. Yanni didn't move. He must not have heard.

Alex turned toward the moan. "Who is there?"

Another moan, but no words. He was certain. It was Coffey.

All his hate for the crooked man beside him was diluted by his sounds of pain. He was alive.

Alex's last image of Jack McKee flashed in his mind. He couldn't save him that day. And he wept for him. But now, Coffey was alive beneath the rubble and Alex felt nothing.

"Coffey, he's alive. I just heard him." He turned his head in his brother's direction.

"Are you sure it's him?" Yanni asked in Greek.

"Neh."

The two brothers stared at each other for some time.

"What if my children were in the dining room that night, Alex?" He spoke in a heated whisper. "Their blood would be on his hands."

And if it weren't for Coffey, Leanna would be here waiting for him. He would never have had to give up on love or marry for convenience. If Coffey's prying eyes weren't around, the Pappas family would not suffer the hardship that came with the fire, nor the animosity fueled by the American miner. If they rescued the man who hated them, Alex was sure life in Castle Gate would continue on as always — one step ahead, but a miserable man trying to push them back.

"Leave him," Yanni mumbled with disgust.

Alex wanted to agree. But he couldn't. What if Alex were the one trapped? Would Coffey rescue him?

He doubted it.

He thought of Tommy's grandmother and the Good Book she quoted. They were all the same, all under the same God's watch. Coffey may not know their shared position, but that didn't make it any less true. Alex couldn't allow ignorance to win. He must not give in to such darkness.

Yanni walked away, assisting a group of men with the stretcher. Alex searched the rocks beside him. Compassion snuffed out his hatred, and he began to dig out the rubble. Coffey's face appeared, badly bruised. His eyes fluttered open then rolled back in his head.

"Stay with me." Alex continued to remove the rubble, uncovering his shoulders. Coffey's gray eyes wobbled open and fixed on Alex.

"You'll be fine. Try and stay awake," Alex whispered.

"I . . . can't breathe."

"I know. Help is on its way. Just stay calm." He examined the load that bore down on Coffey's chest. If Alex's leg was twisted by the fall, he could hardly imagine the damage. He winced at the thought.

"Coffey, don't go to sleep, okay?"

He barely nodded then screwed his face up in pain. "I — I don't think I'll make it."

"Don't say that." What could he do? He could not reach any more rubble, and his leg was throbbing again. All he could do was pray. He squeezed his eyes closed. "Protect this man, Lord. Bring Your peace to him — to me. Please let us see the light of day again. Amen."

He looked down at Coffey.

He just stared at Alex, his eyes brimming. "Thank . . . you."

The scuffle of miners came up from behind them.

"Coffey's here!" someone shouted, and everyone began to work on the rock.

They carefully placed Alex on a stretcher. Yanni came up beside him, giving him a narrow look.

"We would be no better than him," Alex said as he winced with pain.

Yanni's jaw flinched. He placed a hand on Alex's shoulder and smiled. "You, Brother, are better than me."

CHAPTER TWENTY-FOUR

Alex grimaced at the bright sunshine, and he wrapped his arm around his face. Urgent voices spilled on all sides of him, but he couldn't open his eyes until he was in the shade of a covered wagon.

His old friend Will Jacob came up beside him. "Alex, they will take you to Salt Lake City this afternoon. You are one of the lucky ones. A load of coffins just arrived today. We expect at least twenty men have perished."

Alex drew in his first full breath of dust-free air, giving his friend a weak pat on the shoulder.

"There's a young lady who's been anxious to see you, sir." Will tipped his hat and left the wagon, ushering in someone from below.

Kara was a faithful woman. He must thank her for praying. He sure did feel those prayers.

"If only Jack had been as lucky as you,

Mr. Pappas." Leanna's words startled the fatigue right out of his aching bones. He whipped his head up, spied the fair-haired beauty, then groaned, the ache wrapping around his neck.

"Be careful." Her warm hands brushed the curls from his forehead. "You've been through quite an ordeal."

"When did you arrive?" He took her hand and held it to his chest. Her fingers tensed at first, but then she allowed her hand to relax beneath his.

"This morning." She gave him a sorrowful smile. "How are you feeling?"

"The whole of the Castle Gate spires seemed to sit on top of me, but I'll survive." Alex chuckled softly. "But seeing you is something else entirely." His heart was about to burst from his chest.

"I had to see you and make sure you were still —" She grimaced and pulled her hand from Alex's in a gentle, determined way.

"Alive?"

She nodded. "Alex, I also came here to see if there was still a chance —" She gave a nervous glance to the entrance of the wagon then back to him again. "I met Kara. She is so worried about you." Her eyes bubbled with tears. "I realize that I was presumptuous. Even if I had the chance to give Coffey a piece of my mind, I could never hurt Kara or your family."

This is the woman he should be with. She was the one who gave him hope in the dark mine, in his bankrupt faith. Leanna McKee was his heart. "Wait, Leanna —"

"I shall be just fine." She swiped a tear from her eye. "You have a lovely bride, Alex. She is perfect for your family. And as for Coffey, I suppose it would be rather harsh of me to give him an earful when death was so near him today."

"Leanna, there must be a way." He tried to prop himself on his elbows. He grunted and then fell back.

"Please, don't hurt yourself even more. Really there is nothing to discuss. You have found a match, a Greek match. And I shall go to San Francisco. My cousin has a position for me now. It is all working out — perfectly."

A rustle came from the opening, and a man boarded, lugging another stretcher up into the wagon. He slid Coffey beside Alex.

Coffey's eyes were closed and bruises ran along the entire right side of his face. Any ill feeling he had for this man must have been buried beneath the mountain. He only felt sympathy for him.

"I better go," she said with her attention

now focused on Coffey.

"Is that you Mrs. McKee?" Coffey blurted in a weak, hoarse voice, opening his eyes.

"It is, Mr. Coffey," she said. Her ivory skin flushed as if she was either embarrassed or furious. Perhaps she was both.

"I'll not forget your deed, Mr. Pappas." Coffey managed a half smile. "I ain't been much of a man to deserve such a thing."

"We are all men in need of a little grace, Mr. Coffey," Alex said.

"Some of us need it more than most." Coffey nodded at Leanna. "I ain't been very neighborly to you, either. Runned you off, and for that I apologize." He retrieved his hand from beneath the tight blanket pulled over his body, offering it to Alex. "You are a good man, Alex."

Alex flared his nostrils then smiled. He held out his hand and shook Coffey's. "Thank you, sir."

"Now, if you'll excuse me. I'd rather sleep this whole thing off." He settled back and closed his eyes.

Leanna gaped at him. "What happened?"

"More prayer, less reason." Alex winked.

She cocked her head, searching his face. "How did you know?"

"Know? I prayed over Coffey, Leanna. God was close down there."

Her brow tilted in a desperate furrow. "I prayed over you — up here."

"He listened to us both." He smiled wide and reached for her hand.

"I better go." Leanna began to scoot back.

"Please." Alex grabbed her arm. "We can work this out. Most of it is done already. Would you have ever thought that he'd apologize?" He nodded his head at Coffey.

"She needs you, Alex," Leanna whispered. "I cannot get in the way of a family. Not again." She wrestled her arm away and disappeared.

Leanna filled her lungs with the mountain air, her pace brisk as she tried her best to keep her wild emotions under control. Her heart brimmed with gratitude and grief — all for Alex.

Stergios met her, wringing his hands. "He okay?"

She forced a reassuring grin. "Yes, Mr. Pappas, he will be fine."

His blue eyes were vibrant. He placed a hand on her shoulder. "You are good friend to us." He grimaced, opened his mouth as if to continue, and instead, gave her a squeeze and walked away.

Mrs. Pappas and Kara approached from town. Kara must have run down to tell her the news.

"Ah, Leanna!" Alex's mother ran up to her and embraced her with great enthusiasm. She pulled away, her face swimming in emotion. "He safe, he safe." She patted Leanna's cheeks. "You stay now. You family." Her smile fell quickly with a glance to Kara.

A lump formed in Leanna's throat. She could not —

"He is a strong man, Mrs. Pappas," Leanna said. Mrs. Pappas spoke quietly to Kara, shrugging her shoulders. Kara nodded in a thoughtful way.

"Meesus McKee!" Yanni ran up to her. "You come to dinner tonight? Maria and Teddy see you?"

"I would love to," she said, but the tension between Mrs. Pappas and Kara was obvious. All because of her. "But I can't; it wouldn't be fair to Kara."

Leanna had seen the damage of a love triangle with the Scotts. She would not play Mildred's part in all of this.

"Kara would not mind." He smiled just like his brother. "She'll go with Alex to Salt Lake City."

Stergios came up and spoke quickly to Kara. She began to follow him but stopped by Leanna's side. "Thank you, Meesus Mc-

Kee. You are like family to them." Her teeth rested on her lip, and then she said, "I glad I meet you."

The woman continued toward the wagon.

Leanna had come here to fight for love, but perhaps she could settle with the fact that God brought her here to pray, just like Mrs. Pappas said that she wished for. This was enough. To have this final good-bye with the Pappas family without a fire or a fight. She would leave Castle Gate knowing that all was well with the people she loved the most.

She peered back at the wagon. Kara ducked under the canopy, and her soon-to-be father-in-law followed her inside.

Leanna turned to Yanni. "Thank you for the invitation. But it is time for me to leave."

Yanni stepped closer. "But —"

"No, Yanni." Leanna shook her head. "Give the children my love. This is for the best." She gave him a hug and then turned to Mrs. Pappas.

"You are family." The small woman managed in her limited English, her brown eyes intense.

Not anymore. Leanna leaned down and kissed her cheek. "Good-bye, Mrs. Pappas."

A dim light crept from somewhere to the

left side of Alex, casting a myriad of shadows upon the strange ceiling. He imagined his cot was rocking to and fro as it had the whole journey to Salt Lake City. When he turned his head, Kara stood beside him, perfectly still.

"How do you feel?" she spoke quietly.

"The same." He tried to move his body, but it was stiff. "Do I dare look at my leg?" Had they amputated? He couldn't bear the thought, although the mining company doctors were known to lop off limbs for quick repair.

"It is neatly wrapped in a cast. You have nothing to worry about. They will have you up on crutches as soon as you have food and water. And rest, of course." She sat down on a stool.

"You did not have to come, Kara. Where will you stay?"

"Do not worry about me." Her words were cool, oddly confident.

"How can I not worry?" A shadow cast over his thoughts. "You are to be my wife." He forced the words out through his teeth then immediately regretted them as hurt washed over her face. "I am sorry. This has been a hard day." Leanna surrendered because of Kara.

"I know." She lowered her eyes. "Leanna

is a beautiful woman."

"It does not matter." His father emerged from the shadows.

Alex groaned. "Why are you here?"

"Kara cannot come to this city alone."

"You were in the wagon?" A dull ache sprouted down his neck as he tried to remember. "You should be home with Momma. We are fine."

"It is good he is here," Kara said. "There is much to be settled." Once again, her confidence surprised him.

Alex's father wrung his hat in his hands. "You've gone and induced your American ways on this woman."

Alex winced with confusion. "What have I done?"

Kara stepped forward and opened her mouth to speak but was not quick enough.

"She's got it in her head that Leanna is your match more than she is. If only Meesus McKee would stay where she belonged."

"You have nothing to worry about. Even if I begged her to stay, Leanna refuses to hurt you or Kara." A different heaviness than collapsed rock pressed on his chest now.

"She is a good woman," his father admitted quietly.

"Her prayer was powerful, just like Maria

said," Kara added. "Alex, if you love her still, you cannot let her go. Love was something stolen from me back in Greece. All because of money. I cannot expect you to marry me because of a dowry. It is not fair."

Money? How were his heartstrings always attached to money? With his effort to save Helena and now with Kara.

"This is the way it is done," his father muttered.

Alex piped up. "What about love, Papa? The way it is done isn't always the only way."

"Alex, do not speak to me of such things. This is tradition. You are Greek, and Kara is a good Greek bride."

She boomeranged her gaze between the two men. "Mr. Pappas, I know your obligations to accept my father's dowry, but perhaps —"

"Money is of little concern to me." He folded his arms on his chest and began to pace. "But I cannot disappoint your father."

"My father was afraid to disappoint Demetri's with such a dowry as mine." She sank down on the bed next to Alex's shoulder. She whispered to him, "It seems that our fathers, at least, will be happy in this match."

Her heart was tender, and her love for

388

another may be just as strong as his was for Leanna.

"Papa, it is not just me who risks betraying love." His heart began to swell, and he could not keep a smile from creeping on his face. "Kara is in love with another man."

"What will I tell her father?" Papa tossed his hands up. "What will you do, Kara?"

She shrugged her shoulders. "I don't know. My dowry is too small for Demetri's father."

Alex managed to lift his hand and find hers. "You act so strong, so ready to give your life to me."

"That is the perk of being a woman. Our imagination can persuade us that anything is possible, even winning the heart of your husband, eventually."

"She is a good Greek girl." Alex's father pulled out a handkerchief and wiped his forehead.

Her eyes widened, and she kept her gaze on Alex for a good long while.

"Demetri has found where I am and sends letters even." Her brown eyes dulled.

A long sigh escaped Alex's father, and he muttered under his breath, "What will happen to us? The restaurant will be in danger again."

"I don't think it will." Alex's heart

pounded in his chest. Could this be happening? "A collapsed mine reminds men of their humanity — and the chance for mercy. Coffey is of no concern now."

"Coffey? But what about others?"

"We won't allow men to stop us from living, Papa," Alex said. "I will not. Not again."

His father glanced at him then said, "Kara will return to Greece unmarried?"

Kara shrugged her shoulders, her eyes sad and hopeless. She was at the mercy of men and money.

But Alex could change all that.

"I will help you, Kara," Alex said. Money would not stop love anymore. He squeezed her hand. "We will find a way for you to marry Demetri."

Papa grimaced then waved a hand in defeat. Alex just laughed — a long, hearty, praiseworthy laugh that bruised his ribs even more than the rocks.

Joy could not be contained.

"I have to hurry up and get those crutches. Or else my bride might run off to San Francisco."

CHAPTER TWENTY-FIVE

Loud Italian conversation buzzed in the background as Leanna sat with Bethany at a small table in the Castle Gate bakery. The aroma of baked bread filled her with warmth, just as the sunshine did outside. No bitterness chilled her now, she was a new person in this town — a soon-to-be stranger to this place that she'd called her home. Sorrow toed the edge of her resolution. Yet all was as it should be.

"Nothing?" Leanna hoped there would be good news for Bethany.

"No. He refuses to see things my way." Bethany sighed and picked at her cannoli. "We will separate and then —" She bit her lip and looked around. But she didn't have to say the word. "I will be fine once I figure out a respectable way to leave my parents once more."

"You and Tommy should come with me to San Francisco. Find a fresh start."

"Oh, dear. I cannot imagine! Honestly, Leanna, are you sure you want to journey all that way alone?"

"It was my original plan," she said. "Just like you came to my rescue when I needed to leave Castle Gate, my cousin's letter arrived just when my time in Utah was ending." She smiled at her friend. She would miss her just like the Pappas family.

Bethany stirred her tea, the spoon clinking on beat. "My mother was so worried that you would stay and sort things out with Alex." She rolled her eyes. "She has fully accepted the gossip as truth."

"Well, it was true wasn't it?" Leanna's smile pricked one cheek up. "We were so close to —" No, she mustn't think about that. She'd tried not to think about the short-lived plan of elopement. That was foolish. To run away was not brave at all. And if there was one word to describe the man who'd stolen her heart, it was *brave*. Alex Pappas was a brave, kind soul who'd found a good woman to protect and love. "Kara fits in perfectly with the Pappas family."

"It is a shame that you had to give up love for such ninnies as those miners." Bethany sipped her tea and stared off into nothingness.

"Mr. Coffey softened, actually. Practically gave us his blessing." She eyed her own finger, tracing the rim of her teacup.

"What do you mean?"

"At the mine. Supposedly he and Alex sorted their differences." She had recalled Coffey's apology over and over as she tossed and turned these past two nights. "For the first time ever, the man apologized and treated Alex like a human being. He didn't even seem to mind that I was next to him."

Bethany's mouth fell open, and she slammed her empty teacup on the table. "Then why in the world are you leaving?"

"I cannot ruin their marriage, Bethany. Kara has planned this day. I cannot take it away from her. I will not be that woman."

Bethany gave her a long narrow stare. "This is not like Mildred." Hurt invaded her blue eyes. "They are not married, Leanna. You cannot ruin something that isn't there."

"There is something, though. A promise." She finished her tea amid Bethany's disapproving look. "It's time for me to leave. The train will arrive soon."

They paid the baker's assistant and entered the bustle of Main Street. Simultaneously, they opened their parasols and strolled down to the depot.

She looked over her shoulder one last time. The Pappas restaurant was barely visible with all the carts and horses crowding the street.

"Is he back from Salt Lake?" Bethany asked.

"I don't know." She grimaced. "I shall not find out, though. This is for the best."

Bethany tucked her arm in Leanna's. "Can you imagine the uproar if you stayed? What would my mother say about such a match like yours and Alex's? Wouldn't that be a delicious controversy?" She gave a devious smile.

"Oh, Bethany. Don't tempt me to stay out of spite." She laughed and continued forward. "I might not stir up anything around here, but I will demand that you visit me."

"Of course. And thank you for standing up for me." She squeezed her arm close. "You are brave, Leanna. One of the best friends I've ever had, too."

Brave? She smiled to herself. "I know men, and women, who are much braver than I am." They stepped onto the platform of the depot. Bethany faced her. Her skin was blotchy and her eyes were red.

Leanna cupped Bethany's cheek. "Give my love to Tommy, okay?"

"Please write as soon as you get there."

Bethany threw her arms around her.

"Of course."

Leanna turned around, unable to watch her friend leave. Castle Gate would keep all that was dear to her now.

The smell of burning fuel filled the platform of the depot, and she lugged her baggage to a bench. Her first entrance into Castle Gate was nothing like today. She'd followed Jack off the train, scrutinizing the arid mountains and the simply made structures of the town. That was a descent into a dark valley of life, but now she faced a sad departure from a treasured place.

All her memories, good and bad, were at furious war inside her.

Lord, give me strength.

At that moment, the shine of a train lamp twinkled in the distance. She gathered in breath to every corner of her lungs. The long hollow whistle beckoned her to gather up her luggage and retrieve her ticket. The train's rumble shook her, a welcome distraction to all the trapped emotion. Closer, closer still, and then the train squealed to a stop.

A few passengers stepped off the train before the conductor came to the door nearest to her and motioned her forward. "Ticket, please."

Leanna handed the conductor her ticket, he punched it, and she began to approach the stairs.

A train employee appeared in the doorway. "Wait, ma'am. We have a passenger who needs some assistance deboarding. Could you please step aside?"

"Of course." She sighed and waited her turn.

The conductor ran up the steps and hopped down again with a pair of crutches in his hands. The other attendant disappeared again. He returned, escorting his passenger forward. Alex filled the entrance, clutching the man's arm.

"Alex?" Leanna blurted out. "Be careful." She rushed toward him, heat filling her neck and cheeks.

Alex reached for her hand, his strength coursing through her like an electric current. The familiarity in his every feature stole her breath.

With help from the attendant on one side and Leanna on his other, Alex hobbled down the steps and out of the shadow of the car. His brown eyes sparkled beneath untidy curls. "It looks like I was almost too late."

"Too late?" Leanna looked down at her ticket. "It seems your train is mine." Her heart sank at the words. And now a second good-bye. Or a third, really.

Why, Lord? Why now?

Alex just stood there, flashing a large smile as the conductor handed him the crutches. This was wonderful and devastating all at once. Everything inside her wanted to embrace him and tell him how much she would miss him. Yet her determination to leave was muted by the overwhelming desire to stay.

Kara emerged, stealing away Alex's attention. A dark scarf was wrapped around her black-as-coal hair. She wore a big smile also — a joy that only tormented Leanna's aching heart. Leanna turned around to retrieve her bag, trying to hide her bubbling eyes.

"Leanna, I don't think this is your train," Alex said as she composed herself with a deep breath. A tear escaped and fell on her bag. She caught another with the back of her gloved hand.

She swiveled to face him. "Yes, it is. This is the three o'clock train to —" Alex drew closer. "Well. Good-bye, Alex. I wish you all the best —"

Kara interrupted, saying, "No, I go," then patted Alex's arm. As she slipped past, she squeezed Leanna's hand. "You stay." She hurried across the platform and left the depot.

Leanna's stomach flipped. "Where is she going?"

Alex kept his gleaming eyes fixed in Kara's direction. "She is off to find her own love." His gaze captured Leanna's, electrifying the moment with all the love he'd brought to her life in Castle Gate.

Her arms pricked with a sudden wave of expectation. "I don't understand —" She shook her head.

His teeth grazed his bottom lip. "Am I speaking Greek?" He winked. "It so happens that Kara is in love with another man. A cushioned dowry was all she needed to seal her fate, a payment I was willing to make. She goes home to pack and return to Greece."

Leanna's bag slipped from her fingers and thudded on the floor beside her. Her breaths came in short, uneven bursts, and she wasn't sure she could swallow. Bethany's exasperated voice sprung in her mind, *"Then why in the world are you leaving?"*

"All aboard!" The conductor stared at her, but she couldn't move, and it appeared Alex would not let her. He blocked her from the train, his crutches firmly planted on the platform, and his attention undeniably hers.

"Leanna, do you see?" His face beamed with expectancy. "We have no excuse to remain apart now. Coffey is finished with us, and I won't be married" — he stepped closer still — "yet, anyway."

"But your father." Stergios hadn't wavered, even when his own wife seemed to outside the mine. "The man was set in his plan the last time I saw him."

"Plan? We are all foolish to think we have the best plans for ourselves, aren't we? There's something greater nudging us out of the darkness. I'm realizing that after sitting in my own ignorance all these years." A dark cloud passed quickly over Alex's features. "And Papa? Well, after months of fighting with me, he seems ready for a rest." His face relaxed and his loving smile grew wide again. "Don't worry. He knows."

She cupped her hand on his jaw, melting into his loving gaze. "I came here to fight for you, and it seems I gave up rather quickly." Even when Coffey softened toward them both. Only God could change a man's heart, yet she thought it was all up to her. "Is it really true that Kara wants to leave?"

"Yes, it is true. It seems that love wins twice today." He slid his hand over hers and clasped her fingers, pulling them over his heart. "And don't forget, Papa thinks you're pretty, according to Maria."

Leanna laughed, a deep, healing laugh that set off a warmth she'd first discovered around a table in a small Greek restaurant.

He took the ticket from her other hand and shoved it in his front pocket. "This is not part of the plan, Mrs. McKee." He grazed her forehead with his lips. Tender kisses tickled her cheek, then her jawbone, then rested softly on her lips.

"Perhaps you should keep the ticket," Alex said as they pulled apart.

"What?" Her heart skipped and heat filled her cheeks.

"The Pappas house might be a little crowded for a newly married couple, don't you think?" He squeezed her hand.

She laughed again, and they turned away from the conductor, the train, and her last chance to leave Castle Gate. Her heart was a diamond peeking out from its bed of coal, finally bright with all the love she'd found here. On the arm of her beloved Greek miner, she strolled down Main Street for all to see, assured that she had belonged in Castle Gate all along.

ABOUT THE AUTHOR

Angie Dicken is a third generation Greek American, the granddaughter of strong men and women who endured hardship to grow American roots. *My Heart Belongs in Castle Gate, Utah* is set near the birthplace of her grandfather, a Greek coal miner's son, and published 100 years after his birth. Angie is a contributor to The Writer's Alley blog and has been an ACFW member since 2010. She lives with her husband and four children in the Midwest where she enjoys exploring eclectic new restaurants and chatting with friends over coffee.

6/07

ECONOMIC TURBULENCE

ECONOMIC TURBULENCE

Is a Volatile Economy Good for America?

CLAIR BROWN,
JOHN HALTIWANGER,
AND JULIA LANE

THE UNIVERSITY OF CHICAGO PRESS   CHICAGO AND LONDON

CLAIR BROWN is professor of economics and director of the Center for Work, Technology, and Society at the University of California, Berkeley. She is the author of *American Standards of Living, 1918–1988* and a coauthor of *Work and Pay in the United States and Japan.* JOHN HALTIWANGER is professor of economics at the University of Maryland. He is coauthor of *Job Creation and Destruction* and a coeditor of several volumes, including, most recently, *Measuring Capital in the New Economy.* JULIA LANE is senior vice president and director of the Economics, Labor, and Population Department at the National Opinion Research Center at the University of Chicago. She is coauthor of *Moving Up or Moving On* and a coeditor of *Confidentiality, Disclosure, and Data Access.*

The University of Chicago Press, Chicago 60637
The University of Chicago Press, Ltd., London
© 2006 by The University of Chicago
All rights reserved. Published 2006
Printed in the United States of America
15 14 13 12 11 10 09 08 07 06   1 2 3 4 5

ISBN-13: 978-0-226-07632-4 (cloth)
ISBN-10: 0-226-07632-6 (cloth)

Library of Congress Cataloging-in-Publication Data

Brown, Clair, 1946–
   Economic turbulence : is a volatile economy good for America? / Clair Brown, John Haltiwanger, and Julia Lane.
        p. cm.
   Includes bibliographical references and index.
   ISBN-13: 978-0-226-07632-4 (cloth : alk. paper)
   ISBN-10: 0-226-07632-6 (cloth : alk. paper) 1. Business cycles—United States. 2. Statics and dynamics (Social sciences) I. Haltiwanger, John C. II. Lane, Julia. III. Title.
   HB3743.B76 2006
   338.5′40973—dc22

                                                                                        2006012469

TO

RALPH GOMORY

NANCY GORDON

AND

FREDERICK "KNICK" KNICKERBOCKER

WHOSE COMMITMENT TO, AND UNDERSTANDING OF,

THE IMPORTANCE OF THE LEHD AND SLOAN INDUSTRY

CENTERS PROGRAMS MADE THIS BOOK POSSIBLE.

Contents

Acknowledgments

The research for this book was funded by an Alfred P. Sloan Foundation grant to the Urban Institute and the University of Maryland. We gratefully acknowledge the support of the Sloan Foundation as well as the support and encouragement of Gail Pesyna and Michael Teitelbaum, who initially also helped support the formation of the Census Bureau's Longitudinal Employer-Household Dynamics Program (LEHD) in 1998.

Researchers from five Sloan Industry Centers and the U.S. Census Bureau joined forces to examine the impact of economic turbulence on economic growth, job ladders, career paths, and earnings inequality. That partnership led to the writing of seven research papers that underlie the work summarized in this book. Thus, although there are three named authors, the book had many intellectual contributors. Julia Lane led the final drafting of the book, and she led the research on the distribution of earnings. Clair Brown led the research on job ladders and career paths. John Haltiwanger led the research on firm performance. Julia Lane and John Haltiwanger coordinated the researchers at the U.S. Census Bureau, and Clair Brown coordinated the researchers at the Sloan Industry Centers.

Although all participants contributed substantively to the analytical work and the writing of the reports, there were clear areas of specialization between the two groups. Sloan Industry Centers researchers provided the analysis of their industries: Larry Hunter for the financial services industry; Michael Belzer and Stan Sedo for the trucking industry; Clair Brown, Ben Campbell, and Yooki Park for the semiconductor industry; Liz Davis and Tim Park for the retail food industry; and Kathryn Shaw for the software industry. Yooki Park created the Career Path Simulator. Brian McCall provided analysis of the retail food industry as well as the analytical underpinning of the chapter on the earnings distribution. U.S. Census Bureau researchers took primary responsibility for the data creation and analysis: Fredrik Andersson and Matthew Freedman for earnings inequality and career paths; Hyowook Chiang for firm performance and career paths; Cheryl Grim for firm performance; Nicole Nestoriak for firm performance; Kristin Sandusky for earnings inequality and firm performance; and Jeongil Seo for firm performance. Ron Jarmin provided substantial input in all areas.

Special thanks also go to the Census Bureau staff—Steven Roman, Scott Scheleur, Jessica Young, and Tom Zabelsky, as well as Fay Dorsett, Pat Kent, Christopher Pece, Judy Ross-Davis, Anne Russell, Chris Savage, and Tim Winters—and Nicholas Greenia from the Internal Revenue Service for ensuring that the research had, as its predominant purpose, the improvement of economic and demographic surveys and censuses, and for providing invaluable input and guidance.

We also thank the teams from the participating states in the LEHD program for their cooperation in providing data and for their helpful comments on earlier drafts of our research. Particular thanks go to George Putnam, Henry Jackson, Vicky Feldman, Sonya Williams, and Phil Hardiman.

We have benefited from thoughtful comments from Charlie Brown, Erica Groshen, David Stevens, and participants at the 2004 American Economic Association, 2004 NBER Summer Institute, and 2005 Society of Labor Economists meetings, and the UC Berkeley Labor Economics seminar.

We are also indebted to Robin McCullough-Harlin for her indefatigable energy and efficiency in taking care of the logistics associated with the project. We thank Pearl Jusem and Patricia L. Blake for their work on the figures in the text.

Matthew Freedman, Patrick Lane, David Stevens, and Peter Welbrock provided invaluable guidance and editing assistance at multiple stages of the book. We are heavily indebted to them for their willingness to do such a thankless task, their candor and innate good sense. Our editor, Alex Schwartz of the University of Chicago Press, provided extremely sensible and valuable input with good humor. We benefited from research support from the Institute of Industrial Relations at the University of California, Berkeley, and from ITEC-COE at Doshisha University.

This manuscript draws heavily upon the research at the Census Bureau's Longitudinal Employer-Household Dynamics Program (LEHD). This document supports the research and analysis undertaken in part by U.S. Census Bureau staff. The research and analysis are released to interested parties to encourage discussion. LEHD is partially supported by the National Science Foundation Grant SES-9978093 to Cornell University (Cornell Institute for Social and Economic Research), the National Institute on Aging Grant 5 R01 AG018854-02, and the Alfred P. Sloan Foundation. The views expressed herein are attributable only to the authors and do not represent the views of the U.S. Census Bureau, its program sponsors, or data providers. Some or all of the data used in this paper are confidential data from the LEHD program. The U.S. Census Bureau is preparing to support external researchers' use of these data; please contact Jeremy S. Wu, Program Manager, U.S. Census Bureau, LEHD Program, Demographic Surveys Division, FOB 3, Room 2138, 4700 Silver Hill Rd., Suitland, MD 20233, USA (Jeremy.S.Wu@census.gov, http://lehd.dsd.gov).

Overview of the Book

It's better to be a dog in a peaceful time than be a man in a chaotic period.—Chinese proverb

The U.S. economy is both celebrated and reviled for its dynamism. New jobs are constantly created, new firms replace old, and the American economic model is the one adopted around the world. Yet its unceasing and turbulent change creates enormous angst about the loss of jobs, the loss of earnings, and the loss of competitiveness of American firms. At the same time that employment is at an all-time high, CNN reporter Lou Dobbs captures the national angst in his book, *Exporting America*.

What is the overall impact of this change on jobs, workers, and firms? Every week, in every part of the economy and in every corner of the country, some firms shut down and others start up, some jobs are created and others are destroyed, some workers are hired and others quit or are laid off. Giant Food, a fixture in the Washington, D.C., economy, is one example. It shut down its Maryland headquarters in May 2005 and laid off five hundred workers. The local news was full of stories about the demise of good middle-class jobs and how the local community would be hurt.[1] But almost unnoticed in the very same week was a small report that MOM (My Organic Market) was creating fifty new jobs by opening a new store in western Maryland.[2] Of course, the nature of the news industry is to report on visible and traumatic events, which tend to be job losses, worker layoffs, and plant closings. Yet maybe small startups like MOM will turn into many more jobs, although added slowly and over time. And maybe workers laid off at Giant will end up with better jobs. It's also possible that MOM will fail and that workers at Giant will never land the kind of jobs that they had before.

Finding out what happens to jobs, workers, and firms—like Giant workers and workers at MOM's new store—is what this book is about. While stories point out the successes and traumas for individual businesses and in individual lives, decisions need to be based on facts. This book does just that. It uses new information to go beyond anecdotes and establish some facts about economic turbulence and its impact on things that people, and their politicians, worry about: firm survival, worker job ladders and career paths, and the future of middle-class incomes.

The book focuses on five industries that are familiar to all Americans: semiconductors, software, financial services, retail food, and trucking. These industries have been affected by the same sets of forces that have affected all industries in the economy, but to different degrees. The semiconductor industry has experienced rapid technological change combined with restructuring caused by the rise of foundries and startup fabless companies—semiconductor companies that outsource the actual manufacturing—combined with the proliferation of product markets. In software, small startup firms also have played a critical role in the explosion of new products and applications, and these startups are closely linked to dominant firms like Microsoft. In financial services, the range of changes has also been staggering. Regulatory restructuring increased competition both within and between sub-industries and led to industry consolidation during a period of massive technological change, including the introduction of the ATM, widespread use of call centers, and the introduction of online services. In food stores, changes in market structure have been enormous, with power retailers like Wal-Mart playing an increasingly large role. In trucking, deregulation has led to tremendous heterogeneity across firms as they pursue different business strategies and seek to serve different segments of the for-hire transportation market.

The five industries studied here include a wide range of different human resource practices. High-tech, high-skill industries such as semiconductors and software should have more skill development with lower turnover and higher wages than a low-skill service industry such as food stores and a low-skill infrastructure industry such as trucking, which differs again from a high-skill infrastructure service industry such as financial services.

The analysis in this book combines facts gleaned from studying millions of data points on millions of firms and workers, as well as from interviews with firms in each industry to answer some key questions.

1. How much turbulence is there and why does it happen?
2. What is the impact of economic turbulence on:
   a. *Firm performance and survival:* What is the relationship between work-force quality, turnover, and firm survival?
   b. *Firm job ladders:* What has happened to jobs within a firm? Is it still possible to land a good job that pays good initial earnings with good raises? What kinds of firms offer the best job ladders?
   c. *Worker career paths:* What impact has economic turbulence had on workers' lifetime earnings and employment? How much impact does job loss have on a worker's earnings?
   d. *Wage distribution:* What has happened to middle-, low-, and high-income jobs? Are there still "good" jobs? Do new firms pay more or less than the firms that fail?

The next sections provide a brief preview of the answers to these questions, which are discussed in much more detail in later chapters.

What Is Turbulence, Why Does It Happen, and What Is the Impact?

Turbulence is the entire process of economic change: worker reallocation as workers change jobs and job reallocation from firms contracting and shutting down, to firms expanding and starting up. Chapter 2 spells this out in more detail, but the sheer amount of turbulence is staggering. In any given quarter, about one in *four* job matches either begins or ends, one in *thirteen* jobs is created or destroyed, and one in *twenty* establishments closes or is born. Why does it happen? Some turbulence reflects the natural selection processes, and some reflects the fundamental changes in the economy, like globalization, technological change, and deregulation.

Dynamic Selection of Workers

The refrain to a well-known song begins "Take this job and shove it," and one of the most famous lines in television is "You're fired." Put more prosaically, turbulence can be caused by a shuffling of workers across jobs. Firms will hire workers, and workers will accept jobs, but then one or both sides will decide that the job match isn't right. The worker then leaves and is replaced by someone else. In a lot of low-wage industries, like the retail food industry, this *worker reallocation* is quite high because the skills required are easily learned and it is easy to replace workers once they leave. In a lot of high-wage industries, like the semiconductor industry, worker reallocation is lower because the costs of replacement are high.

Wal-Mart has made headlines both because of its low prices and because of its low wages. Other firms, like Costco, have workers lining up to work for them. Different firms, even within the same industry, can have different levels of worker turnover simply because firms choose different personnel strategies. This means that different firms have different levels of wages and different amounts of worker turnover. An article in the *Seattle Times* pointed out the differences between Costco and Wal-Mart:

> A cashier at Costco can make more than $40,000 annually within four years. The average store manager makes $107,000, with a crack at $40,000 in performance bonuses on top. The company also pays hourly workers annual bonuses from $4,000 to $7,000. No wonder they stick around: Turnover at Costco is less than a third the industry average.[3]

Costco follows a high-wage, low-turnover strategy, while Sam's Club, owned by Wal-Mart, has substantially higher turnover and lower wages. The net impact on overall economic turbulence can be substantial: Costco has become one of the ten largest retailers worldwide[4] and has outstripped Sam's Club in terms of employment, which has had the result of lowering worker turnover in the industry.

Dynamic Selection of Firms

PanAm, Montgomery Ward, Bethlehem Steel. There is a long list of firms that have gone out of business in recent years, with an equally long list of new ones. Turbulence can result from new, more productive firms replacing old, less productive ones, even within the same industry. This process, which Joseph Schumpeter called "creative destruction," means that *jobs get reallocated* from one set of firms to another, and accounts for a large fraction of aggregate (industry) productivity growth. In a vivid example of this, some call centers can be closed by firms like Capital One and JPMorgan Chase in the very same city—Tampa Bay—at the very same time that firms like HSBC are opening them.[5]

This turbulent selection process means that economic growth in the U.S. is unsteady and complex. There is much trial and error in companies searching for the "right" way of doing business—the right technology, the right market niche, and the right workforce. As a result, most turbulence occurs within industries: even though more than one in ten jobs are created and destroyed every year in the U.S. economy, only about 10 percent result in employment growing or shrinking across industries.

However, there are big differences across industries. In the software industry, for example, businesses enter and exit quite quickly, but entry and exit rates are much lower in the semiconductor industry.

External Shocks

CNN reporter Lou Dobbs's book *Exporting America* (2004) paints a vivid picture of the third reason for economic turbulence: there are fundamental changes in the way in which goods and services are produced. He focuses on globalization, but others have lamented the impact of technological change and deregulation. Changes like these are much harder to measure in a systematic way, which is why our book focuses on an industry-by-industry analysis. As will become clear in chapter 3, globalization is a driving force in the software, semiconductor, and financial services industries with the relocation abroad of some design, manufacturing, and back office activities; technological change has been important in financial services industry, retail food, and semiconductors as is clear from the advent of ATM machines, scanning technology, and smaller, faster chips. And deregulation has had a major impact in the trucking and financial services industries.

A good way to understand how dramatic economic changes like these affect how business is done is to go and directly talk to firms in the industry. That is precisely what the researchers who contributed to this book did. They talked to dozens of firms in each industry using case study techniques that permitted them to describe very specifically the nature and type of external shocks in each industry.

The combination of this approach and the direct measurement of job and worker reallocation and firm entry and exit can lead to a very different view of the world than one gets by reading the newspaper. To take one example, Austin, Texas, has been featured as an example of the negative impact of globalization because semiconductor employment in that city dropped in four years by about sixteen thousand workers, and one-half of its major semiconductor factories closed.[6] However, the facts do not show that Austin's experience is representative of the industry. The data show that the number of jobs in the semiconductor industry has actually increased, and case study evidence suggests that Austin's job loss was other cities' job gain because the structure of the industry changed substantially.

The Impact

Some things are known about the impact of economic turbulence, but much is not. To start with, not much is known about the relationship between economic turbulence and economic growth. Is the shuffling of jobs across firms and workers across jobs efficient? Does it contribute to economic growth? Chapter 4 begins to answer this question by showing the relationship between the reallocation of workers with varying levels of skill to different types of firms and workers' earnings and firms' performance.

Not much is known about the relationship between economic turbulence and either the job ladders provided by firms or the career paths of workers. Chapter 5 examines the impact of economic turbulence on job ladders by examining the impact of working for high-turnover and low-turnover firms, or for expanding and shrinking firms, on workers' earnings and earnings growth. Chapter 6 looks at how much job change there is in different industries and examines the impact of job change on worker *career paths.*

Finally, not much is known about the impact of economic turbulence on the earnings distribution, particularly what has happened to *low-income, middle-income, and high- income jobs.* A popular concern is that "good" jobs have been lost because the old high-paying firms have been replaced by new firms that pay much less. Chapter 7 examines the evidence on this.

A Preview of the Rest of the Book

Chapter 2 provides an overview of the amount of economic turbulence in the economy,) and chapter 3 surveys the economic change sweeping the five industries. Chapters 4 through 7 are analytical; they discuss the impact of economic turbulence on firms, on firm job ladders, on worker career paths, and on the earnings distribution, respectively. Chapter 8 gives an idea of how the information in the book, and the sources that are used here, can be used in policy analysis. The data appendices provide the background material, including information about the new and rich databases linking outcomes for firms and workers, that underlies the analysis and discussion in this book.

THE IMPACT OF ECONOMIC TURBULENCE ON FIRMS. Firms' survival depends on how they organize themselves. Firms behave differently, and these differences matter for their performance and survival. Different firms organize themselves differently, have different levels of workforce quality and workforce turnover, and these differences have significant effects on *firm performance*. High-productivity businesses have a large share of high-skill workers, with either general skills or experience, and also have low turnover, or churning, of workers. All of these factors independently affect firm survival—businesses with high productivity, low churning, and high skill (especially general skills) are more likely to survive. There are substantial differences across industries—one size does not fit all. For example, low worker turnover is especially important in the semiconductor industry, and having a highly skilled workforce is especially important in the trucking industry. New businesses have a disproportionately important impact in changing production methods, which deserves an important role in the study of entrepreneurship.

There is no "one size fits all" lesson even within an industry, and firms need to be examined within the context of their industry. For example, the popular press makes much of the importance of "small business." Yet small businesses are very different things across industries, and their importance has changed. In the semiconductor industry, for example, industry restructuring has meant that the industry has moved more to fabless semiconductor establishments. These fabless design firms, which are small, highly skill intensive, and volatile, are changing the dynamics of firm performance in that industry. Similarly, in the retail food and trucking industries, large, national chains operate very differently from small, local entities. And large software producers, like Microsoft, are different from small, agile software producers that typically target small market niches.

THE IMPACT OF ECONOMIC TURBULENCE ON JOB LADDERS. Economic turbulence, as measured by firm growth, substantially affects the number and type of jobs offered by firms. The data confirm what one would expect: across industries, large, growing firms provide some of the best job ladders (initial earnings and earnings growth), and small shrinking firms tend to provide the worst job ladders (and few in number). In general, firms with growing employment offer better jobs than shrinking firms, except in trucking, where large, shrinking firms, often unionized, offer some of the best job ladders. Although large firms are the largest supplier of long-term job ladders, the importance of small and growing firms in providing excellent job ladders in semiconductors, financial services, and trucking indicates that these firms may be a growing source of good job ladders over time.

Economic turbulence often results in low initial earnings but higher than average wage growth at a firm, particularly in semiconductors and financial services. The combination of high turnover with high wage growth for workers that stay suggests that firms are sorting workers and workers are deciding whether to stay, within an "up or out" wage-setting system. Another way of thinking of this is that the job market within a firm is like a tournament: workers compete for "good jobs," and those who are selected do well, and those who don't move on to another job.

ECONOMIC TURBULENCE AND CAREER PATHS.   The data show that there are three common career paths (individual earnings trajectories over time) that are observed in each industry. The data are consistent with the popular opinion that loyalists experience better career paths than job changers for all education groups of prime-aged (twenty-five- to fifty-four-year-old) men and women. However, the data also show that, over time, most workers who stay in the labor market are able to improve their career paths through changing jobs until they finally find a relatively good job ladder in a firm, despite not being able to catch up to the loyalists.

Career paths are very different across industries. Just as firm performance varies across industries, career paths for each education-gender group vary greatly across the five industries, with retail food at the bottom and software and semiconductors at the top. In general, workers improved their career paths by *moving into* the software, semiconductor, financial services, and trucking industries, and *by moving out of* retail food. Several underlying economic forces might explain these different outcomes in career paths. One force is individually based: loyalists in good jobs may have superior knowledge or other unobserved characteristics that make them more valuable to their employer than the job changers, who may need to increase their skills through experience before landing a better job. Another force is firm based: firms with good job ladders may operate in nonclearing or rationed labor markets with a wage premium—that is, with a wage higher than the market average, and have a queue of fairly homogeneous and qualified workers waiting for job openings. A third force is market based: firms and workers must learn which workers are good matches for which jobs; in effect, workers must change jobs in order to find a "good match." Most likely it is a combination of these factors.

Many workers continually improve their career paths by finding better job opportunities with other firms, although the typical spell between jobs can be as long as twelve to eighteen months. Although the recent economic downturn has highlighted the costs associated with lost jobs, the long-run evidence is that the consequences of such losses, while important for some workers, are not substantial for most.

ECONOMIC TURBULENCE AND JOB QUALITY.   The popular perception that jobs are vanishing is not correct. There are more jobs in each of the five industries than at the start of the period—and this is not an increase in "bad" jobs. The proportion of low-income workers declined in all five industries. The decline is larger in semiconductors, software, and financial services and smaller in retail food and trucking.

The proportion of high-income jobs increased substantially in high-skilled industries, contrary to fears about the impact of globalization on high-skilled workers. The percentage of high-income workers increased substantially in software, financial services, and especially semiconductors. However, in the retail food and trucking industries, there are *fewer* high-income workers at the end of the period.

A rising tide has lifted all boats in the high-skilled, high-tech industries. Workers in financial services, semiconductors, and software have seen increases in earnings across the board. By contrast, the retail food and trucking industries have experienced an increase in the middle group with fewer workers in the top and bottom groups.

In sum, although turbulence is very often equated with negative factors, this is only half the story. People see workers getting fired, and jobs being lost as firms shut down because that makes news. The other side of the story, workers getting hired and firms starting up and expanding, is not as visible. This book has been written because new data now exist that can measure many dimensions of turbulence: the reallocation of jobs and workers into as well as out of jobs; the entry and expansion as well as the contraction and exit of businesses. The following chapters explain the basic results in much more detail.

CHAPTER TWO

Economic Turbulence: What, Who, and How Much?

Introduction

The facts are breathtaking. In any given quarter, about one in *twenty* establishments opens or goes out of business, and one in *thirteen* jobs begins or ends. And these changes have enormous impact on people's lives. One example is Mark McClellan, who had worked at a Kaiser Aluminum plant in Spokane, Washington, all his life but was out of a job in 2001, when the plant closed. As the *New York Times* reported:

> He still lives in a grand house in one of the nicest parts of town, and he drives a big white Jeep. But they are a facade. "I may look middle class," said Mr. McClellan, who is 45, with a square, honest face and a barrel chest. "But I'm not. My boat is sinking fast."[1]

Newspapers and policy briefs are full of anecdotes like these about job loss. But there are other types of job loss as well. In the summer of 2004, the daughter of one of the authors—a seventeen-year-old high school senior—worked at an ice cream parlor at minimum wage. It was a lousy job by any standards: her hours and work schedule changed every week, she could be called in, or told not to come in, at half an hour's notice, and she took home under $200 a week. Not surprisingly, few workers stayed with the business for long, and she was the only one who stayed the whole summer. The other workers, who were older and had more experience, were able to get better jobs elsewhere. Their job loss reflected a move up, not down, the economic ladder.

The aluminum company and ice cream parlor stories reflect very different types of turbulence, with very different impacts on workers and their jobs, but raise the same questions. What are the different types of economic turbulence, how much is there, and how are workers and firms affected?

Answering these questions is the focus of this chapter. We introduce the measures that are needed to discuss the types of economic turbulence: job creation and destruction, hires and separations, firm births and deaths. We also discuss how much economic turbulence there is, and how different it is across different industries and for workers of different ages. In other words, after reading the chapter you will have a sense of how vulnerable Mark McClellan would be if he were twenty instead of fifty. Or if instead of working for Kaiser Aluminum, he had worked in a different industry. Or if he had been laid off in a boom, instead of a recession.

In sum, this chapter lays out a set of newly available facts about turbulence. These facts will provide a baseline for the next chapters. At the end of the chapter questions will arise like:

·   Why do firms shut down?
·   What has happened to the job ladders provided by firms?
·   What has happened to workers' career paths?
·   What does turbulence mean for middle-, low-, and top-income jobs?

Defining and Measuring Turbulence

There is a ritual in Washington. On the first Friday of every month, at 8:30 AM, the secretary of labor, accompanied by the commissioner of the Bureau of Labor Statistics, reports what has happened to employment in the previous month. The press then dutifully reports whether employment is up or down or has stayed the same. But these numbers, which are typically about net changes in hundreds of thousands of jobs, are just the tip of the employment iceberg, since literally millions of workers will have changed jobs over that period. Even though the numbers signal important changes in levels of economic activity, they're a little like reporting changes in the level of a lake, without information about the rivers that flow into and out of the lake. Not surprisingly, these *turnover* measures are much more dynamic and capture much more economic activity than net changes.

Statistics about net changes in employment don't tell us about how many times the boss at the ice cream store replaces his workers. Statistics about worker turnover do. Counts of worker turnover are created by counting the flow of workers into and out of jobs at a firm as they get hired and as they separate (either because they are laid off or because they quit). The *worker turnover rate* is the average of the hiring rate (the number of workers who are new to the firm in a given quarter or year divided by employment) and the separation rate (the number of workers who left the firm in the previous quarter or year divided by employment).[2]

Statistics about net changes in employment also don't capture how many jobs were lost at shrinking or closing plants like Kaiser Aluminum and how many were created by expanding or new firms The *job turnover rates* used in this book capture the total job destruction (or job creation) from firms shrinking or shutting down (or expanding and starting up). Job turnover counts are measured by counting the flow of jobs to and from different firms as some firms expand and exit and others contract and enter. The *job turnover rate* used for illustrative purposes in this chapter is the average of the job creation rate (the number of jobs added at all expanding firms divided by employment) and the job destruction rate (the number of jobs lost at all contracting firms divided by employment).

What is the difference between job turnover and worker turnover? Simply put, job turnover reflects the shift of jobs across companies, worker turnover the shift of workers across jobs. The worker turnover rate includes both the loss of jobs at Kaiser Aluminum and the replacement of workers at the ice cream store. If employment at the ice cream store didn't change, there would be no job turnover, even though there was worker turnover. So worker turnover represents the ebb and flow of workers and can reflect a worker's life cycle decisions as well as the matching of workers and jobs. *Job turnover*—exemplified by the closing of Kaiser Aluminum—reflects something very different. It represents a shift in demand away from some firms and towards others.

The differences in turbulence across industries and age groups are striking, as figure 2.1 shows for the second quarter of 2003. The first point to recognize *is what a difference the measures make.* The first set of bars in the retail food graph shows that employment for all workers actually declined in that quarter. Yet the job turnover rate was about 6 percent, while quarterly worker turnover was greater than 10 percent. So even though newspapers and magazines would have trumpeted net job losses, the turnover measures show there was enormous turbulence in the flow of workers and the reallocation of jobs across firms underlying the small net decline in jobs. Workers were still getting hired, and jobs were still being created, despite the gloomy aggregate statistics. It's worth remembering, though, that there were a lot of people laid off, just like Mark McClellan.

The second point is that the *age of a worker makes a difference*. Younger workers (aged 25–34 years old) have both more opportunities to be hired and a higher likelihood of being fired than older workers. The second set of bars for each industry shows this clearly: worker turnover for younger workers is 30 to 100 percent higher than job turnover, which can be two or three times higher than net employment growth. Older workers are subject to less economic turbulence, as the third set of bars, for 45–54 year olds, show. Turbulence is a fact of life for younger workers, like high school seniors, but much less likely to concern fifty-year-olds.

The third point is that there are large *differences across industries*. There are some differences in the net employment changes across industries: the financial services industry, for example, was growing rapidly in mid-2003, while retail trade was shrinking. But the worker and job flow differences across industries are also large. Workers in low-skill industries, such as retail food and trucking, are much more vulnerable to economic turbulence than are workers in high-skill industries, such as semiconductors and software. The importance of this for workers' career paths will become clear in later chapters.

In general, from a variety of studies using statistics on job and worker turnover, following set of facts have been established:

· Younger workers are more likely to leave or be hired than older workers. So the ice cream shop experience is typical. Not only is turbulence a fact of life for younger workers, but firms that hire younger workers should expect much more turnover. It is also likely that as America's workforce ages, national turnover rates will drop.
· Worker turnover is higher in low-skill industries (like trucking and retail food) than in high-skill industries (like semiconductors and parts of financial services). In other words, economy-wide turbulence, and job instability, can change simply because the industrial structure is changing.
· Worker turnover rates are substantially higher than job turnover rates. Even when the number of jobs in a firm has not changed, there are still job opportunities, simply because firms need to hire workers who have retired, been laid off or quit. The ice cream shop always had a "help wanted" sign in the window.
· Job turnover is higher in small and young businesses. Small firms are much more volatile in both creating and destroying jobs. Hence, industries that are dominated by such firms are more likely to be affected by economic turbulence than are industries with large, older firms.

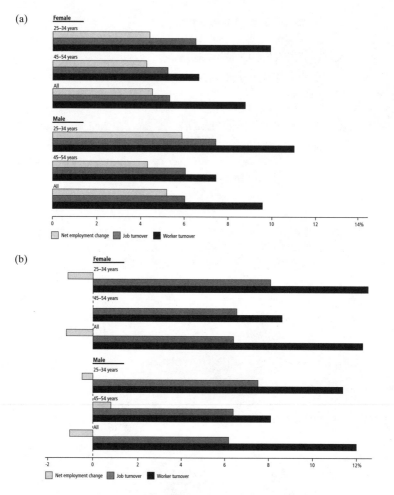

FIGURE 2.1. Net employment change, job turnover, and worker turnover. (a) Financial services. (b) Retail food. (c) Semiconductors. (d) Software. (e) Trucking.

· Most job loss is highly concentrated: more than two-thirds of all lost jobs occur at businesses that shrink more than ten percent, and more than one-fifth of workers whose jobs were destroyed worked at businesses that shut down. This explains one of the reasons for the newspaper headlines that trumpet job loss: because job loss is much more concentrated, it's also much more visible.

The overwhelming impression from these studies is not only that there are enormous rates of worker and job reallocation, but that this reallocation is

(c)

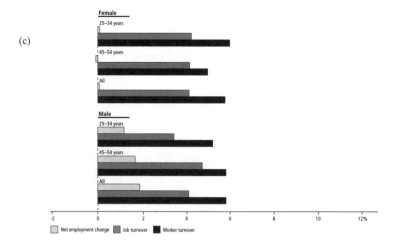

(d)

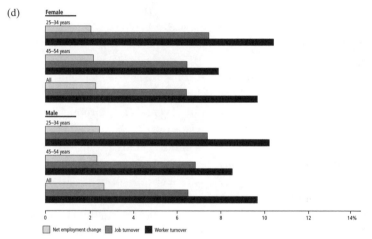

(e)

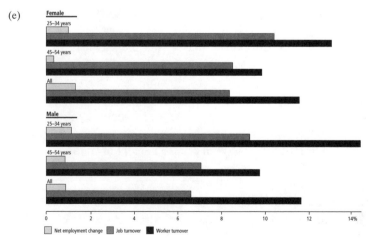

not uniform: particular industries, specific types of firms, and specific types of workers are disproportionately affected by turbulence.

The Birth and Death of Firms

More than one in five jobs that are lost in the U.S. are lost because firms close their doors.[3] Death, like taxes, seems to be inevitable—the average life span of even highly visible, well-established firms, such as Fortune 500 companies, is less than 50 years. However, it comes at different times for firms in different industries, of different sizes, and at different parts of the economic cycle. Young firms are more vulnerable, and thus jobs at young firms are more vulnerable. For the most part, firms are relatively small at birth and then, if successful, exhibit rapid growth in the first several years after entry. Like firm deaths, the patterns of firm births are different across industries and the cycle.

There are striking *differences across industries.* The annual shutdown rate in the trucking industry rose as high as 25 percent, while in the software industry it was below 10 percent in several years (although exit rates for software firms grew rapidly in the late 1990s). The reason for such differences range from deregulation with industry restructuring to changes in domestic or foreign competition.

This brings up an important issue. Although most firms consist of one establishment, about half of workers work for multiestablishment firms with more than 500 workers (about 0.2 percent of the total number of firms). As a result, establishments can shut down either because a parent firm shuts down or because the parent firm downsizes and closes selected establishments. Similarly, new establishments can be born either because an existing firm opens new locations or a totally new firm opens. *Mergers and acquisitions* are also important ways in which firms can enter or exit an industry.[4]

How important are mergers and acquisitions? They represent a substantial part of industry restructuring: about 5 percent of GDP and 48 percent of nonresidential gross investment in 1995.[5] This is spread fairly evenly across most industries, with between 2 and 8 percent of continuing establishments belonging to a different firm over a five-year horizon.

The deregulation of the trucking industry provides a good example of how mergers and acquisitions can change the economic landscape. Federal Express developed from being just an overnight express carrier into a general LTL (less than load) carrier and logistics provider by purchasing another, bankrupt, company named Caliber (which in turn was the heir to an original spinoff organization called Roadway Regionals, which in turn included, among others, Menlo Logistics, Viking, and Roadway Package Service [RPS]). There is no question that this wave of mergers and acquisitions was stimulated by regulatory change. Until 1994, when Congress mandated the deregulation of intrastate truck transportation, many states, especially key large states such as California, Texas, Michigan, and Pennsylvania, retained regulation for intrastate trucking and protected local cartage within those states. After 1994, new and small nonunion carriers took advantage of new opportunities and grew rapidly. In addition, individual owner-operators now could easily apply for and receive forty-eight-state authority, and today about 300,000 drivers own their own trucks. Indeed, as unionized trucking jobs disappeared, many experienced drivers bought their own trucks and attempted to compete in this market by undercutting the rates of existing carriers, and further cutthroat competition ensued. These low-cost operators showed up as an increased number of firm births, and, since they had a greater tendency to operate below cost and go under regularly, also showed up as a greater number of firm deaths. And, in this industry, employment only grew slightly (about 4 percent in more than a decade in the states for which we have data).

The impact of mergers and acquisitions is also clear in the financial services industry. To take one example: in 1998 Citicorp anticipated the Gramm-Leach-Bliley Act by merging with Travelers Group, itself the result of acquisitions and mergers of such businesses as the investment banks Salomon Inc., Smith Barney, and Drexel Burnham Lambert, the insurance company Travelers Life and Annuity, the property and casualty divisions of Aetna, and the retail brokerage and asset management operations of Shearson Lehman. By 2004, it had credit card customers in every state and its expansive branch banking network served retail customers in twenty-two states. First Union and Bank One are also excellent examples. Both of these grew spectacularly over the 1980s and 1990s, mostly as a result of acquisitions. Both overdid it. Bank One (out of Columbus, Ohio) ended up struggling and being bought by JPMorgan Chase & Co. (http://money.cnn.com/2004/01/14/news/deals/jpmorgan_bankone/). JPMorgan itself is an investment bank that previously bought Chase, a commercial bank, which had in turn been through a number of commercial bank mergers. First Union (out of Charlotte, North Carolina) also overshot and

18

CHAPTER TWOCHAPTER TWO

floundered, particularly after its purchase of CoreStates. It merged with Wachovia (also out of North Carolina) in 2001 in what was touted as a merger of equals.

The retail food industry provides a classic example of the impact of competitive forces on both births and deaths within an industry. Wal-Mart's encroachment into food retailing has posed a significant challenge to traditional grocery firms. The National Grocers Association has found that close to 80 percent of supermarket managers identified the super-center format used by Wal-Mart as the major threat to traditional grocery chains. Indeed, Wal-Mart has become the leading firm in the grocery in-dustry, and it continues to garner market share as it builds new stores and expands its product selection. From a base of only ten supercenters in 1993, Wal-Mart expanded to over 1,400 supercenters by the start of 2005. Com-pany plans indicate that it intends to open two hundred new stores every year for the next five years.

Mergers and acquisitions have also been crucially important in retail food: between 1997 and 2000, the four largest food retailers' share rose from 18 to 27 percent of total grocery store sales in the U.S. The number of mergers and acquisitions peaked in the late 1990s as some chains chose to grow through acquisitions, while others (Wal-Mart in particular) contin-ued to open new stores. The Giant Food story, where Giant was taken over by Stop and Go while MOM expands, is part of the retail food landscape. What has been the net effect on jobs? An increase of about 7 percent in just over a decade in the states in which we have data.

Other factors that contribute to high death rates include the forces of *globalization*. In the semiconductor industry, for example, the competitive positions of firms and countries have undergone dramatic changes since 1980, when IBM introduced its first personal computer. Then, in the mid to late 1980s, Japanese firms used their comparative advantage in manufac-turing to grab the lion's share of the market for the memory chips (DRAM). But the 1990s saw the resurgence of U.S. firms, led by Intel, based on improved production methods and product innovation as well as the dominance of the personal computer, or PC.[6] The 1990s also witnessed the rise of Taiwanese foundries, which manufacture chips designed by other companies, and which spurred the growth of new fabless design com-panies, especially in the U.S. Widespread adoption of the Internet and in-troduction of wireless devices challenged the central role of the PC and allowed chip producers from Europe and Asia to gain ground. Further up-heaval is expected with the entry of China to the global industry.[7] In 2002, U.S. firms accounted for about 50 percent of the global market, but the number of companies had dropped from 993 in 1997 to 898 (and the number of establishments had gone from 1097 to 1032).[8]

The software industry is another industry that has been affected by globalization. As a leading researchers in the area, Ashish Arora and Alfonso Gambardella note:

> One rather unexpected phenomenon of the 1990s has been the spectacular growth of the software industry in some non-G7 economies. The first element of surprise is that these are not countries where one would expect to see the growth of what is commonly thought of as a high-tech. The second element is that what the 1990s have shown is not just growth of the industry, but a remarkable growth. In India, for example, software production was virtually non-existent in the early 1980s. Today software employs more than 450,000 employees, sustaining annual growth rates of 30–40% in revenues and employment over more than 10 years. Although less remarkable than India, countries like Ireland and Israel have also had double digit growth. . . . To put these figures in perspective, employment in the U.S. software industry was slightly above 1 million, with sales of around $200 billion.[9]

The number of software establishments has also declined going from 12,090 in 1997 to 9,899 in 2002.[10]

Obviously, *firm size is an important factor.* While even the biggest firms (like AT&T) can die, big firms are much more likely to survive than are small ones because big firms have better access to credit and often have more established markets. Not surprisingly, birth rates are higher for small businesses, because firms are more likely to be born with a small number of employees than a large number. Economy-wide, firms with more than one hundred workers have half the death rate of firms with fewer than twenty workers.[11]

Finally, *timing matters.* The business cycle forces many firms, particularly the least successful ones, out of business, as the volatile jumps in figure 2.2 show. Some industries, such as trucking and software, are particularly cyclically sensitive while others, such as retail food, are less sensitive. The software industry is a classic example. The IT boom spawned an enormous number of new software companies. Indeed, by 1997, there were more firms that had been born in the past five years than had lived longer than five years. In financial services, the bear market in the early 2000s caused a lot of the least productive firms to leave.

"The bear market separated the wheat from the chaff—a lot of marginal brokers left the business," says Ron Cordes, chairman of AssetMark Investment

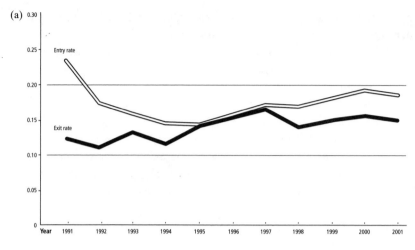

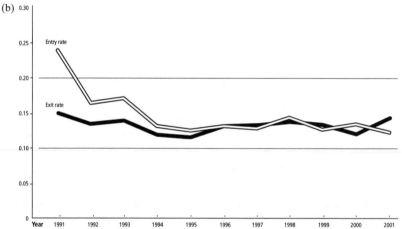

FIGURE 2.2. Entry and exit rates of establishments. (a) Financial services. (b) Retail food. (c) Semiconductors. (d) Software. (e) Trucking.

Services, a San Mateo (Calif.) firm that helps commission brokers make the transition to independent, fee-based financial advisers. And Wall Street's credibility is still smarting in the aftermath of New York State Attorney General Eliot Spitzer taking firms to task for issuing biased reports. That scandal deprived stockbrokers of their chief sales tool.[12]

So a number of basic facts have been established. First, firm entry and exit rates are very different across industries, firm sizes, and parts of the

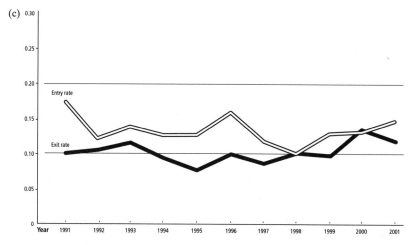

(c)

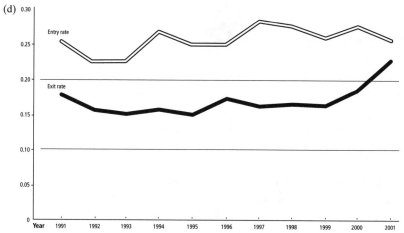

(d)

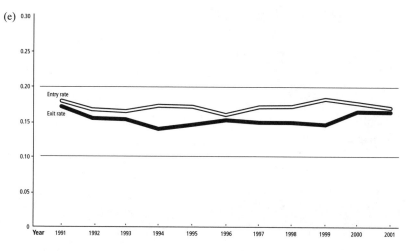

(e)

business cycle, so workers in different firms and different time periods will have very different experiences. In particular, workers who work for smaller and younger firms are much more likely to see their firm exit than workers who work for older and larger firms. Second, although firm entry and exit are common across industries, the primary impetus is different in each. Deregulation has had particularly important effects on firm entry and exit in two industries—trucking and financial services—while heightened domestic competition has been important in the retail food industry, and globalization in the semiconductor and software industries. Finally, although mergers and acquisition activity does not account for a large number of firm births and deaths, it is important economically, particularly in financial services and retail food.

The Bottom Line

Economic turbulence is substantial and pervasive. Job loss, like Mark McClellan's, is part of the constant restructuring of economic activity that is hidden by aggregate statistics.

Some workers are more vulnerable than others. Younger workers are more likely to leave or be hired than older workers. Workers who work in low-skill industries (like trucking and retail food) are more likely to experience turnover than workers in high-skill industries (like semiconductors and parts of financial services). Worker turnover rates are much higher than job turnover rates, and job turnover is higher in small and young businesses.

The impact of closings like Kaiser Aluminum is substantial. Firm deaths are not only an important contributor to job losses, but the rates of firm births and deaths are very different across industries, firm sizes, and parts of the business cycle. Case study research and the large differences across industries suggest that factors such as deregulation, industry restructuring, and globalization are important driving forces in contributing to firm entry and exit. The next chapter examines this part of the economic turbulence story in more detail.

CHAPTER THREE

The Industries

Introduction

The last chapter closed by saying that factors such as deregulation, industry restructuring, and globalization are important sources of economic turbulence. But getting simple measures of these forces is impossible. Government statistical offices do not produce indices of any of these events. Indeed, when the National Academy of Public Administration (NAPA) was charged in 2005 to examine what data could be used to examine off-shoring, a common outcome of globalization, it noted on its website:

> The migration of U.S. jobs off-shore and its impact on America's workforce and economy is neither a new, nor unstudied or unfamiliar, issue. From an economy-wide perspective, this issue has been at the center of frequent national debates about the benefits and costs of economic growth and trade expansion. However, the debates have not produced consensus on the magnitude and significance of the net migration of U.S. jobs off-shore or its impact on U.S. workers and the economy.
>
> The Bureau of Labor Statistics (BLS) and others have undertaken efforts to expand the range of data, but these collections remain fragmentary and hampered by a clear understanding of what needs to be measured.[1]

The approach taken in this book is more holistic. No attempt is made to measure such complex events. The five industries that are under the microscope—financial services, semiconductors, software, retail food, and trucking—have all been buffeted by globalization, deregulation, and increased competition. Since these industries span the economic spectrum from manufacturing to service, from low technology to high technology, and from low skill to high skill, what they have experienced should shed light on the experiences of the economy as a whole. As Gail Pesyna, a program officer for the Sloan Foundation who has thought a great deal about the importance of industry studies points out,

> When one is trying to understand a complex phenomenon—like a workplace, a firm, an industry, or an economy—a good place to start, scientifically speaking, may be with the solid, scientific practices of direct observation and primary data collection. We believe academic research ought to start here in order to study "in-depth" the key questions . . . posed. In other words, to start by observing, talking to, and collecting data from real people in workplaces. Then one can combine that with data on firms within a specific industry, and perhaps aggregate upwards. And then . . . one might begin to look at the differences across industries, or combine this with big, statistical analyses, to get something really interesting.[2]

The next section does just what Pesyna suggests. It takes the work of experts in each industry, who have spent their careers talking directly to businesses, and sketches out an overview of the workforce of the five industries. It then describes the events that have buffeted each of them.

The Five Industries: An Overview

The Workforce

The diversity of the U.S. workforce is mirrored in these five industries. The semiconductor and software industries pay high weekly wages, typically $900 in 2002, and men are 70 percent of their workers (see figure 3.1). By contrast, retail food stores pay low weekly wages, typically $300 in 2002, and hire men and women in about equal proportions. Financial services and trucking pay moderate weekly wages, typically $550 to $600 in 2002, but the financial service workforce comprises over 60 percent women, while the trucking workforce is over 80 percent male.

The level of union representation also varies. Collective bargaining plays an important role in the retail food and trucking industries. Even in these two industries, however, the proportion of workers belonging to a union has declined precipitously over the past twenty years, so that no more than 20 percent of workers were represented collectively in either industry by 2002. Unions represent very few workers in financial services, software, or semiconductors.

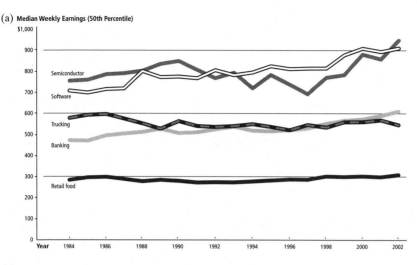

(a) Median Weekly Earnings (50th Percentile)

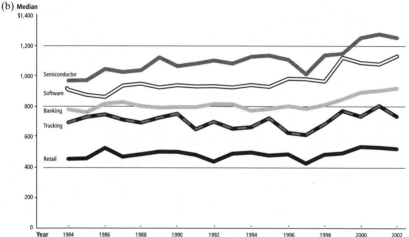

(b) Median

FIGURE 3.1. Median weekly real earnings. (a) All workers. (b) College-educated workers.

Even the most casual observer knows that the education of U.S. workers has risen dramatically over the past two decades, and the returns to education have also increased. The same is true in these five industries. College graduates saw their real weekly earnings rise since the late 1990s, although earnings for high-educated workers grew faster in semiconductors, software, and financial services than in trucking or retail food.

Pay differentials vary across the five industries for the same reasons they vary nationally. One reason is that the education of the workforce varies. Among workers with a high school diploma or less, truckers earn as much as workers in semiconductors and software, and earnings in financial services are catching up. Another reason is that firms in different industries have different pay scales for similiarly educated workers. Less educated workers in retail food earn substantially less than in the other four industries, although they typically also work fewer hours (around thirty-five hours per week, compared with forty or more in other industries). College-educated workers earn more in high-tech than in low-tech industries.

Economic Shocks

Economic shocks like technological change and deregulation have affected jobs and employment for centuries. The poster child industry during the nineteenth-century English Industrial Revolution was the cotton industry, and Luddites smashed cotton machines because they were afraid that machines and new laws were taking away their jobs. Financial services is the poster child industry for the changes in the 1980s and 1990s, dubbed the Second Industrial Revolution.[3] As the entry on "deregulation" in Wikipedia notes:

> Deregulation was a major trend in the United States in the last quarter of the twentieth century. A number of major deregulation initiatives were passed. Some of these were withdrawn quickly (but not quickly enough to avoid major problems), including the deregulation of savings and loans. American savings banks, which were permitted to lend unfettered, had their depositors' funds insured by the federal government, creating a moral hazard. The California electricity crisis was precipitated by price manipulations by companies such as Enron after energy industry deregulation in 1996. Other legislation has been considered more widely successful, including deregulation of transport, and the gas market.[4]

As was pointed out in chapter 2, deregulation is crucial to understanding recent change in the financial services industry, and is typified by two key pieces of legislation. The Interstate Banking and Branching Efficiency Act of 1994 (also known as the Riegle-Neal Act) completed the deregulatory process of extending branch banking across state lines. Five years later, the Financial Services Modernization Act of 1999 (also known as the Gramm-Leach-Bliley Act) formally repealed restrictions imposed by the 1933 Glass-Steagall Act. Glass-Steagall, a remnant of the New Deal era, had been under siege for years. Its provisions formally barred banks, brokerages, and insurance companies from entering each others' industries and separated investment banking from its commercial counterpart. Throughout the 1990s, financial services firms increasingly sought economies of scale and scope as well as cross-market opportunities, which challenged Glass-Steagall limits. The Gramm-Leach-Bliley Act rewrote statutes to accommodate changes in the industry.

The impact of the deregulation on the industry has been profound. The high-water mark for the number of FDIC-insured commercial banks was reached in 1984, when there were 14,496 banks in the U.S. By 1992 this number had dwindled to 11,466, and by 2002 the U.S. had only 7,887 banks. The decline in the number of banks has occurred even as the number of bank branches has grown substantially (from 51,935 in 1992 to 66,185 in 2002). Especially precipitous has been the drop in small institutions: the number of single-unit banks dropped by half between 1992 and 2002 (from 4,647 to 2,319).[5] Consolidation among the subindustries of financial services, such as insurance and investment banking, particularly among large firms, has also accelerated. The economic turbulence that this activity created, however, had little impact on net employment, which actually posted substantial increases.

The massive technological change in the financial services industry was also part and parcel of deregulation. In retail financial services, for example, the proliferation of automatic teller machines (ATMs) and telephone-, home-, and PC-based banking, provide alternative channels for customers, while new back-office technologies have dramatically decreased the costs of handling individual accounts and transactions. The financial services industry accounts for a disproportionately large share of IT investment in the economy.[6]

The *trucking* industry is a low-wage, old economy industry that has also been substantially affected by the impact of deregulation. It is not a large industry: 113,237 establishments employing 1,826,000 workers,[7] although it is obviously critical for the efficient functioning of the economy. Over the past twenty-five years, economic regulations have been lifted, and competition has intensified. Before deregulation, the industry consisted primarily of regulated common carriers that were certified by the Interstate Commerce Commission (ICC) to haul specific commodities between specific city pairs and of contract carriers that were permitted to haul under contract for up to eight shippers. Following the deregulation that began administratively in 1977 and was written into law in the Motor Carrier Act of

1980, markets were separated by freight shipment characteristics into truck-load (TL) markets and less-than-truckload (LTL) markets, which by the middle of the 1980s no longer competed with one another.[8] The changes in the market as a result of both active merger and acquisition activity and the adoption of information technology are well illustrated in the following communication from Michael Belzer, a Sloan industry trucking expert:

> The American Freightways purchase by FedEx might have been the most bril-liant move in trucking in a generation. American Freightways, out of the tiny poor Ozark town of Harrison, Arkansas, may be the most sophisticated IT com-pany in trucking. At least, that is what they looked like to us six years ago when we spent two days there surveying their operation. They had a computer opera-tion that was so sophisticated they could track each shipment's movements at all times and virtually prevent misloads, which is a major cost factor in LTL. This allowed them to exploit one of the most complex paradoxes of modern industry: they could use fantastic up-skilling high-road IT management to de-skill on the manual labor side. AF was feared by all the smaller LTL carriers of the old school as AF moved east and relentlessly cut costs and improved service using IT. The master stroke purchase by FedEx put them in another league.[9]

The software and semiconductor industries, two industries that are often mentioned in the same breath as globalization, are foci of the NAPA study as well as of a 2005 GAO report.[10] The *semiconductor* industry is one of the industries in which the U.S. achieved dominance in the 1980s, and in which even now the U.S. accounts for 50 percent of the global market of $150 billion (with just one company, Intel, accounting for 15 percent).

Firms in this industry develop and produce semiconductors (chips), the electronic devices that provide functionality to computers and an ever-widening array of products. However, the rise of Asian foundries that only do the manufacturing of semiconductors facilitated the rise of Silicon Val-ley startups that only do the design of chips (fabless companies). The semi-conductor industry is a good example of how economic turbulence has led to industry restructuring with improved and lower-cost products.[11]

The *software* industry is another New Economy high-wage industry that has experienced rapid growth and industry restructuring and been enormously affected by globalization. It is hard to overstate how rapidly the industry has grown. Sales in the software industry, which includes programming services, software products, and professional services, sky-rocketed from $155 billion in 1995 to $357 billion in 2001.[12] Employment in the software industry increased nearly fivefold between 1984 and 2002, and doubled in the period since 1992.[13]

At the same time, the nature of the industry has changed rapidly. Vast increases in computing power mean that new software is far more sophisticated, specialized, and powerful because of the huge increases in the processing and storage capabilities of computer hardware. Production of software products has changed as programs are broken down into modules created by independent programmers and as standards for debugging, along with debugging tools, developed. Partly as a result of these changes, software production has also moved out of company IT departments, which developed firm-specific software, into firms specializing in software products, called independent service providers.

Insights about the impact of changing domestic competition and technological change on low-wage, old economy and mature industries can be gleaned from examining the *retail food* industry.[14] At the beginning of the 1980s, the industry consisted primarily of traditional food stores, such as supermarkets, grocery stores, bakeries, meat markets, and convenience stores. Increasingly, the competitive structure of the industry has been transformed with competition from restaurants and from supercenters and "power retailers," such as Wal-Mart, now the largest food retailer in the U.S.[15] This threat has led to increasing consolidation in the market share of the leading retailers with significant impacts on pricing and competitive behavior. Of course, the major technological change that shoppers are familiar with is scanning technology, which has not only transformed the way in which the industry does business, but potentially presages the way in which RFIDs (radio frequency IDs) may change businesses in the future. But retail food stores also adopted supply chain management, with electronic data interchange (EDI) technology and experimented with self-checkout systems, electronic shelf tags, vendor-managed inventory, and frequent shopper/loyalty card programs.

A More Detailed Look at Industry and Workforce Change

Financial Services

The financial services industry[16] now accounts for almost 10 percent of gross domestic product (its sales have grown rapidly from 6.4 percent of the U.S. GDP in 1992 to 8.6 percent in 2001).

The labor force has become much more educated over the past twenty years. In part, the displacement of lower-educated workers reflected technological changes that reduced the number of workers required to fill positions such as tellers, clerks, and transactions processors, which were the jobs traditionally held by women. Technological changes, however, do not explain the entire shift in the educational composition of the financial services workforce. The absolute number of tellers employed in financial services, for example, has declined very little, and not nearly as rapidly as BLS projected. Rather, the educational requirements for particular jobs have been upgraded. Many banks now seek tellers and other customer service representatives with more education, even college degrees, and expect them to incorporate sales work and other kinds of advanced customer service into their jobs. The industry has gradually become a workplace for higher-skilled workers, as the proportion of workers in higher-educated, and higher-paying, occupations has increased, while the proportion in lower-paying positions has decreased. The low wages of the less-skilled workers reflect, at least in part, the weak and poorly coordinated industrial relations system in banking. Union membership density in the banking industry, for example, is less than 1 percent.[17]

Concurrent with these earnings trends has been the destruction of longstanding internal labor markets and career ladders in the industry. High school graduates and workers with some college education have found their routes to advancement blocked, particularly in larger organizations, as formal educational requirements have begun to replace industry and firm experience as prerequisites for high-earning jobs. This trend intensified as merger activity heated up in the 1990s in the banking industry. As larger companies purchased small locally owned firms, local managerial jobs such as those in branches were devalued, and firm experience was increasingly dispensable.

Trucking

Competitive pressures have been considerable in the trucking industry. New, nonunion truckload carriers pay low wages, provide little or no health insurance, and almost never contribute to drivers' pension plans. As a result, new carriers managed to avoid taking on the "legacy costs" that were beginning to overwhelm the old-line carriers. As the industry deregulated, older, unionized firms exited in record numbers, firm death was rampant, and the birth of new nonunion firms changed the complexion of the industry quickly. Indeed, most of the carriers that had existed since the days of horse-drawn teaming were out of business by the end of the first decade of deregulation.[18] In 2002, only car-haul remains as a largely unionized specialized market (much of this due to the unusual skills and equipment required, as well as to the value of the freight hauled).

The industry structure changed further after 1995, when intrastate trucking was deregulated. These changes intensified the competitive effects wrought by deregulatory policies some two decades previously. Until 1994, when Congress mandated the deregulation of intrastate truck transportation, many states (especially key large states such as California, Texas, Michigan, and Pennsylvania) retained regulation for intrastate trucking, protecting local cartage within those states. Once competition began to intensify in the wake of the legislation in 1995, union wages and benefits became increasingly untenable in regional LTL and in local cartage. At the same time, new and small nonunion LTL carriers took advantage of new opportunities and grew rapidly.

The labor market structure in the trucking industry is very different from those in the other industries. Differences by education or across other worker characteristics are much less important in trucking than in the other industries, since formal education above a high school degree is not required for truck driving and the industry workforce has few women or minorities. Truck drivers earn most of their income based on mileage rates, which are similar within a company but differ across companies and are influenced by union collective bargaining and the industry segment. Drivers hauling high-revenue freight (such as LTL and small package freight) earn higher returns and are often unionized. Drivers hauling low-revenue freight, such as intermodal containers, gravel and other raw materials, and produce, have the lowest earnings. Some firms, often those that are unionized, choose a high-productivity, high-cost approach with higher-quality freight carried by better-trained and better-paid drivers. Other firms, most of which are nonunionized, take a low-productivity, low-cost approach and are plagued by high turnover.

The labor force, while low wage, is very different from most, because of the flexible nature of the work. The average 1998 earnings for truck drivers (including local markets and those operating relatively smaller trucks) was $7.01 per hour, and those working more than the sixty-hour legal limit average earned only $6.20 for each hour worked.[19] Opportunities for promotion within a trucking company are limited, and longer tenure usually results in favorable schedules or routes at best. The most common path to better earnings and working conditions is to land a job at a union company, although this strategy has become less viable with the decrease in union jobs.

Semiconductors

The semiconductor industry's history since the early 1970s is a story of steady disintegration of the supply chain as specialized sub-industries, such as those for manufacturing equipment ($25 billion) and design software ($4 billion) have emerged. To understand the changing industry structure in semiconductors, it is useful to review the three distinct stages of semiconductor production: design, wafer fabrication, and assembly. The first stage to arise as a distinct industry was the backend assembly of the fragile wafers into sturdy packages that can be inserted into equipment. U.S. companies began moving their labor-intensive assembly operations to lower-cost locations as early as the late 1960s. Local firms, especially in Asia, took over many of these operations on a contract basis and now dominate the assembly industry, which today has only a small presence in the U.S.

Chip design emerged as a separate industry during the 1980s. Fabless companies design chips and then contract for fabrication by other chip companies. Chip design has also been part of the ongoing debate about offshore outsourcing. The fabless design industry, accounting for over 10 percent of chip revenues, got a big boost with the appearance in the 1990s of independent wafer fabrication companies (foundries), which do not design and sell chips of their own. Chip designers no longer feared sending designs to a possible competitor for fabrication. The foundry model was pioneered in Taiwan, which is still home to the largest share of the $12 billion foundry industry. The U.S., where the chip industry was born, remains home to about a third of fabrication capacity.[20]

The impact on the American labor force of the automation of chip manufacturing coupled with the outsourcing of manufacturing to Asian foundries was that employment became even more dominated by highly skilled engineers. The proportion of the workforce that had graduated college rose from 42 percent of the workforce in 1985 to 57 percent in 2002, and that proportion experienced a 20 percent increase in their earnings over the period. At the same time, workers with high school diplomas (or less) declined from 33 percent to 18 percent of the workforce and watched their earnings gradually deteriorate and then improve so that earnings in 2002 were at the late-1980s level.

With the rise of the fabless/foundry model, the industry came to include small competitive firms alongside large multinational integrated corporations. This diverse group of firms uses employment systems that range from what might be considered as close to a competitive spot market as is possible to traditional internal labor markets. Fabless startups often have competitive, short-term employment relationships that are project-related, and tend to offer high-risk, high-return compensation packages. Multinational corporations offer more secure long-term employment relationships with structured career ladders. Even these secure employment relationships weakened in U.S. companies throughout the 1990s as some older companies experienced hard times early in the decade and as the mobility of engineers increased with the lure of huge profits from stock options if their startups became publicly traded or acquired during the boom late in the decade.

The restructuring did not come without cost—the website www.job-hunt.org notes:

> During the Digital Equipment Corporation ("DEC") layoffs of the early and mid-1990's, over 80,000 people lost their jobs world-wide. Thousands who were "right-sized" out of a job found a very tough job market. In New Hampshire and Massachusetts (near DEC's headquarters), they faced many employers who would not consider hiring them because of their DEC experience. The result in several instances was personal tragedy: homes were lost, marriages broke up, and at least three people are known to have committed suicide with one murder-suicide combination adding an additional victim to the total tragedy.[21]

Software Production

Initially, *software* production was dominated by hardware producers and firms that were the end users. Before the late 1960s, most software companies were small and reliant on government contracts and system development work from hardware companies. Further, they tended to focus on development of high-level languages such as FORTRAN or COBOL and on development tools, such as debugging and automatic test data generation. The late 1960s, however, saw the advent of the independent software industry. This, in turn, ushered in the contemporary era of the software industry, which can be dated to the early 1980s.[22]

The diversity of industries that use software in the U.S. has made it difficult for computer manufacturers to pursue vertical market strategies. Most hardware vendors have retreated from software production or reduced their reliance on it. For example, IBM strongly emphasizes its advantageous collaboration with independent software vendors (ISVs).[23] Furthermore, recent entrants into computer production are minor participants in software production, owing to the large number of ISVs. The prior existence of enormous numbers of small contract programming companies directly led to the current large number of ISVs, as well as the fact that increasingly, software programs can be broken down into modules that can be created by independent programmers. In addition, there are standards for debugging, and software tools used to do debugging, that are more generally applied across programs, and thus used by the independent software providers. Among computer producers, ISV participation has fostered greater product diversity and faster sales growth than producers would have realized from their own in-house production of hardware and software. Moreover, for end users of software, the ISV use also presents an important cost-reducing alternative to internal production of software. These changes are reflected in the rapid growth of software vendors such as Oracle, PeopleSoft, and SAP.

Technological change and globalization have also played an important role in the evolution of the industry. Since the 1980s, the emergence of personal computers with a CRT and a graphical user interface (GUI) made it easier for end users who were not primarily programmers to satisfy some of their own programming needs. The further development of CASE tools, which check for programming errors, meant that many of the lower-skilled programming tasks that software engineers would have assigned to programmers could now be automated. Over time, the nature of programming has changed, so that programs are written in modules, rather than as completely intertwined in-house products. As all of these changes improved the design methodology, programming could be more easily specified and contracted out or outsourced overseas. As measured by imports of IT services, outsourcing overseas grew from $300 million in 1995 to $1.2 billion in 2000.[24] However, while growth in outsourcing may be dramatic, it remains small relative to the size of the U.S. economy at only 0.3 percent of domestic output.

The labor force in the industry has two main professions—programmers, who write or modify programs according to specifications given to them, and software engineers, who develop software architecture, devise algorithms, and analyze and solve programming problems. Offshore contracting, the introduction of advanced object-oriented programming languages, "embedded" programming skills among end users, and automation of code writing have all reduced the demand for simple programming tasks. While the growth in demand for computer programmers has been modest (from 400,000 in 1983 to 600,000 in 1997, then dropping to 499,000 by 2002 before rebounding to 563,000 in 2003), the demand for software engineers, systems analysts, and computer scientists has grown dramatically (from 350,000 in 1983 to a peak of 1.9 million in 2000, then dropping slightly since then).[25] With product cycles as short as six months and frequent job changes, certification is seen as a valuable way to demonstrate technical and professional knowledge. The number of certifications available to IT workers doubled from 200 to 400 between 1997 and 2000.[26]

Large numbers of programmers and software engineers are employed on a temporary or contract basis, because companies demand expertise with new programming languages or with specialized areas of application. Although data do not permit us to measure the full extent of this contracting, some 21,000 out of 675,000 software engineers were self-employed in 2002. In the same year, 18,000 out of 499,000 computer programmers were self-employed.[27] Both of these are relatively high shares among white-collar occupations. A substantial amount of programming has also been contracted to be performed outside the U.S. Between 2001 and 2004, offshore programming jobs may have nearly tripled, from 27,000 to an estimated 80,000.[28]

Retail Food

This is an important industry: 224,300 food stores in the U.S. sold nearly $450 billion worth of food and nonfood products in 2002. Though food retailing had traditionally been a highly competitive industry with thin operating margins, the 1990s featured dramatic changes in the landscape of food retailing that further heightened competition. During this period, an increasing number of retailers from outside the traditional food industry began to compete with supermarkets to sell both food and nonfood items. Such "power retailers" included mass merchandisers (Wal-Mart, Kmart, and Target, for example), warehouse club stores (such as Costco, Sam's Club, and BJ's Wholesalers), and other retailers such as drug stores (e.g., CVS, Eckerd, and Walgreen's) and dollar stores. In fact, Wal-Mart is now the largest food retailer in the U.S. This has been accompanied by relatively slow growth in sales at supermarkets—about 1 percent per year after adjusting for inflation—as the share of food sales accounted for by mass merchandisers, warehouse clubs, and other nontraditional food retailers more than doubled from 9 percent in 1994 to 19 percent in 2002.[29] Traditional food stores are also facing more competition from another source: restaurants and other food service companies. Many grocery stores altered their size, format, and product line to respond to these forces. Individual food stores have grown larger; expanded their offerings of ready-to-eat, organic, and natural food products; offered more nonfood items and services; lengthened hours of operation; and adopted various technological innovations to streamline both back-end and frontline operations.

The 1990s also featured consolidation in retail food. Market shares held by leading food retailers rose markedly: between 1997 and 2000, the four largest food retailers' share rose from 18 to 27 percent of total grocery store sales in the U.S. The number of mergers and acquisitions peaked in the late 1990s as some chains chose to grow through acquisitions, while others (Wal-Mart in particular) continued to open new stores. Two of the largest events in retail food consolidation occurred in 1998, a year that saw the joining Albertsons and American Stores, including the Lucky's brand, as well as top-ranked Kroger's purchase of Fred Meyer. Table 3.1 illustrates the quite rapid switching of market leadership, together with the entry and dominance of Wal-Mart. Foreign ownership of food retailers also increased over this period, with recent figures indicating that foreign-owned companies, such as Ahold, account for about 15 percent of grocery store sales.[30] What is clear is that the traditional retail food sector will continue to face intense competitive pressures due both to changing consumer preferences and to the expansion of other retailers into food sales.

Substantial technological change has occurred in the industry, but it is

TABLE 3.1 **Top North American food retailers, based on sales.**

	1992	1998	2001	2003
1	Kroger	Kroger	Wal-Mart	Wal-Mart
2	American Stores	Albertsons	Kroger	Kroger
3	Safeway	Wal-Mart	Albertsons	Costco
4	Winn-Dixie	Safeway	Safeway	Albertsons
5	Albertsons	Ahold USA	Costco	Safeway
6	A&P	Supervalu	Sam's Club	Sam's Club
7	Food Lion	Fleming Cos.	Ahold USA	Ahold USA
8	Publix	Winn-Dixie	Supervalu	Supervalu
9	Ahold USA	Publix	Fleming	Publix
10	Vons	Loblaw	Delhaize	Loblaw

Sources: Food Institute, *Food Industry Review*, various editions. Note that the earlier years did not include warehouse club and mass merchandiser sales when ranking.

generally not "skill-biased" toward higher-skilled workers. Indeed, much of the technology adopted in the industry, while contributing to the productivity of lower-skilled workers and improving overall efficiency, have not directly increased demand for higher-skilled workers. Nonetheless, retail food businesses increasingly use information technology in supply chain management, with growing adoption of EDI (electronic data interchange) technology. Food retailers also are experimenting with additional in-store technologies, such as self-checkout systems and electronic shelf tags. Rates of technology adoption tend to be higher among stores in self-distributing groups, which operate their own warehouses and distribution networks than in stores supplied by independent wholesalers.

The workforce in the industry is similar to that in the retail industry more broadly, in that there is a flat or bottom-heavy job hierarchy, with large numbers of clerks, cashiers, and stockers, and relatively few managers. The job structure became even more bottom heavy as executive, administrative, and managerial jobs declined 30 percent between 1983 and 1993.[31] This bottom-heavy job structure combined with a prevalence of part-time workers helps explain the low average wages in the retail food industry. Average weekly earnings in the industry were only $365 in 1984, and increased only slightly to $384 in 2002.

Retail industries, including food stores, are generally not known for innovative or high-performance human resources practices. Indeed, the typical food retailer maintains a hierarchical and centralized approach to labor.[32] Anecdotal stories abound of store managers and executives who have worked their way up, but the actual level of upward mobility is constrained by the small number of managerial positions and by lack of training opportunities. One study of supermarkets found that while department heads are often hired from within, store managers are not.[33] Over the past several decades, the predominant type of job in the supermarket industry has changed from a full-time, relatively well-paid position (often unionized) to a job with irregular and part-time hours, low pay, and few options for training and career advancement.[34]

The Bottom Line

Globalization, technological change, and deregulation have different effects on different industries, and so using broad-brush aggregates to describe the impact is misleading. This chapter has used case study evidence to describe the changes occurring in each industry over time and suggested that these five industries are a microcosm of the broader economy.

The next chapters quantify and examine how economic turbulence impacts the performance of firms, the jobs available to workers, and the distribution of income across households.

CHAPTER FOUR

Firms, Their Workers, and Their Survival

Introduction

When Calvin Coolidge declared that the business of American is business, he was absolutely right. Firms are the basic building blocks of the economy: they create—and destroy—jobs, wealth, and income. He could equally well have said the business of America is workers. Bricks, mortar, and machines might have been the keys to business success a hundred years ago, but even then, Henry Ford famously (and successfully) paid workers five dollars a day and got a high-quality workforce and with it a profitable business.

So what explains why some firms, like Costco, follow the Henry Ford model and others, like Wal-Mart, don't? Clearly each firm, and each industry, is different. Each firm chooses a different business model with very different levels of workforce quality and worker turnover rates. Some employers, like Wal-Mart, compete by paying low wages and having low prices. Others, like Costco, compete by attracting, retaining, and motivating good workers at all skill levels.

Firms that get it wrong, like Winn-Dixie, are more likely to fail. There are enormous differences in productivity in firms, even firms within the same industry, and research shows that this is closely related to failure rates.[1] Paradoxically, failure, like greed, can be good. Failing businesses have created a surge in productivity for the retail trade industry, for example, precisely because low-productivity firms, like Winn-Dixie, have shut down and been replaced by new high-productivity firms, like Whole Foods.

Business success has many parents. This chapter examines the link between three of them—*worker turnover, workforce quality,* and *worker pay*—and success as measured by *firm performance.* It will show that more productive firms pay above-average wages to their workers, have a higher-quality workforce and lower turnover, and have more skilled workers, although these relationships vary substantially across industries. It confirms that less productive firms are less likely to survive. It also shows that, even after controlling for the level of productivity and other factors, higher-turnover firms are less likely to survive and firms that maintain high-quality workforces are *less* likely to fail in some industries and *more* likely to fail in others. Single-unit, small, and local establishments are especially hurt by high workforce turnover, while establishments with a national reach are especially hurt by low workforce quality.

Different Paths to Firm Success and Failure

Management consulting firms have multiple specialties—such as marketing, finance, and asset management—but almost all of them offer a specialty in people management. Firms can, and do, choose human resources management (HRM) practices that fit their market strategy. Those that choose a strategy of hiring high-quality workers by paying higher wages will see reduced turnover and increased productivity. Others choose to pay lower wages and experience high turnover. The former strategy will increase profitability if wage increases are less than productivity increases; otherwise the latter strategy makes sense.

Managers have often told researchers that they feel compelled to choose low-wage HRM strategies because of competitive pressures to keep costs down. For example, Larry Hunter's work in the financial services industry has found that some firms choose an approach that deskills and segments the workforce as a "low road" response to risk and complexity.[2] And the pressures resulting from industry restructuring have led firms in other industries to choose low-road paths to economic success. Responses by firms in industries as diverse as manufacturing, telecommunications, hospitality, and health care, interviewed by researchers studying low-wage work, led researchers to conclude, "Most employers have responded to increased economic pressure by reducing costs. For a great many of them, cost-cutting has focused on the wage bill."[3]

But other businesses go the opposite route. *Fortune Magazine* annually reports on the hundred best places to work, and some businesses go to extraordinary lengths to pay workers well and reduce turnover. Just as some firms in the financial services industry follow a low road to success, the Principal Financial Group has been regularly named one of the Fortune 100 best places to work. They provide employees with flexible medical plans, flexible leave programs for caregivers, and "no meeting" Fridays.[4] In another one of the industries studied in this book, the software company AGI has been recognized as one of the leading small- to medium-sized companies to work for by offering a family-friendly work atmosphere with daily breakfasts and lunches served to employees and an on-site laundry. The CEO, Paul Graziani, justifies the generous perks with the high productivity increases the firm has enjoyed with these policies.[5] Similarly, the semiconductor giant Intel has been promoting flexible work schedules and a comprehensive work/life program in its efforts to attract and retain the best workers.[6] Intel is also well known for its stock options, bonuses, and retirement programs designed to reduce employee turnover. And four retail food stores make it into the Fortune "best list," with Wegman's starring at number one.

There are high-road employers even in industries that are not featured in the Fortune 100 list. In the trucking industry, where employee turnover is extremely high, Schneider Trucking has health management as well as other employee assistance programs and has developed innovative ways to communicate with drivers spread out across the country. Benefits coordinators regularly talk to employees while they are on the road or visit their families in their absence, and benefits information is available on the Internet for drivers to access while on the road.[7]

Whatever the path, it is clear that businesses deliberately choose their HRM practices and do so to find the practices that makes them successful. The latter goal is clearly stated by James Sinegal, the founder of the Costco warehouse store chain, who "waves away any grand plan to save the American dream. 'I am not a social engineer,' Sinegal says. And, he doesn't have to be. His most convincing rationale for treating workers well is also the simplest: 'It works.'"[8]

Which HRM practices will prove to be profitable? One size does not fit all, and even a good strategy can fail if it's not well implemented. But HRM practices have to include three key, and related, elements: worker pay, workforce quality, and workforce turnover. Each of these is inextricably linked with firm performance and survival.

Worker pay. Each firm has to decide whether higher wages will motivate

workers to be more productive. Paying workers according to skills and performance, rather than by a rigid pay schedule, is likely to help attract the
most able workers and motivate employees. Businesses that attract, retain,
and motivate the best workers will in turn have higher productivity. But
when all is said and done, HRM practices will be profitable, and lead to
better chances of survival, only if the gains from productivity outweigh the
costs from higher wages.

Workforce quality. Each manager has to decide how important it is to
have a high-quality workforce. Bill Gates hires the best and the brightest
at Microsoft because their work has been critical to its success. Not only is
this true, but his management style is such that he is more productive himself when he can interact with high-quality workers, and high-quality workers are in turn more productive by interacting with him. This type of syn-
ergy, which often occurs between managerial ability and worker ability, can
lead to a positive correlation between workforce quality and survival.[9]
Again, however, this strategy is profitable and successful only if the productivity gains outweigh the costs.

Workforce turnover. All managers know that some worker turnover is
healthy. But levels of turnover that are too high can be devastating if firm-
and industry-specific knowledge is lost or the wrong people leave.[10] One
characteristic of a good manager often emphasized in the literature is the
ability to attract and retain good workers.[11]

Although it is tempting to put firm HRM practices in different boxes,
some caveats apply. Not only do different firms follow different paths, but
sometimes they even follow both at the same time. A popular view is that
Wal-Mart is the classic case of a very successful firm that has followed a
low-wage, high-turnover strategy. As a PBS documentary noted:

> Whereas Wal-Mart employees start at the same salary as unionized employees
> in similar lines of work, they make 25 percent less than their unionized counter-
> parts after two years at the job. The rapid turnover—70 percent of employees
> leave within the first year—is attributed to a lack of recognition and inadequate
> pay, according to a survey Wal-Mart conducted.[12]

Yet Wal-Mart's success is due to a much more complex approach. First,
they combine advanced technologies such as innovative inventory management practices with sophisticated and efficient proprietary software
that manages the flow of goods to their stores. This requires high-skilled
high-wage workers for developing and monitoring the technology. Second,

this advanced technology enables them to hire low-wage, low-skilled workers at the cash register.

And regardless of the HRM practices adopted, strategic decisions can make the difference in whether a firm survives. Good business leaders make good decisions in their responses to changes in economic conditions, in their choices of goods and services to produce, and in their choices of business location, as well as in their HRM practices.

Keeping both of these caveats in mind, the following sections explore the relationship between firm performance, workforce quality, and worker turnover and begin with some basic facts about economic turbulence and firms.

Basic Facts about Economic Turbulence and Firms

Performance, Survival, Entry, and Exit

Wikipedia calls a firm "a loose legal term for a company." The way most people do business with a firm is with one of its physical manifestations: one of its establishments. So, for example, Citibank's local branch is an establishment, while Citibank itself is the firm. Most U.S. firms have only one establishment, but the large, multiestablishment firms are most important in terms of creating income, jobs and wealth. This chapter mostly focuses on outcomes for individual establishments, both because industry classifications are establishment based and because it is more straightforward to measure a number of key outcomes. However, the data permit linking establishments to their parent firms, so one part of the chapter examines the role of large, national chains like Citibank or Wal-Mart.

Measuring firm and establishment performance is a challenge, both because there are so many dimensions that could be used—like profits, sales, value added, growth—and because they can be very difficult to measure. Revenue generated per worker is one of the most straightforward measures, and that is what is used in this chapter.

The enormous difference in performance (revenue per worker, our measure of productivity) across establishments, even establishments within the same industry, is an important fact uncovered by looking at the data Figure 4.1 highlights this.[13] In each of the five industries, one standard deviation difference in productivity is around 70 percent. In other words, an establishment at the threshold of the top 15 percent of firms is 140 percent more productive than a firm at the threshold of the bottom 15 percent; and

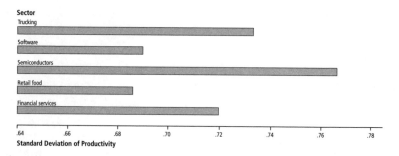

FIGURE 4.1. Dispersion of productivity across establishments within industries.

an establishment at the threshold of the top 2 percent of firms is 280 percent more productive than an establishment at the threshold of the bottom 2 percent.

The obvious question is how the most poorly performing establishments can survive. The answer is that the poor performers by and large don't survive. But less productive firms stay around for several reasons. One reason is that it takes time for firms to decide whether it is worth restructuring poorly performing establishments or to shut them down. Another reason is that a less productive establishment may be located in a geographic region or product market where competition is not intense. Finally, some poorly performing establishments are simply very young, and still going through the trial-and-error process of finding their right path.

Another fascinating fact uncovered after examining histories for establishments in each of the five industries is just how much establishment entry and exit occur. Figure 4.2 shows this over a five-year period.[14] Almost four in ten establishments exit, and about one in three are new in a five-year period. At one end, the less dynamic semiconductor industry had only about one in four of its establishments exit; at the other end, the very dynamic software industry had over half of its establishments born over a five-year period.

It is important to note, though, that the process of establishment survival or failure is likely to be more complex than the simple statistics presented in figure 4.2.

An establishment may exit because its parent firm shuts down or because its parent firm downsizes and closes selected establishments. This distinction is important since even successful firms may find it profitable to close an establishment in one location and open it up in another location. Citibank, like most other financial institutions, does this routinely. Simi-

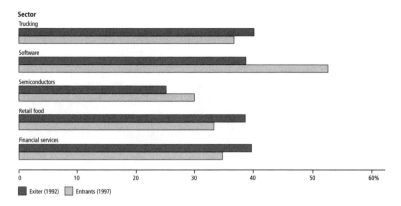

FIGURE 4.2. Entry and exit rates for establishments by industry.

larly, a newly formed establishment may be associated with an existing firm opening new locations or it may be a totally new firm. The retail trade sector is a good example of this: there are many new startup establishments, but much of this entry belongs to national chains like Wal-Mart, Costco, and the ubiquitous Starbucks expanding into new markets.

Even if an establishment physically continues, it may have changed ownership as a result of a merger or acquisition. Great department stores like Marshall Field's and Dillard's, which were owned by May, are taken over by Federated and will become Bloomingdale's or Macy's. Similarly, branch banks that were once First Union become Wachovia. Much (but certainly not all especially in the retail sector) establishment entry and exit is associated with the entry and exit of firms, as most firms have only one establishment. This is not the case, however, for the financial services industry, where particularly intense restructuring and downsizing meant that large numbers of establishments entered and exited, even though many of the parent firms remained in operation. There is a relatively moderate pace of merger and acquisition activity in most industries, with 2 to 8 percent of continuing establishments experiencing a change in ownership over a five-year period. The highest acquisition activity is in financial services (8 percent of continuing establishments) and semiconductors (6 percent).

Entry, Exit, and Performance

Thomas Alva Edison famously said, "I have not failed. I've just found 10,000 ways that won't work." Basic economic principles help explain the complex relationship between performance, entry, and exit. Businesses enter, try different paths, if successful they survive and grow, if not successful, they contract and exit.[15] Accordingly, the economy is constantly replenishing itself with low-productivity exiting businesses being replaced by more productive entering and expanding businesses. For example, in the software industry, entering businesses are, over a five-year horizon, more than 25 percent more productive than the exiting businessess that they replace. This productivity difference between entering and exiting businesses is large by itself and also large compared to the 9 percent productivity gains of continuing businesses over this same five-year period. Taking the difference between the entry and exit difference and the growth rate of productivity for continuing businesses provides an index of the extra productivity grown in the industry coming from entry and exit. In software, this difference-in-difference productivity gap is 16 percent.[16] This pattern implies that *average productivity in the software industry rises substantially as low-productivity exiting firms are replaced by higher-productivity entering firms.*

The entry and exit of establishments raise productivity in four of the five industries, but other factors also play an important role. For example, the substantial increase in overall productivity in semiconductors is associated with productivity increases for continuing businesses and with highly productive entrants replacing much less productive exiting establishments. Continuing businesses over a five-year horizon in the 1990s in semiconductors increased productivity by almost 80 percent. The productivity gap between entering and exiting semiconductor businesses is 116 percent, which is 36 percent higher than the growth in productivity for continuing businesses. This enormous productivity gap reflects the restructuring of the industry, as entrants tend to be fabless startups and leavers tend to belong to integrated companies. The fabless startups that survive have much higher revenue per worker than departing semiconductor establishments.

The major anomaly in this story is the financial services industry, where continuing establishments exhibit substantial productivity declines and entering establishments are less productive than the exiting establishments they are displacing. Exiting establishments have higher measured revenue per worker than continuing establishments; either revenue per worker is not an accurate measure of productivity in financial services or it is poorly measured. Poor measurement may stem from the difficulty of linking the stream of revenue for a financial services firm to a specific establishment. In banking, for example, an establishment is a bank branch, and linking the revenue stream for the bank to a particular establishment is less than straightforward.

Using the data to examine the effect of both firm restructuring (closing and opening establishments) and mergers and acquisitions (ownership changes for existing establishments) shows for most industries that:[17]

- *Firm restructuring is productivity enhancing;* that is, exiting establishments that also entail the exit of the firm are typically the least productive, and entering establishments of continuing firms are more productive than entering establishments of new firms. This pattern of highly productive entering establishments for continuing firms is especially pronounced in retail trade, where the productivity gap between entering establishments for large, national chains and exiting small, single-unit establishment firms is especially large. In short, the displacement of small mom-and-pop stores by the big-box national chain stores has contributed substantially to productivity growth in the retail trade industry.
- *Ownership change is concentrated in more productive establishments;* that is, continuing establishments are more productive both before and after ownership change than establishments that did not change ownership. There is relatively little evidence that the ownership change increases productivity except for establishments in the semiconductor industry. Instead, it is the more productive establishments that change owners.

In general, *industry productivity dynamics are closely linked to firm entry and exit and restructuring.* At the very core of all of this dynamics are firms trying to find the right path. The remainder of the chapter explores how the choices about the workforce and workforce practices contribute to this search for the right path by firms.

Worker Turnover, Workforce Quality, Earnings, and Productivity

Firms across the five industries have very different workforce quality, pay, and worker turnover patterns.[18] Two measures of *workforce quality* are used: a comprehensive measure called "human capital," which reflects the value that the market places on all worker skills (particularly educational attainment, plus problem-solving skills, people skills, social networks, and luck) including experience; and a more narrowly defined measure called "individual skills," which is the human capital measure excluding the contribution of experience.[19] These two measures permit the separation of experience from education and other personal attributes. Table 4.1 documents the proportion of workers in each industry who are above the national median level for each measure.

Software and, to a lesser degree, semiconductor companies have high

TABLE 4.1 **Productivity, workforce quality, churning, earnings, and size by industry.**

Sector	Year	Revenue/worker ($)	Churning rate (%)	Human capital (%)	Person effect (%)	Employment (number)	Payroll/worker ($)
Financial services	1992	143,814	16.8	48.3	57.1	18.9	24,433
	1997	117,857	15.9	61.6	63.1	18.2	23,397
Retail food	1992	138,176	28.7	31.2	46.7	16.1	9,343
	1997	140,355	24.3	40.6	50.3	16.6	9,068
Semiconductors	1992	141,306	13.2	56.6	48.4	82.4	26,873
	1997	555,483	13.2	65.7	53.9	84.5	28,188
Software	1992	116,952	20.2	72.3	74.1	19.0	35,220
	1997	139,924	17.1	79.0	77.0	23.0	38,671
Trucking	1992	97,891	26.9	54.5	39.3	13.9	17,547
	1997	99,313	21.3	67.4	46.0	14.1	17,307

proportions of high-skill workers with both individual skills and experience, and skills in software are better compensated than in semiconductors. By contrast, firms in the retail food industry have high proportions of workers with both low individual skills and little experience. Meanwhile, workers in the trucking industry have surprisingly high levels of experience and low levels of individual skills. The reverse phenomenon is evident in financial services. All of the industries exhibit substantial increases in both measures of workforce quality over the 1990s.

As noted earlier and as seen in table 4.1, average *earnings* are highest in software followed by semiconductors and financial services, then by trucking and finally by retail food. Workers in software generally earn about four times what workers in retail food earn. If workers were roughly paid the value of their marginal products, as predicted by simple economic theory, the rank ordering of industries by revenue per worker should be the same as the rank ordering of industries by payroll per worker, but this is not the case.

The relationship between productivity and workforce quality, churning, and earnings is striking. As seen in figure 4.3, businesses with higher-quality workforces are more productive, as expected.[20] Businesses that are more productive pay higher wages. Businesses with higher churning rates are less productive, which suggests that high levels of turnover might be costly and inefficient for firms. There is also a positive correlation between average pay and workforce quality, between average pay and employer size, and between workforce quality and employer size.[21]

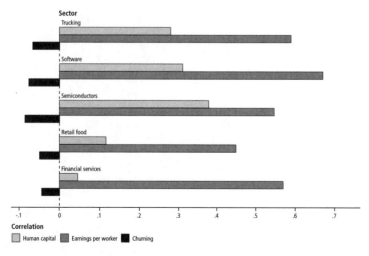

FIGURE 4.3. Correlation of productivity with human capital, earnings per worker, and churning.

Workforce Quality, Churning, and Firm Survival

The next step is to investigate empirically how human resource practices affect firm survival.

Entry, Exit, and Workforce Quality and Turnover

It's trite to say that in a service economy, the company is only as good as its workers. Yet clearly firms like Starbucks and Nordstrom have survived and prospered precisely because their human resource practice is to hire good workers and minimize turnover. The converse can also happen. One of the authors worked in one of the most popular fish and chip shops in Palmerston North, New Zealand (called Jolly Wally's Fish and Chips) when she was a high school student. The manageress trained the "girls," held the secret of the batter recipe, and ran the shop extremely well. But when a new owner bought the business and didn't treat the manageress well, she moved recipe, "girls," skills, and all to another fish and chip shop several blocks away. The first business didn't survive the high turnover and the loss of its high-quality workforce!

How does workforce quality and turnover affect patterns of exit and survival more generally? Figure 4.4a shows that workforce skill is very different across entering, exiting, and continuing establishments. Looking over a five year period in the 1990s, exiting businesses have a lower quality workforce than do surviving businesses, with the difference ranging from about 4 percentage points in semiconductors (not significant) to 19 percentage points in trucking. Entrants in semiconductors have higher-quality workforces, while entrants in retail food and trucking have lower-quality workforces than incumbents. In retail food and trucking, the human capital advantage of incumbents reflects differences in workers' experience rather than individual skill.

Churning rates display a pattern similar to human capital, as illustrated in figure 4.4b. Exiting businesses have turnover rates that are between 4 and 15 percentage points higher than the turnover rate for continuing businesses, and between 2 and 5 percentage points higher than that for entering businesses (except in financial services, where turnover is 2 percentage points *lower* in exiting firms). Continuing businesses have 5 to 10 percentage points lower turnover rates than do entering businesses. The differences in churning rates between entering and exiting establishments on the one hand and continuers on the other hand are especially large in the software and trucking industries.

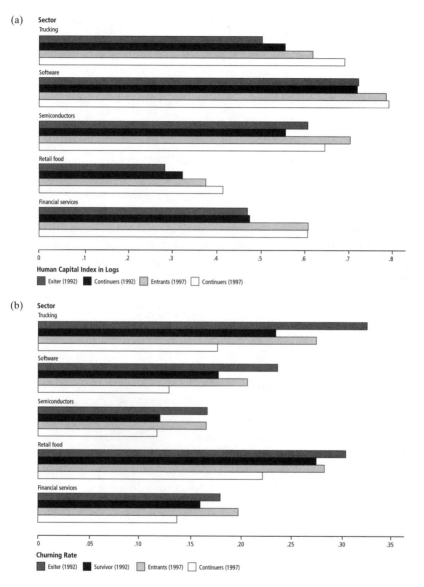

(a)

Sector

Trucking

Software

Semiconductors

Retail food

Financial services

Human Capital Index in Logs

■ Exiter (1992) ■ Continuers (1992) ▨ Entrants (1997) ☐ Continuers (1997)

(b)

Sector

Trucking

Software

Semiconductors

Retail food

Financial services

Churning Rate

■ Exiter (1992) ■ Survivor (1992) ▨ Entrants (1997) ☐ Continuers (1997)

FIGURE 4.4. Differences across continuing, entering, and exiting establishments. (a) Human capital. (b) Churning.

Establishments that survive are more likely to have lower churning rates, to have higher workforce quality, and to be more productive than firms that do not. In general, establishments that exit are less productive and have higher turnover and lower workforce quality than firms that enter. The next section examines the separate effect of each of these factors on survival.

Market Selection: The Role of Firm and Workforce Characteristics

How do firm characteristics and workforce quality and churning interact to affect firm performance and survival? A good approach to answering this question is to examine the relationships for interesting subsectors of the industries, securities brokers within the financial services industry and integrated versus fabless establishments in the semiconductor industry; and for interesting characteristics of firm's product markets.

Quantifying the Impact of Firm and Workforce Characteristics on Survival

The impact of churning and workforce quality on establishment survival is summarized in figure 4.5, which shows quite dramatically that *even controlling for productivity and other establishment characteristics, workforce quality and worker churning significantly affect establishment survival.* In particular, higher-churning businesses are more likely to exit, and the impact of churning is significant across all industries. The magnitude of this effect is large: a 10 percentage point increase in the churning rate increases the likelihood of failure 5 percentage points in the semiconductor industry.[22] These results clearly suggest that high churning businesses are low profit businesses that are more likely to exit. The control factors yield other sensible patterns: larger establishments are less likely to exit and, except for firms in financial services, high-productivity businesses are less likely to exit.[23]

Of course, causality is unclear, since workers anticipating business failure may leave before the business fails, and this may drive up the turnover rate prior to a business exit. A few factors should mitigate such concerns about the interpretation of these findings. For one, the measure of workforce churning that is used abstracts from the net growth rate of firms, so it does not simply capture the downsizing that may occur prior to exit. Second, there is considerable persistence in churning patterns across busi-

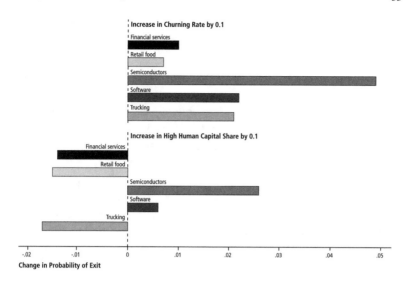

FIGURE 4.5. Impact of human capital and churning on the probability of establishment exit.

nesses. Some businesses have persistently low average churning rates relative to other companies even within the same narrowly defined industry.
One interpretation is that these companies are actively engaging in workforce practices that lower the churning rate in the manner discussed in the
introduction to this chapter.

The impact of workforce quality on firm performance and survival is
less clear-cut, since the high-tech industries behave differently than do
older industries. Establishments with high levels of human capital in financial services, retail food, and trucking are less likely to fail. In semiconductors, establishments with high levels of human capital are more likely to
fail. This seemingly odd pattern most likely reflects the entry and exit of
fabless startup companies, which hire mostly design and other engineers
and so have a higher average human capital than integrated companies,
which hire a wide array of workers. These fabless startups are small and
risky given the fast pace of product innovation in the industry. In software,
an industry also characterized by the rapid entry and exit of startup companies with high-skill labor, the effect is positive but not significant. Software entrants have a smaller support and administrative staff than established companies. Thus, it is not surprising that human capital plays a
different role in the probability of exiting in high-tech industries than in the
other industries.

The inverse relationship between human capital and the probability of exit for the traditional industries points to the importance of a high-quality workforce in long-run firm performance. Interestingly, when the same relationship is estimated including only individual skills as the measure of workforce quality (and excluding the effect of experience), the effect of a higher-quality workforce is to reduce the probability of exit significantly for four of the five industries. In semiconductors, the effect is insignificant, but still positive. Thus, the education and experience component of human capital works differently in software and semiconductors than in other industries. Young, highly skilled workers who know the latest technology are especially valuable in software and semiconductors, and so in these industries it is especially important to distinguish between experience and other dimensions of skills.

The basic message here is that businesses with higher-quality workforces and lower churning are more likely survive. This message does not imply that one size fits all or that these factors are perfect predictors of success or failure. Recall that in the retail food industry, Wal-Mart has succeeded with a low workforce quality and high worker churning strategy while Costco has succeeded with a strategy consistent with these findings. This leads to an obvious question: what is it about Wal-Mart's business plan that permits it to succeed with its low workforce quality and high turnover practices? This analysis suggests that the reason for Wal-Mart's success is that it is at the cutting edge of inventory and distribution management using advanced technology. It may be these other dimensions that permit Wal-Mart to succeed even though its human resource practices would be strong predictors of failure for the average company.

A Deeper Look within Industries

So far, it is clear that firm performance, as measured by the entry of new establishments, exit of old establishments, and growth of continuing establishments, is closely connected to workforce churning and, to a lesser extent, to workforce quality. In general, businesses with high productivity, low worker churning, and high worker quality are more likely to survive.

However, this broad look at industry-wide dynamics sheds little light on how these factors actually play out within each industry, where different economic and political forces are at work. Four detailed characteristics in specific industries are now examined in depth in order to understand better the complex interactions between workforce quality and turnover and firm performance and survival. First, in the financial services sub-industry of securities brokers a better *measure of revenue* and firm performance is used to shed light on firm dynamics. Second, the performance dynamics of *design-only fabless companies* in the semiconductor industry are compared to those of companies with fabrication facilities. Third, the performance of retail food or trucking establishments in *national firms* is examined and compared to that of regional and local firms. Finally, the impact of *establishment and market size* on firm performance in the software industry is analyzed in detail.

Securities Brokers

How does the measurement of firm performance affect the analysis of the financial services industry? Measuring revenue and firm performance in financial services, and especially in banking, is problematic. However, revenue numbers are more reliable and sensible indicators of value added in the narrowly defined securities brokers industry (SIC 6211), since brokers are largely providing a transaction service. This sub-industry within financial services provides a view into how firm performance and firm survival may be related in financial services.

Overall, the patterns are very different for securities brokers than for the remainder of the financial services industry, and in particular, patterns that are more consistent with our findings for the other industries. Overall productivity growth for securities brokers was positive in the 1990s. Not only did productivity increase substantially for industry incumbents, but also entering establishments are much more productive than exiting establishments. These sensible patterns for security brokers suggest that the anomalous findings for the overall financial services industry are likely due to the difficulties of measuring and interpreting revenue per worker for many financial services establishments.

Fabrication vs. Fabless Semiconductor Establishments

Earlier results indicated that productivity and human capital in the semiconductor industry have grown remarkably. To what extent does this reflect the restructuring of the semiconductor industry in the 1990s with the rise of fabless semiconductor companies in the U.S. and the growth of foundries in Asia? Clearly, the fabless startups have workers with high human capital, especially individual skills, and are also small and risky. It is likely that the characteristics and dynamics of the industry have changed substantially, since startups look quite different from large, established integrated establishments (with fabs).

Most entrants in the domestic industry in the 1990s have been fabless establishments, and case study analysis by the Sloan Semiconductor Industry Center suggests that integrated establishments have at least three hundred employees.[24] The number of fabless establishments increased dramatically relative to integrated establishments in the 1990s, but fabless establishments still account for a relatively small share of total industry employment and sales. The fabless establishments are indeed much smaller and more human capital intensive and have higher revenue per worker than integrated establishments. Fabless establishments that entered in the 1990s are especially high-productivity and high-human-capital establishments. Continuing fabless establishments did not exhibit much skill upgrading (they were high skill in the first place). Fabless establishments that exit are likely not to have been able to sell their designs, and so are low productivity, but not especially low skill.

National vs. Regional vs. Local vs. Single-Unit Establishment Firms

The retail food and trucking industries have also been restructuring, albeit in a very different way from semiconductors. The firm organization of these industries has been revamped with the rise of national superstore chains in retail food and the bifurcation between national trucking and smaller locally oriented trucking companies. In retail trade, the rise of box stores from national chains like Wal-Mart and Costco as well as national chains for everything from coffee shops (e.g., Starbucks) and restaurants (e.g., Applebee's and Olive Garden) is ubiquitous. In trucking, large national firms like J.B. Hunt are increasingly running the trucks that are on the interstates doing the long hauling.

Establishments in retail food and trucking have different characteristics and dynamics depending on whether they are part of a large national firm with many establishments across many states, or a regional or local firm. To investigate these differences, establishments are classified into one of four groups:

·   single unit (firm is one establishment)
·   local (establishment is part of a multi-unit establishment firm that operates in only one state)
·   regional (establishment is part of a multi-unit establishment firm that operates in two to five states)
·   national (establishment is part of a multi-unit establishment firm that operates in six or more states).

Most establishments in the retail food and trucking industries are single units, but national establishments account for a disproportionate share of sales. Two-thirds of retail food stores are single units, but these establishments account for only one-third of employment and one-quarter of sales. The share of sales accounted for by establishments from large national chains grew rapidly over the 1990s.

In retail food, national and regional establishments are more productive, are larger, pay higher wages, are more human capital intensive, and are much more likely to survive. Establishments from large national chains increased their productivity advantage both by entry and exit, with an entrant having higher productivity than an exiting establishment, and by smaller productivity losses for continuing national establishments compared to regional. Skill upgrading occurred in all types of establishments, but skill upgrading is especially marked among single-unit establishment firms. Perhaps the only mom-and-pop stores that survived given the intense competition from the large, national chains are those that upgraded the skills of the workers.

Both regional and national establishments exhibit greater churning than local and single-unit establishment firms. Among national establishments, those with especially high churning exited. More human-capital-intensive national establishments are more likely to exit, which may reflect a shift in the composition of national establishments from grocery store chains to superstores over this period of time.

In trucking, national establishments stand out as being larger, more skill intensive, more productive, and lower churning compared to regional and local. However, establishments from national firms lost some of their productivity advantage over the 1990s in the trucking industry as the entry and exit dynamics worked in the wrong direction—the productivity of entering establishments is below the productivity of exiting establishments. All types of establishments exhibited increases in workforce skill and decreases in churning.

Small vs. Large Software Establishments

The software industry has become bifurcated into companies serving two types of markets: those with small, custom-designed software products and those with very large prepackaged software products. To explore the differences across small and large software establishments, establishments are classified into small (twenty or fewer workers) and large (more than 20 workers), since the national average establishment size in software is twenty workers. In the 1990s, large software producers accounted for about 20 percent of the establishments and more than 80 percent of the sales. Large software producers have higher revenue per worker, pay higher wages, are more skill intensive, and have slightly lower churning compared to small producers. These differences between large and small establishments stayed roughly constant over the 1990s except the productivity gap widened, with greater productivity gains for continuing large establishments.

The data also show that productivity has a positive impact on the probability of surviving for large establishments, while churning has an especially large adverse impact for small establishments. These results are consistent with the large packaged producers needing high volume to survive and the small custom producers using designated teams to respond to customer needs and service.

The Bottom Line

Firm performance is tightly linked with workforce quality and churning. Measures of productivity, workforce quality, and turnover are highly correlated across businesses in each of our five industries. High-productivity businesses have a higher proportion of workers with high human capital, including education, individual attributes, and experience. It is not a coincidence that Wegman's, rated number one in the Fortune 100 best places to work, is identified by the *Progressive Grocer* as one of the strongest regional grocery chains.

Firm survival is a function of all of these factors: businesses with high productivity, low churning, and high human capital are more likely to survive. The patterns of these results vary substantially across the five industries. For example, churning is especially important in semiconductors and retail foods while, interestingly, workforce quality is especially important in the trucking and retail food industries.[25] In other words, Ford's five-dollars-a-day model is as instructive today as it was a hundred years ago.

Understanding the detailed characteristics and evolution of each industry helped us to interpret the patterns across industries. Some of the anomalous patterns for the semiconductor industry, for example, seem to be driven by the rise in fabless startups. Software startups with niche products look quite different than their older high-volume counterparts. In retail food and trucking, large disparities exist between the characteristics and dynamics of establishments that are part of national chains as opposed to small, local establishments. Industry knowledge is critical for understanding how firms operate and the outcomes for both the firm and its workers.

Heeding the advice of H. L. Mencken, that complex problems have simple, easy-to-understand, and wrong answers, this chapter has spelled out in detail the complex interrelationship between an establishment's workforce, performance, and survival, and, in turn, industry growth. The next obvious question is: what is the impact of establishment performance on individual workers? This question is addressed in the next two chapters.

CHAPTER FIVE

Firm Turbulence and Job Ladders

Introduction

Are good jobs disappearing? Lou Dobbs in his *Exporting America* (2004) thinks so: in his view too many U.S. companies are sending American jobs overseas and choosing to employ cheap overseas labor.[1] Chinese and Indian software engineers work for Microsoft in Beijing and Bangalore; Intel assembles most of its chips abroad; call centers for American consumers are located in India and the Philippines. Some companies are even more extreme. SeaCode Inc. is one of them: its owners did not even go overseas to employ foreigners. They planned to hire six hundred foreign software engineers to work on a cruise ship three miles off the California coast so that they could avoid paying U.S. wage rates and obeying California labor laws while still having a location close to headquarters and workers in the same time zone.[2]

The America of Horatio Alger seems to be vanishing. Domestic and foreign competition are eroding the number of jobs with high pay and good growth potential. As a *Business Week* article pointed out in 2003:

> There has been much talk recently of the "Wal-Martization" of America, a reference to the giant retailer's fervent attempts to keep its costs—and therefore its prices—at rock-bottom levels. But for years, even during the 1990s boom, much of Corporate America had already embraced Wal-Mart-like stratagems to control labor costs, such as hiring temps and part-timers, fighting unions, dismantling internal career ladders, and outsourcing to lower-paying contractors at home and abroad.[3]

Whatever the causes, there are always news stories about the economic vulnerability of even high-educated people in competitive industries. They often start with anecdotes about people like Sandra ("Candy") Robinson, a software engineer with a BS in electrical engineering, MS in computer science, an MBA, and twenty-three years of experience, who was earning $89,000 when, in January 2001, her company merged with Citigroup and she was laid off. Candy has been out of work ever since. In over two years, she has had only three interviews and no job offers.[4]

But there is a flip side to the picture. For every story about people like Candy, there are other stories about workers who stay with one firm and succeed. Carol Primdahl represents such a story. She received a BS in mechanical engineering and then joined Texas Instruments in 1986. From 1987 through 1993, Carol worked in one of TI's Houston semiconductor manufacturing plants (fabs). In 1995, she was promoted to quality manager at a fab in Dallas. She received an MBA from SMU while working at TI, and has held three other positions within the company.[5]

Which of these sides of the picture is true? The fear described in the *Business Week* article, by Lou Dobbs, and by stories like Candy Robinson's is that complex events like globalization, deregulation, and technological change demolish jobs and the good job ladders, like Carol's, that Americans are used to. The promise implicit in Carol's story is that competition on a global scale will help create strong job ladders like the one she has scaled.

So how much truth is there to the basic fear haunting Americans that "good jobs" have been lost? Defining a "good job" is not easy. Most would agree that TI's Carol Primdahl has a good job because she works in a firm with long-term job ladders that provide career development. Most would also agree that Candy Robinson's job was not so good: her job ladder abruptly ended. But this begs the question: how can a job ladder be defined? In this chapter, three core characteristics are used: job tenure, initial earnings, and earnings growth.[6]

These three characteristics define literally millions of job ladders in millions of firms for tens of millions of workers. In order to tell this chapter's story of the impact of economic turbulence on typical job ladders, those ladders had to be characterized, and then the impact of firm size, growth rates, and turnover had to be measured. Finally, because employment, earnings, and earnings growth are systematically different for workers who differ by gender, age, and skill, the impact had to be measured for different types of workers. Then, and only then, was it possible to describe how economic turbulence—firm expansion and contraction coupled with worker turnover—contribute to job ladders' differences and begin to explain the difference between Candy's and Carol's experiences.

How can these events like globalization, deregulation, and foreign competition be measured and quantified? *The truth is that they can't be.* The best that can be said is that after interviewing key players and studying particular industries, experts have judged that these factors are important to different degrees in different industries. What *can* be measured are the outcomes: how much firms in different industries are expanding and contracting, hiring, and shedding workers, and offering different types of job ladders.

The rest of the chapter spells out some of the ways in which economic turbulence affects job ladders. Some common themes will become clear as you read the next sections.

· *A firm's growth and turnover rates can provide some clues to whether the firm offers "good jobs."* High worker turnover at a firm indicates lower-quality job ladders. Large firms and growing firms provide some of the best job ladders. Conversely, small firms and shrinking firms tend to provide the fewest and the worst job ladders. However, small growing firms often provide excellent job ladders, especially in semiconductors, financial services, and trucking.

· *Even when a company offers good job ladders, only a select group of workers may be able to move "up" onto these ladders.* Many high-turnover firms seem to follow an "up or out" strategy. In all industries except semiconductors, male workers who are able to keep their jobs in high-turnover firms end up earning more than similar workers in low-turnover firms. The fact that firm turnover and the growth in a worker's earnings go hand in hand suggests that some firms follow a strategy for advancing the careers for only a selected group of workers rather than all workers.

· *Men experience better job ladders than women, who are less likely to have good jobs than are men.* In each of the five industries, women's job ladders had lower initial earnings and earnings growth than do men's, even when the women and men have the same education. However, economic turbulence has a similar impact on the job ladders for both men and women.

A Potted History of Job Ladders in Each Industry

How did job ladders evolve, and what are the forces changing them? The answers are different for each industry.

Large semiconductor firms used to be known for establishing job ladders that encouraged the development of worker skills and commitment.

Even in the 1980s, when intense global competition and an ever increasing pace of technological change forced chip companies to be more market driven and performance based, they streamlined operations and downsized through "voluntary early retirement" programs. For example, in 1983, IBM offered workers at five locations a voluntary early retirement program, where workers with twenty-five or more years' experience could receive a bonus of two years' pay over four years. IBM offered voluntary retirement programs again in 1986 and 1989.[7] These programs did not always work as the companies hoped, since often the better workers would opt to leave, and the workers who stayed were often those without good job opportunities elsewhere.

It wasn't until the deep recession in the early 1990s that IBM, DEC, and Motorola, once known for their employment security, finally announced layoffs.[8] The new approach to downsizing included voluntary programs for targeted workers, and if workers did not accept the termination program, they could become subject to layoff. These programs were not seen as voluntary by the workers, although the programs with severance pay were substantially better than being laid off without severance pay. In 1991 and 1992, IBM selected workers eligible for termination that included a bonus of up to a year's salary. Over 40,000 workers were "transitioned" out. Downsizing continued through 1993, and by 1994 actual layoffs were occurring at IBM.[9]

Similar downsizing occurred throughout the semiconductor industry. DEC, the second largest computer company in the late 1980s with over 100,000 employees, began layoffs in the early 1990s. Over 80,000 workers were laid off worldwide during the 1990s, before DEC was acquired by Compaq in 1998.[10] After Compaq was acquired by HP, 14,500 layoffs were announced in 2005.[11]

Then, with the dot.com bust in the early 2000s, massive rounds of layoffs by semiconductor companies occurred again. By the end of 2001, Motorola had laid off nearly 42,900 workers from its 2000 peak of 150,000 employees.[12] The volatile swings in demand meant that the idea of lifetime employment in the semiconductor industry was a thing of the past, although selected workers could still find excellent job ladders with long careers.

The software industry is characterized by two distinct types of firms with different HRM practices. Industry giants, like Microsoft and Oracle, have captured large market shares in specific product markets and produce and revise well-established products. Because they need to hire and retain high-skilled loyal workers who can maintain and expand their software offerings, these firms develop extended job ladders and provide strong incentives for good workers to stay.

Job ladders are very different in those waves of software startups looking to create the next "killer application." These firms occupy market niches that are on the cutting edge of new product development. Product turnover is high, and the startups are small and highly volatile. They are likely to adopt a "star" approach: hire star workers who are especially skilled at a specific application or sales and are highly mobile. If the new product is successful, the firm takes off. If not, the firm contracts and either the product line or the firm itself disappears.[13]

The two different types of strategies have coexisted for a long time. A 1999 *Business Week* story highlighted the pressures on Microsoft:

> After 24 years as a talent magnet, Microsoft is grappling with a brain drain. Even though the software behemoth has one of the lowest turnover rates in the computer industry, some experts believe the loss of key people at all levels in the organization could threaten Microsoft's ability to stay on top of the computer world. For years, company executives have preached that smart employees are their most crucial asset. "This loss of talent is a serious problem, if not the most serious problem Microsoft is facing," says a programmer who left Microsoft this past spring.[14]

Human resource practices have been changing in the retail food industry since the entry of nontraditional food retailers, such as mass merchandisers and warehouse club stores like Wal-Mart and Costco, during the 1990s. Although promotion from within the store or chain was once a very common practice, store managers are now increasingly hired from outside the store and even outside the industry. Many employers continue to express concern about the high level of labor turnover in the industry, but according to the *Progressive Grocer,* most supermarkets "are looking for ways to cut, rather than invest in people."[15] Industry restructuring has led to the development of two-tier wage structures, with most new hires facing lower pay and fewer job advancement opportunities.

The trucking industry has been shaped by unionization, and the Teamsters Union once was almost synonymous with trucking. Unions had significant clout in all corners of the industry. After deregulation began, however, intense competition led to a substantial decline in union density in many markets. Older unionized firms exited in record numbers, and the new nonunion firms changed the complexion of the industry quickly. New nonunion carriers paid low wages with little or no health insurance and no pension plans. The recession of the early 1980s, and the resulting loose labor market, put pressure on both carriers and workers to haul freight for less.

Different practices do exist within the industry, however. For example, J.B. Hunt, one of the nation's three largest truckload (TL) carriers, began a bold experiment in paying for experience when it raised driver wages by 38 percent in 1997, partly in response to a documented 96 percent turnover rate. The resulting improvements in worker quality and retention rates improved both productivity and profits for the company. J.B. Hunt touts its pay and benefits on its Web site:

> At J.B. Hunt, we're committed to providing drivers with the best job in the truckload industry. To demonstrate this commitment, we took a bold leap several years ago and invested in our drivers by giving them a 33% wage increase and the potential to earn up to 41 cents per mile. Since then, industry wages have remained stagnant; and we're baffled that many drivers are still content to earn the equivalent of minimum wage while our drivers receive top dollar!
>
> The job itself doesn't change much from company to company; any carrier will give you a truck, some miles, and a day off once in a while. But your questions remain: What's the condition of the equipment? How much will I earn? Will the miles be there? We excel in each of these categories, and we have one question of our own: Why would you pick up the same freight from the same docks as our drivers and allow yourself to be paid less, year after year? Let us assure you that we will have our fair share of America's freight, and we will get you the miles.
>
> In these times, you can't afford to leave your family in financial uncertainty. We'll give you a paycheck you can count on every week—and remove the worry about whether your check will cash and whether your company will even still be in business. Our stability is something you can rely on, year after year. And we want you to enjoy long-term satisfaction—not just for one year or two, but for ten years, fifteen, or however many years you drive. A 100% conventional OTR fleet, earning two days off for seven on the road, and our permanently assigned equipment option were all put in place to ensure driver satisfaction.[16]

Despite the success of this strategy, the changes made by J.B. Hunt remain the exception rather than the rule in the trucking industry.

The financial services industry also changed its HRM practices as it underwent deregulation and consolidation as big companies bought up small ones. First Union and Bank One are excellent examples. Both of these grew spectacularly over the 1980s and 1990s, mostly as a result of acquisitions. Both overdid it. Bank One ended up struggling, and being bought by JPMorgan Chase & Co.[17] JPMorgan itself is an investment bank which previously bought Chase, a commercial bank that had already been through a series of mergers.

Chase, Citicorp, and Merrill Lynch made big employment cuts in the late 1990s, but usually layoffs are more incremental. Financial services tend to have high enough turnover that employment can be reduced through attrition. For example, First Union restructured its retail division in the second half of the 1990s, but it was able to cut employment through attrition and performance-based cuts rather than layoffs.

Workers with relatively little education had long had opportunities in financial services firms, especially local banks and insurance agencies, to gain skills and advance over time to well-paying positions. But this has become increasingly rare over the past twenty years. Many of the old job ladders in financial services companies have been destroyed amid increasing segmentation of jobs with different educational requirements.[18] For example, large retail banks transitioned to a sales orientation, and their turnover increased both voluntary and forced separations of workers with low sales performance. Turnover remained higher even after the transition because the banks no longer have a civil service mentality. The whole industry begins to look more like investment banking and brokerage houses.

In sum, job ladders in firms have changed in very different ways in response to the economic turbulence sweeping their industries. But there's no question that there is wide variation in HRM practices and firm characteristics among firms within an industry, as well as across industries. The thirty-two companies in our five industries that were featured in Fortune's listing of the "100 Best Companies to Work For" (2005) display a wide range of characteristics—by size (small to large), by employment growth (negative to highly positive), and by voluntary turnover (from 3 percent to 32 percent).[19] Eleven large growing companies and seven small growing companies, which tend to offer the best job ladders, made the list, but so did seven companies that decreased employment over the year. Perhaps most surprising was the variation in voluntary turnover at these good employers, who exhibited both low (3 percent to 6 percent) and high (13 percent to 32 percent) voluntary turnover in software, financial services, and retail food. Only semiconductors did not have any best companies with high turnover; its three best companies all had voluntary turnover no greater than 5 percent.

Sloan Industry Center researchers have certainly found that different firms treat workers differently. Some companies create and reward loyalty. They provide their workers with career development up long job ladders that begin with high initial earnings and provide earnings growth that reflects skill development. As a result, workers provided access to these job ladders tend to stay. Companies like TI Semiconductors, PeopleSoft, USAA Insurance, Wegmans Food Markets, and Roadway Express develop reputations for being good employers. The next section examines whether such firms are the exception or the rule in their industries.

Measuring Job Ladders

Job ladders can best be measured with initial earnings, earnings growth, and tenure, or the length of time a worker is employed at a firm. But because firms offer different types of job ladders by education and the jobs available also vary by age and gender, this means that there are literally hundreds of job ladders in each of the industries. As a result, it was a major task is to identify typical patterns for each group. Fortunately, 70–80 percent of the workforce are between 25 and 54 years old, and so it is possible to separate most workers into two age groups: a "younger" group (aged 25–34 years old) and into a "middle-aged" group (aged 35–54 years old).[20] Because job ladders vary by gender and education, separate categories are created for those groups as well—the education categories being comprised of "low," roughly high school and less; "medium," some college; and "high," college graduate and above.

It was also a major challenge to capture the impact of economic turbulence, like firm employment growth and worker turnover, on each career ladder. The firms are straightforwardly categorized as growing or shrinking; and also by whether they have high or low turnover rates.[21] Growing firms are obviously having jobs reallocated to them from shrinking firms, while high-turnover firms are disproportionately contributing to worker turnover. Firms are also categorized as large or small because the effect of volatility differs by firm size.[22]

The impact on job ladders of both job reallocation across firms as they grow and shrink plus worker turnover within firms was modeled for each of the five industries with twelve categories of workers and eight types of firms (see appendix C for details). In fact, a job ladder and career path calculator was created that describes the impact of each factor on initial earnings, job growth, and final earnings, and this is accessible for all 480 job ladders on this book's Web site, www.economicturbulence.com (you can also calculate your favorite career paths in each industry). Of course, there are too many to be summarized in this chapter, so the following sections explore some basic facts about the most prevalent job ladders and describes common patterns.

Some Facts about Jobs and Firms

Short jobs lasting less than three years are common, and not just in trucking and retail food. Six in ten ongoing jobs for workers aged 25 to 55 years old have lasted less than three years (and even less time in software). American workers are extremely mobile across employers and industries. Although this probably reflects personal decisions to change jobs as well as the company's decision to fire workers, the data do not distinguish between the two. But this worker mobility means that there are lots of opportunities for the first step on the ladder. New hires account for one out of every three jobs in software, retail foods, and financial services, but only one out of every six jobs in semiconductors and trucking.

Long jobs lasting more than five years are less common than short jobs, but long jobs are more common in some industries than others. Even in large growing firms with low turnover, which are known for providing good jobs in their industries, the proportion of workers who keep their jobs for five years or more varies enormously across industries.[23] Surprisingly, the low-wage industries of retail food and trucking are the most likely to have long jobs, where 40 percent of workers have jobs that have lasted at least five years. In the three high-skilled sectors, only one in four workers in the semiconductor industry, only one in five workers in financial services, and a mere one in seven workers in the software industry have jobs that have lasted five years or more.

Not surprisingly, most jobs are in firms where the growth is. Jobs are provided predominantly by growing firms and by large firms.[24] *Growing firms* provided 65 percent to 70 percent of jobs in all five industries in 2001. *Large firms* provided the majority of jobs, from 55 percent in software to 85 percent in semiconductors, except in trucking, where 55 percent of jobs are in small firms. So even though Lou Dobbs lists as many firms as he can find that are outsourcing jobs, much of the impact on the labor market can be gleaned simply by examining what the largest and fastest-growing firms are doing.

But in some industries, stable jobs are hard to find. *Growing firms with low turnover,* the most stable firm type, provide over half (50 percent to 58 percent) of jobs in financial services and semiconductors, but only 38 percent of software jobs, and only 25 to 30 percent of jobs in trucking and retail food. And the proportion of jobs that are in *high turnover* firms, which are likely to be quite unstable, varies dramatically by industry. Over 40 percent of jobs are in high-turnover firms in retail food, compared with only 10 percent of jobs in semiconductor. The trucking industry has a variety of different firm types. *Surprisingly, small growing firms with high turnover* are the largest provider of jobs in trucking and account for 25 percent of jobs. Two-thirds of jobs at these firms last fewer than three years. So although J.B. Hunt may have high visibility and show up in many anecdotes about the trucking industry, the data show that many trucking companies are small companies unknown to the general public.

What Happens to Jobs in Shrinking Firms?

Much of the fear of the loss of good jobs stems from a fear that when firms shrink as a result of competition, workers like Mark McClellan will lose their jobs. But firms can have different strategies. Some firms follow a LIFO strategy (last in, first out), while others follow a FIFO (first in, first out) strategy.

In fact, firms in different industries differ. Case study evidence indicates that in semiconductor companies, experienced (and higher-paid) engineers are replaced by younger engineers with newer skills—a FIFO strategy. This is confirmed by data. Large shrinking semiconductor firms have even fewer long jobs than do large expanding firms. By contrast, shrinking software firms do not reduce their proportion of long jobs, suggesting that, unlike shrinking semiconductor firms, shrinking software companies do not replace experienced workers with new hires. A LIFO approach is common for most firms in financial services and trucking: shrinking firms have more long jobs than do expanding firms, although in retail food, shrinking firms have the same high percentage of long jobs as growing firms.

Why do firms in different industries follow different approaches? Part of it may be cost: higher-wage industries may downsize by replacing experienced workers with lower-cost new hires at an accelerated pace, while shrinking firms in low-wage industries may adjust by simply reducing the number of new hires unless prevented by union contracts. Another possibility is that experienced, better-educated workers in high-tech industries have more options, and so are able to leave, while their counterparts in the low-wage industries have fewer places to go, although the next chapter will show that this scenario is probably not common. Workers who change jobs typically end up with lower incomes than the workers who keep their jobs. Candy Robinson's experience is quite common: even good education and job experience could not guarantee her a good job when she was laid off.

Job Ladders and Workers

The best way to explore the different types of job ladders offered by firms is through graphs, so this section shows some *typical earnings paths* for jobs that have lasted at least five years for each worker and firm type in each industry.[25] What does examining these hundreds of job ladders show?

Growing firms offer better job ladders than do shrinking firms, both to low-educated workers and high-educated workers. Figure 5.1 is a classic example: it shows the typical job ladders faced by middle-aged men in the semiconductor industry. Job ladders for low-educated men are heavily affected by whether they work in a growing or a shrinking firm. Those who land jobs in the growing firms typically start out $5,000 more than low-educated men in shrinking firms and maintain their earnings advantage

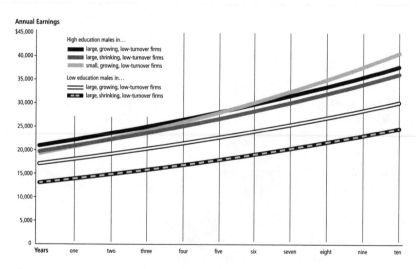

FIGURE 5.1. Job ladders for middle-aged workers in the semiconductor industry.

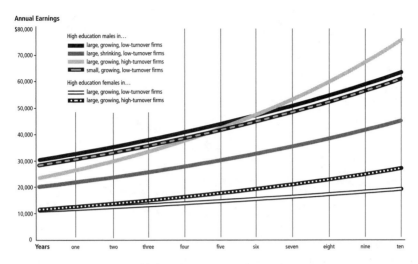

FIGURE 5.2. Job ladders for middle-aged workers in the financial services industry.

over time. The same pattern holds for high-educated men, although the gap is quite a bit less: about $2,000.

Large firms usually offer better job ladders than small firms, although this is not true in the rapidly changing semiconductor industry. *Small low-turnover* firms in this industry, which are likely to be early-stage design companies, mainly hire highly trained technical personnel and offer relatively good job ladders for the college educated. As figure 5.1 shows, these firms offer better job ladders than large growing firms. Although initial earnings are lower, earnings growth is high, and by the end of a decade, the earnings of engineers at these successful startups have passed those of engineers at large growing firms.

High-turnover firms tend to have inferior job ladders, but this is not always the case. In financial services, job ladders for high-educated middle-aged men are better than in high-turnover than in low-turnover (large, growing) firms (see figure 5.2). The men start with lower initial earnings in the high-turnover firms, but they have higher earnings growth and after five years pass the men in the low-turnover firms. However, many of the men in the high-turnover firms are unlikely to keep their jobs long enough to catch up and pass their peers in the low-turnover firms. Women in financial services find that the same is true for them: women in high-turnover growing firms end up with considerably higher earnings at the end of a decade compared to their peers in low-turnover (large, growing) firms.

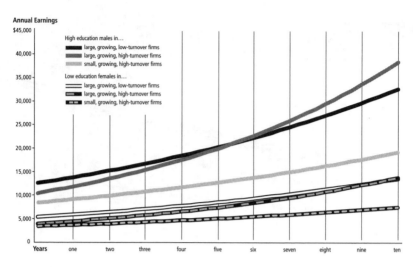

FIGURE 5.3. Job ladders for middle-aged workers in the retail food industry.

The other job ladders in figure 5.2 reinforce the observation that large firms pay more than small (growing) firms, although the difference shown for high-educated middle-aged men is small. They also reinforce the observation that the difference between job ladders in growing and shrinking (large, low-turnover) firms is much greater for these men. In this industry, men who work in growing firms start off with $10,000 more in earnings and end up ten years later with almost $20,000 more.

The most startling difference in these job ladders is between women and men. Even among long-tenured high-educated, middle-aged workers, women earn considerably less than men in financial services, and fare much worse than in the other industries. In large growing firms, men start out earning over twice what women make, and at the end of a decade the men are typically making up to three times what the women make in this white-collar industry once thought a good place for women to work.

In some industries, where a worker works matters even more than the worker's education level. Job ladders in the low-wage retail food industry are a classic example of this (see figure 5.3). The data on both high-educated male and low-educated female (middle-aged) workers in large and small (growing high-turnover) firms show that large firms pay slightly higher initial earnings and have higher earnings growth. At the end of a decade, workers in large firms earn over 80 percent more than comparable workers at small firms. The earnings differences by firm size are so dramatic that low-educated workers (both males and females) in large firms, if they are able to keep their jobs, eventually earn more than their high-educated peers at small firms (not shown). The bottom line is that a bagger who moves up to stocker in a large store will end up making much more than the worker who does a variety of jobs in a small store.

However, initial earnings are important to workers in retail food, since turnover is high and many workers see it as a way to earn money while they go to school or take care of families. *Large growing low-turnover* firms, which are often unionized and provide between 5 and 10 percent of the jobs in this industry (depending upon education and gender), pay initial earnings that are at least 20 percent higher than other types of firms (shown here for high-educated men and low-educated women). Their high-turnover counterparts provide higher earnings growth, but it takes five years for the high-educated men to catch up and almost ten years for the low-educated women to catch up with their peers in the low-turnover firms.

What is the overall picture of the job ladders provided by different kinds of firms to different types of workers? Table 5.1 summarizes this by showing average initial earnings (first row) and average earnings growth (second row) for the two most prevalent education groups for middle-aged men and women. In order to compare the earnings across firms in an industry, row three reports earnings at the end of ten years as a proportion of the earnings of men in the highest education group shown in a growing, large, low-turnover firm.

Starting earnings vary dramatically by type of firm. A typical male worker who is high-educated and gets a job in a growing, large low-turnover financial services firm, for example, will start out at about $30,236 and experience an average earnings growth of 7 percent. A similar worker who gets a job in a firm that is shrinking, but still large and still low turnover, will get only $19,817. And at the end of ten years, that worker will only end up with 70 percent of the earnings that his counterpart had. Earnings also vary by gender. The job ladder is substantially worse for his high-educated female counterpart. She would start at $11,081, her income would grow by about 5.5 percent, and she would end up with earnings that are 30 percent of the male's.

How does this vary across industries? The same set of comparisons in retail food shows that a typical high-educated male worker in retail food who gets a job in a growing, large low-turnover firm, would start out at about $12,483—only 41 percent of the starting pay of his counterpart in

TABLE 5.1 **Job ladders, workers age 35–54.**

	Males					Females				
	+ Growth Large Low T/O	+ Growth Large High T/O	+ Growth Small Low T/O	+ Growth Small High T/O	– Growth Large Low T/O	+ Growth Large Low T/O	+ Growth Large High T/O	+ Growth Small Low T/O	+ Growth Small High T/O	– Growth Large Low T/O
Financial Services										
Medium Education	$19,436	$15,765	$17,688	$18,101	$14,602	$8,780	$8,038	$6,655	$7,256	$7,835
	0.081	0.118	0.087	0.109	0.085	0.062	0.086	0.070	0.090	0.065
	0.69	0.81	0.67	0.85	0.54	0.26	0.30	0.21	0.28	0.24
High Education	$30,236	$23,447	$28,012	$24,119	$19,817	$11,081	$11,479	$8,955	$9,830	$9,937
	0.074	0.117	0.077	0.106	0.082	0.055	0.086	0.060	0.086	0.061
	1.00	1.19	0.96	1.10	0.71	0.30	0.43	0.26	0.37	0.29
Retail Food										
Low Education	$9,401	$7,143	$4,468	$5,628	$8,028	$5,243	$3,880	$3,655	$3,437	$3,488
	0.108	0.141	0.088	0.092	0.123	0.095	0.126	0.060	0.079	0.116
	0.85	0.90	0.33	0.44	0.84	0.42	0.42	0.20	0.23	0.34
High Education	$12,483	$10,339	$8,059	$8,452	$10,230	$7,971	$5,482	$4,542	$4,845	$5,450
	0.096	0.131	0.073	0.082	0.089	0.083	0.116	0.044	0.069	0.082
	1.00	1.17	0.51	0.59	0.77	0.56	0.54	0.22	0.30	0.38
Semiconductors										
Medium Education	$19,458	$13,427	$14,068	$15,517	$16,330	$11,808	$9,600	$7,712	$8,050	$8,630
	0.054	0.063	0.068	0.076	0.061	0.039	0.021	0.048	0.085	0.036
	0.88	0.67	0.74	0.88	0.80	0.46	0.31	0.33	0.50	0.33
High Education	$20,904	$19,391	$19,102	$18,676	$19,530	$12,765	$11,264	$9,694	$8,973	$9,369
	0.059	0.040	0.075	0.055	0.061	0.044	-0.002	0.054	0.064	0.036
	1.00	0.77	1.07	0.86	0.95	0.53	0.29	0.44	0.45	0.36

Software

Low Education	$16,316	$18,174	$15,372	$15,524	$17,074	$10,397	$12,232	$9,348	$10,001	$11,265
	0.078	0.104	0.083	0.099	0.077	0.054	0.082	0.069	0.093	0.061
	0.67	0.97	0.66	0.78	0.69	0.34	0.52	0.35	0.48	0.39
High Education	$22,551	$22,895	$19,898	$22,402	$19,748	$15,204	$14,587	$13,434	$12,205	$14,584
	0.086	0.087	0.074	0.084	0.075	0.062	0.065	0.061	0.078	0.059
	1.00	1.03	0.79	0.97	0.78	0.53	0.53	0.46	0.50	0.49

Trucking

Low Education	$11,519	$9,140	$9,214	$8,798	$10,815	$7,212	$6,040	$5,717	$5,765	$7,700
	0.036	0.077	0.057	0.080	0.063	0.032	0.072	0.078	0.090	0.086
	0.83	0.99	0.82	0.98	1.02	0.50	0.62	0.62	0.72	0.92
Medium Education	$11,946	$9,876	$11,001	$9,669	$11,279	$9,204	$7,931	$7,210	$8,390	$9,005
	0.051	0.073	0.058	0.075	0.075	0.047	0.068	0.079	0.086	0.099
	1.00	1.03	0.99	1.02	1.21	0.74	0.79	0.80	0.99	1.22

Cells contain mean initial earnings, net annualized earnings growth rate across the simulated career path, and simulated final earnings level as a proportion of the corresponding highest-educated male worker shown in a growing, large, low-turnover firm. Benchmark levels of earnings at end of period are financial services, $63,377; retail food, $32,556; semiconductors, $37,699; software, $53,082; and trucking, $19,901.

financial services. But his earnings grow much faster—9.6 percent compared to 7.4 percent in financial services. A high-educated male worker in
a retail food firm that is shrinking, but still large and still low turnover,
would start at $10,230, and, at the end of ten years, would end up with only
77 percent of the earnings of a comparable worker in a growing firm. Earnings also vary by gender. The job ladder is still worse for a high-educated
female in a growing, large low-turnover retail food firm, but the gap is not
nearly as pronounced. She would start at $7,911, her income would grow by
about 8 percent, and she would end up with earnings that are 56 percent of
the male's.

In sum, this table reinforces the results shown earlier for specific job
ladders. The five most important findings are:

*Job ladders are usually worse in shrinking firms, since they initially pay
workers less.* This is clear when the first column is compared with the fifth
and the sixth column with the tenth. Workers of both sexes and all education levels who work in shrinking firms are paid lower initial earnings—
and in some industries, including men in financial services and women in
retail food and semiconductors, substantially less—than similar workers
in growing firms. The main exception is low-educated workers in software.
The only mitigating factor is that earnings growth sometimes offsets the
differences in initial earnings so that earnings in growing and shrinking
firms are nearly the same at the end of ten years: a good example is women
in financial services and low-educated men in retail food. The one industry
that stands out initially as an exception is trucking, since initial earnings are
slightly higher in growing than shrinking firms, but at the end of ten years,
workers in shrinking firms are making 20 to 80 percent more than workers
in growing firms.

*Large, high-turnover firms usually pay less initially than large low-
turnover firms. Workers who keep their jobs in large high-turnover firms are
rewarded with greater earnings growth.* This insight is clear from comparing
the first column with the second and the sixth with the seventh. Women
don't benefit as much as men from working in large high-turnover industries. At the end of ten years men's earnings are much higher in high-
turnover firms compared to low-turnover firms (except in semiconductors,
where earnings for both men and women are lower in high-turnover firms).

*Small high-turnover firms provide better job ladders than small low-
turnover firms* (compare columns three and four, and eight and nine). At
the end of ten years, both women and men who keep their jobs in small
high-turnover firms are earning more than those at the small low-turnover

firms. This evidence suggests that firms with high turnover are providing good job ladders to select workers who benefit from career development in that firm.

Large firms generally provide better job ladders than small firms, except in the trucking and semiconductor industries. A comparison of columns one and three, two and four, six and eight, and seven and nine indicates that job ladders are typically superior in large firms than small for both males and females. Firm size is especially important in the retail food industry. In semiconductors, small growing firms, which tend to be early-stage design companies, provide higher earnings growth than large growing firms.

Women's job ladders in all five industries are worse than men's. They earn less money initially, and their earnings grow more slowly. However, the effects of economic turbulence do not appear to be gender specific: economic turbulence has a similar impact on the job ladders for both sexes across industries.

Summing It All Up

The popular press is right: there are "good" jobs and "bad" jobs. Where workers land a job—which firm, as well as which industry—has a powerful influence on a worker's earnings, in terms of both initial levels and growth rates. But anecdotes aside, good jobs have not disappeared. This chapter, which examined the job ladders offered by hundreds of thousands of firms to millions of workers, identified which types of companies provide the best (and worst) job ladders. It found that firms still exist that could create the next Horatio Alger story. In contrast to the fears raised by Lou Dobbs and *Business Week,* good job ladders exist, particularly in large growing firms. And although large growing firms are the largest supplier of long-term job ladders, small growing firms also provide excellent job ladders in semiconductors, financial services, and trucking.

High-educated male semiconductor workers find the best job ladders in growing firms with low turnover; high-educated women find the best job ladders only in large growing semiconductor firms with low turnover. A woman shouldn't expect to find good job ladders in financial services. Their best jobs are in software, especially for high-educated women, where large growing firms provide the best job ladders for all high-educated software workers.

The best place to go for a worker in the trucking industry is, surprisingly, a shrinking company, although these are obviously jobs that are hard to find. A worker looking for a good job in retail food should look for a job with a large growing firm. A man in the financial services industry can find the best job ladders in financial services if he lands and keeps a job with a growing low-turnover firm (large or small).

Although good jobs do exist, they may not be available to all workers. Human resource practices vary. Some firms can adopt human resource practices in which new hires have to compete for job ladders within the firm. This "up-or-out" situation, where selected workers advance and workers not promoted are terminated or encouraged to find another job, is predominantly found in *expanding* firms. Other human resource practices are established so that experienced workers compete to "survive" or keep their jobs, and may even have to compete not to be replaced by less expensive new hires. This is particularly observable in *shrinking* firms and firms in the semiconductor, financial services, and software industries. Many workers in the software industry in particular experience short jobs lasting less than three years that appear to reflect market wages.

The job ladders found in the low-wage trucking and retail food industries are consistent with three other types of human resource practices: the traditional unionized firm with rule-based job ladders (although two tiers may exist), the nonunion firm that may offer some workers access to job ladders, and nonunion firms that offer competitive market wages. In food services, both the unionized firm and nonunion firm with limited job ladders also rely on market-based temporary and part-time jobs.

The consequences of economic turbulence on job ladders cannot be denied, as Candy Robinson learned—working for a firm that is shrinking, or taken over by another firm, often means that a job ladder can disappear. The impact of this on workers' long-term career paths is the subject of the next chapter.

CHAPTER SIX

Turbulence and Worker Career Paths

Introduction

Everyone knows that career paths—the lifetime pattern of employment and earnings—vary dramatically from one person to the next. Probably the most famous worker in America is Dilbert, stuck in a lousy job while taming his tie and shooting off one-liners. The career path of his creator, Scott Adams, grew out of Dilbert's experience: Adams quit his job as an engineer at Pacific Bell and went on to fame and fortune (although he still gets to shoot off rebellious one-liners). In contrast, the career path that frightens people is Mark McClellan's, mentioned in chapter 2, which ended in job loss and seemed to be the end of a middle-class lifestyle.

Anyone who has watched TV shows like the *Apprentice* knows that sometimes a person's career path depends on what they do (together with the boss's reaction). The words "you're fired" have become immortalized. But anyone who has read books like G. J. Meyer's very popular *Executive Blues* (1995) knows that a career path can also depend on economic turbulence beyond individual control:

> I think I can tell you how it will happen, if it's going to happen to you. The first thing they'll do, when they've made their preparations, is to get you out of your office and into some other room with some geek from Human Resources ... from the moment you pass through his door the HR geek will appear to be in visible pain and eager for you to see it. He wants you to understand that he too is a human being, a nice guy if also a geek, and that his mother didn't raise him for this kind of thing. Anyhow, when the geek has delivered his message and demonstrated the depths of his humanity, he'll get up out of his chair and come around from behind his desk. You'll be drawn up after him by some mysterious force

resembling magnetism—you don't know how it's happening, but all of a sudden you're on your feet and moving—and together the two of you will glide out the door and down the hall to some smaller office that you probably never noticed before, where somebody you've never seen (the outplacement counselor) is waiting to tell you not to worry, everything is going to be fine.[1]

Does it matter? Will everything be fine? As you'd expect, if workers choose to leave, they typically leave for a better job; if they're forced to leave, because the firm is laying people off, shutting down, or simply replacing them, there may be spells without work and they may have lower earnings in their next jobs. In other words, the impact of job loss on workers often depends on who makes the decision to leave—the worker or the firm. But economists argue that even when the firm makes the decision, the results are not necessarily bad. Chapter 4 showed that when jobs are destroyed, new jobs in more productive firms are created, and although firms fire, they also hire. In fact, in theory, *job change can in itself be productive.* There are four reasons for this.

First, it takes time for workers and firms to learn about each other, and it can be good to learn and leave. This is particularly true for highly skilled jobs such as semiconductor or software engineers. Workers need to work at a firm for a time to see if the job will work out. If it doesn't, then leaving the job is a good thing: there's little doubt that Scott Adams was better off leaving Pacific Bell, and Pacific Bell was better off with him gone. The same dynamic is at play even in less-skilled jobs. In truck driving, assembly line work, or retail sales, it is only after some time on the job that workers and their employers learn if they are cut out for each other. If the match is not going to work out, then both sides are often better off if the worker moves on. That's precisely what Donald Trump did on *The Apprentice*. He observed the workers over time, and if they didn't meet his standards, they were fired.

Second, workers can learn different skills from different jobs. Having experience in a semiconductor company with a manufacturing plant is useful to a design engineer when he moves on to a fabless design company. So the skills acquired from different jobs can be useful to employers. In the following example, Silicon Image, a fabless startup that has gone public, obviously found this important:

Robert Bagheri, executive vice president of operations, brings to Silicon Image more than 21 years of experience in manufacturing operations, quality and engineering. Prior to joining Silicon Image in February 2003, Bagheri spent six years as vice president of engineering, operations, quality and reliability at SiRF Technology Inc., a privately held company. While at SiRF, he was responsible for several manufacturing and engineering operations disciplines as well as quality and reliability functions, strategic business direction, long-range planning, vendor selection, contract/terms/pricing negotiations, material/logistics, technology and foundry selection. Earlier, he served as director of product and test engineering operations at S3 Incorporated, where he helped grow the business to a $500 million run rate. Prior to S3, Bagheri held various product engineering and management positions at Zoran, IMP, Microchip Technology and Monolithic Memories Inc. Bagheri holds a bachelor's degree in electrical engineering from Cleveland Institute of Technology.[2]

Third, job change can give less educated workers a chance to move from a low-paying dead-end job to one with a good job ladders. Different companies offer different types of job ladders, and workers will often queue to get jobs with employers who provide good job ladders. Over time workers may gain access to higher-paying firms by patiently waiting for openings to appear.

But most importantly for this book, job change can occur simply because less productive firms shrink or shut down and other firms grow or are born. In November 2005, GM laid off 30,000 workers because it couldn't sell its cars, just as Mark McClellan's aluminum plant shut down four years earlier. Yet, if workers who leave shrinking firms end up in expanding firms and gain better earnings and earnings growth as a result, the job change would eventually have been productive.

Theory aside, what is the evidence on when it is a good career move to change jobs, and when it is better to stick with a job? The answers have not been clear, precisely because there has been so little information available. One set of studies shows that some workers are worse off when they change jobs. Laid-off workers in the California semiconductor industry who moved to other industries ended up with earnings losses. Those who returned to the semiconductor industry received earnings increases similar to those not laid off.[3] Other research on laid-off workers in Pennsylvania found that on average, male workers who were displaced from jobs that they had held a long time lost about $200,000 in earnings over a five-year period.[4] Different demographic groups of workers have different levels of vulnerability. Job loss hurts the least educated workers the most: they are less likely to find new jobs, more likely to find part-time work, and more likely to experience earnings loss than workers with more education.[5]

Another set of studies shows that workers gain. For young males, changing jobs is often a way to move to a higher earnings trajectory.[6] This makes sense, since younger workers are much more able to shop for the best jobs, much as shoppers find shopping for a new car or house is productive or valuable. Low-wage workers also gain, because their jobs are heavily concentrated in just a few low-wage industries. The best way out of their low-wage trap is to change both jobs and industries. The same studies have found very strong differences across demographic groups: for white males and Latino males job change is critical to a transition out of low earnings, primarily because they were more likely to land jobs in better firms.[7]

The information in this chapter provides more answers than have previously been possible. Looking at millions of worker histories provides new insights into the impact of turbulence on a worker's ability to piece together jobs across firms into a career path. It is now possible to examine the movement and stability of millions of workers over more than ten years, describe their career paths, and begin to answer these questions. Not only that, it shows the earnings that the typical worker can expect from different career paths over time.

What Is a Career Path?

As Mae West once said, "I've been rich and I've been poor . . . Believe me, rich is better." Her career path, just like any career path, is the sum of all the jobs she had over her lifetime. Another way of saying this is that it consists of all the job ladders the worker has experienced plus periods without working. For some workers who have only one employer, the career path is a simply the firm's job ladder for that worker. Most workers have more than one job, and documenting the worker's career path as she or he pieces together job ladders across employers as well as periods without employment is a very complex task.

Career paths need to be calculated both for different types of firms and different types of workers. The job ladders that make up a career path vary by what is going on at the firm: a firm's growth or shrinkage and turnover rate are important information in describing career paths as well. Since volatility is more noticeable in a small firm than a large, the size of the firm is also important.[8] Similarly, career paths vary by type of worker, since female and male, young and old, high- and low-educated workers face different opportunities in the labor market. The career paths described in this chapter are for the most common age group: prime-aged workers.[9] Prime-aged workers are divided into two categories: younger (25–34 years old) and middle-aged (35–54 years old). For our research, workers are classified into twelve categories: the two age groups, two genders, and three education levels.[10]

One of the first tasks is to determine how many jobs workers hold over the ten-year period (remember, Robert Bagheri held at least seven jobs in his twenty-one year career). The facts show that most career paths could be classified into one of three types:[11]

· loyalist: worker has only one job in the five industries over the ten-year period;
· job switcher: two jobs over the period (with at least one in the five industries); and
· jobhopper: three jobs over the period (with at least one in the five industries).

The second task is to piece together the career path from worker job ladders and periods without employment. Each worker's job ladder (initial earnings and earnings growth for the number of years the worker held the job) was estimated for each job and this was then used to create the career ladder. The career ladders were then tracked across different types of firms in each industry. Even though the data have been summarized, there are still 180 groups of career paths for the twelve categories of workers with three types of job histories (loyalist, job switchers, and jobhoppers) in our five industries.

The important question of whether job loss is initiated by the worker ("I quit") or by the firm ("You're fired") cannot be answered directly by the type of data used in this book. Even when data on this is collected, firms and workers have different perceptions. In addition, fieldwork suggests that when growing firms force out professional employees, this may not be viewed as voluntary by the worker.[12] However, the data do give some clues as to whether job separations are voluntary or involuntary. For example, job separations in rapidly shrinking firms are more likely to be involuntary than are job separations in rapidly growing firms and industries.

Of course, it is impossible to describe the 180 basic career paths in a single chapter, although the book's Web site (www.economicturbulence .com) has a career path calculator that can be used to do just that. The next sections focus on the "typical" effects of turbulence and discuss the patterns that are most prevalent. (See appendix C.)

How Does Economic Turbulence Affect Career Paths?

What are the most common career paths? How important is economic turbulence? Which paths provide the best outcomes?

Most workers' career paths involve changing jobs. Loyalists rarely account for more than 40 percent, and sometimes as few as 25 percent, of workers in a demographic group. Surprisingly, the low-wage retail food and trucking industries are much more likely to have workers who are loyalists, as is the financial services industry, than the high-tech semiconductor and software industries, where workers are much more likely to be mobile: the most common career path in semiconductors is the job switcher; in software, the jobhopper. Hence, the fear that a job change will occur is grounded in reality.

The summary of millions of data points show that economic turbulence has a big impact on workers' career paths, which vary across industries.

On average, workers who change jobs earn less than workers who don't. Loyalists experience the best career paths in all five industries. However, it is hard to tell whether they get good jobs because they're loyalists, or they become loyalists because they have good jobs.[13]

Workers who start the period in inferior jobs are generally able to improve their career paths through job change. Workers who initially get a bad job draw can usually gain from changing to another job, although they endure periods without any job.

Some patterns for job changers are very evident. Usually workers improved their career ladders by switching into a job in one of the five industries. The most typical pattern for prime-aged workers in semiconductor, software, trucking, and medium-educated men in financial services[14] is to begin the period in a job *outside* the industry with relatively low earnings and earnings growth. They then switch *into* one of the four industries with a better job with higher initial earnings and higher earnings growth. While these workers do better by switching jobs (and industries) than by staying in their original jobs, they do not catch up to the earnings of the loyalists in the new industry.

The pattern is very different for all job changers in retail food and for women and high-educated men in financial services; these workers eventually do better by switching to a job outside the industry. The typical pattern for these workers is to begin the period with an inferior job with low earnings and earnings growth in the industry, and then to switch *out* of the industry, sometimes even initially earning lower pay at the new job. Eventually in their second or third job in another industry they find a better job with good earnings.

In most patterns, job switchers do better on their first job change than do jobhoppers, who must change jobs again to find a comparably good job, and so the job switchers end up with better earnings than jobhoppers at the end of the period.

What does all this mean? Although the "best" career paths are for workers who find a good job and stay with it, workers who must take less well-paying jobs initially can usually find a better job and improve their career ladders over time. The data do not spell out to what extent finding a good job early in one's career reflects the worker's skills and job market knowledge or just plain luck in landing a job with a good employer. For others, the good news is that they probably can find a better job if they keep looking.

Table 6.1 provides the details for middle-aged workers. Like table 5.1 it shows initial earnings (first row) and earnings growth (second row) for the two most prevalent education groups for middle-aged men and women. In order to compare the earnings across firms in an industry, row three reports earnings at the end of ten years as a proportion of the earnings of high-educated loyalist males in the financial services industry (the highest-paid group).

Loyalists have the best career paths, followed by job switchers. Loyalists experience the best career paths in all five industries because they start off with the highest initial earnings, experience good earnings growth, and end the period with the highest earnings. Take, for example, workers in the financial services industry. The typical high-educated male loyalist starts by earning $31,524, and his earnings grow at a rate of about .082 log points or 8.5 percent annual compound rate). By contrast, his counterpart who switches jobs twice (jobhopper) starts at $15,133 (which suggests the job change is probably related to the lower starting wage), and his earnings growth rate is only .020 log points. At the end of the ten-year period, his earnings are only 26 percent of those of his loyalist counterpart. The picture is similar for workers in the semiconductor industry. Although the typical high-educated loyalist male starts at a slightly higher earnings level, $32,714, he enjoys a lower earnings growth rate of .059 log points and ends up with earnings only 83 percent of the earnings of his counterpart in financial services.

TABLE 6.1 **Career paths, workers age 35–54.**

	Males			Females		
	Loyalist	Two jobs	Jobhopper	Loyalist	Two jobs	Jobhopper
Financial services						
Medium-education	$16,874	$10,494	$8,906	$7,456	$5,861	$5,743
	0.085	0.073	0.069	0.065	0.009	0.022
	0.56	0.31	0.25	0.20	0.09	0.10
High-education	$31,524	$30,492	$15,133	$11,538	$8,522	$7,861
	0.082	0.034	0.020	0.061	−0.020	−0.002
	1.00	0.60	0.26	0.30	0.10	0.11
Retail food						
Low-education	$4,555	$4,157	$4,189	$3,037	$2,765	$2,707
	0.083	0.065	0.049	0.111	0.064	0.050
	0.15	0.11*	0.10	0.13	0.07	0.06
High-education	$9,002	$6,883	$6,559	$4,761	$3,945	$3,809
	0.089	0.035	0.051	0.082	0.047	0.033
	0.31	0.14	0.15	0.15	0.09	0.07
Semiconductors						
Medium-education	$29,523	$13,641	$11,295	$11,863	$7,387	$6,631
	0.054	0.056	0.058	0.039	0.030	0.041
	0.71	0.33	0.28	0.25	0.14	0.14
High-education	$32,714	$20,755	$16,498	$13,590	$9,186	$8,430
	0.059	0.048	0.047	0.044	0.028	0.030
	0.83	0.47	0.37	0.30	0.17	0.16
Software						
Low-education	$18,966	$15,226	$11,682	$10,778	$7,610	$6,851
	0.077	0.081	0.081	0.041	0.068	0.073
	0.57	0.48	0.37	0.23	0.21	0.20
High-education	$26,342	$22,743	$19,228	$16,456	$12,358	$11,020
	0.086	0.071	0.065	0.059	0.057	0.052
	0.87	0.65	0.52	0.42	0.31	0.26
Trucking						
Low-education	$7,840	$6,299	$6,203	$5,323	$4,093	$3,902
	0.080	0.046	0.024	0.118	0.094	0.078
	0.24	0.14	0.11	0.24	0.15	0.12
Medium-education	$9,341	$7,439	$7,175	$7,086	$4,991	$5,232
	0.075	0.031	0.012	0.086	0.076	0.062
	0.28	0.14	0.11	0.23	0.15	0.14

Cells contain mean initial earnings, annualized earnings growth rate (in log points) across the simulated career path, and simulated final earnings level as a proportion of the final earnings of the corresponding final earnings of a financial services male high-educated loyalist ($71,242).
*Simulated final job was stretched beyond modal job tenure duration.

How Do Career Paths Vary by Industry and Worker Characteristics?

Although loyalists have the best career paths within their industry, their career paths vary enormously across industries. The best career path found in the five industries is for high-educated male loyalists in financial services. As shown in table 6.1, these men average $71,242 ($31,542 compounded at 8.5 percent) at the end of ten years in financial services, followed closely by their counterparts in software, who earn 87 percent as much, and in semiconductors, with 83 percent. The best career paths for high-educated male job changers are those that end up in the software industry. The worst career paths for high-educated men are in trucking, where they earn one-fourth to one-half of their peers in financial services, depending on the number of job changes.

The best career paths for high-educated women are in software, whether or not they are loyalists or change jobs. They end up with between 42 percent and 26 percent of the earnings of loyalist males in financial services. High-educated women have their worst career ladders in retail foods, where they earn only slightly more than low-educated women after ten years, whether or not they change jobs. High-educated male loyalists also find their worst career ladders in retail foods, although they do not fare as badly as the women.

Low-educated workers, both men and women, find their worst career paths in retail foods and their best career paths in software, whether or not they change jobs. However, very few jobs are available to low-educated women in software, and jobs open to them in our five industries are mainly in retail foods.

Women's initial earnings are much lower than men's, and their career paths are worse. What is vividly demonstrated in table 6.1 is that not only do men make more than women starting out, but men's career paths are generally better than women's in terms of both initial earnings and earnings growth across all industries. Even high-educated women in the software industry who stay loyal to the firm end up with only 42 percent of their male counterpart in financial services, while similar males earn 87 percent. The only industry in which this is not true is the trucking industry, where low-educated women's few job opportunities allow them to catch up to male earnings over time. In financial services, women fare especially poorly compared to men. Women job switchers typically move out of financial service jobs into inferior jobs and must work their way back up to a good job outside the financial services industry.

The age of a worker is also important (this is not reported in table 6.1). The career paths of middle-aged workers are characterized by higher initial earnings and lower earnings growth than the paths of their younger counterparts. The notable exception is software, where the earnings growth of younger workers is extraordinarily high and their earnings exceed the earnings of middle-aged workers at the end of the period. Younger workers experience very high returns to experience, but these returns diminish over time.

Finally, better education usually leads to better career paths, regardless of the industry. Medium-educated male loyalists in financial services earn 56 percent of the end-of-decade earnings of high-educated loyalists; their medium-educated female counterparts earn two-thirds of what their high-educated female counterparts do at the end of ten years. The gap is smaller in the low-wage industries, however. In trucking, the typical low-educated male loyalist ends up with earnings that are at 24 percent of the benchmark; medium-educated male loyalists reach 28 percent of the benchmark. The differences are negligible across education levels for job switchers and jobhoppers. The same is true in the retail food industry. However, less educated workers have higher earnings growth then high-educated workers in retail food, trucking, and financial services. These relationships partially reflect the lower initial earnings of the less educated workers but may also reflect their learning on the job.

How Important Is Economic Turbulence?

Figure 6.1 vividly illustrates the fact that *loyalists have better career ladders than job switchers and jobhoppers.* This shows the typical career paths for middle-aged high-educated men in the financial services industry, which provides some of the best jobs for these men.

The top line shows the typical career path for a loyalist, who works for only one financial services firm over the decade. He begins his job with annual earnings around $30,000, and experiences excellent earnings growth. At the end of ten years, he is earning around $70,000. The job switcher, shown by the middle line, starts out in a job in financial services with earnings the same as the loyalist, but he is in an inferior job with very little earnings growth. Either he is working for a firm that doesn't provide career development or he wasn't selected by his firm to move up a job ladder with increasing skills and responsibilities. After being in this dead-end job for

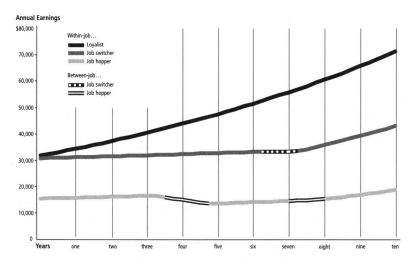

FIGURE 6.1. Career paths for middle-aged, male, high-educated workers in the financial services industry.

over six years, he either quits or is fired and goes without a job for over a year before finally landing a good job in financial services with strong earnings growth. The jobhopper's career path, considerably worse than the others, is shown by the bottom line. He begins at a job in financial services with annual earnings of about $15,000 and with low earnings growth. After working in this job for three and a half years, he goes through a period of one and a half years without a job. Finally, he takes a job outside financial services with lower earnings (around $12,000) and low earnings growth. This job lasts two years, and then he is without a job for a little over a year, before landing a job that offers good earnings growth. Clearly these three typical career paths in financial services indicate very different job experiences for men with similar education and age. The loyalist is a success; the jobhopper struggles.

The key findings *that job changers tend to improve their jobs by changing employers,* and *job switchers experience better job changes than do jobhoppers* is also illustrated by figure 6.1. Not all job changes are equal; some job switching results only in one low earning job being replaced by another; this is the experience for many jobhoppers in their first job change. The jobhopper has lower initial earnings than the job switcher, and the jobhopper must change jobs twice before landing a job with strong earnings growth. The job switcher's second job has strong earnings growth. At the

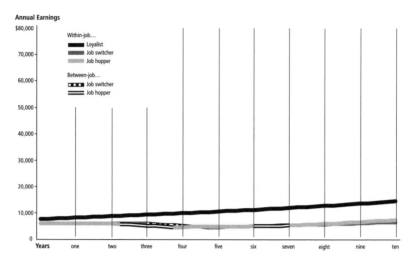

FIGURE 6.2. Career paths for young, female, medium-educated workers in the financial services industry.

end of ten years, the job switcher is earning over $40,000; the jobhopper is earning under $20,000.

The substantial differences that gender, age, and education make in workers' career paths are illustrated in figure 6.2, which shows the career paths for younger medium-educated women in financial services. Their careers are vastly inferior to the careers of their older, better educated male colleagues (figure 6.1), since their labor market outcomes suffer from their being female, younger, and less educated. The female loyalists do not experience much earnings growth, and job switchers do no better than jobhoppers (with only their first job in financial services). However, we saw earlier that even *high-educated middle-aged women* fare poorly compared to their male peers in financial services. At the end of ten years, the high-educated female loyalist is earning only one-third as much as the male loyalist; the female job switcher makes one-sixth as much as the male switcher; and the female jobhopper makes two-fifths as much as the male hopper (not shown). Women have lower earnings growth, which reflects returns to job experience, than men. This is true even for female loyalists, who do not leave the labor force for family reasons, which is often the reason given for their lower earnings growth. Earnings growth for females loyalists is only 75 to 80 percent of the earnings growth for male loyalists in financial services.

The substantial differences across industries is illustrated by comparing the paths for middle-aged high-educated men in three figures: figures 6.1

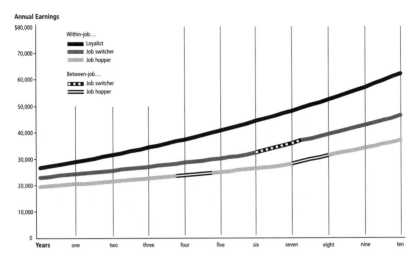

FIGURE 6.3. Career paths for middle-aged, male, high-educated workers in the software industry.

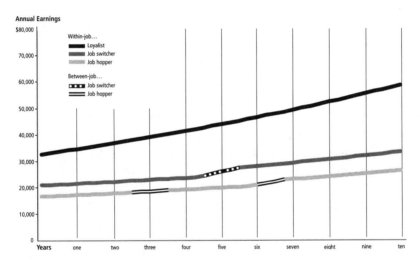

FIGURE 6.4. Career paths for middle-aged, male, high-educated workers in the semiconductor industry.

(financial services), 6.3 (software), and 6.4 (semiconductors). Although these industries are heavy users of technology and high-skilled workers, it is clear that their high-educated workers experience different career paths. Although the male loyalist career paths in software, semiconductor, and financial services are similar, changing jobs is far more lucrative in software than in financial services or semiconductors. Switching into both software

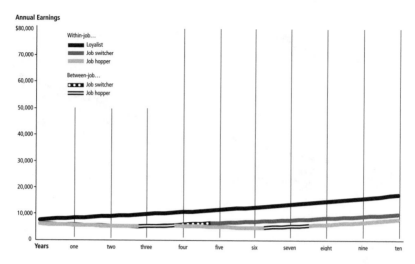

FIGURE 6.5. Career paths for middle-aged, male, low-educated workers in the trucking industry.

and semiconductors after working outside the industry provides a better job with higher initial earnings and earnings growth. The sooner the switch is made, the better the job changers' career path.

Although workers can improve their career ladders over time as they find better jobs, many are working in low-wage and dead-end jobs, and changing jobs is usually a challenging process. *Some jobs even have negative earnings growth.* In trucking, middle-aged low-educated men have negative earnings growth in jobs outside trucking before landing a job in trucking with higher earnings that reflects increases in both wages and hours (see figure 6.5). Although annual earnings are still quite low for male truckers, trucking provides higher incomes for them than do jobs in alternative industries. *Job changing takes time.* In all the figures shown, job changers experience a long period of a year to a year and a half between jobs.[15]

Let us look now at more examples of how workers fare in each industry to understand how this broad set of results actually affects workers' lives.

The Importance of Industry Differences: Stories from the Industries

A repeated theme in this book has been that broad-brush descriptions of the economy are too simple: industry analyses are critical to understanding economic turbulence. In keeping with this, this section delves into the different career paths offered in the different industries.[16]

There are two distinct types of career paths in the *financial services industry:* those of the loyalists; and of the job changers, who begin with a job in financial services followed by another job in financial services (job switchers) or two jobs outside the industry (jobhoppers). Although those who change jobs have lower initial earnings and earnings growth in their financial services job than loyalists, the job change process is not a smooth one. For middle-aged women, changing jobs involves a period without employment and a 16 to 22 percent decline in earnings. The middle-aged high-educated male jobhopper also suffers an earnings loss with job change. Both these men and these women eventually find jobs with good earnings growth, but they never enjoy the earnings of those who stay in the industry.

Workers who manage to *find* and *keep* a good financial services job do very well over the ten-year span. This job path is more common for men than women, who, at substantial cost, are more likely to leave the industry.

Part of this may reflect the technological and strategic changes that have taken place in the financial services industry. As Larry Hunter and his coauthors, Sloan industry experts in financial services, pointed out:

> New technologies profoundly changed the ways in which banks conducted their business and interacted with their customers . . . The evolution of competition and of work organization, in turn, will carry further implications for jobs and earnings . . . In these two banks [that were studied] the introduction of new technologies accompanied explicit changes in education requirements and other kinds of skills . . .
>
> The new emphasis on sales at the expense of service, the increased variability in pay, and the licensure requirements led many incumbents to leave the job, and heightened the importance of external recruiting in establishing skill requirements.[17]

Hunter's research showed that, particularly in large banks, the transition from service-oriented bureaucracies to more aggressive, sales-oriented cultures was rocky for many workers, and some workers did better than others in the new sales environment. Men were more likely than women to find a way to change jobs to improve their position in the new environment. To take one example from Hunter's work, "Ted," an experienced middle-aged worker at a major bank, was asked to broaden his job by taking on sales of a wider range of financial services. Instead, he left the bank and took a position at a smaller regional bank in which he could continue to focus on his specialty area, small business lending. "Andrew" was typical of younger workers, Hunter found, since he took a job at a large bank that provided sales training and licensure support, and he hoped to move on to more a more lucrative sales position in another company.[18]

In contrast, "Jennifer," a successful midlevel branch manager, found her career development stalled in a large bank that had begun to emphasize sales heavily. She finally took a job as a branch manager at a smaller local bank and her earnings suffered. Other women, like "Erma," retired early. Erma, a branch service manager, was a longtime employee and adored by customers and her coworkers. But she had problems with her legs and could not be on her feet enough to perform the tasks that her new sales duties required.[19]

This suggests that some workers (like Erma) who do not perform well in a sales-oriented culture are likely to leave banking. But many don't leave, and like Jennifer find jobs in banking that place less emphasis on sales performance. Unfortunately, these jobs no longer pay very well. Steady advancement through a bureaucracy is less common, and higher earnings are more likely to result from strong sales performance.[20]

Like those in financial services, workers in *semiconductors* also have two distinct career paths for loyalists and job changers. The job changers in semiconductors, however, typically start off with much lower initial earnings in a job *outside* the semiconductor industry and then experience substantial earnings growth (20 to 30 percent for younger and 10 to 20 percent for middle-aged workers) by taking a semiconductor job. Job switchers are on a better career path than jobhoppers, since the job switchers begin with higher pay outside the industry and land a semiconductor job sooner than jobhoppers. Although job changers usually experience higher earnings growth over the decade than loyalists, it is not enough to offset their much lower initial earnings, and so loyalists end the period with substantially higher earnings.

Even though mobility increased among semiconductor companies in the late 1990s, long-term employment still exists for many workers, especially those whose careers are developing well. The management of National Semiconductor, one of the biggest analog companies with almost $2 billion in revenue, vividly illustrates this. Of a team of thirteen senior managers, the majority have been with the company more than twenty years, and several for almost thirty.

Often scientists move into semiconductors to better-paying jobs. In a case study by one of the authors, "Anne," a materials scientist with a Ph.D., improved her pay by switching to a semiconductor company from a more traditional manufacturing company, although she was on-call more in her new job. Electrical engineers tend to switch jobs within the industry to broaden their experiences on new technology and enhance their career development. The introduction to this chapter featured the career path of Robert Bagheri, age forty-nine, who held six jobs before heading operations at Silicon Image. Just in the time spent drafting this book, Robert had taken a new executive position at another semiconductor company.

Younger engineers in Silicon Valley emphasized in interviews how important job change was for continued learning and career development. As "Mark" told one of the authors, "I am more loyal to my professional network than to my company, since that is how I will get my next job." In order to gain experience in chip manufacturing, a chip designer, "Philip," went to work for a large company with a fab, and then he worked at two startups. "Each job has provided me with a new set of skills and has been important in increasing my responsibilities," Philip said.[21]

The *software industry* also exhibits the two distinct career paths observed in semiconductors. Loyalists experience higher initial earnings and the same earnings growth as job changers over time. Overall, job changers experience substantial earnings growth (18 to 26 percent for younger workers and 11 to 20 percent for middle-aged high-educated workers) by landing a software job. Those switching jobs only once usually have higher initial earnings and lower earnings growth than jobhoppers, yet the job switchers end up with earnings that are 20 to 40 percent more than the jobhoppers' earnings.

Long-timers are hard to find in the software industry. For example, Oracle, which advertises itself as the world's largest enterprise software company, has a senior management team of four. Other than Larry Ellison, who founded the company in 1977, none joined the company earlier than 1999. The brief biography of the president of Oracle Corporation is particularly illustrative of the mobility not only within the software industry, but also into (and out of) the industry:

> Safra Catz is President of Oracle Corporation, reporting to Larry Ellison, Oracle's CEO. Ms. Catz has been a member of Oracle's Board of Directors since October 2001, serves on Oracle's Executive Management Committee, and is responsible for global operations. Ms. Catz served as Executive Vice President between November 1999 and January 2004 and as Senior Vice President between April 1999 and October 1999.
>
> Prior to joining Oracle, Ms. Catz was at Donaldson, Lufkin & Jenrette, a

global investment bank that has since merged with Credit Suisse First Boston, where she was a Managing Director from February 1997 to March 1999, and a Senior Vice President from January 1994 until February 1997. Ms. Catz held various investment banking positions from 1986 until January 1994.[22]

Similar career development through jobhopping is just as evident for young software workers as for young workers in the semiconductor industry.

The *trucking industry* exhibits the two distinct career paths observed in semiconductors and software. Loyalists have relatively high initial earnings and good annual earnings growth (5 to 13 percent) in one job with a trucking company; and job changers have lower initial earnings in a job outside trucking, and then experience a large earnings gain (11 to 19 percent) by taking a trucking job.[23] At 8 to 18 percent, earnings growth rates in trucking jobs are substantially higher than in workers' earlier jobs outside trucking, so the sooner the worker enters trucking, the better his career path will be. One possible reason for this is that most of these workers do not have a high school degree, and so obtaining a commercial driver's license, which opens up employment in trucking, represents a significant improvement in job options.

Trucking career paths reflect the variation in HRM practices across firms. As Michael Belzer and Stanley Sedo, Sloan experts in the trucking industry have noted:

> Opportunities for advancement within a company are limited in trucking. While longer tenure may result in favorable schedules or routes, these are marginal improvements, at best. The most common route to better earnings and working conditions is to change companies altogether. However, even this strategy has become increasingly limited with the decrease in the number of available union jobs over time. The lack of returns to tenure in trucking is a primary cause of the high turnover rates in the trucking industry. It is not unusual for firms to have turnover rates in excess of 100% per year.[24]

An article on trucking in *USA Today* gives a snapshot of some of the jobs:[25]

Kathy Shepard is an example of how becoming a trucker improved her career path. She had been laid off from her job in the billing department at a trucking firm. Kathy received her trucking license and was hired less than two weeks later by UPS, where she is making the entry wage of $14.70 an hour, or 34% more than at her last job. At the time she was interviewed for the article, her pay was due to go up to over $30,000 a year.

Carrie Green went into trucking to improve her career path and also to be with her boyfriend Kevin James, a long-time trucker, who said, "You have to like it to be in it." Carrie became a driver four years ago, after she was laid off from Kodak. Now Carrie and Kevin drive together coast-to-coast with their dogs.

Some career paths have upward mobility within trucking, as demonstrated by a vignette about Tracey Edwards in the same article. He went from a driver to a trainer to a recruiter. Each increase in responsibility also brought higher pay.

Although paid much less, workers in the *retail food industry* are similar to workers in financial services in the pattern of their two distinct career paths: the loyalist career path and the job changer path. Loyalists in retail food have relatively high initial earnings and experience good annual earnings growth (5 to 13 percent) in one job.[26] The earnings gap between loyalists and job changers grows over the decade. Job changers begin with an inferior job in the retail food industry followed by one or two jobs outside the industry. For younger workers, switching to a job outside retail food increases their earnings growth. Middle-aged job changers typically experience an earnings loss when they take jobs outside retail food. As in financial services, job changers eventually experience good earnings growth in their second or third jobs outside retail foods, but they never enjoy the earnings of those who stay in the industry.

Beth Wagner is an example of a woman who improved her career path by landing a job in retail foods at Costco and becoming a long-time worker:

> Workers seem enthusiastic. Beth Wagner, 36, used to manage a Rite Aid drugstore, where she made $24,000 a year and paid nearly $4,000 a year for health coverage. She quit five years ago to work at Costco, taking a cut in pay. She started at $10.50 an hour—$22,000 a year—but now makes $18 an hour as a receiving clerk. With annual bonuses, her income is about $40,000. "I want to retire here," she said. "I love it here."[27]

The Bottom Line

Two popular perceptions—that *workers gain big rewards for jobhopping* and that *workers' loyalty to a company pays off*—are both accurate. These apparently contradictory views are actually complementary, and both describe certain segments of the labor market and arise out of different firm strategies. Loyalists tend to be rewarded for staying with one firm (although Dilbert is clearly an exception), but, echoing the results in the last chapter, in many firms workers must jobhop before they get access to a long job ladder that offers career development (like Scott Adams). This is also true for workers who start off in firms offering inferior jobs with relatively low initial earnings and low earnings growth—they must change employers to get a better job. However, the number of jobs that are necessary prior to landing on a good job ladder vary across workers, and their earnings trajectories do not make up for the period when the workers were working on inferior job ladders or were unemployed. Loyalists begin and stay ahead of the job changers.

Despite Mark McClellan's fears, the popular perception of disappearance of good jobs is not valid. The data suggest that the odds are in his favor, although it may take twelve to eighteen months of search. *Many workers are able to continually improve their career paths by finding better job opportunities with another firm.*

The popular perception that low-wage workers are *churning from bad job to bad job* is not accurate, at least in the five industries and thousands of career paths under the microscope. Such a pattern is not dominant—not even in retail food, where many workers leave the industry for better jobs, or in trucking, where a worker's alternative job is worse.

Interventionist policy makers might well use this set of facts to argue that since some workers do not do well in making job transitions, unemployment insurance should have an important role in providing income support for workers during periods of job transition. In addition, interventionists might use the information here to argue for job placement assistance for transitioning workers. Indeed, the evidence in this chapter shows that although workers' career paths are very different, depending on their industry and their current employer, workers who have missed out on obtaining better job ladders can eventually obtain better jobs.

Interventionists might also argue for both micro and macro policy reform to address the consequences of job mobility. The fact that loyalists systematically do better than movers across all industries, even within a group of workers with similar age, sex, and education, raises the obvious question: *are loyalists more capable with special (unobserved) skills or talents compared to job changers, or are loyalists simply lucky to land a job with a company that shares market rents or provides skill development?* If loyalists are more capable, then the onus is on job changers, who must improve their skills before they can land a good job. Interventionist policy makers might then argue that micro policy can potentially help workers with their skill development. If, alternatively, loyalists are those who are lucky to land a coveted good job, and firms are rationing good jobs (i.e., there are many more qualified workers than good jobs), the consequence is that job changers must queue for their chance. Then interventionists would argue for macro policy to expand national employment, so that the number of good jobs increases, which would help more workers land a good job.

Finally, although the reasons need to be examined with further research, it is clear that *most workers were looking for a better job at the beginning of the period, and improved their career paths by changing jobs.* The fear associated with the very visible cost of economic turbulence borne by job losers must be offset by the less visible benefits, uncovered in this chapter, gained by workers who land new (and often better) jobs.

CHAPTER SEVEN

Economic Turbulence and Middle-Income Jobs

Introduction

"A giant sucking sound" was the way Ross Perot described the effect of globalization on middle-income American jobs. The story of the vanishing well-paid job has been a theme of newspaper and magazine articles ever since the series run by the *Washington Post* that said:

> The jobs have had one thing in common: For people with a high school diploma and perhaps a bit of college, they can be a ticket to a modest home, health insurance, decent retirement and maybe some savings for the kids' tuition. Such jobs were a big reason America's middle class flourished in the second half of the 20th century . . . Now what those jobs share is vulnerability. The people who fill them have become replaceable by machines, workers overseas or temporary employees at home who lack benefits . . . Is this just another rocky stretch of the U.S. economy that, if left alone, will foster new industries generating millions of as-yet-unimagined jobs, as it has during other times of upheaval? Or is the workforce hollowing out permanently, with those in the middle forced to slide down to low-paying jobs without benefits if they can't get the education, credentials and experience to climb up to the high-paying professions?[1]

These concerns make sense. While forces of technological change, globalization, and deregulation shaped the economic turbulence described in the previous chapters and may lead to greater productivity, this is hardly reassuring to workers who face the loss of current jobs and suffer uncertainty about the earnings in their future jobs. Tellingly, however, the same

Washington Post article says, "The government doesn't specifically track how many jobs . . . have gone away."

This chapter begins to fill the information gap about lost jobs by answering a number of questions.

· What has happened to the number and type of jobs within each industry through boom and bust?
· Have "good jobs" been replaced by worse jobs as high-paying firms shrink and low-paying firms grow, or is the reverse true?
· Who bears the brunt of economic turbulence—low-income, middle-income, or high-income workers?
· What has happened to the skill level of the workforce?
· Do new jobs pay more than old?

Because all of these effects are interrelated, the chapter also sorts out the separate contributions of each. In doing this, three ancillary points are important. First, *generalizations about changes in what has happened to the numbers and types of jobs are misleading.* Reading through the chapter, it will become clear that although each of the five industries has more jobs for all workers now than a decade ago, and these jobs tend to be higher skilled and higher paying, the positive changes have been greatest in the fastest-growing industries, software and financial services. And, although earnings have increased for low-, middle-, and high-income workers in each industry, the reallocation of jobs has come at a cost to some workers, especially lower-skilled workers who have been displaced.

The second point is that *the people who hold jobs now are often not the same people who held jobs more than a decade ago.* Although this is not surprising given such high rates of worker turnover, the change in who is working is not even across the earnings distribution. Fewer than one in ten of the lowest-income workers who started off in an industry at the beginning of the period is still working more than a decade later, while at least one in five (and sometimes one in two) of the highest-income workers is still employed. Indeed, a small part of the increase in earnings for the low- and middle-income workforce reflects the fact that new entrants have more valuable skills than the workers they replace.[2]

The third thing to keep in mind is that *simple explanations of the impact of changes are misleading.* Many, albeit offsetting, forces affect worker earnings. Firm entry and exit, changes in firm size, and changes in workforce experience all operate in complex and different ways.

Economic Turbulence and Middle-Income Jobs

Economic turbulence affects the quality and quantity of middle-income jobs in four ways. One way is through changes in the types of workers who are hired in an industry. Another is firm entry and exit: for example, firms paying "good" wages can vanish, to be replaced by firms that pay less. Another is that firms can change size: for example, low-paying firms can expand and offer more lower-quality jobs, while high-paying firms can contract and reduce the number of good jobs. Finally, a worker can be reassigned within the firm, to a job with a different title and a different level of responsibility. This chapter, like most broad-based analyses, can look only at the first three of the four. In what follows, a job is a match between an employer and an employee, rather than a specific position within a firm.

Academics disagree about the importance of each of the first three underlying forces. A number of researchers have pointed to the importance of workforce change, particularly the aging of the workforce and changing worker skills.[3] Another set of researchers emphasizes the growth and decline of firms and industries, particularly the loss of manufacturing jobs resulting from globalization.[4] One of the most careful analyses to date notes:

> Across industries, we find that plant survival and growth are disproportionately lower in industries with higher exposure to imports from low-wage countries. Within industries, the higher the exposure to low-wage countries, the bigger is the relative performance difference between capital-intensive plants and labor-intensive plants in terms of survival and growth. Finally, . . . some U.S. manufacturing plants adjust their product mix in response to competition from low-wage countries. Plants facing higher shares of imports from low-wage countries are more likely to switch industries. When plants do switch, they jump towards industries that are on average less exposed to low-wage countries and are more capital and skill intensive.[5]

The overall impact of such changes on low-income workers over the long term is not known, although studies of the low-wage labor market show that where low-wage workers work has a major impact on their earnings and their long-term opportunities.[6]

Firm managers also tell researchers that there is a variety of forces at work. Three industries have substantially changed the types of workers hired. In *semiconductors,* with rapid technological change and automation, the employment of engineers relative to operators increased over the 1990s. In financial services, the proportion of individuals employed in higher-paying occupations has increased while the share of those in lower-paying positions has decreased gradually. And in software, more educated young workers, often with little experience, have been hired.

Meanwhile in almost every industry, new firms have emerged with very different ways of doing business. In the early 1990s, large firms with manufacturing plants dominated employment in the semiconductor industry, but during the 1990s, a significant portion of chip manufacturing moved overseas and small design-only fabless firms sprang up. There are large differences across trucking firms in what they are doing—some ship higher-quality freight with higher-skilled, higher-paid, and often unionized drivers, and others do the opposite. In general, nonunion carriers have replaced unionized carriers, which pay higher mileage rates to their drivers. In retail food, similar patterns emerged through the process of some unionized firms exiting or at least not growing while nonunion firms entered as well as grew. In financial services, restructuring and strategies to segment customers, combined with new human resource management practices, have affected pay within the industry. And the software industry has experienced explosive growth; as many large hardware firms have outsourced the production of software programs to small independent providers of software products or programming services, new products have been emerging rapidly and meanwhile the earnings premium paid to higher-skilled software workers grew.

Basic Facts about Jobs and Earnings

Setting a Baseline

In order to describe the impact of economic turbulence on lower, middle, and higher income jobs, boundaries need to be set for each category. Although any boundaries are arbitrary, many researchers use the bottom 25 percent of jobs to describe bottom or low-income jobs and the top 25 percent of jobs to describe top or high-income jobs, with the middle 50 percent described as middle-income jobs. Because the focus of the book is on what has happened *within* each industry, each threshold is defined separately for each industry.

Of course, there are many different earnings measures that have been used in the past, including hourly, weekly, and annual earnings. Since the focus in this chapter is on the earnings that workers get from their jobs and workers can hold multiple jobs in a year, two very different earnings measures are used here. The first is a narrow measure, which is based on jobs with *dominant employers*. A worker's dominant employer is the firm that contributes the most to his or her earnings in each year. In this case, the earnings measure used is *annualized earnings,* which is an estimate of potential earnings if workers keep their jobs year round without any unemployment or nonwork periods.[7] The second measure used is broader, as it is based on *any* job in a given Sloan industry. In this case, the earnings measure used is *actual annual earnings,* which is simply the sum of quarterly earnings during a given year.[8]

Together, these measures represent the spectrum of the impact of economic turbulence on earnings and jobs. The annualized earnings measure captures less volatility than does actual earnings, because the latter includes the earnings of part-time workers who enter and leave the labor market as they go to school, take care of family, or are unemployed, as well as the earnings from secondary jobs.

Both measures are used precisely because there are important differences in jobs and earnings structures across industries. For example, the retail food industry has many temporary and part-time jobs, but has relatively *few dominant jobs.* In 2003, only 39 percent of all jobs in retail foods were dominant jobs, and only 50 percent of all jobs in trucking were dominant jobs. In contrast, 64 percent of all jobs in software, 78 percent of all jobs in semiconductors, and 89 percent of all jobs in financial services are derived from dominant employers.

What Are the Facts?

The key facts are summarized in table 7.1, which shows what has happened to the growth in the number of jobs and to the earnings thresholds for workers in the bottom, middle, and top income categories.

What has happened to the number and type of jobs within each industry through boom and bust? Every industry has more jobs at the end of the period than at the beginning. The growth in the number of dominant jobs ranges from 130 percent in software, 26 percent in semiconductors and 19 percent in financial services to a much weaker 4 percent in trucking and 7 percent in retail food. Much of the job growth has been in the higher-paying industries. For example, in the fastest-growing industry, software, the median worker made more than three times as much in 2003 (over

TABLE 7.1 **Earnings levels for all workers across industries (1999 dollars).**

		DOMINANT JOBS		
Year	Job growth 1992–2003	75th percentile	Median	25th percentile
Financial services				
2003	19%	$62,479	$37,509	$24,559
1992		$47,780	$30,684	$20,900
Retail food				
2003	7%	$33,144	$21,396	$13,806
1992		$33,635	$21,042	$13,079
Semiconductors				
2003	26%	$98,589	$66,595	$42,208
1992		$66,350	$44,242	$30,206
Software				
2003	130%	$96,281	$68,665	$45,028
1992		$74,851	$52,082	$35,586
Trucking				
2003	4%	$44,504	$34,247	$24,318
1992		$45,033	$33,188	$22,137

		ALL JOBS		
Year	Job growth 1992–2003	75th percentile	Median	25th percentile
Financial services				
2003	13%	$50,343	$28,748	$14,842
1992		$38,896	$23,444	$12,245
Retail food				
2003	13%	$24,708	$13,163	$6,324
1992		$23,622	$12,376	$5,961
Semiconductors				
2003	19%	$92,988	$59,770	$33,535
1992		$61,386	$39,384	$24,304
Software				
2003	111%	$86,016	$54,464	$27,738
1992		$65,469	$41,753	$22,980
Trucking				
2003	−6%	$37,545	$23,656	$11,248
1992		$35,626	$20,727	$9,641

$68,000) as the median worker in one of the slowest-growing industries, retail food, who made $21,396.

In almost all industries, the growth of full-time year-round, or dominant, jobs exceeds the growth of all jobs. In the trucking industry, for example, the number of total jobs actually shrank (by 6 percent), even as the number of dominant jobs grew by 4 percent. One exception is retail food, where all jobs growth is substantially higher than the growth for dominant jobs. This is not surprising, since more than half of all of the jobs in retail food are not dominant jobs but instead reflect secondary or part-time jobs.

Have "good jobs" been replaced by worse jobs as high-paying firms shrink and low-paying firms grow; or is the reverse true? In the fastest-growing industries, the rising tide raised all boats. The top, middle, and bottom earnings thresholds rose. In software, all boats rose by roughly the same amount: the bottom earnings threshold increased by 27 percent (from $35,586 to $45,028), median earnings increased by 32 percent (from $52,082 to $68,665), and the top threshold increased by 29 percent (from $74,851 to $96,281). Although earnings growth occurs for all groups of workers in both the financial services and the semiconductor industries, the earning growth for workers at the top far outpaced the growth for workers at the bottom. The pattern is similar when we use the measure of all jobs earnings, but of course the annual earnings are much lower. In software, for example, the low-income threshold when all jobs are used as the basis is approximately $27,738 (compared to the $45,028 for dominant jobs), and the top threshold is $86,016 (compared with the $96,281 threshold for dominant jobs). In all of the industries, the secondary or part-time jobs should not be viewed as inherently bad jobs. Since these jobs are not the primary job, the number of hours is inherently limited and this may account for the substantially lower earnings.

In the two slowest-growing and lowest-paying industries, retail food and trucking, only low-income workers experienced substantial earnings growth—the earnings threshold rose by a scant 6 percent in retail food (from $13,079 to $13,806) and by 10 percent in trucking (from $22,137 to $24,318). Earnings grew by 2 percent for the median retail food worker and by 3 percent for the median trucking worker over the ten-year period. And the earnings threshold for top-income workers actually declined by 1 percent in both industries. The news is less bleak in percentage terms when the earnings thresholds are calculated for all jobs in these two industries, although, of course, earnings levels are substantially lower. Middle earnings for all jobs in retail food were only around $13,163 in 2003, compared to middle earnings for dominant jobs of $21,396.

As was discussed in chapter 2, very different workers are employed by these disparate industries. For example, retail food workers are considerably younger than workers in other industries and are more likely to work part-time. Both retail food and financial services employ more female workers (47 and 63 percent, respectively) than the other three industries. The two highest-paying industries, software and semiconductors, have more male and older workers, but the low-paying trucking industry has a workforce that is 84 percent male.

In order to compare apples to apples, the same set of statistics is calculated for the jobs and earnings for male workers aged thirty to fifty. This includes workers like Mark McClellan, described in chapter 2, who had lost his well-paid management job and found his boat "sinking fast." This calculation shows that Mark's story is not true for the average worker of his age, which is a reminder that averages can be misleading. The number of jobs held by thirty- to fifty-year-old male workers *increased* in each industry, and shot up by 160 percent in software and 54 percent in semiconductors. Even though the job growth rate is much slower in the low-paid industries over this period, the growth rate for thirty- to fifty-year-old males exceeded the average.

It is true that earnings for workers of Mark's age did not keep pace with the rise for the workforce as a whole. Indeed, for workers in the trucking and retail food industries, earnings for middle-aged men actually declined or stagnated.

Who is working at this firm today vs. who was working at this firm yesterday? Only one in three workers in financial services, one in four workers in retail food, and one in six workers in software who started off in the industry in 1992 is still in the same industry more than a decade later.[9] And even fewer are still with the same firm—for example, only one in fourteen workers in the software industry were with the same firm in 2003, although the rates are around one in six or seven in the other industries.

What happened to workers in low-income, middle-income, and top-income jobs? Many fewer low-income workers remain in their jobs, or in their industries, than high-income workers. The differences in retention patterns across industries and between low- and high-income workers are striking.[10] In the low-skill industries, retail food and trucking, about one in seven of the low-income workforce is with the same industry, and about one in fourteen with the same firm, after more than a decade. More than one in five low-income workers in financial services stay in that high-skill industry, and one in ten with their firm; the figures are similar in the semiconductor industry. Software is the most turbulent—fewer than one in seven low-income workers are still in the same industry more than a decade later, and fewer than one in sixteen with the same firm.

Although these low retention rates for workers at the bottom end of the earnings distribution are to be expected, there are also large differences across industries for workers at the top end. Only one in five high-income software workers is still in the software industry twelve years later, and only one in ten is in the same firm. The same is true in the semiconductor industry; one in four high-income workers are with the same industry and one in eight in the same firm over the same period. This compares with retention rates of about one in three for high-income workers in the retail food, trucking, and financial services industries.

In sum, jobs at the bottom end of the earnings distribution and in low-skilled industries are much less likely to be stable than jobs at the top end and in high-skilled industries. However, *a particularly intriguing finding is that the two industries, software and semiconductors, that have been most affected by globalization and rapid technological change are also the two industries that have the lowest retention rates for workers in the top income category.* Presumably there is both opportunity and incentive to move in many cases (although the IT bust may have meant there were more lost opportunities than incentives).

The other important implication is the flexibility that firms have in changing their workforce. The increase in demand for goods and services in the software, financial services, and semiconductor industries has been accompanied by an expansion in employment, and firms clearly used this expansion to increase the skills of their workforce by hiring more skilled workers. Yet even in the two industries where employment declined (trucking) or stayed the same (retail food), firms have very high short-term turnover rates and the capacity to replace workers who are not as good a match to the firm, due to skills or other factors, as workers quit or are laid off.

What has happened to the skill level of the workforce? The short answer is that the skill level of low- and middle-income workers has increased over time. This is particularly true in the three high-skilled, expanding industries: the greater skill level of new hires relative to workers who left the industry raised the average skill level of workers in the bottom- and middle-income jobs. However, with the exception of the semiconductor industry, new high-income workers were slightly less skilled than the ones who left (see figure 7.1). The answer is quite different in the two low-skill industries. The skill level of the retail food workforce actually declined slightly, while in the trucking industry, the skill distribution became more compressed

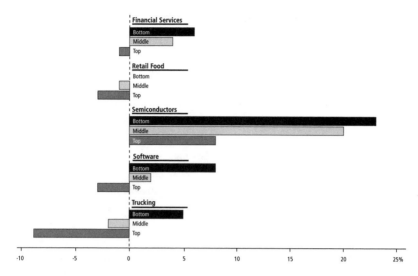

FIGURE 7.1. Skill differences between new and exiting workers.

due to an improvement in the skill levels of workers in the bottom quartile and a decline in the skills of workers in the top quartile

Broadly speaking, the increased earnings for workers in the high-skilled software, financial services, and semiconductor industries at least partially reflects the fact that entrants have higher earnings and higher skill levels than do the workers who leave. The differences between skill levels and earnings of entering and exiting workers are especially high for low- and middle-income workers in the semiconductor industry, where noticeable upskilling occurred. By and large, however, new high-income workers are less skilled than the workers they replace. Similarly, the lack of growth of earnings for workers in the low-skilled retail food industry is at least partly attributable to the fact that there is little difference in the skills of entering and exiting workers.

What is driving these patterns of workforce change? The labor force is becoming more skilled over time as younger generations who are entering the labor force are more educated than the older generations who are exiting. The increased educational attainment of the labor force across generations is a factor that many have suggested is critical for understanding the growth in productivity and earnings in the United States. In this context, this translates into substantial upskilling within low- and middle-income jobs.

Do new jobs pay more than old (or, what has happened to "good" jobs)?

The fear of loss of middle-class jobs reflects concern about the decline in jobs at firms that pay "good wages." As *Business Week* puts it:

> What happens if all those displaced white-collar workers can't find greener pastures? Sure, tech specialists, payroll administrators, and Wall Street analysts will land new jobs. But will they be able to make the same money as before? It's possible that lower salaries for skilled work will outweigh the gains in corporate efficiency.
>
> If the worries prove valid, that could reshape the globalization debate. Until now, the adverse impact of free trade has been confined largely to blue-collar workers. But if more politically powerful middle-class Americans take a hit as white-collar jobs move offshore, opposition to free trade could broaden.[11]

How is it possible to know whether new jobs at new or growing firms pay more than old jobs? An important finding from chapter 4 was that, all else being equal, new firms are more productive than exiting firms and generally pay more. But do they pay more to all workers, to low-income workers, or to high-income workers? The best way to answer this question is to compare the premium paid by entering firms with that paid by exiting firms. This is done by first calculating the pay premium paid by each firm, ranking each firm by that premium (and weighting by the amount of employment in that firm), then categorizing the firms into the bottom quarter, the middle half, and the top quarter, and finally comparing the pay premium paid by the firms.

This exercise, the results of which are summarized in figure 7.2, answers the question. *In two of the three high-skill industries, new firms — at every point of the earnings distribution — pay more than old.* In financial services, entering firms at the bottom quartile pay about 5 percent more to workers than did exiting firms; entering firms at the median and the top quartile pay about 10 percent more than did exiting firms. In the software industry, firms entering in the bottom quartile pay almost 10 percent more than the firms they replace; the median entering firm paid almost 15 percent more than the median exiting firm, and the firms in the top quartile of entrants paid about 20 percent more than exiting firms.

The opposite is the case in the two low-skilled industries, where pay premia declined in the top-paying firms. But those firms that entered at the bottom end in the trucking industry paid more than did the firms that exited, as did entering firms in the middle and those at the bottom of the distribution in retail food.

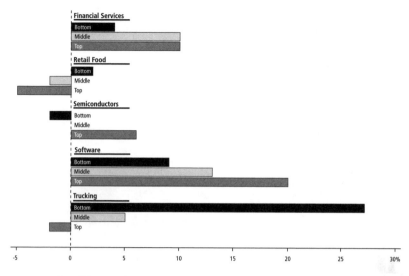

FIGURE 7.2. Pay differences between new and exiting firms.

Why do entering firms pay higher premia than exiting firms? This is an open question but there are a number of intriguing possible explanations. One of the explanations is closely related to the findings in chapter 4. Entering firms are more productive than exiting firms. There is evidence that suggests that firms share their success with their workers; thus, the more productive entering firms share some of that higher productivity with their workers.

Sorting It Out: The Separate Contribution of Worker and Job Reallocation

There have been substantial changes in both the types of *workers* and in the types of *firms* over time, so sorting out the contribution of each of these changes is important. But the sorting-out process is complicated by the fact that over time the way in which workers sort into different firms—their match to firms—may change. If, for example, at the beginning of the 1990's, high-skilled workers were likely to work for high-paying firms, and low-skilled workers were more likely to work for low-skilled firms, and over time the sorting process reversed, there would be quite complex effects on worker earnings.

This section separates out the effect of each of these changes on high-, middle-, and low-income jobs as follows.[12]

· *Worker reallocation* affects the earnings distribution through
    · workforce change: exiting workers with one set of skills can be replaced by entering workers with another set; or
    · change in skill: the skills of continuing workers can increase through increased experience.
· *Job reallocation* affects the earnings distribution through
    · firm entry and exit: firms that enter and exit can have different pay premia; or
    · changing match: changes in the allocation of workers across firms with different pay premia in each industry can result from differential rates of job creation and destruction across firms.

The Results

What was the impact of turbulence on the types of jobs in the workforce? This can best be seen by benchmarking earnings in the initial year: 1992. By definition, 25 percent of the workforce was in the low-income category, 25 percent in the high-income category, with the rest in the middle-income category. In what follows, we answer the question by examining whether each force acted to increase or decrease the proportion of workers in the low-, middle-, and high-income categories. The thresholds used here are time invariant and industry specific. So for this purpose the interpretation is how turbulence has impacted the distribution of low-, medium-, and high-income jobs in each industry.[13] The first panel of figure 7.3 shows how the proportions of low-income workers have changed in each industry over more than a decade; the second panel, the middle-income category; and the third panel, the high-income category.

In each panel, the first set of bars summarizes the total change. The first panel, for low-income jobs, confirms that there are proportionately *fewer low-income jobs:* there is a much lower proportion of workers in that category in each industry than there was in 1992. In the semiconductor industry, the proportion has dropped by over 10 percent; in software and financial services the percentage has dropped by almost the same amount. The proportion has dropped by 2.5 percent even in the low-wage retail food industry. The second panel demonstrates that there are *more middle-income workers in retail food and trucking and fewer in semiconductors, software, and financial services.* And the third panel reveals that there are *more high-income workers in the three high-skilled industries.* In semiconductors, the proportion above the 1992 high-income threshold had grown by more than 25 percent; in software, the high-income proportion has grown by almost 20 percent.

The five subsequent sets of bars describe the separate (marginal) impact of all the other contributing factors. Thus, the second set (workforce change) shows how the proportion of low-income workers is affected by new workers replacing exiting workers. The third set (change in skill) shows the impact of changes in the experience, or age, of the workforce; the next set, the impact of firm entry and exit; and the next set, the impact of the changing match between workers and firms.

What is the impact of workforce change? The second set of bars in each panel shows quite dramatically that there is almost none. If there been no worker entry and exit (i.e., had the workforce been the same during the entire period and all other factors been held constant), the earnings distribution in each industry would have changed very little. This pattern might seem a bit surprising given the earlier finding that the entrants to the labor force have more skill than the exiters—apparently the increasing skill led to increases in earnings within each of the three income earnings categories rather than to shifts among the categories.

What are the effects of skill changes? The next set of bars shows the impact of changing skill (primarily due to the aging of the workers) on the earnings distribution. Changes in skill acted to *reduce the proportion of workers below the low-income threshold and push substantially more workers above the high-income threshold.* This is true for each industry, but is particularly striking in the semiconductor industry.

The closing of Kaiser Aluminum is what pushed Mark McClellan out of the ranks of the middle class. What do the data tell us about the effects of firm entry and exit. For each industry, new firms' higher pay compared to the pay of the exiting firms has reduced the proportion of low-income workers—particularly in trucking—and increased the proportion of middle-income workers. There is little impact at the top end of the distribution. Two findings are remarkable. One is that, despite the stories in the popular press, the *entry and exit of firms acts to increase the size of the middle class,* not decrease it. This pattern is consistent with chapter 4, which showed that more productive firms tended to enter and less productive ones tended to exit and suggests that greater firm productivity is shared with workers. The other remarkable finding is that the impact is not con-

(a)

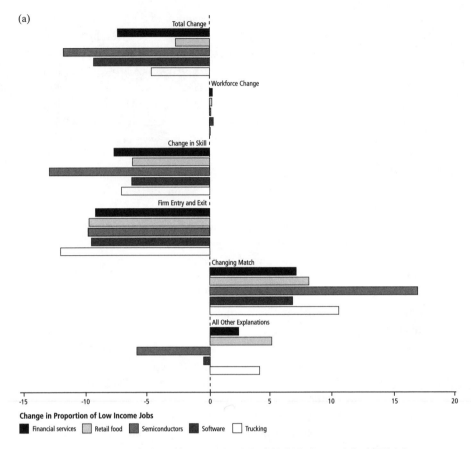

FIGURE 7.3. Sources of Change. (a) Low-income jobs. (b) Middle-income jobs. (c) High-income jobs.

fined to high-skilled industries. Indeed, the greatest impact of firm entry and exit on middle-income workers is in retail food and trucking, the two low-skilled industries.

What is the impact of job reallocation as firms grow and shrink? The re-allocation of workers among continuing firms goes to the heart of the im-pact of firm expansion (job creation) versus firm contraction (job destruc-tion) for continuing businesses. Surprisingly, it is job reallocation among continuing businesses that has had a big negative impact on middle-income workers and has increased the proportion of low-income workers, particu-larly in the semiconductor industry. Compared to shrinking firms, growing firms account for growth in low-income jobs. Part of this story may be that among incumbents the rapidly growing firms are often the young busi-

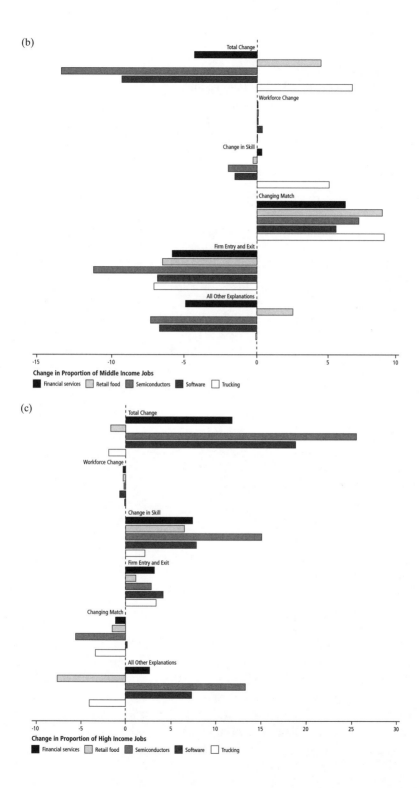

(b)

Total Change

Workforce Change

Change in Skill

Changing Match

Firm Entry and Exit

All Other Explanations

Change in Proportion of Middle Income Jobs

■ Financial services ☐ Retail food ▨ Semiconductors ■ Software ☐ Trucking

(c)

Total Change

Workforce Change

Change in Skill

Firm Entry and Exit

Changing Match

All Other Explanations

Change in Proportion of High Income Jobs

■ Financial services ☐ Retail food ▨ Semiconductors ■ Software ☐ Trucking nesses who have found the right path for their product or location. Such rapidly expanding firms might be firms that pay lower premia than large, mature incumbent firms. So in order to reconcile the opposite effects of entry and exit and job reallocation of continuing businesses, it is important to emphasize the different reference groups. For entry and exit, what matters is the pay premia for entering businesses relative to exiting businesses. For job reallocation, what matters is the pay premia for growing vs. shrinking (or at least firms that are not growing).

If the impacts of firm entry and exit and the expansion and shrinking of continuing firms are combined the effect is to increase the proportion of middle-income workers in the two low-skilled industries, retail food and trucking; to have almost no impact on financial services; and to decrease the the proportion of middle-income workers in both semiconductors and software. The combined impact is to increase substantially the proportion of high-income jobs in software and financial services, but to decrease that proportion in semiconductors.

These findings suggest that low-wage workers have been adversely affected by reallocation of jobs from high- to low-paying firms, while the opposite is true for high-wage workers, except in semiconductors. Overall, the positive effects for high-income workers are outweighed by the negative effects for low-income workers.

The last set of bars shows the impact of the residual—that is, of all explanations not accounted for by the wage decomposition, as well as possible measurement errors.[14]

The Bottom Line

This chapter has explored the impact of economic turbulence on low-, middle-, and high-income jobs over more than a decade.

The popular perception that jobs are vanishing is not correct. There are more jobs in each of the five industries than at the start of the period.

The increase in jobs is not an increase in "bad" jobs. The proportion of low-income workers declined in all five industries. The decline is larger in semiconductors, software, and financial services, and small in retail food and trucking.

The proportion of high-income jobs increased substantially, contrary to fears about the impact of globalization on high-skilled workers. The percentage of high-income workers increased substantially in software, financial services, and especially semiconductors. However, in the retail food and trucking industries, there are *fewer* high-income workers at the end of the period.

A rising tide has lifted all boats in the high-skilled, high-tech industries. Workers in financial services, semiconductors, and software have seen increases in earnings across the board. By contrast, the retail food and trucking industries have experienced an increase in the middle group with fewer workers in the top and bottom groups.

What were the main factors driving these changes? We found that while there were differences across industries, some factors stood out. In particular, even in industries in which the aggregate earnings distribution changed very little over the decade, there are large and offsetting changes in the underlying four components.

Worker entry and exit has had very little impact on changes in the earnings distributions. The evidence shows that there has been upskilling via worker entry and exit but this has had little impact on the distribution of earnings across broad earnings categories. In financial services and software, the increase in age (and experience) of continuing workers increased earnings across the board.

In contrast, *firm entry and exit* tended to reduce dramatically the percentage of low-income workers. This is largely offset by the *firms growing and shrinking,* which tended to increase the proportion of low-income workers as growing firms paid higher wages then shrinking firms.

The offsetting effects from these different factors make it difficult to make broad generalizations about the impact of economic turbulence on the distribution of earnings. What is clear is that the tremendous churning of jobs and workers, combined with the large differences in pay premia across firms, has a large impact on the earnings of an individual worker.

So the newspaper stories are right: it is not only important to find out why some firms have different pay premia for similar workers, but also to find out whether high premia firms will vanish in the future. The fate of an individual worker like Mark McClellan is a great example. He, like all workers, should anticipate that his skills and talent for hard work would be rewarded. And what this chapter shows is that, for most workers, this has been the case. But all workers should know that precisely because different firms pay different amounts, positive or negative outcomes for the firms that they find themselves employed with can and will have a large impact on their earnings and employment outcomes. So the fate of Mark McClellan was as much tied to the fate of his employer, Kaiser Aluminum, as to his own skills and talent.

West Virginia's governor, Joe Manchin III, is on the record as saying,

"Wherever there is one job on the verge of being lost, I will fight to save it. Wherever there is one company looking to grow in West Virginia, I will fight to make that growth a reality." The bottom line from this chapter is that policy makers are right to be concerned about gaining and losing "good" jobs. Tight connections between the fate of the workers and the fate of their employers are unavoidable, and some workers have been hurt by the loss of "good" jobs. But despite all the different forces of globalization, competition, deregulation, and turbulence faced by firms and workers in each of the five industries, the bottom line from this chapter is that the net result has been to increase the number of jobs and increase earnings across the board.

CHAPTER EIGHT

Conclusions and Implications
for Policy

The Chinese proverb advised being a dog rather than a man in chaotic times. The seven chapters that preceded this one don't provide any evidence on the value of being a dog, but do suggest that, for most, being a man is not so bad. The chaotic change that leads firms to grow and shrink, and workers to change jobs, eventually lead to a more productive and stronger economy.

Of course, economic turbulence affects some much worse than others. Some observers, such as Larry Elliott, the economics editor of the *Guardian,* are particularly skeptical about the value of flexibility:

> [T]here's the result of the French referendum on the European constitution, seen as thick-headed luddites railing vainly against the modern world. What the French needed to realise, the argument went, was that there was no alternative to the reforms that would make the country more flexible, more competitive, more dynamic. Just the sort of reforms that allowed Gate Gourmet to sack hundreds of its staff at Heathrow after the sort of ultimatum that used to be handed out by Victorian mill owners. An alternative way of looking at the French "non" is that our neighbours translate "flexibility" as "you're fired".[1]

The difference in focus between French and Anglo-American policy makers is indeed stark. French policy makers have consistently responded to their public's concern about unemployment with strict rules that constrain laying off workers while allowing the growth of an informal labor market for immigrants. The strict rules in France about whether and how firms can lay off workers is in strong contrast to the rules in both the United

States and the United Kingdom. Advocates of the French system argue that it preserves "good jobs" for citizens; advocates of the Anglo-American system argue that it creates a productive economy that provides openings for jobs that can be pathways to success.

This book sheds light on this debate by describing the labor market interactions of millions of workers and firms. The chapters in the book describe the components of economic turbulence in five industries that in many ways represent archetypes for other U.S. industries, and then examine the impact of turbulence on firms, workers, and the mix of high-, middle-, and low-income jobs.

The industries studied are characterized by pervasive change and economic turbulence. Workers enter and leave the labor market; they are reallocated across firms; firms expand and contract; and firms start up and die. The value added of this book is that it examines the *interactions of all of these factors simultaneously*. As a result, the book documents, for the first time, the many different ways in which worker and firm outcomes interact.

A strong tie exists between economic turbulence and firm outcomes. Even within these five industries, different firms have different ways of organizing themselves and their workforce practices. There is neither a magic bullet nor only one successful organizational structure: different firms even in the same industry have alternative paths to success. However, these different approaches have consequences, and some patterns emerge. For example, firms with excessively high turnover and low-skilled workforces are less likely to survive. But the economic turbulence associated with different choices has some long-run economic benefits. That is, economic turbulence results in stronger industries, as more productive firms tend to replace less productive ones. Recall the example from the trucking industry in chapter 3: American Freightways was feared by the smaller LTL carriers as it moved east and relentlessly cut costs and improved service through sophisticated use of IT.

Although there are costs to workers like Mark McClellan who are caught up in the adjustment process, most workers handle economic turbulence well. Over time, their job changes result in improved jobs, although job change often involves a period without work. Workers who initially find a good job with a firm—for whatever reason—typically do better than workers who change jobs. When workers do lose these good jobs because of firm downsizing, they may end up in an inferior job. Those workers who start out on bad job ladders with low earnings and low earnings growth usually are able to land on better job ladders by changing jobs.

And finally, although many factors contribute to changes in the mix of high-, middle-, and low-income jobs in the five industries, what happens to firms—their entry and exit plus their growing and shrinking—primarily determines the mix of jobs. This is because different firms pay different wages to workers with similar skills, and so changes in the number of jobs offered by different firms change the mix of earnings across jobs.

Broad-brush economy-wide descriptions, while tempting, can be extremely misleading. The analysis of the five industries in this book makes it clear it is important to use a bottom-up approach on an industry-by-industry basis. While some results appeared to hold consistently across the industries, most outcomes and their interpretation needed to be guided by an understanding of the particular industry context.

This chapter provides a summary of the key contributions of the book as well as a discussion the possible policy lessons.

Key Contributions

Basic Facts

The footprint of economic turbulence is large and pervasive. More than 20 percent of workers either begin or end a job each quarter, and up to one-half of this churning of workers reflects the churning of jobs among firms as they grow and shrink. Additional job churning occurs as firms enter and leave an industry. Over a five-year horizon, in all five industries at least 25 percent of establishments exit and at least 30 percent are recent entrants.

The amount of turbulence varies by worker, firm, and industry characteristics. Low-skilled younger female workers in low-tech industries are much more likely to have turbulent careers than their high-skilled older male coworkers. Similarly, entry and exit rates are much higher for young, small firms than for larger established businesses. However, firm size is an example where analysis must be grounded in an industry-specific context. In the semiconductor industry, for example, firm size is often a proxy for whether the company has manufacturing facilities; firm size reflects different product markets in software; and firm size in retail food and trucking reflects different organizational structures as well as different product markets.

Case study researchers have found substantial variations in firms' human resource management (HRM) practices, both among and within industries. In particular, firms appear to make systematic choices in their worker mix and job ladders that simultaneously determine the turnover and earnings of their workers. The fact that large and persistent differences exist across firms in their patterns of worker turnover, workforce skill, and job ladders is very consistent with these findings. In retail food, for example, Costco has followed a strategy of paying workers well and working with a union because it works, while Wal-Mart has followed a completely different strategy—which works for Wal-Mart.

Economic Turbulence and Firms

Firm survival changes with worker skills and turnover. Even after taking productivity, size and a variety of other factors into account, workforce skills and churning affect the likelihood of businesses surviving. As always, however, broad generalizations need to be tempered by industry-specific knowledge, since one size does not fit all. In particular, the two very high–human capital industries—software and semiconductors—are exactly those where human capital does not matter for firm survival. In the case of both industries, firms must be distinguished by their business models in order to predict survival: small software and semiconductor companies are often risky startups that hire only high-educated programmers and engineers.

Impact on Workers

The analysis of literally millions of worker histories and hundreds of career paths for workers and job ladders for firms leads to the reassuring finding that although turbulence imposes short-run costs, in the long-run job change leads to improved jobs for most workers. The evidence does not support the popular notion that *"low-wage workers churn from bad job to bad job"*—not even in retail food, where many workers leave the industry for better jobs, or in trucking, where a worker's alternative job is usually worse. The apparently contradictory views, *"big rewards exist for jobhopping"* and *"loyalty pays off,"* are actually complementary. Some workers, such as loyalists like Carol Primdahl, the engineer with TI, are rewarded for staying with one firm; but in many firms these workers compete to gain access to a long job ladder that offers career development. Workers who do not gain access to these long job ladders, for whatever reason, do better by changing employers. These workers, who start off with relatively low initial earnings and low earnings growth, often in a different industry, must change jobs to get a better job. The evidence suggests that workers vary in how many jobs it takes before they land on a good job ladder with career development, and their earnings trajectories cannot make up for the period when they were working on inferior job ladders or were unemployed.

The type of firm makes a difference in both job ladders and career paths. Workers generally find the best job ladders in growing large low-turnover businesses. Small growing high-turnover companies also provide good job ladders, except in retail food. Worker turnover and firm job ladders do not have a straightforward relationship. Turnover generally goes with lower initial earnings in large firms but with higher initial earnings in small firms. High-turnover firms generally have higher earnings growth than do low-turnover firms. Altogether, after ten years of job tenure, earnings are higher at high-turnover firms than at low-turnover firms for the workers who kept their jobs (except semiconductors, where the opposite relationship holds). Although this finding is a concern, it is counterbalanced by the fact that initial earnings are more important than earnings growth in high-turnover firms where few workers stay long and by the evidence that high-turnover businesses are less likely to survive.

High-, Low-, and Middle-Income Jobs

Although a major concern has been that "good jobs" (meaning high-paying jobs) have been lost as a result of economic turbulence, this is not the case. Analysis of the earnings and skill levels of workers, together with the wage premium paid by new, continuing, and exiting firms over more than a decade, provides a new perspective on the impact of turbulence on jobs and workers. The general idea that low-wage workers have suffered as a result of economic change does not hold up. Although there is high worker turnover at the bottom end of the earnings distribution, low-wage workers have typically gained ground. These changes are particularly large in software and to some extent in trucking and semiconductors, while in retail food the improvement is much more modest. The generally held notion that there are more high-wage workers in the high-wage industries does hold. However, there is not a monolithic cross-industry pattern of changes in the earnings distribution. Indeed, inequality increased in the three high-skilled industries and decreased or was unchanged in the two low-skilled industries.

Changes in the types of jobs that workers hold are quite complex, and reflect substantial changes in offsetting factors. This complexity reflects the fact that different firms pay different premia to similarly skilled workers, and thus the changing mix of firms has important implications for the changing mix of high-, middle-, and low-income jobs.

Policy Lessons

These results have important implications for policy in at least five areas. Future research using both matched employer-employee data and industry-level analyses can help improve policy decisions in each of these areas.

1. Information about economic dynamics helps inform policymaking.

Although job destruction and job loss are much more visible than job gains and worker hires, the public and their leaders need to be aware that both are occurring at the same time. Statistical indicators that summarize the economic turbulence and its impact on firms and workers should be produced by the U.S. statistical agencies and made broadly available on a timely basis. Specific measures that are useful include measures of worker churning, job churning, and firm churning at both national and local levels and broken out by worker (e.g., gender, age, education, and experience) and firm (e.g., industry and size) characteristics. Moreover, directly connecting measures of churning to the outcomes for workers and firms allows insights such as the earnings and productivity at new vs. exiting firms. Leaders at the federal, state, and local levels, as well as the business community and workers, would all benefit from timely information summarizing the patterns of economic turbulence and the ongoing changes in their respective industries and communities.

2. High turnover rates and low workforce skill adversely impact firm survival.

Although different firms do choose different management practices, and while there are alternative paths to survival, some ways are more successful than others. A basic message to the business community is that human resource practices appear to be critically important for firm success. Businesses with especially high worker turnover and especially low workforce skill perform more poorly and are less likely to survive, even after controlling for a number of other factors. The finding on worker turnover is robust across all five industries, although the finding on workforce skill does not hold for the high-tech, high-skilled industries—software and semiconductors—because of the many small startups in those industries employ mostly high-skilled programmers and engineers. Some of those high-tech startups have very high payoffs but many fail. Most workers caught up in the economic turbulence from the high turnover of startups appear to handle it well, as career paths in these industries exhibit positive income changes from changing firms.

An interventionist policy might include active engagement in improving the skills of the workforce, since this will enhance both workers and firms. An open question is whether the government has any role in supporting the ability of businesses to implement successful HRM practices, since this also improves the outcomes for workers and firms.[2]

3. Most workers eventually find successful career paths — but some do not.

Although one of the perceived costs of economic turbulence is the disappearance of the good jobs provided by large growing firms, the ability of most workers to improve their career paths by finding better job opportunities with another firm is impressive. One word of caution here is that the analysis in this book has not focused on the career paths of workers with very long spells of unemployment, or those who are not able to look for work. In the U.S., long-duration spells of unemployment are relatively rare, but experiencing long unemployment is inevitably a costly and difficult process for the workers involved.

The ubiquitous and ongoing economic turbulence that workers face, combined with the fact that job change usually involves a period without a job, suggests that if interventionist government policies are to be implemented to help workers, they should take this turbulence into account. For example, government policies that aid in training and helping workers search for jobs might well be designed with the knowledge that there is a good chance that the new job a worker finds may not last. Also workers have different experiences in finding another job after firms shut down. For example, semiconductor engineer Robert Bagheri was able to continue his career development after a experiencing a plant closure as a young worker, while Mark McClellan, the aluminum company manager, was unable to quickly find another job after experiencing a plant closure as a middle-aged worker.

The findings in this book suggest that workers who find "the right job" do well, so workers should ultimately be looking for a good long-term job. However, the high pace of turbulence and the finding that many workers move up via this turbulence is consistent with the view that training and job search assistance should not be geared towards finding the right job per se but rather should provide the worker with skills and with information that facilitates adapting to the ongoing changes as the worker seeks a long-term career job.

The payoff from turbulence for both workers and firms in the long run suggests that policies, like the French approach, that directly or indirectly stifle change and mobility are not likely to be successful over time in a dynamic economy. However, the information provided in this book would provide justification for those who believe that it is necessary to provide some assistance and insurance to buffer the adverse impact of economic turbulence. It would certainly be consistent with one of the current policies in place in the U.S.: namely, the unemployment insurance system, which provides temporary income benefits to those who have suffered an involuntary job loss. Of course, the evidence would also reinforce the views of many who argue that the challenge for the unemployment insurance system and related support programs is to provide the appropriate amount of insurance for the risks induced by economic turbulence without distorting the incentives for job change.

4. The dynamics of the distribution of high-, middle-, and low-income jobs reflects complex processes.

Economic turbulence acts in complex and sometimes offsetting ways to change the number and distribution of high-, middle-, and low-income jobs. The finding that the dispersion of earnings is reduced as new firms offer higher pay premia than exiting firms is one interesting aspect of this complexity. This finding, coupled with the analysis of firm job ladders, supports the popular view that it is not only who you are but where you work that determines your earnings. Those designing and evaluating policies to aid low-income workers, whether job search, training, or welfare-to-work policies, should use data like those presented in this book in considering how the policies impact the types of firms that employ low-income workers. Future research in this area should focus on understanding the factors behind firm pay premia and how the distribution of firms by pay premia has been changing over time by firm and worker characteristics.

5. Industry analysis is critical for interpreting micro-data.

This book has clearly demonstrated the importance of industry-specific knowledge in interpreting large-scale micro-data in order to develop correct and useful understanding and policy. Business and government leaders should beware of glib generalizations, because understanding the impact of economic turbulence on the workplace is difficult when organizational structure, technological change, regulations, and economic forces vary tremendously across industries. For example, a worker at a small, high-turnover retail establishment has a very different career path than a worker at a small, high-turnover software establishment. In-depth studies of what's happening within detailed industries, extended to more industries than the five included here, combined with large national data sets, are necessary to understand what is happening in the economy.

The research presented in this book should constitute only a first step along the road that integrates industry-level research with data at the statistical agencies to help workers and their business and government leaders understand and improve economic outcomes.

Appendix A: The Data

This book has explained the importance of the dynamic interaction between workers and firms in contributing to American economic growth. Firms are constantly redefining and reinventing themselves, and workers are constantly shuffled from less productive to more productive firms. The resulting challenge to U.S. statistical agencies has been to provide information that describes this rapidly changing environment to policy makers. The ideal data set—which would contain information on workers, firms, and the dynamic interaction between the two—has never hitherto been available. This book is the first to exploit data from a new program at the U.S. Census Bureau that not only captures the interaction of workers and firms, but also incorporates new measures of job and worker dynamics as well as workforce quality.

The rich empirical micro data set we use is complemented by the industry expertise of academics affiliated with the Sloan Industry Centers. The aim of these centers is to create an academic community that understands industries and to encourage a direct approach to the companies and people of each industry for data and observations. A core principle of the industry centers is that observation-based work by well-informed academics will, in the long run, lead to practical contributions to the industries studied. The industry centers have developed tremendous expertise in the innermost workings of their industries through such observation-based work.[1]

The Centers that are participating in this work have extensive knowledge of their industries. The Sloan Industry Center on the retail food industry, for example, has used a supermarket panel of grocery stores to research the effect of management and training practices on the wage distribution, career ladders, and skill levels in the retail food sector; the Sloan–UC Berkeley Competitive Semiconductor Manufacturing Program

has collected data on thirty-nine semiconductor fabrication plants in the
U.S., Asia, and Europe during the 1990s through a series of two-day site
visits; the Sloan Trucking Industry Program has collected and analyzed
data on both firms and workers between 1997 and 1999 to understand the
link between firm performance strategies and driver outcomes; the Software Program is just beginning to look at key skill issues in its new center.

This appendix describes the basics of the data set, focusing in particular
on its unique components. We then turn to describing the construction of
the key measures of economic turbulence, workforce turnover, and firm
entry and exit. We conclude by illustrating the main measurement challenges in evaluating worker and firm outcomes, describing in detail both
the advantages and limitations of our new data in depicting the dynamic
interaction between workers and firms.

The Source of the Information in the Book

The data that we use here capture the interaction between firms and workers over time for (almost) the universe of workers and (almost) the universe of firms. How is this done? The Census Bureau already collects data
on households and businesses with products including aggregate (e.g., national, industry, state, county) statistics on a large variety of variables including output, employment, income, earnings, capital expenditures, and
poverty. In addition, the Census Bureau produces separate analytical micro data sets on households and businesses. The Longitudinal Employer-
Household Dynamics (LEHD) program at the Census Bureau brings the
household and business data together at the micro level using universe
state level wage record data to create a comprehensive and unique resource for new analysis (see figure A.1). The key characteristic of these
data is that they describe both sides of the labor market –both the demand
side and the supply side. This feature is necessary for understanding the
interaction of the employment and earnings outcomes of workers and the
productivity and survival outcomes of firms. This is the first comprehensive
data set that permits such analysis for U.S. workers and firms.[2]

Data Details

The key integration record in this case is unemployment insurance (UI)
wage record. Every state in the U.S. collects quarterly employment and

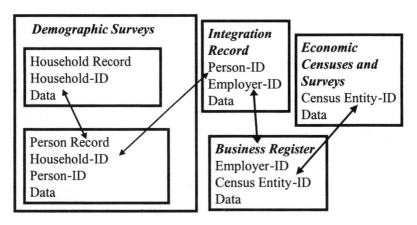

FIGURE A.1. The Longitudinal Employer-Household Dynamics program.

earnings information through its state employment security agency to manage its unemployment compensation program, enabling us to construct a quarterly longitudinal data set on employers. The employer's four-digit Standard Industrial Classification code is then added from another administrative file. Virtually all business employment is covered.

The advantages of UI wage record databases are numerous. The data are frequent, longitudinal, and potentially universal. The sample size is generous and reporting is more accurate than survey-based data. Longitudinal earnings and employer files can be constructed for individuals at quarterly intervals. The key advantage of having virtually universal data is that we can track movements of individuals to different employers and the consequences of these movements on earnings. It is also possible to construct longitudinal data sets using the employer as the unit of analysis.

Perhaps the main drawback to the UI wage records data is the lack of even the most basic demographic information on workers. The integration with Census Bureau data overcomes this in two ways. First, the micro data can be linked to administrative data at the Census Bureau containing information such as date of birth, place of birth, and gender for almost all the workers in the data set. Second, as will be discussed in the next section, staff at the LEHD program at the Census Bureau have exploited the longitudinal and universal nature of the data set to estimate both worker and firm fixed effects as new measures of workforce quality.

The information in the UI wage records is also quite limited with regard to characteristics of the employer. The Census Business Register has limited information on total employment, payroll, industry classification, sales, and geographic location on each business. However, because the UI data contain information about all the workers in each business, it is possible to create detailed information about the demographic characteristics of the workforce at each business, together with information on the demographic characteristics of worker and job flows into and out of the business. In addition, detailed information on firm inputs, outputs, and performance is available in the economic census years—primarily 1992 and 1997.

The work in this book uses data from six geographically dispersed states with a wide variety of industries and workforces[3]—California, Florida, Illinois, North Carolina, Pennsylvania, and Texas—which are home to just under 40 percent of the U.S. workforce. The data that we use begin in the early 1990s (for three of the states) and ends in 2003.

A major advantage of the data set is its sheer size: the data include 854,593,228 observations on some 57,823,057 individuals and 2,913,197 businesses.

Definitions

The very turbulence of economic activity that is the focus of this book creates substantial definitional challenges. Most obviously, the constant flow of workers into and out of jobs and industries makes it difficult to impose a static concept like "works in the software industry" or "works in retail food" on an inherently dynamic process. However, because our interest in part is in the impact of firm and industry changes on workers, we impose a requirement that the employer and the employee should be substantively attached to each other.

To be more specific, we use a concept of the "dominant employer" or the "dominant job." The definition of a dominant employer is the employer from which a worker has generated the most earnings in a given period. The job of a worker associated with her dominant employer is the dominant job. Depending on the research questions, we use either a quarter or a year as our time period. We require that a worker's "dominant employer" be in the relevant sector.[4] In addition, we focus on workers who have real quarterly earnings of at least $250.

Similarly, because we do not observe hours worked in the data but instead only observe quarters worked, quarterly earnings reported in UI data may not be a good earnings measure when we examine earnings inequality or calculate earnings growth over time. In some cases, earnings may be three-month earnings and, in other cases, they may be one-month earnings. To overcome this problem, we have constructed "full-quarter" earnings for a quarterly measure and "annualized" earnings for an annual measure.

First, the worker is considered full-quarter employed in quarter t if positive earnings are reported in quarters $t - 1, t,$ and $t + 1$. Then her earnings in quarter t is considered "full-quarter" earning. We still do not know whether she worked full-time or part-time during quarter t. However, she is more likely to have worked all three months during that quarter regardless of her full-time status. Therefore, this measure is more comparable across workers than the simple quarterly earnings measure.

Continuous employment during quarter t means having an employment history with positive earnings for either $t - 1$ and t or t and $t + 1$. Employment spells that are neither full quarter nor continuous are designated discontinuous. If the individual was full-quarter employed for at least one quarter at the dominant employer, the annualized earning measure is computed as four times average full-quarter earnings at that employer (cumulative full-quarter earnings divided by the number of full quarters worked). This accounts for 84% of the person-year-state observations in our eventual analysis sample. Otherwise, if the individual was continuously employed for at least one quarter at the dominant employer, the annualized earnings are average earnings in all continuous quarters of employment at the dominant employer multiplied by 8 (i.e., 4 quarters divided by expected employment duration during the continuous quarters of 0.5). This accounts for 11% of all observations. For the remaining 5%, annualized earnings are average earnings in each quarter multiplied by 12 (i.e., 4 quarters divided by an expected employment duration during discontinuous quarters of 0.33). This "annualized" earnings measure is, for each worker, the full-time full-year earnings equivalent and is used as the dependent variable in the decomposition of each individual's "wage" into person effect, firm effect, and an experience component.[5]

A major advantage of our data over survey-based data is that our ability to link directly to firm identifiers makes it possible to identify accurately the industries within which people work. However, it is worth noting that the blurring of employment definitions is mirrored in the blurring of industry definitions. For example, the shift towards fabless semiconductor establishments as the primary form of semiconductor establishment in the U.S. over the 1990s has raised a variety of questions about where such establishments are and should be classified. Table A.1 identifies the four-digit

TABLE A.I **Sector SIC definitions.**

Sector	1987 SICs
Financial services	6021, 6022, 6029, 6035, 6036, 6061, 6062, 6081, 6099, 6111, 6141, 6153, 6159, 6162, 6163, 6712, 6211, 6221, 6231, 6282, 6289, 6311, 6321, 6324, 6331, 6351, 6361, 6371, 6399, 6411
Retail food	5399, 54, 5541
Semiconductors	3674, 3559
Software	7371, 7372, 7373
Trucking	4212, 4213, 4214

industries that we use for this analysis, but the concern about possible mismeasurement of industry boundaries is a topic that we discuss in chapter 4.

Finally, although we generically speak about "businesses" or "employers," the unit of observation is typically the establishment—the physical location at which output is produced. However, our data permit the linking of establishments with parent firms, and many of our firm-specific exercises exploit this information. In chapter 4, for example, we distinguish between entering establishments that are new firms and entering establishments for existing firms. In terms of basic measures such as revenue, employment, payroll, firm linkages, and survival, the primary sources of information are the Economic Censuses and the Business Register. However, it is worth bearing in mind that the workforce quality and workforce turnover measures described below are developed from the matched employer-employee data sets from the LEHD program. These data are indexed by business identifiers that can differ from those on the Census Business Register for some businesses. We integrate these measures at the establishment-level with our Census-based measures by matching LEHD data to Census data at the federal Employer Identification Number (EIN), county, and two-digit SIC level of aggregation. For most businesses, this match is at the establishment level. When the match is at higher level of aggregation (e.g., for a firm that has multiple establishments in the same county and same industry), we aggregate the establishment-level detail from the LEHD data and link to the Economic Censuses. Underlying this linkage is the assumption that the workforce quality and workforce churning are the same across establishments in the EIN, county, two-digit industry cell.

The Use of New Measures

Describing Economic Turbulence

The turbulence that we want to describe takes two forms: the reallocation of jobs from one set of businesses to another, and the reallocation of workers across a fixed set of jobs. The driving force behind job reallocation is often precisely the types of economic shocks that were described in chapters 2 and 3, including changes in cross-industry demand (away from one sector and towards another) or changes in the competitive structure of the industry and deregulation. The result is typically that less productive firms contract and die (job destruction) and more productive firms enter the market or expand (job creation). Meanwhile, the reallocation of workers across job slots is likely to change in response to technological change and changing human resource practices.

The measures that we use reflect these concepts. Job creation is defined as the employment gains (including those from firm births) from one point in time to another, and job destruction is defined as the employment losses (including those from firm deaths) from one point in time to another.[6] Job reallocation is the sum of job creation and destruction and as such is a summary measure of all job flows for a period of time. Worker reallocation, or churning, is a measure of excess worker reallocation over and above job reallocation.[7] This measure at the business level is given by the sum of the accession and separation rates (net of job reallocation at the establishment level) and captures the component of worker turnover that is in excess of that needed to accommodate any net changes in the number of workers in the business. Whether it represents any excess in an efficiency sense is an open theoretical question and part of our investigation.

The magnitude of these flows is huge. As is evident from table A.2, which provides a sample of the quarterly worker and job flows for one local area in one quarter, even when net job change is negligible—about 0.15 percent of employment in the first column—job creation can be substantial—about 6.5 percent. Separation rates are also astoundingly high, at almost 22 percent of base employment. This picture of enormous job and worker flows is even more stunning when we examine the patterns for younger workers. Small changes in net employment for twenty-two- to twenty-four-year-old males mask 16 percent job creation rates and 40 percent separation rates, as seen in the second column. As seen in the third column, net job losses for the same demographic group in accommodation and retail food masks a separation rate of some 50 percent.

TABLE A.2　**Quarterly workforce indicators: Philadelphia, Pennsylvania 2003:3.**

	All workers	Males 22–24	
	All industries	All industries	Accommodation and retail food
Total employment	1,802,845	49,669	5,600
Net job change	2,910	734	−245
Job creation	117,340	7,967	869
Separations	391,772	19,693	2,851

Source: QWI Online (http://lehd.dsd.census.gov/led/datatools/qwiapp.html).

Describing Workforce Quality

No study of the American workforce would be complete without a discussion of workforce quality. Yet standard econometric measures of workforce quality—typically only years of education or experience—are inadequate because they fail to capture differences in school quality, region, and program of study.[8] It has been pointed out that quantifying unobserved skill differences—like problem solving skills, people skills, or other unobserved ability—is necessary to describe the changing sets of skills necessary in a rapidly evolving, exceedingly complex, and increasingly service-oriented economy.[9] The development of the new skill measures at the LEHD program has begun to address some of these concerns. These individual-level measures, which can be derived only from universal longitudinal data on employers and employees, capture the market value of the portable component of skill by separating out the sources of earnings variation into the contribution of firm characteristics (where one works) and the contribution of worker characteristics (skill measures). For the latter, we further decompose our skill measures into the contribution of the "person effect," which is the time-invariant portable component of a person's wage (capturing time-invariant characteristics like ability and education), and the experience component, which represents the skills and education acquired in the workforce. The development of these measures has added extraordinary power to economists' ability to explain the workings of the labor market. The tools that were used before, which were often based only upon worker surveys, typically could explain only about 30 percent of earnings variation. These new tools—based on the new data on employers and employees—are able to explain about 90 percent of earnings variation.

We use these components of earning in two different ways. In chapter 4, we use proportions of workers within establishments whose human capital measures are higher than the economy-wide median level. In that case, we care only about the ordinal ranking of individual workers' human capital measures. On the other hand, in chapter 6, human capital measures are treated in cardinal fashion so that the magnitude of difference in human capital matters.

Table A.3 provides some preliminary evidence on why these new measures are so powerful. The table decomposes industry wage premia—i.e., the percentage by which the wage in a given industry is higher than the average wage—into the two main sources: workforce human capital and firm wage-setting policies. The first set of rows analyze the highest-paying industries. Clearly the highest-paying industry—security, commodity, and brokers and services—is high paying both because it has high-quality workers and because firms within the industry pay a premium to those workers. Specifically, according to the table, security, commodity, and broker and service workers have earnings that are 82 percent higher than the

TABLE A.3 **Sources of Industry Earnings Differentials.**

SIC	Name	Industry wage premium	Premium attributable to workforce human capital	Premium attributable to firm wage-setting policy
		Highest-paying industries		
62	Security, commodity, and brokers and services	82%	34%	37%
67	Holding and other investments	70%	34%	27%
48	Communication	63%	7%	52%
49	Electric, gas, and sanitary services	54%	0%	55%
81	Legal services	54%	18%	31%
		Lowest-paying industries		
58	Eating and drinking places	−45%	−12%	−38%
1	Agriculture-crops	−35%	−10%	−31%
72	Personal services	−33%	−12%	−24%
79	Amusement and recreation services	−32%	−8%	−28%
70	Hotel and lodging services	−32%	−17%	−19%
54	Food stores	−30%	1%	−30%

Source: John M. Abowd, "Unlocking the information in integrated social data," *New Zealand Economic Papers* 36 (June 2002): 9–31.

average market wage. Using our decomposition of earnings, we attribute 34 of the 82 percent to the worker characteristics, 37 of the 82 percent to firm's paying higher wages on average, and the remaining 11 percent to unobserved factors. However, another high-paying industry—electricity, gas, and sanitary services—has high wages entirely because firms in the industry pay its workers much higher than average. The workers themselves are of roughly the same quality as the rest of the workforce. This is the firm wage premium referred to in the book. Similar results emerge when we analyze low-wage industries in the second set of panels. Eating and drinking establishments, for example, both hire workers of lower than average quality and pay them less. However, firms in another very low-wage industry—food stores—actually hire workers of above average quality, but pay them less.

In addition to the decomposition of earnings into person effects, experience effects, and firm effects, we also exploit additional information about the workers. As previously mentioned, we measure gender and age for the universe of workers. For subsets of workers that are also included in specific surveys (e.g., the CPS, SIPP, or the decennial census), we also gather a rich array of additional worker characteristics, including occupation and education. While it is not the focus of much of the analysis in this book, in some cases we exploit specific samples where we are able to directly observe occupation and education. In other cases, we take advantage of analyses performed by LEHD staff to generate imputations of key characteristics like education based upon statistical imputation models estimated from subsamples where we have direct measures of those characteristics.

Measuring Firm Outcomes

Administrative data sources provide only limited information on firms. The main survey-based data we use to examine businesses more in depth in this book are the 1992 and 1997 Economic Censuses, which are in turn linked to the Longitudinal Employer Household Dynamics (LEHD) databases. Variables available from Economic Censuses include revenue, employment, payroll, establishment identifiers, and firm identifiers.

These data permit us to measure some economic outcomes for firms particularly well, such as the entry and exit of establishments and the organization of establishments into firms, as well as revenue, employment, job flows, worker flows, earnings, and workforce composition. For firm performance, the measurement of entry and exit dynamics is important, as a key indicator of performance is survival.

However, our measures of productivity (as in much of the micro and aggregate literature) are crude at best. For what we denote productivity in what follows, we measure gross output per worker, where gross output is measured as gross revenue deflated with a detailed industry deflator. This crude measure of labor productivity is closely related to the measures of gross output per unit of labor that are published by the Bureau of Labor Statistics (indeed, the BLS typically uses gross revenue data from the Census Bureau as the primary source data for gross output) and is used extensively in the literature. For some industries, gross output per worker is not a bad proxy for productivity. For example, for the manufacturing sector, a variety of studies have shown that labor productivity measured in this manner is highly correlated with carefully measured multifactor productivity (with careful treatment of the measurement of output and inputs including physical capital, labor, and materials). However, for non-goods-producing industries, gross output per worker measures of productivity are sometimes problematic. Recent studies have shown that in some service industries, measures of labor productivity based upon gross output per worker at the aggregate level have yielded implausible negative productivity growth in the 1990s.[10] The problems with gross output per worker are especially severe in those industries where the product or service is difficult to measure. A related problem is that in some sectors it is especially difficult to allocate the output of a firm to individual establishments. In our case, these problems are particularly severe in the financial services sector. In what follows, we explore the limitations of our measures for this and other industries.

To gain some perspective on the measurement challenges for our industries in terms of measuring productivity, figure A.2 depicts the BLS output per hour index for key four-digit industries that are part of the five somewhat broader sectors that are the focus of this study. A log scale for the vertical axis is used because of the dramatic increases in the productivity index for the semiconductor industry. The latter is largely driven by the tremendous decreases in the price index of semiconductors measures that take into account the enormous efficiency/quality improvements in semiconductors (via hedonic price indices). At the other end of the scale, the official BLS indices suggest little or even declining productivity for food stores, commercial banks, and trucking. As noted above, it is not uncom-

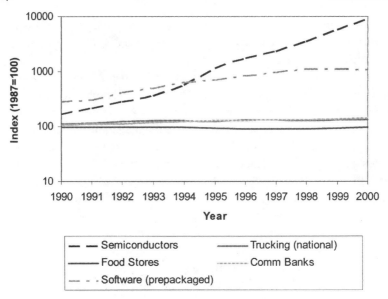

FIGURE A.2. BLS output per hour indices.

mon to find only modest or even declining productivity for many non-goods-producing industries in the 1990s. An open question is the extent to which this poor productivity performance is real as opposed to merely a reflection of mismeasurement. This question is particularly difficult to answer in sectors such as financial services, where output is a particularly slippery concept.[11]

Another related problem is that our revenue measure is gross revenue. While for some industries we can measure value added at the firm level for a sample of firms (especially for manufacturing industries), we focus our attention on gross revenues since this measure is readily available for all businesses. Given our focus on the impact of entry and exit of firms and establishments, this is important, as value-added measures are often not available for small and young businesses. Value added per worker would be the preferred concept, but a number of studies have shown that value added per worker is highly correlated with gross output per worker across firms *within* the same industry. An obvious limitation is that gross output per worker measures in levels (as opposed to growth rates) are not comparable across industries. This limitation is particularly pertinent for the retail food industry. In retail food we measure gross revenue per worker, not taking into account the cost of the goods sold (as we do not measure gross margins at the micro level). Much of the gross revenue in retail food (and in retail more generally) is accounted for by the cost of goods sold. As such, we find that gross revenue per worker is very high relative to gross revenue per worker in the software and semiconductor industries, which is quite misleading. For the most part, we focus on the growth of revenue per worker or we only consider variation within industries so that this problem with measurement levels across industries is not relevant.

A firm outcome that we measure quite accurately is survival. The longitudinal links in our files permit measuring the survival of establishments and firms very accurately. In our analysis, we explore the determinants of survival for both firms and establishments. Moreover, our links across establishments into composite firms are very accurate as well, so we can explore the relationship between ownership change of an establishment and the characteristics of the workers of the business.

Summary

The data used in the analyses reported in this book are newly developed longitudinal matched employer-employee data for the U.S. The data permit measuring and studying the interaction of firms and workers and examination of the implications of this interaction for a rich set of outcomes. For firms, we can measure performance via measures of both productivity and survival. We can also measure their human resource practices in a variety of ways, including the composition of their workforces by age, gender, and human capital. Further, we can evaluate the structure of wages within each firm and study patterns of job and worker turnover. For workers, we can measure employment and earnings outcomes in a comprehensive, longitudinal manner. Thus, we can piece together individual workers' job ladders and career paths as well as associated changes in earnings. In addition, we can fully characterize the distribution of earnings across workers taking into account both the characteristics of workers and the characteristics of firms.

Appendix B: Chapter 4 Background

This appendix contains supplementary material for chapter 4.

TABLE B.1 **Marginal effects on probability of exit.**

	Financial services	Retail food	Semiconductors	Software	Trucking
Single-unit dummy	**−0.131**	**0.039**	−0.093	**−0.098**	**−0.112**
	(0.011)	(0.008)	(0.059)	(0.025)	(0.020)
Size	**−0.078**	**−0.072**	−0.019	−0.017	**−0.049**
	(0.003)	(0.005)	(0.016)	(0.010)	(0.008)
Revenue/worker	**0.066**	**−0.110**	−0.015	**−0.038**	**−0.067**
	(0.005)	(0.006)	(0.036)	(0.019)	(0.011)
Churning	**0.100**	**0.069**	**0.494**	**0.219**	**0.206**
	(0.032)	(0.019)	(0.175)	(0.064)	(0.033)
Human capital	**−0.135**	**−0.151**	**0.261**	0.064	**−0.170**
	(0.027)	(0.023)	(0.105)	(0.066)	(0.036)
N	23,160	15,682	428	2,044	4,318

Estimation is based on probit with stay/exit as dependent variable. Standard errors are in parentheses. Boldface numbers are statistically significant. Controls: four-digit SIC.

TABLE B.2 **Productivity differences and probability of exit (securities brokers).**

Establishment	Revenue/ worker	Estab/firm (year)	Revenue/ worker		Probability of exit
Exiter (1992)	**−0.405** (0.040)	Exiter/exiter (1992)	**−0.442** (0.052)	Single-unit dummy	0.017 (0.039)
		Exiter/survivor (1992)	**−0.294** (0.052)	Size	**−0.092** (0.011)
Survivor (1992)	**−0.266** (0.033)	Survivor/different (1992)	−0.008 (0.071)	Revenue/ worker	−0.012 (0.023)
		Survivor/same (1992)	**−0.260** (0.035)	Churning	**0.170** (0.042)
Entrants (1997)	**−0.254** (0.034)	Entrants/entrants (1997)	**−0.139** (0.040)	Person effect	**0.442** (0.099)
		Entrants/continuer (1997)	**−0.339** (0.046)		
Continuers (1997)	0.000 (—)	Continuer/different (1997)	**0.303** (0.071)		
		Continuer/same (1997)	0.000 (—)		
R^2	0.030	R^2	0.042		
N	4,097	N	4,097	N	1,734

Standard errors are in parentheses. Boldface numbers are statistically significant. Controls: four-digit SIC.

TABLE B.3 **Marginal effects on probability of exit in semiconductors.**

	Group	
Single-unit dummy		−0.102
		(0.061)
Size	Fabless	0.015
		(0.035)
	Fabbed	−0.024
		(0.018)
Revenue/worker	Fabless	0.028
		(0.045)
	Fabbed	0.007
		(0.038)
Churning	Fabless	0.344
		(0.260)
	Fabbed	0.414
		(0.214)
Person effect	Fabless	−0.158
		(0.224)
	Fabbed	0.090
		(0.135)
N		428

Estimation is based on probit with stay/exit as dependent variable. Standard errors are in parentheses. Controls: four-digit SIC.

TABLE B.4 **Marginal effects on probability of exit.**

	Group	Retail food	Trucking
Single-unit dummy		**−0.375**	**−0.274**
		(0.030)	(0.086)
Size	Single unit	**−0.056**	**−0.049**
		(0.008)	(0.010)
	MU local	**−0.111**	**−0.122**
		(0.009)	(0.027)
	MU regional	**−0.043**	−0.013
		(0.012)	(0.027)
	MU national	**−0.090**	**−0.043**
		(0.009)	(0.017)
Revenue/worker	Single unit	**−0.081**	**−0.074**
		(0.007)	(0.011)
	MU local	**−0.122**	**−0.093**
		(0.009)	(0.026)
	MU regional	**−0.150**	**−0.110**
		(0.011)	(0.026)
	MU national	**−0.183**	**−0.079**
		(0.009)	(0.020)
Churning	Single unit	**0.197**	**0.252**
		(0.023)	(0.035)
	MU local	0.000	**0.472**
		(0.047)	(0.197)
	MU regional	−0.094	0.009
		(0.079)	(0.172)
	MU national	−0.085	0.082
		(0.053)	(0.145)
Person effect	Single unit	**−0.084**	**−0.144**
		(0.025)	(0.042)
	MU local	**−0.203**	−0.087
		(0.054)	(0.192)
	MU regional	**−0.219**	−0.210
		(0.099)	(0.157)
	MU national	**0.223**	**−0.399**
		(0.074)	(0.111)
N		15,700	4,319

Estimation is based on probit with stay/exit as dependent variable. Standard errors are in parentheses. Boldface numbers are statistically significant. Controls: four-digit SIC.

TABLE B.5 **Marginal effects on probability of exit in software.**

		Size
Single-unit dummy		**−0.094**
		(0.025)
Size	Small	−0.027
		(0.025)
	Large	−0.019
		(0.019)
Revenue/worker	Small	−0.029
		(0.020)
	Large	**−0.052**
		(0.026)
Churning	Small	**0.304**
		(0.078)
	Large	0.020
		(0.112)
Person effect	Small	−0.065
		(0.073)
	Large	0.125
		(0.116)
N		2,045

Estimation is based on probit with stay/exit as dependent variable. Standard errors are in parentheses. Boldface numbers are statistically significant. Controls: four-digit SIC.

Appendix C: Chapters 5 and 6 Background

Measuring Firm Job Ladders and Worker Career Paths: Summary

Structuring an analysis of worker earnings and employment outcomes creates obvious measurement challenges—precisely because the movements of the workforce are so dynamic. In brief, we simulate prototypical career paths in the five industries over the period 1992 through 2001. We focus on two groups of prime-aged workers: younger prime-aged (25–34 years old) and middle-aged prime-aged (35–54 years old), in order to avoid data problems associated with many younger and older workers not being in the sample for many quarters. This category includes 70 to 80 percent of all workers. This restriction obviously has differential impacts in different industries—particularly retail food. We divide each age group into three education groups, roughly approximating high school and less ("low"), some college ("medium"), and college graduate and above ("high"), and also have separate groups for females and males. We categorize employers by characterizing whether workers' jobs are in firms with the most typical firm characteristics (size, excess turnover, and growing or shrinking).

One challenge that we face in piecing together career paths is left- and right-censoring. In 1992, many job spells had already been ongoing and in 2001 many are still ongoing. To overcome this challenge, many of our results for career paths are based upon spells that begin after 1992. Moreover, the estimates of the earnings-tenure profiles in the analysis that we present in chapters 5 and 6 are based upon underlying regression models with many controls including controls for right-censoring.

Measuring Firm Job Ladders and Worker Career Paths: Details

The career path and job ladder simulations are based primarily upon the results of within-job and between-job wage growth regressions for each of the
five industries, hereafter referred to as the WJWG and BJWG regressions,
respectively. These regressions provide estimates for earnings growth by
different job types (defined by duration, employer, and employee characteristics). We then take the modal characteristics of various career paths and
construct simulated ten-year earnings growth trajectories for each.

WJWG and BJWG Regressions

The data for the WJWG and BJWG regressions are drawn from the LEHD
program data of matched employer-employee records based on UI wage
records of California, Illinois, and Maryland. Quarterly earnings are observed for almost all workers in those three states. Our sample runs from
the first quarter of 1992 to the fourth quarter of 2001.

The unit of observation for the WJWG regression is a job spell. Each
worker is assigned to one full-quarter-dominant employer in each quarter
that positive earnings of at least $250 (2001 dollars) are observed. The
dominant employer is the employer who pays the highest earnings to a
worker in a given quarter. The worker is considered full-quarter employed
at quarter t if positive earnings are reported in quarters $t - 1, t,$ and $t + 1$.
The job spell's starting quarter is the first full quarter when positive earnings are reported for a given employer-employee match, and the ending
quarter is the last full quarter for which positive earnings are reported for
that employer-employee match, provided that the employee did not have
full-quarter earnings at another dominant employer in the interim. The annualized log earnings change from the starting quarter to the ending quarter of employment, deviated from the national mean earnings growth during the period, defines the job spell's within-job earnings growth.[1] Job spell
length is divided into four tenure groups: less than one year, one or more
years but less than three years, three or more years but less than five years,
and five or more years. Spells are also classified as left, right, and uncensored. We also include the following on each job observation:

- worker characteristics:
    - gender;
    - age in 1995 (in four groups: 18–24, 25–34, 35–54, 55–65); and

- education in 1995 (low, with no college education; medium, with some college, but without a bachelor's degree; and high, with at least a bachelor's degree; education categories vary across the Sloan industries).
- employer characteristics:
  - in or out of Sloan industry (see below);
  - mean employer size over the job spell ($\leq$100 employees, $>$100 employees);
  - mean employer churning over the job spell ($\leq$20% or $>$20%), defined as:

$$\frac{(Accessions + Separations - |\Delta Employment|)}{Average\_Employment(t, t-1)}; \text{ and}$$

  - net employment growth over the job spell ($<0, \geq0$).

Employers are defined at the SEIN (state employer identification number) level, which is the establishment for single-unit establishment firms. For multi-unit establishment firms, the definition of SEIN units is state specific; generally, however, the SEIN unit is smaller than firm.

We divide the job observations into five samples, one per industry, with some overlap. Each sample contains *all* of the job spells for a given worker if that worker had at least one full-quarter-dominant employer in that industry during the sample period. Therefore, if a worker has one job in retail food followed by one job in trucking, *both* observations will appear in *both* samples. In the retail food sample, the first job will be "in" industry, and the second will be "out"; it will be reversed in the trucking sample. In each sample and for each of the five sectors, we regress the WJWG measure on worker characteristics including gender, age, education, and job tenure as well as appropriate censoring variables and employer characteristics.

The BJWG is similarly estimated. The unit of observation for the BJWG regression is a spell between two full-quarter jobs before and after a job switch. The variable of interest is the annualized log earnings change between the last full-quarter earnings at the old job and the first full-quarter earnings at the new job. In the regression specification, we do not consider the length of the nonemployment spell, but include the employer characteristics of both the old job and the new job.[2]

Regression Specifications

Two specifications were estimated for each group of workers (defined by industry and employer characteristics) to characterize within-job wage growth and between-job wage growth.

WJWG: by industry, firm characteristics (size, turnover, employment growth), and in/outside industries.

$$\text{WJWG}_{in} = \text{sex}_i + \text{censor}_{in} + \text{age}_i + \text{education}_i + \text{tenure}_{in} + \varepsilon_{in}$$

BJWG: by industry, firm characteristics (size, turnover, employment growth) and in/outside industries of old and new jobs.

$$\text{BJWG}_{in} = \text{sex}_i + \text{censor}_{in} + \text{age}_i + \text{education}_i + \varepsilon_{in}$$

Career Path Simulation

To simulate career paths in each industry, we first find the modal tenure profile and employer characteristics for each career path of interest, then use the results from our WJWG and BJWG regressions to simulate the earnings growth profiles of each career path.

Within each industry and worker type (by gender, age, and education group), we define three career path types: "loyalists" who hold one job, "two-time movers" who hold two jobs, and "three-time movers" who hold three jobs over the period. We exclude workers with more than three jobs from the analysis. Conditional on the number of jobs, the industry, and worker characteristics, we first find the modal sequence of jobs held within and outside of the industry (e.g., the modal young, high-educated male three-time movers in the semiconductor industry holds two jobs outside of the semiconductor industry followed by one job in semiconductors). Conditional on this job sequence, and that the first job is not left-censored, we then compute the mean first full-quarter earnings as the initial earnings level for the specified career path. Also conditional on the job sequence, we find the modal tenure group and employer characteristics (size, churning, and growth) for each job in the sequence, and the mean duration of nonemployment spells between each job. This procedure thus defines, for each industry-worker career path type, the modal sequence of jobs, with within- and between-job durations and associated firm characteristics. Using the WJWG and BJWG regressions, we obtain the estimated wage growth rates within and between each job in the sequence, assuming that the final job in each sequence is right-censored and that the other jobs are uncensored.

In order to provide comparisons of earnings profiles, we use this data to simulate career paths spanning exactly forty quarters. As the modal career paths defined above only specify tenure *groups* for each job, we assign a specific number of quarters to each job in order to total forty quarters. First, each job was assigned the median duration for the specified tenure group (e.g., eighteen months for a job in the one- to three-year tenure group). Additional quarters were then added or subtracted evenly across all of the jobs in the career path in order for the total between- and within-job time to equal forty quarters, provided the within-job duration within each job did not fall outside the amount specified by that job's modal tenure group. In the event that this was insufficient to extend the career path to forty quarters, the job in the highest-tenure group was extended to the required duration. Career paths where such an extension was required were:

trucking: loyalists and two-time movers low-educated young women
retail food: loyalists and two-time movers low-educated young women
      two-time movers medium-educated young women
      two-time movers low-educated older men
software: loyalists and two-time movers in all younger groups, except high-educated
      men (loyalists only)
semiconductors: none
financial services: none

Job Ladder Simulation

For the job ladder analysis, earnings growth is the predicted value of the WJWG regression for the specified job tenure. Initial earnings are the mean initial earnings for the specified cell, using the same variables as in the WJWG regression (firm characteristics, demographic group, and job tenure). Ongoing jobs are jobs that are right-censored in 2001; completed jobs are all uncensored jobs during the sample. Cells containing fewer than fifty observations comprise fewer than 5 percent of jobs for the gender/age/education group, or contain fewer than 0.5 percent of the total 5+-year jobs for the industry, are not considered in the analysis unless otherwise specified.

Appendix D: Chapter 7 Background

Chapter 7 describes the implications of economic turbulence on the distribution of earnings within industries, with a particular focus on the impact of turbulence on middle-class jobs. In this appendix, we describe the definitions of variables used in the chapter and the methodology for decomposing the sources of changes in the earnings distribution.

Definitions

As discussed in chapter 2 and in appendix A, administrative data are immensely useful to the extent that they are longitudinal, accurate, and nearly universal. However, they have several limitations, one of which relates to the measure of earnings we have in the data set. Indeed, an important characteristic of the administrative data we use is that earnings refer to quarterly earnings, and we have no information on either wage rates or hours and weeks worked. Thus, there are a large number of ways the LEHD data may be used to characterize the distribution of annual earnings and of the level of workforce quality in each industry. Several concepts are useful in understanding the final measures of earnings that we use.

Dominant Employer

The data set can be used to calculate summary statistics of the earnings and skill distributions for workers in each sector and each year. However, since some workers have multiple jobs in a year, we use their dominant employer to identify which sector they work in. A worker's dominant employer is the SEIN (state employer identification number—this is the state UI administrative unit) that contributes the most to the worker's earnings in each year. Thus, each worker employed during a year has one (and only one) dominant employer per year.

Full-Time Workers

We use data from Current Population Survey in combination with LEHD state data to impute whether or not a worker is employed full-time in each year at his main job (analogous to the dominant employer concept used in LEHD state data). We use CPS variables to perform this imputation using a logit model, and the dependent variable was taken from the CPS question of whether or not the respondent was employed full-time at the main employer last year.

Three characteristics of the findings suggest that this imputation was quite successful. First, the standard errors on the coefficients were very small. Second, for individuals found in both the CPS and the LEHD state data, the imputation results were very similar to the observed outcomes. Third, for all individuals, the predicted probabilities of working full-time were clustered into two groups such that predicted probabilities for all members of one group were extremely high and the predicted outcomes for the second group were extremely low. More discussion of this imputation can be found in John M. Abowd, Paul Lengermann, and Kevin McKinney, "The measurement of human capital in the U.S. economy" (Working paper, March 2003, Cornell University; http://instruct1.cit.cornell.edu/~jma7/abowd_lengermann_mckinney_20030402.pdf, accessed February 26, 2006), hereafter ALM.

Methodology

Measuring Earnings

Because we do not observe hours worked in the data but instead only observe quarters worked, we constructed the "annualized" earnings measure, which is, for each worker, the full-time full-year earnings equivalent. This variable is adjusted for discontinuities in labor market attachment during the year and is used as the dependent variable in the decomposition of the individual's "wage" into person effect, firm effect, and an experience component.

First, we define full-quarter employment in quarter t as an employment history with positive earnings for quarters $t - 1, t,$ and $t + 1$. Continuous employment during quarter t means an employment history with positive earnings for either $t - 1$ and t or t and $t + 1$. Employment spells that are neither full quarter nor continuous are designated discontinuous. If the individual was full-quarter employed for at least one quarter at the dominant employer, the annualized wage is computed as four times average full-quarter earnings at that employer (total full-quarter earnings divided by the number of full quarters worked). This accounts for 84 percent of the person-year-state observations in our eventual analysis sample. Otherwise, if the individual was continuously employed for at least one quarter at the dominant employer, the annualized wage is average earnings in all continuous quarters of employment at the dominant employer multiplied by eight (i.e., four quarters divided by an expected employment duration during the continuous quarters of 0.5). This accounts for 11 percent of all observations.

For the remaining 5 percent, annualized wages are average earnings in each quarter multiplied by 12 (i.e., four quarters divided by an expected employment duration during discontinuous quarters of 0.33). For additional details, see ALM.

Measuring Skill

The details of the skill measures are contained in ALM. In the reported statistics, there are three measures reported: overall skill, the person effect, and the experience effect. Note the overall skill measure is the sum of the person effect, the experience effect, and a reference constant (see in particular equation (25) in ALM). Also note that by construction, the grand mean of the person effect is zero, which means that some workers (groups) have negative person effects. All components are from a log specification, so differences across workers (groups) are interpretable in terms of log differences.

When computing the worker and firm fixed effects, only dominant job spells held by workers who are between eighteen and seventy years old and who are imputed to work full-time at that job are used. Thus, only workers who have been imputed to work full-time in at least one job will have a valid person effect. However, once calculated, these measures may be applied to any job spell (dominant or other, full-time or other) held by the worker.

Defining groups of workers

The data sets include year- and sector-specific earnings and skill distributions summary statistics for all workers with a dominant employer in that sector, who are imputed to work full-time in that year, and who have real earnings of at least $250 in at least one quarter of the year.

This sample decision makes a difference in some industries. In semiconductors, for example, 82 percent of all dominant jobs held at any point in the year are held by full-time workers who are working at the end of quarter one. This fraction is substantially higher than in retail food, where only 55 percent of dominant jobs are held by full-time workers employed at the end of quarter one. The shares for trucking, financial services, and software all lie between these two extremes.

As noted above, only workers who are imputed to work full-time at least once in the period of time covered by the LEHD data have values for the skill measures. Thus, these worker and job counts will almost always be smaller than worker and job counts for the earnings measures. Recalling that all skill counts are conditional on a worker having worked full-time at least once, it is not surprising that the current full-time and point-in-time restrictions have a smaller impact on the count of dominant jobs for the skill measures than we observe for the earnings measures. This is true in all sectors. For retail food, the share of dominant jobs held by full-time workers working at the end of quarter one is now 78 percent, given that the worker is observed to work full-time at least once. The share in semiconductors, however, essentially remains unchanged by this condition.

Regardless of whether we consider the count of jobs with an earnings measure or the count of jobs held by workers with skill measures, the fraction by which the job count increases when we include all jobs as opposed to dominant jobs only is identical in each sector.

A comparison of these counts across sectors provides information on the relative amount of job changing and multiple jobholding in each sector relative to other sectors. Surprisingly, the amount of variation across sectors in this fraction is not large. The count of all jobs is between 127 percent of dominant jobs (in semiconductors) and 140 percent of dominant jobs (in trucking).

Finally, recall that the count of dominant jobs for the skill measures is smaller than the count of dominant jobs for earnings measures because only workers who have worked full-time at least once have skill measures. However, regardless of the difference in magnitude between the two counts, the fraction by which the job count increases when we include all jobs is identical. This suggests that within each sector, workers who have worked full-time at least once are perhaps neither more nor less likely to change jobs or to hold multiple jobs.

Describing the Earnings Distribution

Rather than report percentiles of the actual distributions of these earnings and skill measures, we report percentiles of the "smoothed" distributions using a kernel density estimator. We use these smoothed distributions both because the smoothed distributions may correct for noise/measurement error and for disclosure purposes. Tests indicate that the characteristics of the actual and the smoothed distributions are quite similar.

The methodology for decomposing the sources in the earnings distribution is provided in Andersson et al. (2006).[1]

Notes

Chapter One

1. Marc Fisher, "Giant looks more and more like a dinosaur," *Washington Post,* May 5, 2005, B1.
2. Associated Press, state and local wire, May 2, 2005, dateline Frederick, Maryland.
3. Lynda V. Mapes, "Good business: Two local companies are proving it pays to do well by workers," *Seattle Times,* January 16, 2005, domestic news section. p. 14.
4. Ibid.
5. Dave Simanoff, "Tampa among 3 cities vying for call center," *Tampa Tribune,* May 5, 2005.
6. Crayton Harrison, "Austin economy still wired to semiconductor industry," *Dallas Morning News,* September 22, 2004.

Chapter Two

1. Timothy Egan, "No degree, and no way back to the middle," *New York Times,* May 24, 2005, A15.
2. Employment here represents the average of reference period employment in the firm and previous period employment in the firm. In the economics literature, worker turnover is sometimes defined as the sum of accessions and separations to reflect the overall number of transitions, and job turnover is likewise defined as the sum of job creation and destruction to reflect the overall number of changes in opportunities. Our definitions are obviously closely related. These alternatives bound the number of workers impacted by the worker and job turnover respectively. Note that in some of the succeeding chapters, we also define excess worker turnover at the firm level as the sum of accessions and separations at the firm minus the absolute value of net change at the firm. This "excess" measure thus captures the extra churn-

ing of workers at the firm over and above that necessary to accommodate net changes at the firm. For further discussion, see Steven J. Davis and John Halti-wanger, "Gross job flows," in *Handbook of Labor Economics,* ed. Orley Ashenfel-ter and David Card (Amsterdam: North-Holland, 1999), and Steven J. Davis, John Haltiwanger, and Scott Schuh, *Job Creation and Job Destruction* (Cambridge: MIT Press, 1996).

3. Any discussion of the birth and death of firms should recognize that there is a difference between an establishment, which is a single physical location at which business is conducted or services or industrial operations are performed, and a firm, which includes all establishments under the same operational control. In 2001 there were about 5.7 million firms and just over 7 million establishments in the U.S. In our discussion of specific results we try to be careful about this distinction but for expo-sitional reasons we often use the term "firm" to refer to either firms or establish-ments.

4. In what follows note that changes in ownership associated with mergers and acquisitions do not inherently imply the entry and exit of establishments.

5. Gregor Andrade, Mark Mitchell, and Erik Stafford, "New evidence and per-spectives on mergers," *Journal of Economic Perspectives,* 15, no. 2 (2001): 103–20.

6. Jeffrey T. Macher, David C. Mowery, and David A. Hodges, "Back to domi-nance? U.S. resurgence in the global semiconductor industry," *California Manage-ment Review* 41, no. 1 (1998): 107–36.

7. Greg Linden, Clair Brown, and Melissa Appleyard, "The net world order's influence on global leadership in the semiconductor industry," in *Locating Global Advantage: Industry Dynamics in the International Economy,* ed. Martin Kenney and Richard Florida (Stanford: Stanford University Press, 2004).

8. Semiconductor and Related Device Manufacturing 2002, Economic Census, U.S. Bureau of the Census, Table 1.

9. Ashish Arora and Alfonso Gambardella, "The globalization of the software industry: Perspectives and opportunities for developed and developing countries," NBER Working Paper no. 10538, National Bureau of Economic Research, 2004, 1.

10. Software Publishers 2002, Economic Census, U.S. Bureau of the Census, Table 2.

11. Although much has been written about the job-creating prowess of small businesses, one of the authors has argued elsewhere that this rests on misleading in-terpretations of the data, since many previous studies of the job creation process rely upon data that are not suitable for drawing inferences about the relationship between employer size and job creation. That same work notes that small plants and firms account for most newly created and newly destroyed manufacturing jobs and that survival rates for new and existing manufacturing jobs increase sharply with employer size. See Steven J. Davis, John Haltiwanger, and Scott Schuh, *Job Crea-tion and Destruction* (Cambridge: MIT Press, 1996), chap. 4.

12. Amey Stone, "Death of a stock salesman," *Business Week Online,* April 7,

2005 (http://www.businessweek.com/bwdaily/dnflash/apr2005/nf2005046_9224 _db016.htm).

Chapter Three

1. NAPA, http://www.napawash.org/pc_management_studies/ongoing_offshoring .html, posted February 7, 2005. The approach taken by NAPA is to describe what data are available and make recommendations for more data collection. The GAO and Sloan's Offshore Working Group have also issued reports on the data needed to analyze the impact of offshoring on U.S. jobs and economy.

2. Gail Pesyna, SBE/CISE workshop, March 15, 2005 (http://vis.sdsc.edu/sbe/ reports/SBE-CISE-FINAL.pdf).

3. Michael C. Jensen, "The modern Industrial Revolution: Exit and the failure of internal control systems," *Journal of Finance* 48 (1993): 831–80.

4. See http://en.wikipedia.org/wiki/Deregulation.

5. Data taken from FDIC and available at http://www2.fdic.gov/hsob/HSOBRpt .asp?state=1&rptType=1&Rpt_Num=1.

6. Lorin M. Hitt, Frances X. Frei, and Patrick T. Harker, "How financial firms decide on technology," in *Brookings-Wharton Papers on Financial Services 1999*, ed. Robert E. Litan and Anthony M. Santomero (Washington: Brookings Institution Press), 93–136.

7. These figures underestimate the contribution of truck transportation to the overall economy, since they include only the employees of the so-called for-hire firms within the industry. The figures exclude trucking operations that occur within other industries, such as manufacturing and retail, as well as self-employed owner-operators.

8. Michael H. Belzer, "Collective bargaining in the motor carrier industry," *Contemporary Collective Bargaining in the Private Industry,* ed. Paula B. Voos (Madison, WI: Industrial Relations Research Association, 1994), 259–302.

9. Personal communication from Michael H. Belzer, August 15, 2005.

10. General Accounting Office, Offshoring of Services: An Overview of the Issues, November 2005, Report GAO-06–5, U.S. Government Accountability Office (http://www.gao.gov/htext/do65.html).

11. Clair Brown and Greg Linden, "Offshoring in the semiconductor industry: A historical perspective," in *Offshoring White Collar Work,* ed. Susan Collins and Lael Brainard (Washington: Brookings Institution, 2005), 279–333.

12. Douglas S. Meade, Stainslaw J. Rzeznik, and Darlene C. Robinson-Smith, "Business investment by industry in the U.S. economy for 1997," Bureau of Economic Analysis U.S. Census Department, Industry Economics Division, November 2003 (http://www.bea.gov/bea/ARTICLES/2003/11November/1103% 20Investment .pdf).

13. In some ways, this understates the size of the industry, because virtually every company involved in information technology, from hardware producers to end users, writes software. Measurement of the industry's activity via sale of software services and packaged software does not include the investment in software-creating activities within organizations. The magnitude of these activities is indicated by the fact that more programmers are employed outside the business service (which includes software) industry than within this industry. In 2002, according to the Bureau of Labor Statistics, only 81,000 computer programmers and software engineers worked in the software publishing industry, out of over one million total computer programmers and software engineers (http://www.bls.gov/oco/cg/cgs051.htm).

14. Some definitions of the retail food industry include the food service industry, e.g., restaurants. In this study, the food service industry is not included in the retail food industry.

15. A supercenter is defined by the Food Institute as a large food/drug store combined with a mass merchandiser under one roof, where food items account for less than 40 percent of the selling area.

16. The industry consists of three main subindustries: banks and savings and loans, securities and commodities firms, and insurance companies.

17. For a discussion of industry change, and a matched pair case study, see Larry W. Hunter, "Transforming retail banking: Inclusion and segmentation in service work," in *Employment Practices and Business Strategy,* ed. Peter Cappelli (New York: Oxford University Press, 1999), 153–92, and Larry W. Hunter, Annette Bernhardt, Katherine L. Hughes, and Eva Skuratowicz, "It's not just the ATMs: Firm strategies, work restructuring, and workers' earnings in retail banking," *Industrial and Labor Relations Review* 54 (2001): 402–24.

18. Norman A. Weintraub, "ICC regulated motor carriers of general freight under NMFA that terminated general freight operations from July 1, 1980 to October 31, 1992," IBT Economics Department Report (Washington: International Brotherhood of Teamsters, 1992).

19. Michael H. Belzer, Kenneth L. Campbell, Stephen V. Burks, Dale Ballou, George Fulton, Donald Grimes, and Kristen Monaco, *Hours of Service Impact Assessment* (Ann Arbor: University of Michigan Transportation Research Institute and Federal Highway Administration, Office of Motor Carriers and Highway Safety, 1999).

20. Robert C. Leachman and Chien H. Leachman, "Globalization of semiconductor manufacturing," *Locating Global Advantage: Industry Dynamics in the International Economy,* ed. Martin Kenney and Richard Florida (Stanford: Stanford University Press, 2004), 203–31.

21. http://www.job-hunt.org/about.html.

22. Albert Endres, "A synopsis of software engineering history: The industrial perspective" (Position Papers for Dagstuhl Seminar 9635 on History of Software

Engineering, 1996); Edward Steinmueller, "The U.S. software industry: An analysis and interpretive history," in *The International Computer Software Industry*, ed. David C. Mowery (Oxford and New York: Oxford University Press, 1995), 15–52.

23. For an example, see http://www.developer.ibm.com/tech/isvadvantage.html.

24. Data drawn Digital Economy 2000, Economics and Statistics Administration, Office of Policy Development, U.S. Department of Commerce Bureau of Economic Analysis, June 2000 (http://permanent.access.gpo.gov/lps53674/2000/digital .pdf, 55–60).

25. U.S. Department of Labor, Bureau of Labor Statistics, *Occupational Outlook Handbook*, 2004.

26. http://www.computer.org/certification/cert_for_you.htm.

27. U.S. Department of Labor, Bureau of Labor Statistics, *Occupational Outlook Handbook*, 2003.

28. Stephen Baker and Manjeet Kripalani, "Software," *Business Week Online*, March 1, 2004 (http://www.businessweek.com/magazine/content/04_09/b3872001 _mz001.htm).

29. Food Institute, *Food Industry Review 2003* (Elmwood Park, NH: American Institute of Food Distribution, 2003).

30. Phil R. Kaufman, "Food retailing," U.S. Food Marketing System, 2002, AER-811, U.S. Economic Research Service, U.S. Department of Agriculture (http:// www.ers.usda.gov/publications/aer811/aer811e.pdf).

31. Gerald R. Moody, "Information technology and economic performance of the grocery store industry," Economics and Statistics Administration, Office of Policy Development, U.S. Department of Commerce, ESA/OPD 97-1, 1997 (http:// ssrn.com/abstract=37747).

32. Avner Ben-Ner, Fanmin Kong, and Stacie Bosley, *Workplace Organization and Human Resource Practices: The Retail Food Industry* (St. Paul: University of Minnesota, Retail Food Industry Center, 2000).

33. J. P. Walsh, *Supermarkets Transformed* (New Brunswick: Rutgers University Press, 1993).

34. Katherine L. Hughes, "Supermarket employment: Good jobs at good wages?" IEE Working Paper no. 11, April 1999 (http://www.tc.columbia.edu/centers/iee/ PAPERS/workpap11.pdf).

Chapter Four

1. The results in this chapter draw very heavily on Benjamin A. Campbell, Hyowook Chiang, John Haltiwanger, Larry W. Hunter, Ron Jarmin, Nicole Nestoriak, Tim Park, and Kristin Sandusky, *Firm Performance, Workforce Quality, and Workforce Churning*, working paper, U.S. Bureau of the Census, Suitland, MD, 2005 (http://www.economicturbulence.com/data/papers/wp-firmperf.pdf). The details of

measurement and the statistical analysis underlying much of the discussion can be found in this paper. Some of the key tables from this analysis are provided in appendix B. The results in this chapter are based upon data for 1992 and 1997 using data from the Economic Censuses and unemployment insurance (UI) wage record data for California, Illinois, and Maryland.

2. Others choose a "high road" path and are competitive with the "low road" firms. Frances X. Frei, Patrick T. Harker, and Larry W. Hunter, "Retail banking," in *U.S. Industry in 2000: Studies in Competitive Performance* (Washington: National Academy Press, 1999), 179–214.

3. Eileen Appelbaum, Annette Bernhardt, and Richard J. Murnane, "Low-Wage America: An Overview," in *Low-Wage America: How Employers Are Reshaping Opportunity in the Workplace*, ed. Eileen Appelbaum, Annette Bernhardt, and Richard J. Murnane (New York: Russell Sage Press, 2003), 10.

4. "The Principal Financial Group: simply (one of) the best," January 7, 2004 (http://www.principal.com/about/news/fortune010704.htm).

5. "50 best small and medium companies to work for in America named at SHRM annual conference," June 28, 2004 (http://www.scienceblog.com/community/older/archives/K/2/pub2387.html).

6. Jill Elswick, "Having it their way: Intel's benefit plan emphasizes choice and flexibility," *Employee Benefit News*, March 1, 2003.

7. Karen Lee, "Trucking firm takes benefit portability to new heights," *Employee Benefit News*, July 1, 2000.

8. Lynda V. Mapes, "Good business: Two local companies are proving it pays to do well by workers," *Seattle Times*, January 31, 2005.

9. Some evidence in favor of this idea using LEHD data is provided in John M. Abowd, John Haltiwanger, Ron Jarmin, Julia Lane, Paul Lengermann, Kristin McCue, Kevin McKinney, and Kristin Sandusky, "The relation among human capital, productivity, and market value," in *Measuring Capital in the New Economy*, ed. Carol Corrado, John Haltiwanger, and Don Sichel (Chicago: University of Chicago Press, 2005), 153–204.

10. See, e.g., John C. Haltiwanger, Julia I. Lane, and James R. Spletzer, "Wages, productivity, and the dynamic interaction of business and workers," *Labour Economics* (in press).

11. Indeed, a series of papers show that the higher the average educational level of production workers or the greater the proportion of nonmanagerial workers who use computers, the higher the plant productivity. See, in particular, Casey Ichinowski, Kathryn Shaw, and Giovanna Prennushi, "The effects of human resource management practices on productivity: A study of steel finishing lines," *American Economic Review* 87 (1997): 291–313 (reprinted in Edward Lazear and Robert McNabb, eds., *Personnel Economics* [Cheltenham, U.K.: Edward Elgar Press, 2004]), and Sandra E. Black and Lisa M. Lynch, "How to compete: The impact of workplace practices and information technology on productivity," *Review of Economics and Statistics* 83 (2001): 434–45. See Timothy F. Bresnahan, Erik Brynjolfs-

son, and Lorin M. Hitt, "Information technology, workplace organization, and the demand for skilled labor: Firm-level evidence," NBER Working Paper no. 7136, 1999, for related results.

12. PBS, "Store Wars: When Wal-Mart Comes to Town," February 2, 2004 (http://www.pbs.org/itvs/storewars/stores3.html).

13. While this measure is quite simple, it has been shown in recent research that it is highly correlated with more sophisticated measures of firm performance such as measures of total factor productivity. See Lucia Foster, John Haltiwanger, and C. J. Krizan, "Aggregate productivity growth: Lessons from microeconomic evidence," in *New Directions in Productivity Analysis*, ed. Edward Dean, Michael Harper, and Charles Hulten (Chicago: University of Chicago Press, 2001), 303–63.

14. We directly calculate the proportion of firms that existed in 1992, and survived until 1997 (survivors), as well as the proportion that did not survive (exiters). We can also calculate the proportion of firms in 1997 that entered the industry between 1992 and 1997 (entrants).

15. It is an open question as to whether entrants should be as productive as continuers. There are conflicting effects, some of which can make entrants more productive than incumbents and some that can make them less so. For example, new entrants can start their business with the best technology available (the vintage effect), incumbents have more time to learn from their previous production processes (the learning effect). If the vintage/learning effect dominates, then entrants/incumbents are more productive.

16. This productivity gap is calculated from a simple regression where the dependent variable is productivity and the right-hand-side variables are year effects and dummies for entering and exiting establishments.

17. Tables and figures underlying this summary of findings can be found in Campbell et al., *Firm Performance*.

18. In the statistical analysis underlying the discussion our measure of revenue per worker is real gross output per worker. The measure is gross revenue deflated with an industry deflator per worker. Real earnings per worker is measured by deflating payroll with the CPI and dividing by the number of workers at the business.

19. The overall human capital measure is the measure developed and discussed by Abowd, Lengermann, and McKinney, "The measurement of human capital in the U.S. economy."

20. See Campbell et al., *Firm Performance*, for details on the statistical correlations discussed here.

21. Ibid.

22. The fabless/integrated differences are important here since the new fabless entrants have higher turnover than the continuing integrated companies.

23. These results are from the estimation of a probit model relating factors that are associated with the exit of an establishment from one economic census to another (i.e., over a five-year horizon). In figure 4.5, we show the impact of a 10 percentage point (0.1) change in churning and human capital rate on the probability of

exit. The results from this probit estimation are reported in Campbell et al., *Firm Performance*. We also control for firm structure with a single-unit dummy. In most sectors, single-unit establishments are less likely to fail after controlling for size, productivity, churning, and workforce quality. This is consistent with the Holmes and Schmitz hypothesis that single-unit establishment firms may be, holding other factors constant, less willing to close since closing down the establishment implies closing down the firm while this is not the case for establishments belonging to a multi-unit establishment firm. Thomas J. Holmes and James A. Schmitz, Jr., "On the turnover of business firms and business managers," *Journal of Political Economy* 103 (1995): 1005–38.

24. In order to do the analysis, any semiconductor establishment that entered after 1987 and upon entry had fewer than three hundred employees was classified as a fabless establishment, and all others were classified as integrated establishments.

25. Recall that there are some inherent measurement problems. In particular, measuring output and productivity in the financial services industry is problematic. However, revenue per worker has reasonable properties in selected sub-industries like securities brokers.

Chapter Five

1. See http://www.cnn.com/CNN/Programs/lou.dobbs.tonight/book.html.
2. Mike Hiltzik, "Shipping out U.S. jobs—to a ship," *Los Angeles Times*, May 2, 2005.
3. Aaron Bernstein, "Waking up from the American dream: Meritocracy and equal opportunity are fading fast," *Business Week*, December 1, 2003.
4. See http://www.spectrum.ieee.org/careers/careerstemplate.jsp?ArticleId =n070103.
5. See http://engr.smu.edu/students/lunch/bios/primdahl.html.
6. The results in this chapter are based upon data for 1992–2003 using UI wage record data for California, Illinois, and Maryland.
7. See http://www.allianceibm.org/news/jobactions.htm.
8. Some of the observations about specific firms here likely reflect divisions of these large, complex firms beyond their production of semiconductors. Even so, the patterns discussed reflect the impact of globalization on high-technology products.
9. See http://www.allianceibm.org/news/jobactions.htm.
10. See http://en.wikipedia.org/wiki/Digital_Equipment_Corporation; http://www.job-hunt.org/about.html.
11. See http://www.networkworld.com/topics/layoffs.html.
12. See http://www.bizjournals.com/austin/stories/2001/12/17/daily22.html.
13. This discussion borrows heavily from Fredrik Andersson, Matthew Freed-

man, John Haltiwanger, Julia Lane, and Kathryn Shaw, "Reaching for the stars: Who pays for talent in innovative industries?" (working paper, Stanford University, 2005).

14. Michael Moeller, "Outta here at Microsoft: The software giant is losing key talent to the Internet" (http://www.businessweek.com/1999/99_48/b3657197.htm).

15. Meg Major, "The people gap," *Progressive Grocer,* November 1, 2003, 20, quoting Prof. Richard George, St. Joseph's University, Philadelphia.

16. See http://www.jbhunt.com/careers/drivingcareers/index_drcareer.html.

17. See "$58B bank deal set" (http://money.cnn.com/2004/01/14/news/deals/jpmorgan_bankone/).

18. Larry W. Hunter, "Transforming retail banking: Inclusion and segmentation in service work," *Employment Practices and Business Strategy,* ed. Peter Cappelli (New York: Oxford University Press, 1999), 153–92.

19. From Fortune's 2005 list of "100 Best Companies to Work For" (http://money.cnn.com/2005/01/07/news/fortune500/best_companies/). The company's national characteristics cannot be directly compared to the firm characteristics in our sample, since job ladders are described at the establishment or workplace level. Fortune's companies have a national full-time workforce of at least one thousand workers.

20. This has the additional advantage of avoiding the data problems associated with many younger and older workers not being in the sample for many quarters. We exclude workers under twenty-five years old, who are often involved with finishing school and working part-time, and seniors, who are often confronting retirement decisions. We exclude workers with more than three employers in order to simplify the analysis, since they are a small number of prime-aged workers. We defined workers as working in an industry if they had at least one full-quarter-dominant employer in that particular Sloan industry between 1992 and 2001. Observations are at the job level that is defined by a match between an employer and an employee over certain time periods. An employer is identified by the SEIN (state employer identification number) level, which is establishment for single-unit but not necessarily for multi-unit establishment firms. In general, SEIN is smaller than firm: establishment $\leq$ SEIN $\leq$ firm within a state. SEIN is state specific and thus is different in each state. An employee is uniquely identified by the PIK (person identification number).

21. Turnover is the excess worker reallocation concept defined in chapter 2.

22. *Size:* large ($\geq$100 workers) and small ($<$100 workers); *employment growth:* positive (employment same or increased) or negative (employment declined) over the period of each job (i.e., if the job lasted from t_1 to t_2, sign(firmsize(t_2) $-$ firmsize(t_1)). "Growing or shrinking" is measured by the job spell, so that a job is in a growing firm if employment at the firm increases (or remains the same) during the worker's job there (as measured by employment at beginning and end of job observation). The distribution of job observations across net employment growth by industry is:

Growth	financial services	retail food	semiconductors	software	trucking
−	29.2%	31.9	33.7	32.8	35.3
0	12.6%	18.6	7.6	14.6	15.2
+	58.1%	49.5	58.7	52.6	49.4

Turnover: high (turnover is at least 20% above the turnover predicted by change in employment) or low (turnover is less than 20% above the turnover predicted by change in employment).

23. Large growing firms with low turnover have 50% of jobs in semiconductors, almost 40% in financial services, 20% to 25% in software and retail food, and 12% in trucking.

24. Part of this is by construction, since for any sample of ongoing job spells, they are more likely to be observed in a larger firm (more workers by construction) and, conditional on size, a growing firm (i.e., an expanding firm will tend to have more workers). While these basic patterns are to be expected, it is useful to understand the magnitudes of these patterns and even more importantly the variation of these patterns across industries, employee characteristics, and other employer character-istics (e.g., turnover).

25. The full set of graphs is also available on the book's Web site.

Chapter Six

1. G. J. Meyer, *Executive Blues: Down and Out in Corporate America* (New York: Franklin Square Press, 1995), 25.

2. See http://www.siliconimage.com/aboutus/team.aspx.

3. Paul Ong and Don Mar, "Post-layoff earnings among semiconductor work-ers," *Industrial and Labor Relations Review* 45 (1992): 366–79.

4. Louis S. Jacobson, Robert J. LaLonde, and Daniel G. Sullivan, "Earnings losses of displaced workers," *American Economic Review* 83 (1993): 685–709. The earn-ings loss of $80,000 in their study has been converted to 2005 values.

5. Henry Farber, "Mobility and stability: The dynamics of job change in labor markets," in *The Handbook of Labor Economics,* vol. 3, ed. Orley Ashenfelter and David Card (Amsterdam: Elsevier Science, 1999), 2439–84.

6. Robert Topel and M. P. Ward, "Job mobility and the careers of young men," *Quarterly Journal of Economics* 107 (1992): 441–79.

7. Fredrik Andersson, Harry J. Holzer, and Julia Lane, *Moving Up or Moving On: Workers, Firms, and Advancement in the Low-Wage Labor Market* (New York: Russell Sage Press, 2005).

8. See chapter 5, notes 21 and 22, for definitions of terms.

9. Analyzing prime-aged workers allows us to avoid data problems associated with many younger and older workers not being in the sample for many quarters. We exclude workers with more than three employers in order to simplify the analysis, since they are a small number of prime-aged workers. See chapter 5, note 20, for definitions of workers and jobs.

10. The results in this chapter are based upon data for 1992–2003 using UI wage record data for California, Illinois, and Maryland. Career paths for other workers are provided on our website: economicturbulence.com.

11. The proportion of all workers in the sample (not just prime-aged) holding 1–3 jobs is 71% in software, 74% in semiconductors, 76% in financial services, 78% in trucking, and 82% in retail food.

12. Kenneth J. McLaughlin, "A theory of quits and layoffs with efficient turnover," *Journal of Political Economy* 99 (1991):1–29, points out that there is little operational distinction between voluntary and involuntary job change. Some of the disagreement between employers and employees in surveys reflects the different incentives the UI laws give to the two sides.

13. The careful reader comparing the results in this chapter to those in chapter 2 might be surprised by these findings as worker turnover rates are much higher in retail trade and trucking than in other industries. To reconcile these findings, it is important to emphasize that for worker turnover the unit of observation is a match, and short-duration matches count as much as long-duration matches in the definition of worker turnover. In contrast, the discussion here is about a worker's career, and we are ranking predominant career patterns within the industry. Moreover, the career path comparisons made here control for gender, age, and education.

14. High-educated men in financial services tend to experience the same type of path as the women. However, high-educated male job switchers stay in the industry in finding their second, and better, job.

15. The measurement of these time intervals reflects the requirement that a worker is considered to be at a job once the worker has been at the job for a full quarter. Even taking this into account it is clear that one of the costs of jobhopping is that it takes time.

16. A full set of tables and figures for all career path and job ladder types for all industries can be found at economicturbulence.com.

17. Larry W. Hunter, Annette Bernhardt, Katherine L. Hughes, and Eva Skuratowicz, "It's not just the ATMs: Technology, firm strategies, jobs, and earnings in retail banking," *Industrial and Labor Relations Review* 54 (2001): 411.

18. From fieldwork conducted by Larry W. Hunter and Eva Skuratowicz as part of their research at the Sloan Financial Services Industry Center at the University of Pennsylvania.

19. Eva Skuratowicz and Larry W. Hunter, "Where do women's jobs come from? Job resegregation in an American bank," *Work and Occupations* 31, no. 1 (2004): 73–110.

20. Larry W. Hunter, "Transforming retail banking: Inclusion and segmentation in service work," in *Employment Practices and Business Strategy,* ed. Peter Cappelli (New York: Oxford University Press, 1999), 153–92.

21. From fieldwork conducted by Clair Brown and Benjamin A. Campbell as part of their research at the Sloan Semiconductor Industry Center at University of California, Berkeley.

22. See http://www.oracle.com/corporate/pressroom/html/scatz.html.

23. Two characteristics of our data set are particularly relevant for the trucking industry. First, since most drivers are paid by the mile and enforcement of regulations concerning hours of service is spotty at best, the increase in earnings may be the result of working more hours. There is some evidence that truck drivers operate with target earnings in mind. If this target cannot be reached in other low-wage employment, the option of working longer hours in trucking may be attractive. Second, the total amount of observed time in the sample may be less than forty quarters, and this is true whether the last job is right-censored or uncensored, i.e., if the worker is still observed in a job or has left the sample. A large proportion of workers in the trucking industry are owner-operators, who are classified as self-employed, and so their earnings are not reported by any firm, and therefore not observed in our sample. The simulated career paths in trucking are sensitive to right-censoring of the last job. However, 70 percent of all long trucking jobs (five years or longer) in the sample are ongoing in 2001; only 30 percent were completed earlier. The completed jobs all had negative earnings growth, which indicates that these workers are in troubled companies and have left (or been terminated) in order to find a job with better prospects.

24. Personal communication, August 2004.

25. Barbara Hagenbaugh, "Truckers needed to keep economy rolling," *USA Today,* October 12, 2004.

26. The simulated career paths in retail food are sensitive to right-censoring of the last job. Almost 60 percent of long retail food jobs in the sample are ongoing in 2001. Although the completed jobs may have had higher initial earnings than the ongoing jobs, their earnings growth rates are all negative, which indicates that these workers were in troubled companies and had left (or been terminated).

27. Steven Greenhouse, "How Costco became the anti-Wal-Mart," *New York Times,* July 17, 2005, BU1.

Chapter Seven

1. Griff Witte, "As income gap widens, uncertainty spreads: More U.S. families struggle to stay on track," *Washington Post,* September 20, 2004, A01.

2. Improved skills are not a factor in the increased earnings for high-income workers: the skill set of incoming workers is actually lower than the earnings of the workers they replace.

3. David Card and John E. DiNardo, "Skill-biased technological change and rising wage inequality: Some problems and puzzles," *Journal of Labor Economics* 20, no. 4 (2002): 733–83.

4. Andrew B. Bernard and J. Bradford Jensen, "Understanding increasing and decreasing wage inequality" (unpublished paper, Yale University, 1998).

5. Andrew Bernard, Brad Jensen, and Peter Schott, "Survival of the best fit: Exposure to low wage countries and the (uneven) growth of U.S. manufacturing plants," *Journal of International Economics* 68 (2006): 235.

6. Fredrik Andersson, Harry J. Holzer, and Julia Lane, *Moving Up or Moving On: Workers, Firms, and Advancement in the Low-Wage Labor Market* (New York: Russell Sage Press, 2005).

7. We include a worker's real annualized earnings, defined as the average of full-quarter earnings in a given year from the dominant employer in that sector multiplied by four, where the dominant employer is defined as the employer contributing the most to the worker's annual earnings, where the worker has been imputed to work full-time in that year. We impute a worker to have worked full-time in a year if we have identified her or him as likely to be working at the end of the first quarter of the year and he or she has real annualized earnings of at least $1,000 for the year.

8. We include real annual earnings from all jobs that are in one of the five Sloan sectors and that are at least $1,000 for the year.

9. These are within-state retention rates; thus, a worker who moves across state lines but stays in the same industry is not counted as staying in the same industry.

10. It is a little misleading to compare retention rates across industries, since larger industries, such as financial services, are, almost by definition, likely to retain higher proportions of their workforce. For this reason, firm retention rates are more comparable.

11. Pete Engardio, Aaron Bernstein, and Manjeet Kripalani with Frederik Balfour, Brian Grow, and Jay Greene. "The new global job shift," *Business Week,* February 3, 2003, http://www.businessweek.com/magazine/content/03_05/b3818001.htm.

12. The details of the approach are described in appendix D. In the discussion that follows, the annualized earnings measure is used, and hence there is a one-to-one correspondence between a job and a worker. The terms "low-income worker" and "low-income job" are hence used almost interchangeably.

13. The studies on earnings inequality have found that much of the action in terms of changes over time is a within-industry phenomenon. Moreover, the primary value added of our data is that we can drill down deep inside of industries and look at the interaction of specific firms and workers. Between-industry changes in the distribution of jobs are relatively easy to measure and study from standard data sources.

14. Residual explanations seem to be especially important in accounting for the large increase of high-income workers in semiconductors and for the decrease of high-income workers in retail food.

Chapter Eight

1. Larry Elliott, "Edwardian summer," *Guardian,* August 18, 2005, http://www .guardian.co.uk/comment/story/0,3604,1551325,00.html.

2. The agricultural extension services in the twentieth century are largely viewed as a success. In the 1990s, the government did experiment with a form of manufacturing extension services via the MEP program to offer training to manufacturing businesses about best practices with more mixed success. Evaluating the success of such programs is, of course, quite difficult since such programs are typically not controlled experiments.

Appendix A

1. See www.sloan.org.

2. For more information on the data set, see http://lehd.dsd.census.gov.

3. The program currently partners with a total of 34 states, comprising 76 percent of the U.S. workforce.

4. A comprehensive discussion of the rationale for and consequences of this choice is provided in Fredrik Andersson, Harry J. Holzer, and Julia Lane, *Moving Up or Moving On: Workers, Firms, and Advancement in the Low-Wage Labor Market* (New York: Russell Sage Press, 2005), and John M. Abowd, Paul Lengermann, and Kevin McKinney, "The measurement of human capital in the U.S. economy" (Working paper, March 2003, Cornell University; http://instruct1.cit.cornell.edu/ ~jma7/abowd_lengermann_mckinney_20030402.pdf).

5. The annualized earnings measure that we use and the decomposition of this measure into these effects is based upon the methodology developed by Abowd, Lengermann, and McKinney, "The measurement of human capital."

6. Steven J. Davis and John Haltiwanger, "Gross job flows," *Handbook of Labor Economics,* ed. Orley Ashenfelter and David Card (Amsterdam: Elsevier, 1999), 2711–805.

7. Simon Burgess, Julia Lane, and David Stevens, "Job flows, worker flows, and churning," *Journal of Labor Economics* 18, no. 3 (2000): 473–502.

8. Daniel Aaronson and Daniel Sullivan, "Growth in worker quality," *Economic Perspectives,* no. 4 (2001): 53–74. ·

9. Casey Ichinowski, Kathryn Shaw, and Giovanna Prennushi, "The effects of human resource management practices on productivity: A study of steel finishing lines," *American Economic Review* 87: 291–313 (reprinted in *Personnel Economics,* ed. Edward Lazear and Robert McNabb [Cheltenham, U.K.: Edward Elgar Press, 2004]).

10. See, e.g., Carol Corrado and Lawrence Slifman "Decomposition of productivity and costs," *American Economic Review* 89 (1999): 328–32, and William Gul-

lickson and Michael J. Harper, "Bias in aggregate productivity trends revisited," *Monthly Labor Review,* March 2002, 32–40.

11. As will become apparent below, our biggest problem with productivity measurement is also with financial services. We should note in this regard that BLS uses the gross revenue measures that we use for all of our sectors *except* for financial services (for the latter they attempt to measure the service flow from financial service providers). Even with their alternative approach, there are anomalous results for the financial services sector.

Appendix C

1. We use the deviation about the national mean to control for a calendar effect on earnings.

2. WJWG and BJWG are both annualized measures. Suppose we want to calculate a wage growth rate from quarter s (E_s) to quarter t (E_t). Then the wage growth rate (whether it is WJWG or BJWG) is defined as

$$WG_{s,t} = \frac{[\log(E_t) - \log(E_s)]}{(t - s)/4}$$

The length of the nonemployment spell is incorporated in the denominator. The BJWG measure calculated in this fashion. Since we use earnings from "dominant" employers, the denominator of BJWG is always positive.

Appendix D

1. Fredrik Andersson, Elizabeth Davis, Matthew L. Freedman, Julia I. Lane, Brian P. McCall, and L. Kristin Sandusky, "Decomposing the sources of eranings inequality within and across industries," February 2006, mimeo, NORC/University of Chicago, http://client.norc.org/jole/SOLEweb/Decomposing%20Sources%20%of%20Earnings%20Inequality%202002-10-2006.pdf.

Bibliography

Aaronson, Daniel, and Daniel Sullivan. 2001. Growth in worker quality. *Economic Perspectives,* no. 4: 53–74.

Abowd, John M. 2002. Unlocking the information in integrated social data. *New Zealand Economic Papers* 36 (June): 9–31.

Abowd, John M., Robert H. Creecy, and Francis Kramarz. 2002. Computing person and firm effects using linked longitudinal employer-employee data. Cornell University Working Paper.

Abowd, John M., John Haltiwanger, Ron Jarmin, Julia Lane, Paul Lengermann, Kristin McCue, Kevin McKinney, and Kristin Sandusky. 2005. "The relation among human capital, productivity, and market value." In Carol Corrado, John Haltiwanger, and Don Sichel (eds.), *Measuring Capital in the New Economy.* Chicago: University of Chicago Press, pp. 153–204.

Abowd, John M., John Haltiwanger, and Julia Lane. 2004. Integrated longitudinal employee-employer data for the United States. *American Economic Review* 94: 224–29.

Abowd, John M., John Haltiwanger, Julia Lane, Kevin McKinney, and Kristin Sandusky. 2005. Within and between firm changes in human capital, technology, and productivity. Working paper, University of Maryland, http://www.econ.umd.edu/~haltiwan/ahlms_20050527_SOLE.pdf; accessed February 26, 2006.

Abowd, John M., Francis Kramarz, and David N. Margolis. 1999. High wage workers and high wage firms. *Econometrica* 67: 251–334.

Abowd, John M., Paul Lengermann, and Kevin McKinney. 2003. The measurement of human capital in the U.S. economy. Working paper (March), Cornell University. http://instruct1.cit.cornell.edu/~jma7/abowd_lengermann_mckinney_20030402.pdf, accessed February 26, 2006.

Acemoglu, Daron. 2002. Technical change, inequality, and the labor market. *Journal of Economic Literature* 40: 7–72.

Aghion, Philippe. 2002. Schumpeterian growth theory and the dynamics of income inequality. *Econometrica* 70: 855–82.

Akerlof, George A., and Janet L. Yellen. 1990. The fair wage-effort hypothesis and unemployment. *Quarterly Journal of Economics* 105: 255–83.

Akhavein, J. D., A. N. Berger, and D. B. Humphrey. 1997. The effects of megamergers on efficiency and prices: Evidence from a bank profit function. *Review of Industrial Organization* 12: 95–139.

Andersson, Fredrik, Elizabeth Davis, Matthew L. Freedman, Julia I. Lane, Brian P. McCall, and L. Kristin Sandusky. 2006. "Decomposing the sources of eranings inequality within and across industries." February, mimeo, NORC/University of Chicago, http://client.norc.org/jole/SOLEweb/Decomposing%20Sources%20 %20of%20Earnings%20Inequality%202002–10–2006.pdf (accessed April 4, 2006).

Andersson, Fredrik, Matthew Freedman, John Haltiwanger, Julia Lane, and Kathryn Shaw. 2005. Reaching for the stars: Who pays for talent in innovative industries? Working paper, Stanford University.

Andersson, Fredrik, Harry J. Holzer, and Julia Lane. 2005. *Moving Up or Moving On: Workers, Firms, and Advancement in the Low-Wage Labor Market.* New York: Russell Sage Press.

Andrade, Gregor, Mark Mitchell, and Erik Stafford. 2001. New evidence and perspectives on mergers. *Journal of Economic Perspectives,* 15(2): 103–20.

Appelbaum, Eileen, Annette Bernhardt, and Richard J. Murnane (eds.). 2003. *Low-Wage America: How Employers Are Reshaping Opportunity in the Workplace.* New York: Russell Sage Foundation.

Arora, Ashish, and Alfonso Gambardella. 2004. The globalization of the software industry: Perspectives and opportunities for developed and developing countries. NBER Working Paper no. 10538, National Bureau of Economic Research.

Aw, Bee Yan, Xiaomin Chen, and Mark Roberts. 2001. Firm-level evidence on productivity differentials and turnover in Taiwanese manufacturing. *Journal of Development Economics* 66: 51–86.

Baily, Martin Neil, Eric J. Bartelsman, and John Haltiwanger. 1996. Downsizing and productivity growth: Myth or reality? *Small Business Economics* 8: 259–78.

Baily, Martin Neil, Eric J. Bartelsman, and John Haltiwanger. 1997. Labor productivity: Structural change and cyclical dynamics. NBER Working Paper no. 5503.

Baily, Martin Neil, Charles Hulten, and David Campbell. 1992. Productivity dynamics in manufacturing establishments. *Brookings Papers on Economic Activity: Microeconomics* 1: 187–249.

Baker, George, Michael Gibbs, and Bengt Holmstrom. 1994. The wage policy of a firm. *Quarterly Journal of Economics* 109: 921–55.

Baker, Stephen, and Manjeet Kripalani. 2004. "Software." *Business Week Online,* March 1; http://www.businessweek.com/magazine/content/04_09/b3872001 _mz001.htm; accessed April 3, 2006.

Bartelsman, Eric J., and Phoebus J. Dhrymes. 1998. Productivity dynamics: U.S. manufacturing plants, 1972–86. *Journal of Productivity Analysis* 9(1): 5–34.

Bartelsman, Eric J., and Mark Doms. 2000. Understanding productivity: Lessons from longitudinal microdata. *Journal of Economic Literature* 38: 569–94.

Batt, Rosemary, Larry W. Hunter, and Steffanie Wilk. 2003. How and when does management matter? Job quality and career opportunities for call center workers. In E. Appelbaum, A. Bernhardt, and R. J. Murnane (eds.), *Low-Wage America: How Employers Are Reshaping Opportunity in the Workplace.* New York: Russell Sage Foundation, pp. 270–316.

Becker, Gary S. 1964. *Human Capital: A Theoretical and Empirical Analysis, with Special Reference to Education.* New York: Columbia University Press.

Belzer, Michael H. 1994. Collective bargaining in the motor carrier industry. In Paula B. Voos (ed.), *Contemporary Collective Bargaining in the Private Industry.* Madison, WI: Industrial Relations Research Association, pp. 259–302.

Belzer, Michael H. 2000. *Sweatshops on Wheels: Winners and Losers in Trucking Deregulation.* New York: Oxford University Press.

Belzer, Michael H. 2002. Trucking: Collective bargaining takes a rocky road. In Paul F. Clark, John T. Delaney, and Ann C. Frost (eds.), *Collective Bargaining: Current Developments and Future Challenges.* Champaign, IL: Industrial Relations Research Association, pp. 311–42.

Belzer, Michael H., Kenneth L. Campbell, Stephen V. Burks, Dale Ballou, George Fulton, Donald Grimes, and Kristen Monaco. 1999. *Hours of Service Impact Assessment.* Ann Arbor: University of Michigan Transportation Research Institute and Federal Highway Administration, Office of Motor Carriers and Highway Safety.

Belzer, Michael H., Daniel A. Rodriguez, and Stanley A. Sedo. 2002. *Paying for Safety: An Economic Analysis of the Effect of Compensation on Truck Driver Safety.* Washington: United States Department of Transportation, Federal Motor Carrier Safety Administration.

Ben-Ner, Avner, Fanmin Kong, and Stacie Bosley. 2000. *Workplace Organization and Human Resource Practices: The Retail Food Industry.* St. Paul: University of Minnesota, Retail Food Industry Center.

Berger, Allen N. 2003. The economic effects of technological progress: Evidence from the banking industry. *Journal of Money, Credit, and Banking* 35: 141–76.

Berger, Allen N., R. S. Demsetz, and P. E. Strahan. 1999. The consolidation of the financial services industry: Causes, consequences, and implications for the future. *Journal of Banking and Finance* 23: 135–94.

Berger, Allen N., W. C. Hunter, and S. G. Timme. 1993. The efficiency of financial institutions: A review and preview of research past, present, and future. *Journal of Banking and Finance* 17: 221–50.

Berger, Allen N., A. K. Kashyap, and J. M. Scalise. 1995. The transformation of the U.S. banking industry: What a long, strange trip it's been. *Brookings Papers on Economic Activity* 2: 55–218.

Berger, Allen N., and Loretta J. Mester. 1997. Inside the black box: What explains differences in the efficiency of financial institutions? *Journal of Banking and Finance* 21: 895–947.

Berger, Allen N., and Loretta J. Mester. 1999. What explains the dramatic changes in cost and profit performance of the U.S. banking industry? Wharton Financial Institutions Center Working Paper 99-10.

Berman, Francine, and Henry Brady. 2005. Final report: NSF SBE-CISE workshop on cyberinfrastructure and the social sciences. http://vis.sdsc.edu/sbe/reports/SBE-CISE-FINAL.pdf, accessed April 5, 2006.

Bernard, Andrew B., and J. Bradford Jensen. 1998. Understanding increasing and decreasing wage inequality. Unpublished paper (Yale University).

Bernard, Andrew B., J. Bradford Jensen, and Peter Schott. "Survival of the best fit: Exposure to low wage countries and the (uneven) growth of U.S. manufacturing plants" *Journal of International Economics* 68 (2006): 219–37.

Bernstein, Aaron. 2003. Waking up from the American dream: Meritocracy and equal opportunity are fading fast. *Business Week* (December 1).

Betancourt, Roger, and David Gautschi. 1993. The outputs of retail activities: Concepts, measurement, and evidence from U.S. Census data. *Review of Economics and Statistics* 75: 294–301.

Black, Sandra E., and Lisa M. Lynch. 1996. Human capital investments and productivity. *American Economic Review* 86: 263–67.

Black, Sandra E., and Lisa M. Lynch. 1998. The new workplace: What does it mean for employers? *Industrial Relations Research Association Papers and Proceedings, 50th Meeting,* 60–97.

Black, Sandra E., and Lisa M. Lynch. 2001. How to compete: The impact of workplace practices and information technology on productivity. *Review of Economics and Statistics* 83: 434–45.

Black, Sandra E., and Lisa M. Lynch. 2002. What's driving the new economy? The benefits of workplace innovation. NBER Working Paper no. w7479.

Bresnahan, Timothy F., Erik Brynjolfsson, and Lorin M. Hitt. 1999. Information technology, workplace organization, and the demand for skilled labor: Firm-level evidence. NBER Working Paper no. 7136.

Brown, Clair (ed.). 1997. The competitive semiconductor manufacturing human resources project: Final report (phase I). CSM-38. Institute of Industrial Relations, University of California, Berkeley.

Brown, Clair, and Benjamin A. Campbell. 1999. The impact of technological change on the internal labor market structure of a semiconductor firm. Sloan CSM-HR Working Paper, University of California, Berkeley.

Brown, Clair, and Benjamin A. Campbell. 2001. Technical change, wages, and employment in semiconductor manufacturing. *Industrial and Labor Relations Review* 54: 450–65.

Brown, Clair, and Benjamin A. Campbell. 2002. The impact of technological change on work and wages. *Industrial Relations* 41(1):1–33.

Brown, Clair, and Greg Linden. 2005. Offshoring in the semiconductor industry: A historical perspective. In Susan Collins and Lael Brainard (eds.), *Offshoring White Collar Work.* Washington: Brookings Institution, pp. 279–333.

Brown, Clair, Greg Pinsonneault, and Dan Rascher. 1999. The use of new technology and human resource systems in improving semiconductor manufacturing performance. Center for Work, Technology, and Society, University of California, Berkeley.

Budd, John W., and Brian P. McCall. 2001. The grocery stores wage distribution: A semi-parametric analysis of the role of retailing and labor market institutions. *Industrial and Labor Relations Review* 54: 483–501.

Bulow, Jeremy, and Lawrence Summers. 1986. A theory of dual labor markets with application to industrial policy, discrimination, and Keynesian unemployment. *Journal of Labor Economics* 4(3): 376–414.

Burgess, Simon, Julia Lane, and David Stevens. 1998. Hiring risky workers: Some evidence. *Journal of Economics and Management Strategy* 7(4): 669–76.

Burgess, Simon, Julia Lane, and David Stevens. 2000. Job flows, worker flows, and churning. *Journal of Labor Economics* 18(3): 473–502.

Caballero, Ricardo J., and Mohamad L. Hammour. 1994. The cleansing effect of recessions. *American Economic Review* 84: 1350–68.

Caballero, Ricardo J., and Mohamad L. Hammour. 1996. On the timing and efficiency of creative destruction. *Quarterly Journal of Economics* 111: 805–52.

Campbell, Benjamin A. 2004. Is working for a start-up worth it? Evidence from the semiconductor industry. Working paper, Center for Work, Technology, and Society, Institute of Industrial Relations, University of California, Berkeley.

Campbell, Benjamin A., Hyowook Chiang, John Haltiwanger, Larry W. Hunter, Ron Jarmin, Nicole Nestoriak, Tim Park, and Kristin Sandusky. 2005. *Firm Performance, Workforce Quality, and Workforce Churning.* Working paper, U.S. Bureau of the Census, Suitland, MD. http://www.economicturbulence.com/data/papers/wp-firmperf.pdf, accessed February 10, 2006.

Campbell, Benjamin A., and Vince Valvano. 1997. Wage structures in the electronics industry. In Clair Brown (ed.), *The Competitive Semiconductor Manufacturing Human Resources Project: Final Report (Phase I).* Berkeley, CA: Institute of Industrial Relations and Engineering Systems Research Center.

Cappelli, Peter. 1999. *The New Deal at Work.* Boston: Harvard Business School Press.

Card, David, and John E. DiNardo. 2002. Skill-biased technological change and rising wage inequality: Some problems and puzzles. *Journal of Labor Economics* 20(4): 733–83.

Carrington, William J. 1993. Wage losses for displaced workers: Is it really the firm that matters? *Journal of Human Resources* 28(3): 435–62.

Carrington, William J., and Asad Zaman. 1994. Interindustry variation in the costs of job displacement. *Journal of Labor Economics* 12(2): 243–75.

Caves, Richard E. 1998. Industrial organization and new findings on the turnover and mobility of firms. *Journal of Economic Literature* 36: 1947–82.

Corrado, Carol, and Lawrence Slifman. 1999. Decomposition of productivity and costs. *American Economic Review* 89: 328–32.

Davis, Steven J., and John Haltiwanger. 1991. Wage dispersion within and between manufacturing plants. *Brookings Papers on Economic Activity: Microeconomics* 1: 115–80.

Davis, Steven J., and John Haltiwanger. 1999. Gross job flows. In Orley Ashenfelter and David Card (eds.), *Handbook of Labor Economics.* Amsterdam: North-Holland, pp. 2711–805.

Davis, Steven J., John Haltiwanger, and Scott Schuh. 1996. *Job Creation and Job Destruction.* Cambridge: MIT Press.

Demsetz, Rebecca S. 1997. Human resource needs in the evolving financial sector. *Current Issues in Economics and Finance* 3(13).

Denison, Edward. 1974. *Accounting for United States Economic Growth, 1929–1969.* Washington: Brookings Institution.

DiNardo, John E., Nicole Fortin, and Thomas Lemieux. 1996. Labor market institutions and the distribution of wages, 1973–1992. *Econometrica* 64: 1001–1004.

Disney, Richard, Jonathan Haskel, and Yvla Heden. 2000. Restructuring and productivity growth in U.K. manufacturing. *Economic Journal* 113: 666–94.

Doeringer, Peter, and Michael Piore. 1971. *Internal Labor Markets and Manpower Adjustment.* New York: D.C. Heath.

Doiron, Denise J. 1995. Lay-offs as signals: The Canadian evidence. *Canadian Journal of Economics* 28(4a): 899–913.

Doms, Mark, Ron Jarmin, and Shawn Klimek. 2003. IT investment and firm performance in retail trade. Working paper 2003-19, Federal Reserve Bank of San Francisco.

Dumas, Mark W. 1997. Productivity trends in two retail trade industries, 1987–95. *Monthly Labor Review,* July, 35–39.

Dwyer, Douglas. 1997. Productivity races I: Are some productivity measures better than others? Center for Economic Studies Working Paper, CES 97-2.

Dwyer, Douglas. 1998. Technology locks, creative destruction, and non-convergence in productivity levels. *Review of Economic Dynamics* 1(2): 430–73.

Egan, Timothy. 2005. No degree, and no way back to the middle. *New York Times* (May 24).

Elliott, Larry. 2005. Edwardian summer. *Guardian* (August 18).

Ellis, Richard, and Lindsay B. Lowell. 1999. Assessing the demand for information technology workers. *Core Occupations of the U.S. Information Technology Workforce.* New York, NY: Commission on Professionals in Science and Technology; United Engineering Foundation, http://www.cpst.org/IT-4.pdf.

Ellis, Richard, and Lindsay B. Lowell. 2003. The outlook in 2003 for information technology workers in the USA (August). http://www.cpst.org/ITUpdate.pdf; accessed February 26, 2006.

Elswick, Jill. 2003. "Having it their way: Intel's benefit plan emphasizes choice and flexibility." *Employee Benefit News,* March 1.

Endres, Albert. 1996. A synopsis of software engineering history: The industrial perspective. Position Papers for Dagstuhl Seminar 9635 on History of Software Engineering.

Engardio, Pete, Aaron Bernstein, and Manjeet Kripalani with Frederik Balfour, Brian Grow, and Jay Greene. 2003. The new global job shift. *Business Week* (February 3).

Ericson, Richard, and Ariel Pakes. 1995. Markov perfect industry dynamics: A framework for empirical work. *Review of Economic Studies* 62(1): 53–82.

Fallick, Bruce C. 1996. A review of the recent empirical literature on displaced workers. *Industrial and Labor Relations Review* 50: 5–16.

Farber, Henry. 1999. Mobility and stability: The dynamics of job change in labor markets. In Orley Ashenfelter and David Card (eds.), *The Handbook of Labor Economics*, vol. 3. Amsterdam: North-Holland, pp. 2439–84.

Ferris, Gerald R., M. Ronald Buckley, and Gillian M. Allen. 1992. Promotion systems in organizations. *Human Resource Planning* 15: 47–68.

Fisher, Marc. 2005. Giant looks more and more like a dinosaur. *Washington Post*, May 5, B1.

Food Institute. 2003. *Food Industry Review 2003*. Elmwood Park, NH: American Institute of Food Distribution.

Food Marketing Institute. 2002. *FMI Technology Review Highlights 2002*. Washington: Food Marketing Institute.

Forbes, J. B., and S. E. Wertheim. 1995. Promotion, succession, and career systems. In G. R. Ferris, S. D, Rosen, and D. T. Barnum (eds.), *Handbook of Human Resource Management*. Cambridge, MA: Blackwell, pp. 494–510.

Fortin, Nicole, and Thomas Lemieux. 1997. Institutional changes and rising wage inequality: Is there a linkage? *Journal of Economic Perspectives* 11(2): 75–96.

Foster, Lucia, John Haltiwanger, and C. J. Krizan. 2001. Aggregate productivity growth: Lessons from microeconomic evidence. In Edward Dean, Michael Harper, and Charles Hulten (eds.), *New Directions in Productivity Analysis*. Chicago: University of Chicago Press, pp. 303–63.

Foster, Lucia, John Haltiwanger, and C. J. Krizan. 2002. The link between aggregate and micro productivity growth: Evidence from retail trade. NBER Working Paper no. 9120.

Frei, Frances X., Patrick T. Harker, and Larry W. Hunter. 1999. Retail banking. In David C. Mowrey (ed.), *U.S. Industry in 2000: Studies in Competitive Performance*. Washington: National Academy Press, pp. 179–214.

Frei, Frances X., Patrick T. Harker, and Larry W. Hunter. 2000. Inside the black box: What makes a bank efficient. In S. Zenios and P. Harker (eds.), *The Performance of Financial Institutions*. New York: Cambridge University Press, pp. 259–311.

Fried, Harold O., Knox Lovell, and P. Vanden Eeckaut. 1993. Evaluating the performance of U.S. credit unions. *Journal of Banking and Finance* 17: 251–66.

Fritsch, Conrad F. 1981. Exemptions to the Fair Labor Standards Act, Transportation Industry. In *Report of the Minimum Wage Study Commission*. Washington: U.S. Government Printing Office, vol. 4, 151–86.

Gant, John, Casey Ichinowski, and Kathryn Shaw. 2002. Social capital and organizational change in high-involvement and traditional work organizations. *Journal of Economics and Management Strategy* 11(2): 289–328.

Gibbons, Robert, and Lawrence F. Katz. 1991. Layoffs and lemons. *Journal of Labor Economics* 9(4): 351–80.

Greenhouse, Steven. 2005. How Costco became the anti-Wal-Mart. *New York Times* (July 17).

Griliches, Zvi, and Haim Regev. 1995. Productivity and firm turnover in Israeli industry: 1979–1988. *Journal of Econometrics* 65: 175–203.

Gullickson, William, and Michael J. Harper. 2002. Bias in aggregate productivity trends revisited. *Monthly Labor Review,* March, 32–40.

Hagenbaugh, Barbara. 2004. Truckers needed to keep economy rolling. *USA Today* (October 12).

Haltiwanger, John. 1997. Measuring and analyzing aggregate fluctuations: The importance of building from microeconomic evidence. *Federal Reserve Bank of St. Louis Economic Review* January/February, 55–78.

Haltiwanger, John, and Ron Jarmin. 2000. Measuring the digital economy. In E. Byrnjolfsson and B. Kahin (eds.), *Understanding the Digital Economy*. Cambridge: MIT Press, pp. 13–33.

Haltiwanger, John C., Julia I. Lane, and James R. Spletzer. 2001. Productivity differences across employers: The role of employer size, age, and human capital. *American Economic Review* 89: 94–98.

Haltiwanger, John C., Julia I. Lane, and James R. Spletzer. In press. Wages, productivity, and the dynamic interaction of business and workers. *Labour Economics.*

Harrison, Crayton. 2004. Austin economy still wired to semiconductor industry. *Dallas Morning News,* September 22.

Hiltzik, Mike. 2005. Shipping out U.S. jobs—to a ship. *Los Angeles Times* (May 2).

Hirsch, Barry, and Edward Schumacher. 2004. Match bias in wage gap estimates due to earnings imputation. *Journal of Labor Economics* 22(3): 689–722.

Hitt, Lorin M., Frances X. Frei, and Patrick T. Harker. 1999. How financial firms decide on technology. In Robert E. Litan and Anthony M. Santomero (eds.), *Brookings-Wharton Papers on Financial Services 1999*. Washington: Brookings, pp. 93–136.

Holmes, Thomas J., and James A. Schmitz, Jr. 1990. A theory of entrepreneurship and its application to the study of business transfers. *Journal of Political Economy* 98: 265–94.

Holmes, Thomas J., and James A. Schmitz, Jr. 1995. On the turnover of business firms and business managers. *Journal of Political Economy* 103: 1005–38.

Hopenhayn, Hugo A. 1992. Entry, exit, and firm dynamics in long run equilibrium. *Econometrica* 60: 1127–50.

Howland, Marie, and George E. Peterson. 1988. Labor market conditions and the reemployment of displaced workers. *Industrial and Labor Relations Review* 42: 109–22.

Hughes, Katherine L. 1999. Supermarket employment: Good jobs at good wages? IEE Working Paper no. 11 (April). http://www.tc.columbia.edu/iee/PAPERS/workpap11.pdf, accessed February 26, 2006.

Hunter, Larry W. 1999. Transforming retail banking: Inclusion and segmentation in service work. In Peter Cappelli (ed.), *Employment Practices and Business Strategy*. New York: Oxford University Press, pp. 153–92.

Hunter, Larry W, Annette Bernhardt, Katherine L. Hughes, and Eva Skuratowicz. 2001. It's not just the ATMs: Firm strategies, work restructuring, and workers' earnings in retail banking. *Industrial and Labor Relations Review* 54: 402–24.

Ichinowski, Casey, and Kathryn Shaw. 1999. The effects of human resource systems on productivity: An international comparison of U.S. and Japanese plants. *Management Science* 45: 704–22.

Ichinowski, Casey, and Kathryn Shaw. 2003. Beyond incentive pay: Insiders' estimates of the value of complementary human resource management practices. *Journal of Economic Perspectives* 17(1): 155–78.

Ichinowski, Casey, Kathryn Shaw, and Giovanna Prennushi. 1997. The effects of human resource management practices on productivity: A study of steel finishing lines. *American Economic Review* 87: 291–313. Reprinted in *Personnel Economics*, ed. Edward Lazear and Robert McNabb (Cheltenham, U.K.: Edward Elgar Press, 2004).

Jacobson, Louis S., Robert J. LaLonde, and Daniel G. Sullivan. 1993. Earnings losses of displaced workers. *American Economic Review* 83: 685–709.

Jarmin, Ron S., Shawn D. Klimek, and Javier Miranda. 2001. Firm entry and exit in the U.S. retail sector, 1977–1997. Working paper, U.S. Bureau of the Census, Center for Economic Studies, http://webserver01.ces.census.gov/index.php/ces/1.00/cespapers?down_key=101704; accessed February 26, 2006

Jensen, Michael C. 1993. The modern Industrial Revolution: Exit and the failure of internal control systems. *Journal of Finance* 48: 831–80.

Jorgenson, Dale W., F. Gollop, and B. M. Fraumeni. 1987. *Productivity and U.S. Economic Growth*. Cambridge: Harvard University Press.

Jorgenson, Dale W., and Kevin J. Stiroh. 2000. Raising the speed limit: US economic growth in the information age. *OECD Economics Department Working Paper 261*. OECD Economics Department

Jovanovic, Boyan. 1982. Selection and the evolution of industry. *Econometrica* 50: 649–70.

Juhn, C., K. Murphy, and B. Pierce. 1993. Wage inequality and the rise in returns to skill. *Journal of Political Economy* 101: 410–42.

Katz, L., and D. Autor. 1999. Changes in the wage structure and earnings inequality. In O. Ashenfelter and D. Card (eds.), *Handbook of Labor Economics*, vol. 3. Amsterdam: North-Holland, pp. 1463–555.

Kaufman, Phil R. 2002. Food Retailing, U.S. Food Marketing System, 2002, AER-

811. U.S. Economic Research Service/U.S. Department of Agriculture. http://www.ers.usda.gov/publications/aer811/aer811e.pdf, accessed February 26, 2006.

King, Robert, and Tim Park. 2004. Modeling productivity in supermarket operations: Incorporating the impacts of store characteristics and information technologies. *Journal of Food Distribution Research* 35: 42–55.

Kinsey, Jean. 1998. Concentration of ownership in food retailing: A review of the evidence about consumer impact. Working paper no. 98-04. Food Industry Center, University of Minnesota.

Kletzer, Lori G. 1989. Returns to seniority after permanent job loss. *American Economic Review* 79: 536–43.

Kletzer, Lori G. 1998. Job displacement. *Journal of Economic Perspectives* 12(1): 115–36.

Kochan, Thomas, Harry C. Katz, and Robert B. McKersie. 1994. *The Transformation of American Industrial Relations.* Ithaca, NY: ILR Press.

Lane, Julia, Alan Isaac, and David Stevens. 1996. Firm heterogeneity and worker turnover. *Review of Industrial Organization* 11: 275–91.

Lazear, Edward P., and Paul Oyer. 2003. Internal and external labor markets: A personnel economics approach. NBER Working Papers 10192. National Bureau of Economic Research.

Leachman, Robert C., and Chien H. Leachman. 2004. Globalization of semiconductor manufacturing. In Martin Kenney and Richard Florida (eds.), *Locating Global Advantage: Industry Dynamics in the International Economy.* Stanford: Stanford University Press, pp. 203–31.

Lee, David S. 1999. Wage inequality in the United States during the 1980s: Rising dispersion or falling minimum wage. *Quarterly Journal of Economics* 114: 977–1023.

Lee, Karen. 2000. "Trucking firm takes benefit portability to new heights." *Employee Benefit News,* July 1.

Lemieux, Thomas. 2004. Increasing residual rage inequality: Compositional effects, noisy data, or rising demand for skill? Working paper, University of British Columbia.

Lerman, Robert. 1997. Reassessing trends in U.S. earnings inequality. *Monthly Labor Review,* December, 17–25.

Levinson, Harold M. 1980. Trucking. In Gerald G. Somers (ed.), *Bargaining: Contemporary American Experience.* Bloomington, IL: Industrial Relations Research Association Pantagraph Printing, pp. 99–150.

Levy, F., and R. J. Murnane. 1992. U.S. earnings levels and earnings inequality: A review of recent trends and proposed explanations. *Journal of Economic Literature* 30: 1333–81.

Linden, Greg, Clair Brown, and Melissa Appleyard. 2004. The net world order's influence on global leadership in the semiconductor industry. In Martin Kenney and Richard Florida (eds.), *Locating Global Advantage: Industry Dynamics in the International Economy.* Stanford: Stanford University Press, pp. 232–57.

Liu, Lili, and James R. Tybout. 1996. Productivity growth in Chile and Columbia: The role of entry, exit, and learning, in Mark J. Roberts and James R. Tybout (eds.), *Industrial Evolution in Developing Countries: Micro Patterns of Turnover, Productivity, and Market Structure.* New York: Oxford University Press for the World Bank, pp. 73–103.

Longitudinal Employer-Household Dynamics Program, Employment Dynamics Estimates Project. 2002. Technical Paper no. TP-2002–05.

Macher, Jeffrey T., David C. Mowery, and David A. Hodges. 1998. Back to dominance? U.S. resurgence in the global semiconductor industry. *California Management Review* 41(1): 107–36.

Mapes, Lynda V. 2005. Good business: Two local companies are proving it pays to do well by workers. *Seattle Times* (January 31).

McKinsey Global Institute. 2001. *U.S. Productivity Growth 1995–2000.* Washington: McKinsey Global Institute.

McLaughlin, Kenneth J. 1991. "A theory of quits and layoffs with efficient turnover." *Journal of Political Economy* 99:1–29.

Meade, Douglas S., Stainslaw J. Rzeznik, and Darlene C. Robinson-Smith, "Business investment by industry in the U.S. economy for 1997," Bureau of Economic Analysis U.S. Census Department, Industry Economics Division, November 2003. http://www.bea.gov/bea/ARTICLES/2003/11November/1103%20Investment .pdf; accessed April 6, 2006.

Meares, Carol Ann, and John Sargent, Jr. 1999. *The Digital Work Force: Building Infotech Skills at the Speed of Innovation.* U.S. Department of Commerce, Office of Technology Policy. Washington: U.S. Government Printing Office.

Melitz, Marc. 2003. The impact of trade on intra-industry reallocations and aggregate industry productivity. *Econometrica* 71: 1695–725.

Melitz, Marc. 2005. When and how should infant industries be protected? *Journal of International Economics* 66: 177–96.

Meyer, G. J. 1995. *Executive Blues: Down and Out in Corporate America.* New York: Franklin Square Press.

Moeller, Michael. Outta here at Microsoft: The software giant is losing key talent to the Internet. http://www.businessweek.com/1999/99_48/b3657197.htm, accessed March 7, 2006.

Moody, Gerald R. 1997. Information technology and economic performance of the grocery store industry. Economics and Statistics Administration, Office of Policy Development, U.S. Department of Commerce. ESA/OPD 97–1. http://ssrn.com/ abstract=37747, accessed February 26, 2006.

Nakamura, Leonard. 1998. The measurement of retail output and the retail revolution. Federal Reserve Bank of Philadelphia, Working Paper 98-5.

Neal, Derek. 1995. Industry-specific human capital: Evidence from displaced workers. *Journal of Labor Economics* 13(4): 653–77.

Nguyen, Sang, and Michael Ollinger. 2002. Mergers and acquisitions and productivity in the U.S. meat products industries: Evidence from the micro data. CES-WP-02–07.

Olley, G. Steven, and Ariel Pakes. 1996. The dynamics of productivity in the telecommunications equipment industry. *Econometrica* 64: 1263–97.

Ong, Paul, and Don Mar. 1992. Post-layoff earnings among semiconductor workers. *Industrial and Labor Relations Review* 45: 366–79.

Osterman, Paul. 1996. *Broken Ladders*. New York: Oxford University Press.

Podgursky, Michael, and Paul Swaim. 1987. Job displacement and earnings loss: Evidence from the displaced worker survey. *Industrial and Labor Relations Review* 41: 17–29.

Prendergast, Canice. 1996. What happens within firms? A survey of empirical evidence on compensation policies. NBER Working Paper 5802, National Bureau of Economic Research.

Rodriguez, Daniel A., Marta Rocha, Asad Khattak, and Michael H. Belzer. 2003. The effects of truck driver wages and working conditions on highway safety: A case study. *Transportation Research Record,* no. 1883: 95–102.

Royalty, Anne Beeson. 1996. The effects of job turnover on the training of men and women. *Industrial and Labor Relations Review* 49: 506–21.

Ruhm, Christopher J. 1991. Are workers permanently scarred by job displacements? *American Economic Review* 81: 319–24.

Schoeni, Robert F., and Michael Dardia. 1996. Wage losses of displaced workers in the 1990's. Technical Report, RAND Corporation.

Schoeni, Robert F., and Michael Dardia. 1997. Earnings losses of displaced workers in the 1990s. JCPR Working Papers 8, Northwestern University/University of Chicago Joint Center for Poverty Research.

Schuh, Scott, Michael Klein, and Robert Triest. 2003. *Job Creation, Job Destruction, and International Competition.* Kalamazoo: Upjohn Institute.

Sheridan, J. E., J. W. Slocum, R. Buda, and R. Thompson. 1990. Effects of corporate sponsorship and departmental power on career tournaments: A study of interorganizational mobility. *Academy of Management Journal* 33: 578–602.

Sieling, Mark, Brian Friedman, and Mark W. Dumas. 2001. Labor productivity in the retail trade industry, 1987–99. *Monthly Labor Review,* December, 3–14.

Simanoff, Dave. Tampa among 3 cities vying for call center. *Tampa Tribune.* May 5.

Simpson, John D., and Daniel Hosken. 2001. Have supermarket mergers raised prices? An event study analysis. *International Journal of Business* 8: 329–42.

Skuratowicz, Eva, and Larry W. Hunter. 2004. Where do women's jobs come from? Job resegregation in an American bank. *Work and Occupations* 31(1): 73–110.

Steindel, Charles, and Kevin J. Stiroh. 2001. Productivity: What is it and why do we care about it? Staff Reports 122, Federal Reserve Bank of New York.

Steinmueller, Edward. 1995. The U.S. software industry: An analysis and interpretive history. In David C. Mowery (ed.), *The International Computer Software Industry.* Oxford and New York: Oxford University Press, pp. 15–52.

Stone, Amey. Death of a stock salesman. *Business Week Online* (April 6). http://
www.businessweek.com/bwdaily/dnflash/apr2005/nf2005046_9224_db016.htm;
accessed February 26, 2006

Topel, Robert, and M. P. Ward. 1992. Job mobility and the careers of young men.
Quarterly Journal of Economics 107: 441–79.

Trevor, C. O., B. Gerhart, and J. W. Boudreau. 1997. Voluntary turnover and job performance: Curvilinearity and the moderating influences of salary growth and
promotions. *Journal of Applied Psychology* 82(1): 44–61.

Triplett, Jack E. 1999. Economic statistics, the new economy, and the productivity
slowdown. *Business Economics* 34(2): 13–17.

Triplett, Jack E., and Barry P. Bosworth. 1999. The Solow productivity paradox: What
do computers do to productivity? *Canadian Journal of Economics* 32(2): 309–34.

Triplett, Jack E., and Barry P. Bosworth. 2000. Numbers matter: The U.S. statistical
system, and a rapidly changing economy. Brookings Policy Brief no. 63 (July).

Triplett, Jack E., and Barry P. Bosworth. 2001. Productivity in the services sector. In
Robert M. Stern (ed.), *Services in the International Economy.* Ann Arbor: University of Michigan Press, 23–52.

Triplett, Jack E., and Barry P. Bosworth. 2001. What's new about the new economy?:
IT, economic growth, and productivity. *International Productivity Monitor* 2
(spring): 19–30. A longer version of this paper appeared in Heidemarie C. Sher-
man (ed.), The Impact of the Internet Revolution on International Economic
Relations and Society, Tokyo Club Papers no. 14.

Triplett, Jack E, and Barry P. Bosworth. 2003. Productivity measurement issues in
services industries: Baumol's disease has been cured. *Federal Reserve Bank of
New York Economic Policy Review* 9(3): 23–33.

Tybout, James R. 1996. Heterogeneity and productivity growth: Assessing the evi-
dence. In Mark J. Roberts and James R. Tybout (eds.), *Industrial Evolution in
Developing Countries: Micro Patterns of Turnover, Productivity, and Market
Structure.* New York: Oxford University Press for the World Bank, pp. 43–72.

U.S. Department of Labor, Bureau of Labor Statistics. *Current Population Survey.*
Various issues.

U.S. Department of Labor, Bureau of Labor Statistics. *Occupational Outlook
Handbook.* Various issues.

U.S. Economic Research Service. 2000. Consolidation in food retailing: Prospects
for consumers and grocery suppliers. *Agricultural Outlook* (August). http://www
.ers.usda.gov/publications/agoutlook/aug2000/ao273g.pdf.

U.S. Economic Research Service. 2002. http://www.ers.usda.gov/Briefing/Food
MarketStructures/papers.htm (page updated July 1); accessed February 26,
2006.

U.S. Economic Research Service. 2003. http://www.ers.usda.gov/Briefing/Food
MarketStructures/foodretailing.htm (page updated May 17).; accessed February 26, 2006.

Walsh, J. P. 1993. *Supermarkets Transformed*. New Brunswick: Rutgers University Press.

Weinberg, Bruce A. 2001. Long-term wage fluctuations with industry-specific human capital. *Journal of Labor Economics* 19(1): 231–64.

Weintraub, Norman A. 1992. ICC regulated motor carriers of general freight under NMFA that terminated general freight operations from July 1, 1980 to October 31, 1992. IBT Economics Department Report. Washington: International Brotherhood of Teamsters.

Witte, Griff. 2004. As income gap widens, uncertainty spreads: More U.S. families struggle to stay on track. *Washington Post* (September 20).

Index

Note: Italicized page numbers indicate figures and tables.